RaeAnne Thayne finds inspiration in the beautiful northern Utah mountains, where the *New York Times* and *USA TODAY* bestselling author lives with her husband and three children. Her books have won numerous honors, including RITA® Award nominations from Romance Writers of America and a Career Achievement Award from *RT Book Reviews*. RaeAnne loves to hear from readers and can be contacted through her website, www.raeannethayne.com.

After thirty-five years as a nurse, **Patricia Davids** hung up her stethoscope to become a full-time writer. She enjoys spending her free time visiting her grandchildren, doing some long-overdue yard work and traveling to research her story locations. She resides in Wichita, Kansas. Patricia always enjoys hearing from her readers. You can visit her online at patriciadavids.com.

New York Times Bestselling Author

RaeAnne Thayne

SPRINGTIME IN SALT RIVER

HARLEQUIN BESTSELLING AUTHOR COLLECTION

ISBN-13: 978-1-335-14492-8

Springtime in Salt River

Copyright © 2018 by Harlequin Books S.A.

The publisher acknowledges the copyright holders of the individual works as follows:

Springtime in Salt River
Copyright © 2017 by RaeAnne Thayne
First published as Taming Jesse James by Silhouette Intimate Moments in 2002

Love Thine Enemy
Copyright © 2006 by Patricia Macdonald

Recycling programs for this product may not exist in your area.

HARLEQUIN®

www.Harlequin.com

Printed in U.S.A.

CONTENTS

SPRINGTIME IN SALT RIVER

RaeAnne Thayne

To Maureen Green, Chris Christensen,
Jennifer Black and Carrie Robinson,
my sisters and my best friends.
For all the clothes, parenting tips, yard sales
and side-aching, milk-out-of-your-nose laughfests
we've shared over the years. I love you!

Chapter 1

Jesse James Harte was in deep, deep trouble.

"You playin' or are you just gonna sit there lookin' pretty?" the scrappier of his two opponents asked with a fearless smirk.

Jesse glared at his cards, trying to figure out his options. They didn't look any cheerier than they had a few moments ago.

"Come on. We're waitin'."

"Yeah, yeah. Hold your water." He looked at his hand one last time, then back at the two troublemakers across the table from him. His throat was parched and he needed a drink in the worst way, but he didn't dare turn his back on these two desperadoes. Not for a second. The two of them were as terrifying as any hardened criminal he'd ever come up against.

Finally he knew he would have to do something, and

quick. He set down the only possible card he could—jack of hearts. As soon as it left his hand, he knew it was a mistake. A triumphant shout rang through the room and a queen of hearts slapped onto his jack.

His niece Lucy gave a shriek of excitement. "Ha! That was her last card. You lose, Uncle Jess! Told ya you'd never be able to beat Dylan at crazy eights. She's the best. The absolute best."

"The winner and still undefeated champ-i-on!" Dylan Webster, Lucy's stepsister of less than a month, jumped from the chair across from his desk and did a little hip-jiggling victory dance around his office.

Jesse leaned back in his chair and watched their celebratory gyrations out of narrowed eyes. "You cheated. I can't figure out how, but you must have cheated. Worse than a couple of Wild West card sharks, that's what you are. Come in here after school acting all sweet and innocent, saying you just stopped in to say hello, and then you bilk me out of two Snickers bars. You think I don't know what's going on?"

Dylan batted her eyes at him. "Who, us? Would we do something like that?" That one was going to be a heartbreaker just like her mom, when she put on a few more years.

"I ought to lock you both up right now and throw away the key," Jesse growled. "Teach you to mess with the Salt River chief of police."

The girls just giggled at him.

"Come on. Best two out of three." He scooped up the cards and started shuffling them. "Better yet, I'll teach you how to play a real game. How about blackjack?"

"We already know how to play," Dylan assured him.

"How about acey-deucy? No? Sit back down, then."

He did a fancy little flourish with the cards that sent them cascading between his hands in a rainbow. His little card trick was rewarded with two pairs of wide eyes.

"Cool!" Lucy exclaimed. "Where'd you learn to do that?"

"Years of practice, beating the pants off your dad. He stinks at cards. Always has. And you can tell him I said so, too." He grinned and she giggled back.

"Will you teach me how to do it?"

"Sure, if you give me the first bite of that Snickers bar."

Before she could answer, a knock sounded at the door.

"Yeah?"

His dispatcher, receptionist and all-around pain in the neck shoved open the door and stood in the doorway, all four feet ten inches of her.

"Chief, you got company," Lou Montgomery barked.

"Yeah?"

"Says it's important."

"Send him in, then."

"Her," a new voice interjected. Compared to Lou's rotgut-rough voice, this one was as soft and smooth as water rippling over rocks. He knew that voice. He opened his mouth to answer, but before he could, the girls beat him to it.

"Ms. McKenzie!" they shrieked in unison, and rushed to greet his visitor, their fourth-grade teacher. She gave them a strained smile but accepted their hugs graciously.

"What are you doing here?" Dylan asked.

The pretty teacher looked uncomfortable. "I… I just had some business to discuss with Chief Harte."

Something she obviously didn't want to share with two nosy little girls. Before the terrible twosome could interrogate her about it, Jesse stepped in. "Ladies, I'll have to take a raincheck on the poker lessons. Aren't you supposed to be cleaning out the stalls at the clinic, anyway?"

They both groaned, but picked up their backpacks. "Bye, Ms. McKenzie," they chimed in unison.

"Thanks for the Snickers bars." Dylan smirked at Jesse on her way out the door.

As soon as they left, Ms. McKenzie raised a delicate eyebrow at him. "Poker lessons?"

Despite that sexy voice of hers, the schoolmarm tone still made him feel as if he'd just been caught throwing spitballs. He cleared his throat. "Uh, guilty. What can I say? I'm a bad influence. Sit down. How can I help you?"

After a brief hesitation, she walked across the office with that slight, barely perceptible limp that had been driving him crazy with curiosity since she'd moved to town at the beginning of the school year.

She slipped into the chair across the desk from him and folded her hands carefully on her lap, her green eyes focused on some point just to the left of his face.

He fought the urge to look over his shoulder to see what she found so fascinating back there. Judging by their few brief encounters since her arrival in Salt River eight months ago, he had the uncomfortable feeling she wasn't looking at anything in particular, just away from him.

For some reason, he seemed to make Sarah McKenzie nervous, although for the life of him he couldn't figure out what he'd done to her.

The last time he'd seen her had been nearly a month ago at his brother Matt's wedding to Dylan's mother, Ellie. At the reception the schoolteacher hadn't moved from the corner for most of the evening. In a pale peach dress and with all that sun-streaked blond hair piled on top of her head, she'd looked cool and remote and scrumptious enough to gobble up in one bite.

When he'd finally decided to ignore her blatant back-off signals and asked her to dance, she'd stared at him as if he had just dumped a glass of champagne all over her, then topped it off by stomping on her fingers.

She hadn't said anything for several painfully long moments, then she had jumped to her feet and stammered some excuse about how she needed to check on something. Next thing he'd known, he'd seen her driving out of the church parking lot as if she was trying to outgun a tornado.

He pushed the memory away. So the pretty, enigmatic Ms. McKenzie didn't want to dance with him. So what? He was a big boy now and could handle a little rejection once in a while. His little sister, Cassidy, probably would have said it was good for him.

Not that any of that had a thing to do with the reason she was sitting in front of him trying not to wring her hands together nervously.

"Is there something I can help you with, Ms. McKenzie?" he asked again in his best casual, friendly-policeman voice.

She drew in a breath, then let it out in a rush. "I want you to arrest someone."

It was the last thing he expected her to say. "You do?"

Her soft, pretty mouth tightened. "Well, I'd prefer if

you could drag him behind a horse for a few hundred miles. But since I don't think that's very likely to happen, given civil rights and all, I suppose I'll have to settle for seeing the miserable excuse for a man locked away for the rest of his natural life."

"Does this miserable excuse for a man have a name?"

She hesitated for just a few beats, just long enough to nudge his curiosity up to fever pitch. "Yes," she finally said coolly. "Yes, he does have a name. Seth Garrett."

His jaw dropped. "The mayor? You want me to arrest the mayor?"

"I don't care if he's the president of the United States. He belongs in jail."

He leaned back in his chair. "Care to tell me why, before I rush over there with my handcuffs? I'm not saying I won't do it—I'd just like to be able to give the man a reason."

She stood up, her hands clenched tightly into fists and a glare on those delicate, fine-boned features. "This is not a laughing matter, Chief Harte. If you refuse to take me seriously, I'll… I'll find someone who will. The FBI, maybe, or the Wyoming State Police."

She was serious! She wanted him to march into the mayor's office and haul him off to jail. What could she possibly have against Seth Garrett, one of the most well liked and respected men in town? He doubted the man even jaywalked.

Still, he knew she wouldn't have come here without a reason, and it was his job to listen to it. "I'm sorry, ma'am. You just took me by surprise, that's all. I didn't mean to make light of this. Sit down. What do you think he's done?"

Sarah slid into the chair again and knotted her hands

together tightly. She wasn't sure what was more to blame for their trembling—this seething fury writhing around inside her or the sick lump in her stomach at having to face the man in front of her.

She *did* know she shouldn't have come here. Jesse Harte made her so blasted nervous she couldn't think straight, and she had known before she even walked into his office that she would make a mess of this.

In the past eighteen months she had worked hard to overcome the lingering fragments of nightmare that haunted her. She wanted to think she had become almost functional again, hiding the worst of her panic attacks behind a veneer of control.

But for some reason Jesse Harte always seemed to punch a hole in the paper-thin wall of that facade, leaving her nervous and upset.

It wasn't him, exactly. Or, at least, she didn't think so. He seemed gentle enough with the girls. It was kind of sweet, actually, to see such a hard-edged cop teasing giggles out of two ten-year-old girls.

For a month she hadn't been able to shake the image of him in his dark Western-cut suit at his brother's wedding, dancing with each of the girls in turn and looking big and solid and completely masculine.

That was most of what made her nervous. He was just so big. So completely, wholly male—intimidating just by his very size and by the aura of danger that surrounded him.

With the combination of that dark-as-sin hair, those startling blue eyes and that wicked smile, Jesse Harte drew the lustful eye of every woman in town. If it weren't for the badge on his tan denim shirt, it would be difficult to remember he was on the right side of the law. All he needed was a bushy mustache and a low-slung gun belt hanging on his hips to look like the outlaw she heard he was named for.

He sent her nerves skittering just by looking at her out of those blue eyes and she hated it, but she had no one else to turn to. She had a child to protect, and if that meant facing her own personal bogeyman, she would force herself to do it, no matter the cost.

Besides her unease around the police chief, it didn't help her nerves to know she could be risking her job. When she had taken her concerns to the principal, Chuck Hendricks had ordered her to leave well enough alone. She was imagining things, he said, making problems for herself where she didn't need to.

It was a grim reminder of what had happened in Chicago. She had been warned then about stepping in where she had no business. But then, just as now, she hadn't had a choice.

"Can I get you a glass of water or something?"

She blinked and realized the police chief was waiting for some kind of an explanation for her presence here. "No. No, thank you. I'm fine."

"You ready to talk now?"

She took a deep breath, then met his gaze directly for the first time since she'd entered his office. "Mr. Garrett's stepson is in my class."

"Corey Sylvester?"

"I take it you know him."

Despite her worries over Corey, that blasted smile of his sent her stomach fluttering. "This is a small town, Ms. McKenzie. Not much slips by the eagle eye of the Salt River P.D. What's Corey done now?"

"Oh, no. He hasn't done anything."

He chuckled wryly. "That's a first."

"What do you mean?"

"Only that the boy's had his share of run-ins with local authorities."

Another person might have asked what possible crimes a child of ten could have committed to bring him to the attention of the local police chief. Not Sarah. She had seen much, much worse than Corey Sylvester could even contemplate. In Chicago, children as young as eight dealt drugs and sold their bodies on street corners and murdered each other for sport.

She thought of a pretty girl with glossy braids and old, tired eyes, then pushed the memory aside.

This was rural Wyoming, where children still played kick-the-can on a warm spring night and the most excitement to be found was at the high school baseball diamond.

That's why she had come here, to find peace. To immerse herself in the slow, serene pace of small-town life.

To heal.

"Corey has done nothing," she assured the police chief. "He's a troubled young boy and I... I believe I know why."

"I'm assuming this has something to do with his stepfather, otherwise you wouldn't be here looking for the mayor's head on a platter, right?"

Her jaw clenched as she remembered what she'd seen at school that day. "Corey has all the characteristics of an abused child. I believe his stepfather is the one abusing him."

Chief Harte leaned forward, suddenly alert as an alpha wolf scenting danger. She started to shrink back in her chair, but quickly checked the movement. She wouldn't cower. Not if she could help it.

"That's a very serious allegation, Ms. McKenzie. You have any evidence to back that up?"

She felt sick all over again just thinking about it. "Corey's been in my class for two weeks now and—"

He interrupted her with a frown. "Only two weeks? School's out in another month. Why would he transfer into your class so late in the year when the session's almost over?"

Because he'd gone through all three of the other fourth-grade teachers and each one refused to allow him back into her class. She was his last stop on the road before expulsion.

"He had some difficulties with the other teachers. But that doesn't matter. What concerns me is that in those two weeks he has come to school twice with black eyes and once with stitches in the corner of his mouth. That's just not normal wear and tear for a boy his age."

"Corey's not like most boys."

"He's certainly a little high-strung, but he's still a child."

After a moment of studying her out of those vivid blue eyes, the police chief pulled a notebook from his pocket and began writing in it. "Two black eyes and stitches in his mouth. That's what you said, right?"

She nodded. "When I asked him about his first injury, he became extremely evasive. He refused to look me in the eye and mumbled some obviously fictitious story about falling off his bike. His second black eye came from falling out of a tree, he said."

"And the stitches?"

"Yet another fall off his bike. He said he did a face plant on the concrete."

"It's possible he's telling the truth. Maybe he's just accident-prone. When I was a kid, I once spent a whole summer at the clinic in town getting patched up from one accident or another."

She had a disturbing mental image of a dark-haired little boy with those blue eyes and the devil in his grin, but she quickly pushed it away.

"Corey is a rough-and-tumble kind of kid, Ms. McKenzie," the chief continued. "It's only natural that he'll suffer a few scrapes and bruises along the way."

"But four serious accidents in two weeks? Doesn't that stretch the bounds of credibility a little even for you, Chief Harte?"

He checked his notebook. "Four? You only mentioned three."

"I was getting to that. Today, during our last recess of the day, he ripped his shirt on the playground fence. He refused to let me help him, but through the tear in his shirt I saw what looked like bruises on his shoulder."

"Bruises?"

"Like from a man's hand squeezing viciously hard." She didn't add that she'd once had similar bruises. And that even though they had faded more than a year ago, she could sometimes still feel them.

He blew out a breath, and for the first time she began to think maybe she wasn't fighting a losing battle. He scribbled a few more notes in his book, then glanced at her again. "What makes you suspect the mayor is behind all of this?"

"When Corey transferred into my class, I examined his school records so I could be familiar with his situation. Until midway through the second grade, Corey's teachers all loved him and he had wonderful grades. The comments in his report cards were things like 'always willing to help others.' 'A joy to have in class.' 'Creative and imaginative.'"

"He's imaginative, all right. Last winter during a cold spell he poured water in the keyhole of every store on Main Street so the locks would freeze. Took us half a day to thaw everything out."

"His behavior in class began to change dramatically, coinciding quite noticeably around the time I understand his mother married Mayor Garrett. Almost overnight, a bright, artistic child turned angry and destructive. I believe there's a connection."

"A lot of kids have trouble adjusting to divorces and remarriages. Doesn't mean they're being abused."

She glared at him, feeling as if she'd lost all the headway she thought she'd gained. Why wasn't he taking this seriously? She had been through this for more than an hour with Principal Hendricks and she had had just about enough of Salt River's good-old-boy network. She had no doubt that's why she seemed to be hitting a brick wall here. Nobody wanted to rock the boat, especially when powerful people were on board.

"Do you care about this child's welfare at all? Or is he just one more juvenile delinquent to you?"

He blinked at her sudden attack. "Sure I care about him. But I just can't jump into a major investigation based on speculation and conjecture."

Speculation and conjecture? She'd given him ample cause to investigate. Wasn't he listening to her at all?

Furious, she glared at him, completely forgetting that the man was supposed to intimidate her. "You mean you don't want to alienate the mayor by pursuing an investigation against him. Isn't that right?"

She narrowed her gaze thoughtfully. "That's it, isn't it? I think I'm beginning to understand. Seth Garrett is an important man around here. Tell me, Chief Harte, are you more concerned about keeping your job or in protecting a little boy?"

As soon as the words escaped her tongue, she knew they were a mistake. A monumental mistake. The police chief's blue eyes hardened. His easy charm disappeared, leaving only raw anger.

"Be careful, ma'am," he murmured.

She clasped her hands together tightly in her lap to hide their renewed trembling. Where had that outburst of hers come from?

The old Sarah might have said something exactly like that, would have faced down a hundred Jesse Hartes if she had to. But she had been gone for a long time. The timid mouse she had left behind never would have risked baiting a man like him.

Some vestige of her former self must have been lurking inside her all this time. What's more, she was amazed to suddenly discover she wasn't willing to run away just because of his threat, implied or otherwise. Corey deserved to have someone on his side.

Even if that someone was only a timid mouse.

She stood up again. "If you're not willing to investigate, I told you, I'll find someone who is."

After a moment's hesitation, he stood, as well. "I didn't say I wasn't going to investigate. I'll look into the matter. I'll talk to the boy, talk to Seth and Ginny. But I have to warn you, I'm not sure how far I'll get. These cases can be difficult to prove, especially if the child won't cooperate. And knowing Corey, I can pretty much guess how it will go."

"Please let me know what happens." She walked toward the door.

"Oh, I'll be in touch, Ms. McKenzie," the police chief said. "You can be sure of that."

That's exactly what she was afraid of, Sarah thought as she walked out of his office.

Chapter 2

It was nearly six when Jesse pulled into the Garretts' driveway. He climbed out of the department Bronco and gazed up at the house, all three stories of it.

Somebody had been busy with spring cleaning, judging by the way the windows gleamed gold in the dying sun, without a streak. The place radiated warmth and elegance, from its perfectly manicured gardens to its cobblestone sidewalk.

The house was only a few years old, but a lifetime away from the miserable one-bedroom trailer halfway up Elk Mountain where Ginny and Corey had lived during her marriage to Hob Sylvester.

Jesse had worked for the county then as a deputy sheriff and he'd always hated going out on domestic disturbance calls there. He could still remember the tangible feeling of despair that permeated the thin, pain-

fully bare walls, and his constant, frustrating attempts
to convince Ginny to get out of the situation.

Oh, she would try. He knew that. She would move
out for a few days or a week or two. But Hob still had
enough high school football star in him to sweet-talk
her back.

Hob hadn't always been a son of a bitch, and maybe
that was one of the things that kept Ginny hanging on.
Once he'd been all charisma and slow, cowboy charm,
the high school football standout everybody pegged to
go pro. It hadn't worked out that way. Something went
wrong—Jesse wasn't sure what—and a few years later
Ginny got pregnant.

Jesse figured Hob must have seen it as just one more
dirty trick played on him by fate. He'd done the right
thing by marrying her, or what was considered the right
thing by society, anyway. It sure as hell hadn't been the
right thing for Ginny. Hob had spent the next six years
drinking hard and taking his bitterness out on her.

For more than a few of those years, Jesse had been
just like him. It was a chapter in his life he hated to
even remember, how after his parents' deaths he'd spent
many a night at the Renegade, trying to drown his guilt
any way he could.

Jesse pushed the memory away. Anyway, Hob was
gone. He'd taken up with a cocktail waitress from Idaho
Falls about four years ago and the two of them had
headed for Vegas, last Jesse heard.

Ginny had landed on her feet, that's for sure. Ended
up marrying her divorce attorney and now she and her
kid lived in one of the fanciest houses in town and she
drove a Range Rover and shopped at all the ritzy designer stores in Jackson Hole.

He thought of Sarah McKenzie's accusations. He really hoped she was wrong. Ginny deserved a happy ending, after what she'd been through.

As he walked up the front steps, the intoxicating smells of spring drifted around him—sweet lilac bushes, damp, musty earth and meat sizzling on somebody's grill nearby.

Salt River was his town and he was fiercely protective of it. When he was a kid, he couldn't wait to get out. He'd been stupid enough to think the slow pace of a small town was strangling the life out of him. Once in a while he still hungered for something more than ticketing jaywalkers and breaking up the occasional bar fight, but he owed a debt to the people of this town.

One he'd be a long time repaying.

Besides, he couldn't imagine living anywhere else on a beautiful, warm spring night like this. It was just about perfect, with kids jumping on a trampoline down the street, people working in their yards or reading the paper on their front porches, and sprinklers thumping happily all across town.

Not *quite* perfect, he amended. He still had the matter of Sarah McKenzie's suspicions about Corey Sylvester to contend with.

He rang the doorbell and had to wait only a few seconds before Ginny Garrett answered.

Her face still retained most of the beauty that had won her the prom queen tiara in school. It brightened when she saw him, but her expression just as quickly grew wary. "What has Corey done now?" she asked, her voice resigned.

"Nothing. Least, nothing that I know about yet. That's not why I'm here, anyway."

"Oh. Well then, Seth's not home, I'm afraid. He had a late meeting with a client."

"Actually, I wanted to speak with you."

Again, wariness vied with curiosity in her expression. "Come in, then," she finally said. "We can talk in the living room."

She led the way through the big house. Jesse had been there plenty of times on business with the mayor, but he always felt out of place amid the creamy whites and fancy furniture—afraid to move wrong in case he broke something expensive.

"Where's Maddie?" he asked, of Corey's six-month-old half sister.

"Napping. Finally." Ginny rolled her eyes. "I know it's almost bedtime anyway, but it's been one of those days. She's teething and has been running me ragged today. Would you care for something to drink? A pop or something?"

"No. I'm fine. I'd just as soon get this over with."

She glanced at him. "That sounds pretty ominous. What's this about, Jess?"

He sighed heavily. Damn, he didn't want to do this. Ginny had been his friend for a long time—the first girl he'd ever kissed, way back in the second grade.

After the car accident that had killed his parents and left him in the hospital for nearly a month, she'd been one of the few people who didn't offer him empty platitudes. Or, worse, who acted as if nothing had happened, when his whole life had just been ripped apart.

She had offered simple, calming comfort and he had never forgotten it.

Since then, she'd been to hell and back and had

worked hard to make something out of her life. How could he tell her about Ms. McKenzie's suspicions?

"Come on, Jess. Out with it. You're scaring me."

He blew out a breath, then met her worried gaze squarely. "How do Corey and Seth get on?"

Her brow furrowed. "What kind of question is that? They get along fine."

"All the time?"

She continued to look puzzled. "Certainly they have their differences, I suppose. Corey can be difficult sometimes and he has a hard time with authority—you should know that as well as anybody. But Seth tries hard to be a good father. Why do you ask?"

Damn, this was tough. "There's been an allegation that Corey is being abused."

She stared at him, the color draining from her face until her skin just about matched the white of the sofa she was sitting on. "Abused? By Seth?"

He nodded grimly.

"This is some kind of sick joke, right? Who would say such a terrible thing? It's not true. Absolutely not true."

"It's not completely unfounded, Gin. I understand he's had several injuries in the last few weeks."

"He's a boy. A boy who gets into more than his fair share of mischief, but still just a boy. He has accidents."

"You have to admit, it looks pretty suspicious, that many injuries in such a short period of time."

"No. You're wrong." She jumped up and began to pace around the room. "Who is saying such terrible things? Who would want to hurt us like this?"

For a moment he debated telling her it was Sarah McKenzie, then he discarded the idea. Sarah still had to teach Corey in her class for the rest of the school year and he didn't want to stir up trouble for her where he didn't need to. "At this point, let's just say it's a concerned citizen. I swear, it's no one with a hidden agenda, just somebody who cares about your son's welfare."

"Well, they're wrong. Dead wrong."

Sometimes he really hated this job. "I'm sorry, but I have to ask you, Ginny. Have you ever seen Seth hurting your son or do you have any reason to believe he might do so when you're not around?"

Her mouth compressed into a thin line. She was quiet for several long moments. When she finally spoke, her voice was low and hurt. "How can you even think such a thing, Jess? You, of all people, should know better. You know what it was like for us before. Do you honestly think, after what my son has been through, that I would stand by and do nothing while it happens all over again?"

He believed her. How could he do anything else, faced with such complete, passionate sincerity?

"Seth is a good man," she went on. "He's decent and caring and in the last two years he's been a wonderful father to Corey. He loves him, just as much as he loves Maddie. He even wants to adopt him!"

He sat back. "I'm sorry, Ginny. I had a hard time believing it, too, but I had to follow through and investigate."

"I understand."

"Did Corey have an explanation for being so accident-prone lately?"

Before she could answer, the front door opened and they heard the chink of keys being placed on a table in the hall.

Ginny paled a shade lighter. "That will be Seth. This is going to kill him, to have someone accuse him of such a thing."

"Ginny?" the mayor called from the entry. "Why is a police Bronco parked in the driveway?" A moment later, he poked his head into the living room. He frowned when he saw Jess. "Chief! Is something wrong?"

"Seth, you'd better sit down," Ginny began.

With a puzzled frown the mayor took a seat next to her. After Jesse reluctantly explained the purpose for his visit, Seth appeared just as shocked as his wife.

"It's absolutely not true," he said vehemently. "You must know that. I would never lay a hand on the boy."

"I had to investigate, Seth."

"Of course you did." He frowned. "It must have taken great courage for someone to step forward with those kinds of suspicions. Too many people just look the other way, not wanting to get involved. I'd like to know who instigated this."

Again Jesse thought of Sarah McKenzie and her nervousness in his office. He found himself strangely reluctant to mention her involvement, again using the excuse that she still had to teach Corey for the rest of the school year and it might make things awkward for her.

Rather than answer Seth, he opted to change the subject instead. "Something is still going on with Corey and I think we need to find out what. That many accidents in such a short time is pretty suspicious. Do you think someone else might be hurting him?"

Ginny looked as if she might be sick. Seth must have seen it, too. He grabbed her hand and squeezed tightly. "Who?" he asked. "Who would do that?"

"I don't know. Maybe someone at school. Has Corey

given you any reason to think he's being bullied? Or that he's been fighting with any of the other boys?"

"If anyone is beating on him, it's probably that Connor boy." Seth's voice dripped disgust.

"Luke's kid?"

Ginny nodded. "He's always hanging around with Corey. But he's in junior high school! What does he want with a ten-year-old?"

Dusty Connor had been in just as many scrapes with the law as Corey. Where Corey's shenanigans leaned toward the clever and mischievous, Dusty's were usually plain mean.

"I don't know, but I think we need to find out," Jesse said.

"How?"

Before he could answer her, they heard the sound of a door slamming, then a voice from the kitchen of the house. "Mom, I'm home," Corey called.

"We're in the living room," Ginny answered. "Come in here, please."

They heard a loud, exasperated sigh and then Corey wandered into the room. With a basketball under his arm and dressed in baggy shorts, a T-shirt and high-top sneakers, he looked like most of the other ten-year-olds in town except for a black eye and all that attitude radiating from him like heat waves off a sidewalk.

"What's for din—" he started to ask, then his gaze landed on Jess. For one brief instant, pure panic flickered across his expression, but he quickly hid it behind belligerence. "I didn't do nothin'."

Interesting. Now, why would the kid suddenly break a sweat just at the sight of a cop when he'd always been a cocky little wise guy, even when Jesse or one of the five officers in his department caught him red-handed up to something?

What was he messed up in now that had him so jumpy? Whatever it was, Jesse had a bad feeling about it. He obviously needed to keep a better eye on the kid.

He raised an eyebrow. "What makes you so sure you're in trouble?"

"I'm not?" Corey's voice cracked on the second word.

"Should you be?"

"No. I told you, I ain't done nothin'."

"Haven't done anything," Ginny corrected quietly.

"Whatever."

"Good," Jesse said, thinking fast. "Because I need your help."

All three of them stared at him. To Ginny and Seth, he sent a reassuring smile. He'd been a cop a long time and the one thing he'd learned was to trust his instincts. He could start interrogating the boy about his injuries—the black eyes, the cut, whatever bruises the school-teacher had seen that afternoon.

But judging by his experiences with Corey, he was sure the kid wouldn't tell them a thing. He would turn closemouthed and uncooperative and give Jesse the same bull he'd been giving everybody else about his injuries.

On the other hand, if he could spend a little time with Corey—convince the kid to trust him—maybe Jesse could get to the bottom of this.

"I'm in need of a partner for a couple days. You interested?"

The boy looked baffled. "A partner?"

"Yeah. I'm coming to school next month to talk

about crime prevention." That much was true, at least. The annual visit had been scheduled for weeks. The rest he was making up as he went along.

"I was thinking I could use somebody who knows his way around to help me out," Jesse went on. "Give the other kids some pointers about how to stay safe and out of trouble."

"Me? You want *me* to help you?"

"Why not?"

The boy looked as if he could think of a million reasons why not, but there was also an unmistakable curious light in his eyes.

Jesse decided to play on that. "You don't have to do it if you don't want to, but I could really use your help. If you agree to help me, you'll need to come to the station a few times so we can figure out what we're going to do. What do you think?"

"Sounds lame."

"Maybe. That's why I need your help. You can make me sound cool enough that the kids will listen to me."

"You want me to help you be *cool?*"

He had to fight a triumphant grin at the unwilling fascination in the boy's eyes at the idea. "Yeah. Think you can handle it?"

"I don't know, Chief." The kid sent him a sidelong look. "Could be a pretty tough job."

Jesse laughed. "I think you're man enough to handle it."

Corey chewed his lip, and Jesse could just about see the wheels turning in his head as he tried to figure out all the angles. He held his breath, waiting for the boy's answer. After a few beats, Corey shrugged his bony shoulders. "Sure. Why not?"

"Great. Meet me at my office tomorrow after school."

"Whatever. Can I go now?" he asked his mother.

Ginny nodded. As soon as they heard footsteps pounding up the stairs, both of the Garretts turned to him.

"What was that all about?" Seth asked.

"It was a spur-of-the-moment thing. I figured maybe if I have a chance to talk one-on-one with him, he might open up a little and tell me what's going on."

"Are you sure Corey would be willing to do this?" Ginny asked with a frown. "And even if he does, how do you know he'll talk to you?"

"Well, even if he doesn't open up and talk to me about whatever's going on with him, maybe he'll learn something himself about staying out of trouble."

A strident cry echoed through the house suddenly. "There's Maddie." Ginny rose from the couch.

Jesse stood, as well. "I'll get out of your hair, then."

"Would you like to stay for supper? We're having fried chicken and mashed potatoes."

The offer of some decent home cooking for a change had his mouth watering.

He used to drop by the family ranch two or three nights a week when Cassie lived there with Matt and Lucy. She was divine in the kitchen. But after Matt's wedding, Cassie had surprised them all by taking a job at a dude ranch north of town and moving out. Since Jesse didn't want to bug the newlyweds while they were busy setting up house, for the past month he'd had to make do with his own pitiful attempts at cooking.

As much as he wouldn't mind staying for supper, he suddenly decided he'd much rather stop in to see Sarah

McKenzie again. She was probably wondering what had happened with Corey.

And he had a powerful hankering to see if he could figure out what had put those shadows in her pretty green eyes.

Every muscle in her body ached.

That would teach her to spend two solid hours yanking weeds and hauling compost. Sarah winced at the burn in her arms as she tried to comb the snarls out of her hair. Even after a long, pounding shower with water as hot as she could stand, her muscles still cried out in protest.

She was so out of shape, it was pathetic. After the attack, she had become almost manic about trying to rebuild the damage that had been done to her body. Maybe on some subconscious level she had thought if she were stronger or faster she could protect herself. She had followed her physical therapy routine religiously, working for hours each day to regain strength.

Eventually, though, she had become so frustrated at the reality of her new, permanent limitations that she had eased off.

After she came to Salt River, it had been so exhausting at first just keeping up with her students she hadn't had energy to exercise. Eventually, she fell into a busy routine that didn't leave much time for anything but school.

Still, she should have made time. Working out in the yard shouldn't leave her knee on fire and the rest of her throbbing muscles jumbled into one big ache.

It had seemed like a good idea at the time. She thought working in the garden after school might calm her nerves, just as it always did. But she was just as edgy and upset as she had been at the police station.

By now, Chief Harte had probably spoken with the Garretts. She should be relieved, and she was. She *was*. Whoever was hurting that child deserved to be punished. She knew that and believed it fiercely. At the same time, she couldn't help the nervousness that had settled in her stomach and refused to leave, or the tiny voice that called her crazy for getting involved at all.

Hadn't she learned her lesson? Hadn't Tommy DeSilva taught her in savage, brutal detail what happened to nosy schoolteachers who didn't mind their own business?

She pushed the thought away. Once more she had a child to protect—it wasn't simply a case of turning in a vicious criminal. She had made the right decision, eighteen months ago and today. She had done what she had to do. The only thing she *could* have done.

She didn't want to think about it. Any of it. After quickly pulling her hair into a ponytail to keep it out of her face, she limped from the bedroom to the kitchen, her knee crying out with every step.

Dinner was the usual, something packaged out of the freezer and intended to be eaten in solitude. What was more pitiful than shoving a frozen dinner in the microwave, then eating it in front of the television set alone? she wondered.

She had to get out more, she thought as she finally settled on a low-fat chicken-and-rice meal. It was a vow she made to herself with grim regularity, but she never seemed to do anything about it. When was the last time she'd shared an evening meal with someone besides Tom Brokaw? She couldn't even remember.

She never used to be such an introvert. In Chicago she'd had a wide, eclectic circle of friends. Artists, social activists, computer geeks. They went to plays and poetry readings and Cubs games together.

At first her friends had tried to rally around her, with cards and gifts and visits in the hospital. Unable to face their awkwardness and pity, she had pushed them all away, even Andrew.

Especially Andrew.

She had given him back his ring when she was still in the hospital, and he had taken it with a guilty relief that shamed both of them.

She didn't blame him. Not really. That day had changed her, had shattered something vital inside her. Eighteen months later she still hadn't made much progress repairing it.

She knew her friends and family all thought she was running away when she decided to take a teaching job in small-town Wyoming. She couldn't deny there was truth to that. She *had* been running away, had searched the Internet for job listings in small towns as far away as she could find.

But escaping Chicago and the grim memories of that fateful morning had been only part of the reason she had come here.

She needed to be in a place where she could feel clean again.

The microwave dinged. Grateful to escape her thoughts, she reached in with a pot holder to pull out her dinner just as the doorbell chimed through the little house.

She'd heard the sound so seldom that it took her a moment to figure out what it was. Who could be here?

Her heart fluttered with wild panic for just an instant, but she took a quick, calming breath. She had nothing to worry about, not here in Salt River.

Setting her plate on the table, she made her way out of the kitchen and down the hall to the door, careful not to put too much stress on her knee. At first all she could see through the peephole was a hard, broad chest, but then she saw the badge over one tan denim pocket and realized it must be Chief Harte.

Her heart fluttered again, but she wasn't completely sure it was only with panic this time. Why did the man have such an effect on her? She hated it. Absolutely hated it!

The bell rang—impatiently, she thought—and with one more deep breath, she opened the door.

His smile sent her pulse into double time. "I was just driving home and thought I'd check in with you and let you know how things went at the mayor's place."

As much as she'd like to, she knew she couldn't very well talk to him through the screen door "I…come in." She held the door open, wishing she were wearing something a little more professional than a pair of faded jeans and an old Northwestern sweatshirt.

The small foyer shrank by half as soon as he walked inside. There was absolutely no way she could stand there and carry on a half-rational conversation with him looming over her, looking so big and imposing. The house she rented was tiny, with a living room only a few feet larger than the entry. Where else could they go?

"It's a nice night," she said impulsively. "We can talk outside. Is that all right?"

She took his shrug for assent and led him through

the house to the covered porch, flipping on the recessed lights overhead as they went through the door.

The back porch had become her favorite spot lately. She hadn't realized how closed in and trapped she'd been feeling during the harsh Wyoming winter until the relentless snow finally began to give way to spring.

As the temperatures warmed, she discovered she liked to sit out here in the evenings and look up at the mountains. Their massive grandeur comforted her, in some strange way she couldn't define.

A few weeks ago she'd found some wicker furniture in the shed and dragged it up the porch stairs. She'd purchased matching cushions and hung baskets overflowing with flowers around the porch to create a cozy little haven. She'd been very pleased with the results, but now, trying to see the place through Chief Harte's eyes, she felt awkward. Exposed, somehow.

He sprawled into one of the wicker chairs, completely dwarfing it. "This is nice," he murmured. "Hell of a view from here."

"I imagine you're used to it, since you grew up in Star Valley."

His mouth quirked into a half smile that did more annoying things to her nerves. "I've seen those mountains just about every day of the last thirty-three years and they still sometimes take my breath away."

She wouldn't have expected such an admission from him. It made him seem perhaps a little softer, a little less intimidating, to know they shared this, at least.

Before she could come up with an answer, he settled back into his chair and stretched his long legs out in front of him until his boots almost touched one of her sneakers. Closing his eyes, he looked for all the world as if he were settling in for the night.

"This is really nice," he repeated.

She cleared her throat, suddenly not at all sure she wanted Jesse Harte lounging so comfortably on her back porch. "So what happened at the Garretts? Did you make an arrest?"

"No. Sorry to disappoint you, but the mayor is still a free man. And it looks like he's going to stay that way."

She stared at him. "Why?"

He opened one eye. "He and Ginny both said he'd never hurt the boy, and I believe them."

"Just like that?"

"Just like that."

Renewed fury pounded through her. It had all been for nothing—risking her job and tangling with the man she had spent eight months doing her best to avoid. For nothing.

Despite her own nightmares, she had done the right thing by going to the proper authority and he had basically laughed in her face.

Calm down, Sarah.

A corner of her brain sent out strident warning bells that she was going to say or do something she would regret, but she ignored it, lost to everything but her anger.

"I can't believe this," she snapped. "If I ever wanted to commit a crime, Salt River, Wyoming, would obviously be the place for it. All I have to do is swear to the police chief that I didn't do anything and I'll be home free."

He dropped his relaxed pose as easily as a snake shedding his skin and straightened in the chair. "Now, wait a minute…"

"Of course, maybe I'd have to be a powerful person like the mayor so I can get away with it," she went on, as if he hadn't spoken. "Apparently, holding political office around here gives a person the right to do whatever he darn well pleases."

"I can see where you'd think that, but you're wrong. Dead wrong. If I thought for one minute Seth had given that boy so much as a hangnail, you can be damn sure I wouldn't let him get away with it."

"Lucky for him, then, that he managed to convince you he didn't do anything. I'd like you to leave now, Chief Harte."

She whirled away from him with an angry, abrupt movement, completely forgetting that her knee was in no condition to withstand the stress of such a quick motion.

She heard an ominous pop, then she had the sudden, sick sensation of falling as her knee gave out.

One instant she was tumbling toward the hard wooden slats of the porch, the next she heard an alarmed "Hey!" and found herself wrapped in strong male arms, shoved back against a hard, muscled chest.

For a moment she froze as she was surrounded by heat and strength, helpless to get away. And then panic took over. *He* had held her just like this, from behind, with her arms locked at her sides.

Instantly she was once more in that dingy Chicago classroom, with its dirty windows and broken desks and stale, tired air.

Not again. She wouldn't let this happen again.

She couldn't breathe, suddenly, couldn't think. Her

heart was racing, adrenaline pumping like crazy, and only one thought pierced her panic.

Escape.

Somehow, some way, this time she had to escape.

Chapter 3

What in the hell?

Jesse held an armload of kicking, fighting female and tried to figure out what had set her off like this.

All he had tried to do was keep her from hitting the ground when she started to topple. One minute she'd been standing there, her pretty mouth hard and angry as she ordered him out of her house, the next she had turned into this wild, out-of-control banshee, flailing her arms around and twisting every which way.

He figured her bum leg must have given out and that's what had made her start to fall. The way she was fighting him, she was only going to hurt it even more—and maybe something else, too.

She wanted out of his arms. He could respect that. Only problem was, if he let her go now, she would still hit the ground.

"Take it easy, ma'am," he murmured softly, soothingly, the way he would to one of Matt's skittish colts. "It's okay. I'm only trying to help. I won't hurt you."

Carefully, moving as slowly as he could manage with his arms full of trouble, he eased her down to the floor. The lower to the ground they moved, though, the more frenzied she fought him. Through the delicate skin at her wrists he could feel her pulse trembling and she was breathing in harsh, ragged gasps.

He finally was close enough to the wooden slats of the porch that he could release her safely. As soon as she was on solid ground, he moved back, crouching to her level a few feet away. "See? No harm done."

For a moment she just stared at him, her big green eyes dazed and lost. She blinked several times, her small chest heaving under that soft old sweatshirt as she tried to catch her breath.

He knew exactly when she snapped back into the present—her eyes lost that frantic, fight-or-flight look and a deep flush spread from her neck to her cheekbones like bright red paint spilling across canvas.

"I... Oh."

In those expressive eyes he could see mortification and something deeper. Almost shame.

She cleared her throat and shifted her gaze to the ground. "I'm so sorry." Her voice was small, tight. "Did I hurt you?"

"Nope." He tried to smile reassuringly, for all the good it did him, since she wouldn't look at him. "I've run into much tougher customers than you."

"I don't doubt that," she murmured, a deep, old bitterness in her voice.

Her hands still shook and he had to fight the urge

to reach out and cover those slender, trembling fingers with his.

She wouldn't welcome the comfort right now. He knew she wouldn't. And she'd probably jump right through the porch roof if he obeyed his other sudden, completely irrational impulse—to reach forward and press his mouth to that wildly fluttering pulse he could see beating quickly through an artery at the base of her throat.

"You want to tell me what that was all about?" he asked instead.

She still refused to meet his gaze. "You just startled me, that's all. I don't like being startled."

Yeah, like a wild mustang doesn't like rowels dug into his sides. Eyes narrowed, he watched her for several more seconds, then realized she wasn't going to tell him anything more about the reason for her panic.

"How's the leg?"

"The…the leg?"

"That's what started this whole thing, remember? You turned to walk away from me and it must have given out. I tried to keep you from falling and you suddenly went off like a firecracker on the Fourth of July."

The blush spread even farther. "I'm sorry," she whispered again. "Thank you for trying to help."

She reached out and used a chair for leverage to stand, then tested her weight gingerly. "It's my knee, not my leg. It gives me trouble sometimes if I move too quickly."

Was that the reason for that slight, mysterious limp of hers? What had caused it? he wondered. An accident of some kind? The same accident that made her spirit seem so wounded, that put that wild panic in her green eyes when somebody touched her unexpectedly?

He had a thousand questions, but he knew she wouldn't answer any of them. "Sit down. Need me to call Doc Wallace and have him come take a look at it?"

"No. I'm fine. It should be all right in a few moments."

"Can I bring you something, then? A glass of water or juice or something? A pillow, maybe, to put that leg on?"

She sat down and gave him an odd look, as if she didn't know quite what to make of the Salt River police chief trying to play nurse. "No, I told you, I'm fine. It's happened before. Usually, if I can just sit still for a few moments it will be all right."

After a moment he shrugged and sprawled into the wicker chair across from her. "In that case, you're in no condition to kick me out, so I'll just sit here with you until you're back on your feet. Just to make sure you don't need a doctor or anything."

"That's not necessary. I told you, I'll be perfectly fine."

"Humor me. It's my civic duty. Can't leave a citizen of the good town of Salt River in her hour of need. Now, where were we?" Jesse scratched his cheek. "Oh, that's right. I was telling you what happened at the mayor's."

"You mean you were telling me what *didn't* happen," she muttered. Her fiery color began to fade, he saw with satisfaction, until it just about matched those soft pink, early climbing roses around her back porch that sent their heady aroma through the cool evening air.

"We covered that. What I didn't have a chance to tell

you is that I think you're right. Something's definitely going on with that kid."

Her green eyes widened. "You agree with me?"

"Someone is behind all those little 'accidents' of his, but I'm not convinced it's the mayor."

"Who, then? Surely not his mother?"

He snorted. "Ginny? Hell—" he paused "—er, *heck* no."

"You don't need to guard your tongue around me, Chief Harte. I've heard a few epithets in my time. Probably some that would make even you blush."

"I doubt that. Anyone who uses words like 'epithets' couldn't have heard too many raunchy ones."

"You'd be surprised what you can hear in a school hallway."

"You teach the fourth grade," he exclaimed, appalled. "How bad could the cuss words get?"

Her lips curved slightly, but she straightened them quickly, before the unruly things could do something crazy like smile, he figured. "I didn't mean my students here, although I still certainly hear some choice language from them occasionally."

"Where, then?"

"Where what?" She shifted her gaze down again, her fingers troubling a loose thread in her jeans.

Why did she have to be so damn evasive about everything? Getting information out of the woman was as tough as trying to get those blasted climbing roses to grow in January.

"Where did you hear the kind of words that could make a rough-edged cop like me blush?"

She was silent for a moment, and then she took a deep breath and met his gaze. "Before I came to Wyoming, I taught for five years at a school on Chicago's south side."

All he could do was stare at her. He wouldn't have been more shocked if she'd just told him she used to be an exotic dancer.

The fragile, skittish schoolmarm who jumped if you looked at her the wrong way used to walk the rough-and-tumble hallways of an inner-city school? She had to be joking, didn't she? One look at her tightly pursed mouth told him she wasn't. Before he could press her on it, though, she quickly changed the subject.

"If you don't believe Corey's being abused, what sort of trouble do you think he's involved with?"

He barely heard, still focused on her startling disclosure. Why did she leave Chicago? Did it have anything to do with her panicky reaction to him earlier? Or with her knee that still gave her trouble if she moved the wrong way?

With frustration, he realized his burning curiosity was going to have to wait. Judging by that withdrawn look on her face, she wasn't about to satisfy it anytime soon.

He gave a mental shrug. He'd get the information out of her sooner or later. He was a cop. It was his job to solve mysteries.

"I don't know," he said, in answer to her question about Corey. "But whatever it is, I doubt it's legal. He sure looked scared when he came home and found me sitting with his parents."

"What do you plan to do next?"

"Try to find out what he's up to. I figured maybe if I can talk to him one-on-one, he might open up a little more."

"I take it you have a plan."

He nodded. "I'm coming to the grade school next month to talk about crime prevention, and he's going to be my assistant. I expect it will take us several days to get ready, which ought to give me plenty of time to find out what's been going on with him."

"And he agreed to help you?"

"He wasn't too crazy about it at first, but he finally came around. I think it will be good for him." He paused. "If someone is hurting that kid, I'll find out, Sarah. I promise you that."

She gazed at him, green eyes wide and startled at his vehemence. Tilting her head, she studied him closely as if trying to gauge his sincerity. Whatever she saw in his expression must have satisfied her. After a few moments she offered him a smile. Not much of one, just a tentative little twitch of her lips, but it was definitely still a smile.

He felt as jubilant as if he'd just single-handedly brought every outlaw in the Wild West to justice.

"Thank you," Sarah murmured, her voice as soft as that spring breeze that teased her blond hair like a lover's hand.

"You're welcome," he answered gruffly, knowing damn well he shouldn't be so entranced by a tiny smile and a woman with secrets in her eyes.

"And I'm sorry for the terrible things I said to you," she went on. "I had no right to say such things. To judge you like that."

He had to like a woman who could apologize so sweetly. "You're a teacher concerned about one of her students. You were willing to do what you thought was the right thing, which is more than most people would in the same situation."

She didn't seem to take his words as the compliment he intended. Instead, her mouth tightened and she looked away from him toward the wooden slats of the porch.

What the hell had he said to make her look as if she wanted to cry? He gave an inward, frustrated sigh. Just when he thought he was making progress with her, she clammed up again.

He ought to just let it ride. Sarah McKenzie was obviously troubled by things she figured were none of his business. But something about that lost, wounded look that turned her green eyes murky brought all his protective instincts shoving their way out.

"Something wrong?" he asked.

"No," she said curtly. "Nothing at all."

"How's the knee?"

She looked disoriented for a moment, then glanced down at her outstretched leg. "Oh. I think it's feeling much better." Gripping the arms of the wicker rocker, she rose to her feet and carefully tested it with her weight. "Yes. Much better."

She was lying. He could tell by the lines of pain that bracketed her mouth like sagging fence posts.

"You sure?"

"Yes. Positive. I'm fine. I appreciate all your help, Chief Harte, but I'm sure you have better things to do than baby-sit me."

He couldn't think of a single one, especially if he stood half a chance of coaxing more than that sad little smile out of her. But she obviously wanted him gone, and his mama hadn't raised her kids to be rude. Well, except for Matt, maybe.

Anyway, he'd have another chance to see those green eyes soften and her soft, pretty mouth lift at the corners. And if an excuse to see her again didn't present itself, he'd damn well make one up.

"If you're sure you're okay, I'll leave so you can get back to the supper I dragged you away from. It's probably cold by now."

She grimaced. "I'm afraid it's not much of a meal, hot or cold. A frozen dinner."

It broke his heart to think of her sitting alone here with her solitary dinner. If he thought for a second she'd agree to go with him, he'd pack her into his Bronco and take her down to the diner for some of Murphy's turkey-fried steak.

But even though he had willingly left the ranch work to Matt, he had still gentled enough skittish mustangs in his time to know when to call it a day. He had a feeling he was going to have to move very slowly if he wanted to gain the schoolteacher's trust.

Asking her to dinner would probably send her loping away faster than the Diamond Harte's best cutter after a stray.

No hurry. He could be a patient man, when the situation called for it. He would bide his time, let her know she had nothing to fear from him.

Meanwhile, he now had two mysteries on his hands: Corey Sylvester and whatever mischief he was up to. And Sarah McKenzie.

The pretty schoolteacher had scars. Deep ones. And he wasn't about to rest until he found out who or what had given them to her.

Chapter 4

The nightmare attacked just before dawn.

She should have expected it, given the stress of the day. Seeing Corey Sylvester's bruises, the visit to the police station that had been so reminiscent of the extensive, humiliating interviews she had given in Chicago, and two encounters with the gorgeous but terrifying Jesse Harte.

It was all more than her still-battered psyche could handle.

If she had been thinking straight, she would have tried to stay up, to fight the dream off with the only tool she had—consciousness. But the sentence diagrams she was trying to grade worked together with the exhausting stress of the day to finish her off. After her fourth yawn in as many minutes, she had finally given up. She was half-asleep as she checked the locks and turned off the lights sometime around midnight.

Sleep came instantly, and the dream followed on its heels.

It was as familiar to her as her *ABC*s. Walking into her empty classroom. Humming softly to the Beethoven sonata that had been playing on her car CD. Wondering if she would be running on schedule after school to meet Andrew before the opening previews at the little art theater down the street from her apartment.

She unlocked her classroom door and found him waiting for her, his face hard and sharp and his eyes dark with fury.

She hadn't been afraid. Not at first. At first she'd only been angry. He should have been in jail, behind bars where he belonged.

The detective she had made her report to the afternoon before—O'Derry, his name had been—had called her the previous evening to let her know officers had picked up DeSilva. But he had also warned her even then that the system would probably release the eighteen-year-old on bail just a few hours later.

She knew why he had come—because she had dared step up to report him for dealing drugs and endangering the welfare of a child. She imagined he would threaten her, maybe warn her to mind her own business. She never guessed he would hurt her.

How stupid and naive she had been in her safe, middle-class world. She had taught at an inner-city school long enough that she should have realized anyone willing to use a nine-year-old girl to deliver drugs to vicious criminals would be capable of anything.

"How did you get in?" she started to ask, then saw shattered glass from the broken window all over the floor and the battered desks closest to it. How was she supposed to teach her class now with cool October air rushing in? With the stink and noise of the city oozing in along with it?

Before she could say anything more, he loomed in front of her. "You messin' with the wrong man, bitch."

Still angry about the window, she spoke without thinking. "I don't see a man here," she said rashly. "All I can see is a stupid punk who hides behind little girls."

He hissed a name then—a vicious, obscene name—and the wild rage in his features finally pierced her self-righteous indignation. For the first time, a flicker of unease crawled up her spine.

He was high on something. He might be only eighteen, but that didn't mean anything on the street. Punk or not, a furious junkie was the most dangerous creature alive.

She started to edge back toward the door, praying one of the custodians would be within earshot, but DeSilva was faster. He beat her to the door and turned the lock, then advanced on her, a small chrome handgun suddenly in his hand.

"You're not goin' anywhere," he growled.

She forced herself to stay calm. To treat him coolly and reasonably, as she would one of her troubled students. "You won't use that on me. The detectives who arrested you will know who did it. They'll arrest you within the hour."

"Maybe. But you'll still be dead."

"And the minute you fire a shot, everybody in the place is going to come running. Are you going to kill them all, too?"

He squinted, trying to follow her logic, and she saw

his hand waver slightly. Pushing her advantage, she held out her own hand. "Come on. Give me the gun."

For several long moments he stared at her, a dazed look on his face as if he couldn't quite figure out what he was doing there. Finally, when she began to feel light-headed from fear, he shoved the gun back into his waistband and stood there shaking a little.

"Good. Okay," she murmured. "Why don't you sit down and I'll get you a glass of water?" *And maybe slip out and call the police while I'm at it,* she thought.

"I don't want a glass of water," he snarled, and without warning he smacked her hard across the face.

The force and the shock of it sent her to her knees. The next thing she knew, he had gone crazy, striking out at her with anything he could reach—the legs of her wooden chair, the stapler off her desk, the stick she used to point out locations on the map during geography.

She curled into a protective ball, but still he hit her back, her head, her legs, muttering all the while. "You have to pay. Nobody narcs on Tommy D and gets away with it. You have to pay."

A particularly hard hit at her temple from the large, pretty polished stone she used as a paperweight had her head spinning. She almost slipped into blessed unconsciousness. Oblivion hovered just out of reach, like a mirage in the desert. Before she could reach it, his mood changed and she felt the horrible weight of his hands on her breasts, moving up her thighs under her skirt, ripping at her nylons.

She fought fiercely, kicking out, crying, screaming, but as always, she was helpless to get away.

This time, before that final, dehumanizing act of brutality, the school bell pealed through the dingy class-room and she was able to claw her way out of sleep.

The ringing went on and on, echoing in her ears, until she realized it was her alarm clock.

She fumbled to turn it off, then had to press a hand to her rolling, pitching stomach. The jarring shift between nightmare and reality always left her nauseated. She lurched to her feet and stumbled to the bathroom, where she tossed what was left of her dinner from the night before.

After she rinsed her mouth, she gazed at herself in the mirror above the sink. She hardly recognized the pale woman who stared back at her with huge, haunted green eyes underlined by dark purplish smears. Who was this stranger? This fearful person who had invaded her skin, her bones, her soul?

Gazing in the mirror, she saw new lines around her mouth, a bleakness in her eyes. She looked more hungover than anything else, and Sarah despised the stranger inside her all over again.

She hated the woman she had become.

For the past eighteen months she had felt as if she were dog-paddling in some frigid, ice-choked sea, unable to go forward, unable to climb out, just stuck there in one place while arctic waters froze the life out of her inch by inch.

How long? How long would she let a vicious act of violence rule her life? She pictured herself a year from now, five years, ten. Still suffering nightmares, still hiding from the world, burying herself in her work and her garden and her students.

She had to be stronger. She *could* be stronger. Hadn't

she proved it to some degree by going to Chief Harte the day before with her concerns about Corey?

She couldn't consider it monumental by any stretch of the imagination. Still, she had done something, even if it was only to kick just a little harder in her frozen prison.

Beginning today, things would be different. She would *make* them different.

If she didn't, she knew it was only a matter of time before she would stop paddling completely and let herself slip quietly into the icy depths.

Her resolve lasted until she arrived at school and found Jesse Harte's police Bronco out front.

She cringed, remembering how she had fought and kicked at him the day before in the middle of another of those nasty flashbacks. He must think she was completely insane, the kind of woman who boiled pet rabbits for kicks.

Maybe she wouldn't even see him.

Maybe the vehicle belonged to a totally different officer.

Maybe an earthquake would hit just as she reached the doors to the school and she wouldn't be able to go in.

No such luck. Inside, she found Jesse standing in the glass-walled office taking notes while Chuck Hendricks—the principal of the school and the bane of her and every other Salt River Elementary teacher's existence—gestured wildly.

Whatever they were talking about wasn't sitting well with Chuck, judging by his red face and the taut veins in his neck that stood out like support ropes on a circus tent.

Jesse didn't see her, she saw with relief. She should have hurried on to her classroom, but the temptation to watch him was irresistible. The man was like some kind of dark angel. Lean and rugged and gorgeous, with rough-hewn features and those unbelievably blue eyes.

She pressed a hand to her stomach, to the funny little ache there, like a dozen tiny, fluttering birds.

"He's yummy, isn't he?"

Coloring fiercely, Sarah jerked her gaze away as if she'd been caught watching a porn movie. She had been so engrossed in watching Jesse that she hadn't even heard Janie Parker walk up and join her.

"Who?" she asked with what she sincerely hoped was innocence in her tone.

The art teacher grinned, showing off her dimples. "Salt River's favorite bad-boy cop. Jesse Harte. The man makes me want to run a few stop signs just so he'll pull me over. He can write me all the tickets he wants as long as I can drool over him while he's doing it."

Janie was probably exactly his type. Petite and curvy and cute, with a personality to match. Sarah had a quick mental picture of the two of them together, of Jesse looking down at the vivacious teacher with laughter in those blue eyes, just before he lowered that hard mouth to hers.

The image shouldn't depress her so much. She quickly changed the subject. "What's got Chuck's toupee in such a twist?" she asked.

It was exactly the kind of thing the Before Sarah would have said, something glib and light and casual. But it was obvious from Janie's raised eyebrows that she didn't expect anything remotely glib from the stiff, solemn woman Sarah had become.

The rest of the faculty must think she had no sense of humor whatsoever. How could she blame them, when she had given them little indication of it?

She also hadn't tried very hard to make friends. Not that she hadn't wanted friends—or, heaven knows, needed them—but for the first time in her life, she hadn't been able to work up the energy.

This was one of the things she could change, if it wasn't too late. Starting today, she would go out of her way to be friendly to her fellow teachers. If anybody dared invite her anywhere after she had spent six months rebuffing all their efforts, she wouldn't refuse this time.

"Somebody broke in to the school last night," Janie finally answered.

Sarah immediately regretted her glibness. "Was it vandals?"

"Nothing was damaged as far as anybody can tell, but they got away with the Mile High Quarter Jar."

She suddenly realized that was the reason the foyer in front of the office looked different. Empty. "How? That thing must have weighed a ton!"

As a schoolwide project, the students were collecting money for the regional children's medical center and were trying to raise enough quarters to cover a mile if they were laid in a straight line.

They still had a way to go, but had raised nearly fifteen hundred dollars in quarters.

Janie shrugged. "Either we've had a visit from a superhero-turned-bad or they must have used a dolly of some kind."

"How did they get in?"

"A broken window in Chuck's office. That's probably why he's so upset. Forget the kids' money, but if he knows what's good for him, Chief Harte darn well better catch the villains who dared scatter glass all over His Holiness's desk."

Broken glass littering a desk like shards of ice.

Sarah drew a quick breath and pushed the memory aside. She forced a laugh, which earned her another surprised look from the other teacher.

Jesse couldn't have heard it inside the office, but he lifted his head anyway.

His gaze locked onto hers and a slow, private smile spread over his features like the sun rising over the Salt River range.

A simple smile shouldn't have the power to make her blush, but she could feel more color seeping into her cheeks. Still, she managed to give him a hesitant smile in return, then quickly turned away to find Janie watching the interaction with avid interest.

"Whoa. What was that all about?"

Sarah blushed harder. "What?"

"Is there something I should know about going on between you and our hunky police chief?"

"No. Of course not! I barely know the man."

"So why is your face more red than Principal Chuck's right now? Come on. Tell all!"

"There's nothing to tell." Without realizing it, she used the same curt tone she would with an unruly student. "Excuse me. I have to get to class."

Janie's tentative friendliness disappeared and she donned a cool mask. "Sorry for prying."

Sarah felt a pang as she watched it disappear. She remembered her vow to make new friends and realized she was blowing it, big time. "Janie, I'm sorry.

But really, nothing's going on. Chief Harte is just… we're just…"

"You don't have to explain. It's none of my business."

"Honestly, there's nothing to explain. I just always seem to act like an idiot around him," she confessed.

"Don't we all, sweetheart? What is it about big, gorgeous men that zaps our brain cells?"

The warmth had returned to Janie's expression, Sarah saw with relief. She wanted to bask in it like a cat sprawled out in a sunbeam.

But she knew she would have to work harder to make a new friend than just a quick conversation in the hallway. Gathering her nerve, she smiled at the other teacher. "Are you on lunch duty this week?"

"No. I had my turn last week."

"Would you like to escape the school grounds for a half hour and grab a quick bite sometime?"

If she was shocked by the invitation, Janie quickly recovered. "Sure. Just name the day."

"How about Friday?"

"Sounds perfect."

It was a start, Sarah thought as she walked to her classroom. And somehow, for just a moment, the water surrounding her didn't seem quite as cold.

Jesse tuned out Up-Chuck Hendricks and watched Sarah make her slow way down the hall toward her classroom. She was still favoring her leg, he saw with concern. Her walk was just a little uneven, like a wagon rolling along with a wobbly wheel.

He shouldn't have taken her word that everything was okay the night before. He should have insisted on hauling her to the clinic, just to check things out.

What else was he supposed to have done? He couldn't force her to go to the doctor if she didn't want to. He'd done what he could, sat with her as long as she would let him.

It amazed him how protective he felt toward her. Amazed him and made him a little uneasy. He tried to tell himself it was just a natural—if chauvinistic—reaction of a man in the presence of a soft, quiet, fragile woman. But deep down he knew it was more than that. For some strange reason he was fascinated by Sarah McKenzie, and had been since the day she moved to Star Valley.

He'd dreamed about her the night before.

He imagined she would be horror-struck if she knew the hot, steamy activities his subconscious had conjured up for them to do together. Hell, even *he* was horror-struck when he woke up and found himself hard and ready for action. She wasn't at all his type. So why couldn't he seem to stop thinking about her?

"Are you listening to me?"

"Sure." He snapped his attention back to Chuck Hendricks, chagrined that he'd let himself get so distracted from the investigation by the soft, pretty Sarah McKenzie.

He also didn't like the fact that the principal could make him feel as if he had somehow traveled twenty years back in time and was once more the troublemaker du jour in Up-Chuck's sixth-grade class.

"What are you going to do to get to the bottom of this?" Hendricks snapped. "These criminals must be caught and punished severely. I can tell you right where to start. Corey Sylvester."

The principal said the name with such seething animosity that a wave of sympathy for the kid washed through Jesse. He knew all too well what it was like to be at the top of Chuck's scapegoat list.

"Why Corey?" he asked.

"It's exactly the sort of thing he would do. After thirty-five years of teaching hooligans, I know a bad apple and I can tell you that boy is just plain rotten."

The principal didn't seem to notice the sudden frown and narrowed gaze of one of those former hooligans. "Besides that," he went on, "I saw him hanging around by the jar yesterday before lunch recess. It's the second or third time I've seen him there. I know he was up to no good."

"Maybe he was putting some quarters in."

Hendricks harrumphed as if the idea was the most ridiculous thing he'd ever heard. "I doubt it."

Jesse felt a muscle twitch in his jaw. He would have liked to tell Up-Chuck exactly what he thought of him, but he knew that wouldn't help him solve the case of the missing quarters. "I'll talk to him. But I've got to tell you, my instincts are telling me you're on the wrong track. I don't think he did it. Or if he did, he couldn't have acted alone."

"Why not?"

"Do the math, Chuck." His smile would have curdled milk, but his former teacher didn't seem to notice. "Corey weighs no more than sixty-five pounds. A jar with six thousand quarters would weigh a whole lot more than that. He wouldn't even be able to wrestle it onto a dolly by himself, let alone push the thing out of the building."

He paused to give the information time to sink through Hendricks's thick skull. "Then you have the matter of getting it out of here. You think he could haul a dolly weighing that much all the way to his house?"

"Well, he probably had help. Most likely that trouble-making Connor kid. You'll probably find both of them spending the loot all over town on any manner of illegal—not to mention immoral—activity."

Yeah. Paying for booze and hookers with quarters always went over real well. "Thanks for all the leads. I'll do my best to get the money back for the kids."

The principal sniffed. "I sincerely hope you do."

Jesse sighed. Having Chuck on his case over this was going to be a major pain in the keister until he found the culprits.

Chapter 5

He managed to put off talking to Corey Sylvester for nearly two hours.

Finally he had to admit that he had nobody left to interview. He had talked to the janitor and the assistant principal, to several of the faculty members and the custodial staff. He had interviewed the residents of the three houses across the street from the school to see if any of them had heard or seen anything in the night, and he had Lou notifying local merchants and banks to give him a buzz if anybody brought in an unusual number of quarters.

He had half a mind to wrap up the initial canvas right now and forget about Corey Sylvester. It stuck in his craw that he had to treat the kid like a suspect just because Chuck Hendricks had decided to peg him as that year's scapegoat.

Jesse knew how it felt to be the kid everybody looked to when trouble broke out. He knew what it was like to be blamed any time anything came missing, to be sent to the principal's office for something he didn't have a thing to do with, to know that most people figured you would never amount to much.

He knew the deep sense of injustice a ten-year-old can experience at being unjustly accused.

He loved his older brother, but he had to admit he'd been a tough act to follow in school. Matt had been every teacher's dream. The best athlete, the best student. Trustworthy, loyal and all the rest of the Boy Scout mumbo jumbo.

Jesse, on the other hand, had struggled in school. He'd been a whiz at math, but words on a page just never seemed to fit together right for him. Reading and spelling had always been torture, right on into high school. In his frustration, maybe he'd developed a bad attitude about school, but that didn't mean he'd been a bad kid.

After a while, he'd got so tired of trying and failing to measure up to Matt's example that it had seemed easier to just give up and sink to everybody's expectations.

While his parents had still been alive, he had managed to stay out of serious trouble just because he knew how his mom's face would crumple and his dad would look at him with that terrible look of disappointment.

After they'd died, everything had changed and he'd become all Chuck predicted for him.

He hated having to feed the principal's stereotypes about Corey Sylvester by interviewing the kid, especially when he was trying to find out what was going on with him. But Hendricks had said he'd seen the kid by the coin jar. What kind of a cop would he be if he

ignored a possible lead, just because the source of that
lead was a bitter, humorless man who had no business
working with children?

He had a duty to follow up, and he had worked hard
the past three years to prove he was the kind of police
chief who tried his best to meet his obligations.

At least he could make the interrogation as subtle as
possible. And on the upside, pulling Corey out of class
would give him a chance to see Sarah McKenzie again.

While he had been busy chasing down nonexis-
tent leads to the theft, the students had descended on
Salt River Elementary. Up and down the hallway he
could hear the low murmur of voices in classrooms, the
squeak of chalk on chalkboards, the rustling of paper.

As he passed each doorway on the way to Sarah's
room, he could see teachers lecturing in the front of
their classes and students bent over their work.

Walking the hallways brought memories, thick and
fast, of his own school years. This was a different school
than the one he'd attended. The board of education had
bonded for a new building ten years earlier and de-
molished the crumbling old brick two-story structure
to build this modern new school, with its brown brick
and carpeted walls.

It might be a different building, but it smelled just as
he remembered from his own school years, a jumbled
mix of wet paper and paste and chalk, all mingling with
the yeasty scent of baking rolls that floated out from
the cafeteria.

Ms. McKenzie's classroom was the last one on the
right. He smiled at the whimsical welcome sign over
her door, featuring a bird knocking at the door of an
elaborate birdhouse.

He could hear her musical voice from inside and he paused for a moment to listen. She was talking in that soft, sexy voice about fractions. Despite the benign subject matter, her voice somehow managed to twine through his insides like some voracious vine.

How could he get so turned on by a shy school-teacher talking about fractions, in a building full of kids?

He watched her through the little square window set into her door, trying to figure out her appeal. She was soft and pretty in a pale blue short-sleeve sweater set and a floral skirt. Her sun-streaked hair was held back on the side by some kind of clip thing, but it fell long and luxurious to the center of her back, just inviting a man to bury his hands in it.

And that mouth. Full and lush and soft enough to make even a priest have to spend a few extra minutes in confession.

But she was still much too innocent for a wild, somewhat-reformed troublemaker like Jesse Harte.

He clamped down hard on his unruly imagination and opened the door to her classroom.

Sarah turned toward him at the sound and her big green eyes widened. Interesting. Now, what made her cheeks turn pink and her breathing speed up a notch?

Before he could put his crack investigative skills toward figuring it out, he was attacked. Lucy and Dylan ambushed him from the left, throwing their arms around him and jabbering like two monkeys in a zoo.

They fired questions at him one after another. "Uncle Jess! What are you doing at school? How long will you be here? Can you stay and have school lunch with us? Can we use you for sharing today?"

He opened his mouth to pick one question to answer, but Ms. McKenzie beat him to it. "Girls," she interjected firmly, "I know you're excited about your uncle visiting our classroom. I'm sure it's a real treat for all of us, but you need to take your seats again."

He raised his eyebrows when they immediately obeyed and hurried back to their desks. Wow. The woman knew how to run a tight ship. Who would have thought someone as meek as she seemed to be could command instant order with her students?

"Can we help you with something, Chief Harte?"

He was pretty sure that tight schoolmarm voice shouldn't turn him on so much, especially with a classroom full of interested fourth graders looking on. It shouldn't be able to slide through his bones, settle in his gut.

He was a bad, bad boy and the idea of pulling her silky hair from its clip, undoing that sweater a button or two and seeing if he could make even more color soak that honey-soft skin appealed to him far more than it should.

He was sick.

He had to be, to entertain prurient fantasies about a sweet, shy schoolteacher like Sarah McKenzie.

He reined in his rampaging thoughts, shifted his weight and turned his attention to the class. He recognized most of the students from around town. Near the back he found Corey Sylvester, sitting alone and looking very aloof. The boy met his gaze warily, then looked down at the book open on his desk.

Was he acting guilty or just resigned to what he had already figured out was coming?

Jesse couldn't tell. How would the kid react if he singled him out in front of his whole class? If he yanked him out into the hall and started grilling him like a suspect? It sure as hell wouldn't put the kid in any kind of mood to chat about who or what was causing his mysterious accidents.

Chuck Hendricks and his suspicious little mind could go to the devil, he decided abruptly. He would run this investigation his own way.

He turned back to Sarah with a smile. To his guilty amusement, the color dusting her cheeks turned a darker shade. "I'm sorry to interrupt, Miss McKenzie. Could I take a few moments of your class time?"

"I…of course."

"Thanks. I'll make it brief and then you can get back to whatever you were doing."

"Math," his new niece, Dylan, said with a disgusted sigh. The implication in her voice was obvious: *Take as long as you want. We don't mind.* He swallowed a sympathetic grin and turned to the rest of the class.

"I suppose you've all heard by now that somebody broke in to the school last night and took the money you've been collecting for the hospital."

As he expected, the students buzzed with reaction, from boos and hisses to shocked exclamations by those who hadn't heard. He registered them all, but kept his gaze on Corey. Unless he was mistaken, Corey looked as upset as the rest of the class.

A redheaded boy covered in freckles—Paul Turner's kid, if Jesse wasn't mistaken—raised his hand. "You catch who did it yet, Chief?"

"Not yet. But I'm going to, I promise you that. I'll need your help, though."

Jackie Allsop, who had won the Little Buckeroo

mutton-bustin' competition at the county fair two years running, raised her hand. "Are you puttin' a posse together?"

He swallowed another grin. "Something like that. See, the way I figure it, it's not right that somebody can come in and take something that you all and your friends have worked so hard to earn. Money you intended to be used to help sick kids. It's not fair. It makes me mad and it should make you mad, too."

Their outraged reaction filled the room. Out of the corner of his gaze, he saw Sarah frown. Uh-oh. Before she could step forward to quiet her students, he held up his hands. The students immediately quieted. "I appreciate your spirit. That's what it's going to take to catch whoever did this because, to be honest with you, we don't have a lot to go on right now."

"How can we help, Uncle Jess?" Lucy asked in her soft voice.

He smiled at her. "Good question, Luce. I want all of you to use your eyes and your ears for me. You have to promise me you won't do anything dangerous, though. If you hear anything you think might help us find whoever took the money, you need to let a grown-up know, okay? Either tell your mom and dad or Miss McKenzie or me. What are some of the things you could be on the lookout for?"

For the next few moments all the children—even the quiet ones—vied with each other to give suggestions, and Sarah watched their enthusiasm with amazement. Jesse had quite a way with children. She should have expected it by the adoration Lucy, and now Dylan, had for him, but she was still surprised at the way her students hung on his every word.

He managed to stir up participation from the entire class as if he had been teaching all his life.

She was going to have a tough time trying to get them to focus on fractions after this kind of excitement, she thought with a sigh. Who was she kidding? Forget the kids. She would be lucky to get through math herself today.

"Thanks for all your great ideas." To her relief, Jesse started to wrap things up. "Now I have to get back to work trying to find out who did it. Remember, if you hear or see something that might help solve the case, who are you going to tell?"

"A grown-up!" the class chorused.

He turned the full power of his smile on them. Even though she was just out of range of it, Sarah still felt the impact of that smile sizzle clear down to her toes. Darn it. The man had no business coming into her classroom and sabotaging her concentration like this.

To her dismay, when he finished addressing the class he headed toward her. "Can I talk to you out in the hall for a minute?" he asked, his voice low enough to send shivers rippling down her spine.

Out in the hall? Just the two of them? When she felt as rattled as seed pods in a strong breeze?

She could handle it, she reminded herself. She was turning over a new leaf and putting all her anxieties behind her. Right? A few minutes alone in the hall with Jesse Harte would be fine. Completely fine.

"Of course," she answered coolly. "Students, turn your attention to today's math assignment. If you have any questions about the work sheet, I'll be back in a few moments to answer them."

Ignoring their grumbles, she set her teacher's guide on her desk, then led the way out into the hall.

Jesse followed her with the strangest look on his face. If she didn't know better, she might have thought it was masculine interest, but of course it couldn't be.

He seemed extremely fascinated by her hair, though. She spent a brief, horrible moment wondering if she'd smeared paint in it while she was preparing the art supplies for the day. She almost reached a hand to check, then let it fall to her side, feeling extremely foolish.

"My students are waiting, Chief Harte," she finally said. "How may I help you?"

"Jess. Call me Jess. Everybody does."

Yes, she knew. Jesse James Harte, the outlaw cop. "If this is about the stolen money, Chief Harte—er, Jess—I'm afraid I can't help you. I don't know anything."

"It's more about one of your students. I need to ask your advice."

She stiffened. "Do you suspect one of my students was involved?"

"Up-Chuck is convinced Corey stole the money."

"Up-Chuck?" she asked, momentarily diverted.

"Er, Principal Hendricks. Sorry. You know what they say about old habits. It's been a long time since sixth grade, but it's still tough for me to think of him as anything else."

She could just imagine him in sixth grade, cocky and tough and rebellious.

A teacher's worst nightmare.

And a sixth-grade girl's biggest fantasy.

She jerked her mind away from that dangerous road. "What possible reason does he have to accuse Corey, besides the fact that he blames the poor boy for every single thing that goes wrong in this entire school?"

"He says he's seen Corey hanging around the jar several times in the last week, looking at the coins inside."

She bristled. "Since when does looking at something make you a criminal? If that's the case, arrest me now. Sometimes I like to walk through the art galleries in Jackson and dream about owning some of the works hanging there. That must make me some kind of international art thief, right?"

"Which ones?"

"Which ones what?"

"Which art galleries do you like?"

"What difference does it make?" she asked impatiently. "My point is, I can't believe you would base your entire investigation on the suspicions of a nasty, small-minded little man."

"I didn't say I agreed with him," Jesse protested. "I'm just telling you his theory."

"So that's why you're really here? To interrogate a child?"

She knew she sounded judgmental, shrewish even, but she didn't care. All her hard work trying to gain Corey's trust these past few weeks would be for nothing if she handed him over to Chief Harte like a trussed goose for Christmas dinner.

"I'd like to talk to him, not interrogate him. I would have pulled him out of class, but I figured the rest of your students didn't need to speculate about why the two of us might need to have a little chat."

She narrowed her gaze at him, studying him closely. She didn't know him nearly well enough to know whether he was telling the truth, but she would have to trust her instincts. All she could see gleaming out of his deep blue eyes was sincerity.

"That was very thoughtful of you," she murmured. "Corey has a hard enough time getting along with his classmates. To be marked as a thief would make him a pariah. I'm afraid children don't readily understand the concept of innocent until proven guilty."

"Neither do certain principals I could name."

She smiled. "Right."

He returned her smile with a grin that made him seem much more like that mischievous sixth grader he'd referred to earlier. Her pulse fluttered wildly and she finally dropped her gaze to her hands. "I really do need to get back to my class. Is there anything else I can help you with?"

"Yeah. I'm still going to have to talk to Corey so I can clear him as a suspect and get on with the investigation. I just wanted some advice on the best tack to take with him. You seem to have a rapport with him."

"I don't know about that." She thought about the boy's surliness since he had come into her class. He had begun to unbend a little, but she knew she still had a long way to go before earning his trust.

"Is there some time during the day I could talk to him without the rest of the class around?" Jesse asked.

She thought a moment. "Yes, actually, there is. Around twelve-thirty, during lunch recess. You could talk to him then. He has to stay in because he didn't turn in his homework folder last week. It's, um, one of our classroom rules." Why did she suddenly feel so defensive, as if she were the strictest teacher in the school?

Jesse didn't seem to notice. "Sounds like a plan. And

I'll bring you lunch so I have an excuse for being here. That way he'll think I'm only here to see you."

She wasn't at all sure she wanted her students to think she and Chief Harte had something going. They didn't. Of course they didn't. Two people couldn't possibly be more mismatched—he caught criminals for a living and she was afraid of her own shadow.

"Murphy's got a special on fettuccine Alfredo this week," Jesse went on. "How does that sound?"

"Lunch is really not necessary, Chief Harte. I'm sure you can come up with another excuse for dropping in to the classroom."

"It's the least I can do for your help." He gave her another one of those devastating smiles, the ones that made her feel as if her legs had no more substance to them than Mr. Murphy's fettuccine.

Arguing with him would make her sound even more like an idiot. Besides, she had a sneaking suspicion Jesse Harte was fairly used to getting his own way.

Lunch wouldn't hurt her. Hadn't she just been thinking how tired she was of eating alone? Here was her chance for a little conversation.

But as she watched him walk away down the hall with that purposeful stride, she had the sudden, terrifying certainty that she had just agreed to dine with the devil.

Chapter 6

He couldn't remember when he'd ever looked forward so eagerly to taking a statement. But then again, few of his interviews had the fringe benefit of including lunch with a sweet, pretty schoolteacher who blushed like a rose in full bloom.

Whistling in anticipation, Jesse reached into the back seat of his vehicle and grabbed the bag of takeout he had just picked up from the diner. As a rule, Murphy didn't normally fix takeout, but Jesse had had no qualms about cashing in some favors the café owner owed him. He now had two servings of Murphy's world-famous fettuccine Alfredo and all the trimmings in his possession.

He just hoped he could convince Sarah to eat it with him.

He wanted to talk to Corey about the missing money, but he also wanted to get to the bottom of the mystery that was Sarah McKenzie. This seemed like a golden opportunity to do it.

For the second time that day he walked through the front doors of Salt River Elementary. Through the glass walls of the office he could see Chuck wagging his finger at some hapless student slumped in one of the hard plastic chairs.

The principal spied Jesse as soon as he walked inside. Chuck froze in midwag, then changed the gesture to a crooked-finger demand for Jesse to come into his office. Pretending he didn't notice, he continued down the hall toward Sarah's room. Let Up-Chuck come find *him* if he was itching to have a chat so badly.

The school was much more quiet now than it had been earlier in the morning, probably because all the kids were either at lunch or out on the playground for recess.

At Sarah's classroom he peeked around the corner, through the open doorway. She was the only one in the room, bent over her desk with a black gradebook in front of her and her hair a shimmering gold curtain flowing down her back.

That sinfully gorgeous hair ought to be against the law. It seemed such an erotic contrast with both the innocent schoolroom setting and her frown of concentration that he had to swallow hard.

A few seconds later she sensed his presence. She looked up and he thought he saw just a quick flash of jittery awareness before she blinked it away and gave him a polite smile instead. Too bad. He preferred jittery awareness any day.

He held up the bag from the café. "I brought lunch.

Murphy makes a killer Alfredo sauce. Do we have time to eat before Corey comes in for detention?"

She frowned. "Fifteen minutes or so. But I thought I told you not to bother with lunch."

"Hmm. And I thought I told you I wanted to bother. Come on, Sarah. Humor me."

She sighed but didn't argue, which he took as a relatively positive sign. He held the bag up again. "Murphy put together the works for us. Salad, bread sticks and pie for dessert. Where do you want it?"

With another sigh, she scanned the classroom. "That worktable back by the computers is empty. We can sit there."

The next few moments were spent pulling up chairs and setting out containers. Murphy was a saint. He had even included paper plates and plastic dinnerware, something Jesse hadn't even thought about.

The one thing neither he nor Murphy had covered was a beverage, but Sarah solved the problem by going to a minirefrigerator behind her desk and pulling out two bottles of water.

He piled food on a plate for her, then did the same for himself, all the while aware of her sitting across the table watching him with the same wariness in her big eyes that he'd seen in Corey Sylvester's.

The food was divine, just as he expected. The sauce was rich and creamy, the bread sticks just crispy enough and the salad was fresh and tasted like springtime.

Sarah didn't eat enough to keep a kitten alive, though. Maybe that was the reason the bones at her wrists seemed so fragile.

"Do you always push your food around your plate," he finally asked, "or is it the company?"

She looked up, startled. "I'm sorry," she said. "The food is wonderful. Delicious. And it was very thoughtful of you to bring it. I guess I'm not very hungry right now."

Maybe she was just painfully shy. Maybe he was torturing her by continuing to force himself on her when she was obviously so nervous around him. The kindest thing would probably be to quit pestering her, to just stay out of her way.

He wasn't at all sure why the idea was so repugnant to him. And anyway, the few times he'd seen her with other people she'd been friendly and composed. He was the only one who seemed to make her edgy and uptight, and damned if he didn't want to know why—and what had put those shadows in her eyes.

Besides, he hadn't been kind in a long, long time.

"So tell me about Chicago," he asked abruptly.

She nearly knocked over her water bottle. "Wh… what?"

"Chicago. What was it like teaching there?"

She was silent for a several moments and he thought she was going to ignore the question, then she smiled softly. "It was great. Really great. I loved my students. It was an incredible feeling to know I could make such a difference in their lives."

"You taught elementary school?"

"Yes. Third grade, a year younger than my students here. It was a fairly rough neighborhood and some of my students lived in the most hideous conditions you can imagine. Without heat or running water, even. And I suspect that for many of them, school lunch was the only square meal they had all day. But despite their hardships, they all had so much promise. They were starving for far more than food. They needed someone to show them what they could achieve in life."

"And you tried to do that?"

"As best I could. Sometimes it was tough, I won't deny that, but I loved the challenge. I found that with a little creativity, I could usually find something that interested them—sports or animals or music or whatever—and individualize each student's curriculum around his or her interests. It really worked."

When the subject was teaching, she glowed with enthusiasm, with bright energy, and he couldn't take his gaze off her. She was like some rare, precious flower that bloomed only under exactly the right conditions. Now that he'd seen her vivid petals unfurl, he knew he wouldn't be content with just this one fleeting glimpse.

"Why didn't you stay?" he asked.

Wrong question. He regretted it instantly when her animation died just like a frost-killed blossom. That haunted look flashed across her eyes again before she quickly shuttered them.

"Every job has its good and bad points." Her voice was stiff and bleak.

"True enough. My job is usually great, but every once in a while I have to deal with the Chuck Hendrickses of the world."

Her expression thawed a little. "What are you complaining about? I have to deal with him every day."

He smiled even as he fought the wholly inappropriate urge to press his lips to the corner of that mouth that lifted so endearingly.

As if she could tell exactly what he was thinking, her breathing quickened and she became fascinated with the pasta she twirled around and around her fork.

"What about you? Have you always wanted to work in law enforcement?"

His own smile slid away as he thought of those days and months and years when the only thing he wanted was another drink to dull the guilt. He doubted a woman like Sarah McKenzie would know anything about a world so sordid and dark.

"Would it shock you if I told you I decided to become a cop one night when I was in jail?"

Her gaze flew to his, then she colored again. "How am I supposed to answer that? No matter what I say, I sound like a prissy schoolteacher. You're making that up, right?"

He laughed, but it held little humor. "It's true. I was twenty-one years old and in the joint again for a D and D—drunk and disorderly. This time I'd made the mistake of planting a right hook on the officer who came to break up the bar fight I was relishing at the time of my arrest, so old Chief Briggs added assaulting a police officer to my charges."

He sipped at his water bottle. "Unfortunately, I didn't have enough cash on me to pay the necessary bribe and persuade Salt River's finest to look the other way. That's the way things worked in those days."

"That's terrible!"

"Carl Briggs, the previous police chief, ran his own little fiefdom. He was a real prize. Anyway, I realized that arrest would stick on my record and there wasn't a thing I could do about it."

"And that was a turning point for you?"

He nodded. "I can remember lying on that scratchy wool blanket in my cell and looking out the little window at the night. I was hungover and battered and bleeding from the bit of extra attention I received from a couple of nightsticks. I felt like an old man. In that moment, I decided I was tired of being on the wrong side of the law. At the rate I was going, I was going to end up dead or doing some hard time in the state pen, so I decided right then that things would change."

He gave her a wicked smile. "I was a bad boy when I was younger, Ms. McKenzie. The kind your mama probably warned you about."

She raised her eyebrows. "Since we've already established that I sound like a prissy schoolteacher, I must ask. Just how, exactly, have you changed since then?"

Damned if she didn't make him feel fourteen years old still lighting bottle rockets in the mayor's mailbox. He laughed. "You're probably right. I'm still a hell-raiser. I just try to do it on the right side of the law this time."

Once more that flicker of awareness flashed across her green eyes like distant lightning on a July night. His gaze landed on her mouth, tracing the curve of her lips.

As he watched, her pink tongue darted out to lick that little indentation in the center of her top lip where mouth met skin. It was a completely guileless gesture, probably a nervous reaction to him staring at her mouth, but it reached right into his gut and gave a hard tug.

His pulse seemed suddenly thick and heavy through his veins. Like a slow trickling creek in the middle of August.

He wanted to be the one licking at her lips. Gliding over that lush, soft mouth, tasting whatever memory of butter and cream remained from Murphy's killer Alfredo sauce.

No. He couldn't.

But his body was already angling toward her, his head already leaning to hers. Her eyes widened with alarm—or was it anticipation?—then her lips parted slightly.

He took that as assent. What the hell else could he do? He would die if he didn't kiss her. His mouth was almost to hers when the sound of her classroom door opening echoed in the room like a gunshot.

Sarah froze, exhaling a puff of air that skimmed over his lips as erotically as their might-have-been kiss, then she jerked away from him as if he'd yanked her hair.

She turned toward the door, fierce color spreading over her cheeks in a hot, angry tide. "Corey! Come in."

The boy sauntered into the classroom, his usual air of defiance and belligerence firmly in place. Sarah didn't seem to notice. "Uh, thank you for coming so quickly," she said distractedly. "Did you have time to finish your lunch?"

Corey shrugged. "Much as I could stand."

"Was it awful?"

"Chipped beef on toast. Yuck. Least they had apple crumble for dessert."

"Good for you to come up with a bright side to chipped beef on toast!" She smiled at Corey and Jesse realized with mild shock that she genuinely cared about the kid, despite the troublemaker attitude he wore as proudly as Jesse wore his badge. It was obvious from her smile and her body language and the affection in her eyes. What's more, Corey knew it was real, and he obviously adored her for it.

Jesse remembered her passionate defense of the boy against Chuck's suspicions earlier in the day and her willingness to go to the authorities with her fear about Corey's home life.

To his chagrin, he experienced a flash of sudden and completely unreasonable jealousy. It wasn't only the grim knowledge that she would probably never look at him with that same affection. He suddenly realized he couldn't remember any of his teachers ever looking at him like that, ever being willing to stand up for him or take his side of things. If they had, he probably would have liked school a whole lot more.

So what made Sarah different than the other teachers Corey had gone through?

Maybe she had a soft spot in her heart for bad boys.

"What's the chief doin' here?" Corey asked.

Jesse answered before Sarah could. "Having lunch with Ms. McKenzie. We're friends." At least, he thought he wanted them to be.

Corey took in the scattered plates and takeout containers on the table, then looked back at the two of them. His sharp little face twisted into a frown. "Yeah? I didn't know stupid cops had any friends."

Now, where did that sudden animosity come from? "Some of us even get married and have families, amazingly enough," Jesse answered.

Corey looked completely aghast at the idea. As his gaze darted between the two of them, Jesse realized something else enlightening. The tough kid of Salt River Elementary had a crush on his pretty blond teacher.

Sarah seemed oblivious to it. "If you're still hungry, I have some pasta left. You're more than welcome to eat it, Corey."

"Looks like chipped beef on noodles," he muttered.

"It's much better," she assured him, but the boy didn't look convinced. "How about some pie, then?"

This was obviously much more appealing to Corey. He grabbed for a piece with a mumbled thanks and dug right in to it.

"I have to finish recording a few grades," Sarah said after a moment. "When you're done with your pie, why don't you wash your hands and clean out Raticus's cage? I'm sure Chief Harte would love to give you a hand with our class pet."

"Oh, yes. Love to," he said dryly. A pet rat. Great. Still, it was a chance for a little private time to talk to Corey and he couldn't pass up the opportunity, even if it entailed cleaning out a rodent's cage.

His job apparently was to hold the rat while Corey put new paper in the bottom of his cage and refilled the water and food dishes. Jesse held the animal gingerly.

In his year spent at the police academy, he had never expected to end up in a fourth-grade classroom holding a rat.

He held Raticus up closer. The rat watched him out of beady little eyes, his whiskers and pink tail twitching. "Does this charming little rodent bite?" Jesse asked.

Corey snorted. "Only if you bite him first."

"I think it's safe to say that's not going to happen anytime soon."

The boy's amusement was fleeting. He quickly returned to glowering. "Don't you have crime to fight or somethin'?"

"I'm on my lunch hour."

"I thought you said you wouldn't rest until you found whoever stole the school money."

The rat wiggled around in his hands and Jesse had to tighten his grip. "I'll find him. Don't worry about it."

"Who said I was worried? I don't care about any stupid quarter jar for any stupid hospital."

"You put any quarters in that stupid jar?"

Corey refused to meet his gaze as he poured food into a small dish. "So what if I did? It was my own money. My mom gave it to me so I could get a pop on my way home from school."

Damn Chuck Hendricks and his suspicious little mind. The only reason Corey had been hanging around the quarter jar was to covertly drop some coins in.

Chuck couldn't even give the kid credit for good intentions when the evidence was right in front of his face. He had to attribute ulterior motives to everything.

The kid had sacrificed his own wants and needs to help sick children the only way he knew how.

Jesse's chest felt suddenly tight. He wanted to give the kid's shoulder a squeeze, to tell him he was proud of him for caring, but he checked the impulse—not just because his hands were full of rat, but because he'd been that cocky kid once upon a time, afraid to show any emotion.

Corey wouldn't welcome the gesture, wouldn't know how to deal with it, any more than Jesse would have at that age.

He cleared his throat. "As I said to the class before, it burns me that somebody took that money that you and the rest of the kids worked so hard for. You haven't heard anything about who might have taken it, have you?"

"Why would you think I know anything?"

Jesse weighed his words. "A street-smart kid like you

keeps his ear to the ground. You probably know more about what goes on in this town than I do."

Corey snorted. "That's not too tough."

"If you hear anything, you'll let me know, right?"

"Whatever." The boy reached for the rat to return him to his clean cage and Jesse handed it over willingly.

The two of them watched Raticus settle in for a moment, then walked together back to Sarah's desk.

"All done?" she asked.

"Yeah," Corey said.

"Thank you. Lunch recess is almost over. Why don't you work in your handwriting notebook until the other children return?"

He made a face but returned to his desk, leaving Jesse and Sarah alone at her desk.

He gestured toward the hall, where they could talk without the boy overhearing. "Did you learn anything?" she asked when they were out of range.

"He wouldn't have taken the money. Not after he sacrificed his own after-school treat so he could put some change in the jar."

"I knew it." Satisfaction glinted in her green eyes. "Now what?"

"I get the pleasure of telling Chuck he's crazy." He grinned.

She smiled back and his gaze froze on her mouth, the memory of their almost-kiss surging through his veins like the whiskey he didn't drink anymore.

He could do it. Right now. Could dip his head and taste her, right here in the middle of the elementary school hallway.

He almost did. He was just a hairbreadth away from

dipping his head to hers and taking that sweet mouth. At the last minute, reality returned with stunning force.

"I've got to run," he said abruptly, stepping back. "Thanks for lunch."

"I…you're welcome."

What was he doing? he asked himself as he walked out of the building. He had no business trying to steal a kiss from her—not once, but twice. No business imagining that incredible golden hair sliding through his fingers, no business wondering about that slender body underneath her demure clothes.

She had wanted him to kiss her, both times. He had seen it in the softening of her mouth, in the wary attraction sparkling in her eyes like Christmas lights.

But he wouldn't. She was too sweetly innocent for a man like him. Too fragile. If he kissed her, she wouldn't have the first idea how to handle it.

Sarah McKenzie wasn't his type. He would hurt her. He might not mean to, but he would. That's just the kind of woman she was.

If he were smart, he would put all his energy into keeping those kinds of inappropriate thoughts about her right out of his head.

She simply had to stop thinking about Jesse Harte.

Hours later, alone in her silent little house with the curtains drawn tightly against the dark, rainy night, Sarah couldn't keep her mind off the man, off those brief moments in her classroom and later in the hallway when she thought—feared? hoped?—he would kiss her.

It had taken hours to even make a dent in reading the weekly assignments for Writer's Workshop. She tried hard to concentrate. But every few pages she would find herself back in that classroom, inhaling the masculine, woodsy scent of his aftershave, watching the muscle in his jaw twitch, trying fiercely to remember to breathe when that mouth started to lower to hers.

What would she have done if he'd kissed her? Would she have panicked? Found herself back in the throes of a flashback she couldn't control? Or would she have welcomed it, reveled in it?

She had wanted desperately to find out. She still did, if she were honest with herself.

She sighed. Might as well wish for the moon while she was at it. A man like Jesse Harte wouldn't possibly be interested in a woman like her.

He was the most eligible bachelor in Salt River. Every woman in town probably swooned over him. He radiated strength and power. Vitality.

Was that why she was so attracted to him? Because he seemed to represent everything she was not? She was a timid, prissy schoolteacher afraid of even Raticus. It was no wonder Jesse hadn't followed through on the look in his eyes and kissed her.

She set her red pencil down, depressed all over again. She ought to just go to sleep—it was past midnight, after all, and she was far from being productive.

The idea of facing that solitary bed, with those cold, lonely sheets and an empty pillow and nightmares lurking in the corners was about as appealing as sleeping out in the rain. But she had to recharge her batteries somehow if she had any hope of coping with thirty unruly ten-year-olds the next day.

She began her nightly ritual, checking and double-checking the locks on the windows and doors. At the back door she paused, looking out the small window at the drizzly night and the little backyard she was slowly transforming into a garden.

A cat yowled somewhere, a dog barked sharply in answer, and the wet breeze fluttered the silvery wind chimes she'd bought the week before in Jackson. She smiled a little at the small-town quiet she had come to love and was just ready to head to her room when a blur of movement outside the glow of the porch lights caught her attention.

She stiffened as her eyes adjusted to the dark, as the blur became a more solid shape.

Cold fear turned her blood to ice.

Someone was out there!

Chapter 7

"Would you like another cookie, dear?"

Jesse ground his back teeth. At this rate he'd be here all night. "No, thank you, Mrs. Lehman. It's late. Why don't we just get to your report?"

"Are you sure? I know they're your favorites."

One of the hazards of working his whole life in the same small town where he grew up was that everybody thought they knew every single thing about him. For one terrible summer when he was nine, Doris Lehman had attempted to give him piano lessons. They had both barely survived the ordeal.

At least she didn't appear to hold a grudge.

"Thanks, anyway, but I'm full." Jesse fought back a yawn and tried to stay focused. Working three double watches in a row would kill him if Mrs. Lehman's butter-rich shortbread cookies didn't do the job first.

Ignoring him, she hoisted her tiny frame out of her chair using her carved, ivory-handled cane and creaked toward the kitchen, her yippy little poodle dancing around her feet. It was past midnight, but the elderly woman was still fully dressed and looked as elegant as if she were on her way to the opera.

"I'll just put a few cookies in a bag, dear, and you can take them with you for later."

With a resigned sigh, Jesse followed her and the poodle into her kitchen. Mrs. Lehman was in the mood to chat. She did this every few weeks or so, called him or his officers to her house on some trumped-up disturbance call. Most of the time he didn't mind. She'd been lonely since her husband, Ed, had died three years earlier and he had instructed his officers to visit with her for a while, no matter how outlandish the complaint, just to make sure she was okay.

He sighed again. It wasn't always easy to follow your own advice.

"That's very nice of you, Mrs. Lehman," he said. "Now, about what you thought you saw tonight...?"

She shook her cane at him, damn near poking his eye out. "Don't use that tone of voice with me, young man, like you're just humoring a crazy old bat by even being here. I saw what I saw. No question about that."

"Can we go over exactly what you saw, then?"

"Not if you're going to patronize me."

He huffed out a breath. He was too blasted tired for this tonight. "What did you see, Mrs. Lehman?" he asked patiently.

She squinted at him for a moment, then finally spoke, apparently satisfied that his interest was genuine. "Lights, up on Elk Mountain. This is the third night in a row I've seen them. They don't belong there."

"Maybe it's high schoolers out four-wheeling or somebody spotlighting for deer."

"I don't think so. These lights didn't move at all. And they didn't look normal, either, I'll tell you that."

"What do you mean?"

"Just what I said." She shifted her gaze around the room as if she feared eavesdroppers, then she lowered her voice. "I think I might know what they're from."

"What?" He leaned forward, pitching his own voice low.

"Aliens."

He leaned back, blinking hard. Maybe Mrs. Lehman needed to have her medication levels checked. "Aliens?"

"Right."

"What gives you that idea?"

"I know all about government conspiracies, young man. About Roswell and Area 54 and black helicopters. I watch *The X-Files,* you know."

"And you think Salt River is in the middle of some kind of alien invasion?"

"I think you need to drive up there to Elk Mountain and check it out. But you'll have to be careful. Don't go alone, whatever you do. Who knows what would happen if they caught you?"

"I shudder to think," he said, hiding his amusement. Mrs. Lehman might have some crazy ideas, but she was usually harmless. "Thanks for calling this to our attention. Technically, Elk Mountain would be the county's jurisdiction, though. Lucky for me, any alien problem would be Sheriff Mitchell's responsibility."

"What are you going to do?"

"Why don't you give me a call the next time you see the lights so I can look up there too and pinpoint exactly where they're coming from and I'll check it out. Okay?"

Before she could answer, the radio at his waist crackled. He pressed the button. "Yeah. Harte here."

His evening dispatcher's voice crackled through the static. "Chief, I have a report of an attempted break-in. Four-oh-four Spruce Street."

His pulse lurched. That was Sarah's address!

"Maybe it's the aliens!" Mrs. Lehman exclaimed, her brown eyes bright with horrified excitement. "Maybe they're looking for some poor soul to use for their experiments."

He was already heading for the door. "I certainly hope not. Look, Mrs. Lehman, I'm the only officer on duty tonight. Can you give your report tomorrow at the station?"

"Why, certainly, dear. You'd better hurry. Here. Don't forget your cookies."

He drove the three blocks to Spruce Street in record time. Every light in Sarah's little gingerbread house was blazing when he pulled up. He shut off the engine and raced to the door, then pounded hard.

"Sarah? It's Jess. Open up."

It took a painfully long time for her to come to the door, while a hundred grim scenarios flashed through his brain. Finally, just before he would have knocked the damn thing down, the lace curtain in the small window fluttered, then her face peered out, her features wary.

Her eyes widened with recognition—and a vast, glimmering relief, he thought—then he heard the snick of a lock. A moment later, she opened the door to him.

"Chief Harte. Thank you for responding so quickly," she murmured.

He might have expected her to be hysterical, judging by her panicked reaction to him the other day. Her face was pale, but otherwise she seemed calm. On closer inspection, he could see that her hands trembled slightly, like a child who has been too long out in the cold.

She wore a robe patterned in rich jewel tones, which only seemed to make her skin look more fragile, a ghostly, bloodless white.

The sudden, powerful urge to gather her up, tuck her against his chest and keep her safe and warm there forever erupted out of nowhere, scaring the hell out of him.

Knowing it was completely inappropriate—not to mention that it would probably terrify her senseless—he struggled into his concerned-but-dispassionate-cop routine. "I had a report of a possible break-in at this address."

The emerald lapels of her silky robe rose and fell when she breathed deeply, as if fighting for control. "I… Yes. That's right."

"Are you all right?"

"Yes. Fine." She fidgeted with the sash on her robe. "I just feel so silly. I shouldn't have bothered you."

"Of course you should bother us. That's why we're here."

"I'm not even sure I saw anything now. It was so dark."

"Why don't we sit down and you can tell me exactly what you thought you saw?"

After a moment's hesitation, she chose a rose-colored wingback chair near the cold fireplace and perched on the edge, hands clasped tightly together in her lap. He took the couch and stretched his long legs out, then pulled his notebook from his breast pocket.

"How long ago did you see the intruder?"

Her hands fluttered. "I told you, I'm not even sure it was someone trying to break in."

"That's what I'm here to figure out, sweetheart. How long ago?"

"Fifteen minutes, maybe."

"And what happened?"

She closed her eyes as if trying to re-create the events in her mind. "I was grading papers at the kitchen table and couldn't concentrate."

Her gaze met his suddenly, then two bright spots of color appeared high on her cheekbones, making him wonder what, exactly, had destroyed her concentration.

She quickly jerked her gaze away. "I decided to go to bed. I was just turning off the lights and checking the locks. I thought I saw something move. I figured it was a cat or something, but then I... I saw a man standing there."

"Standing where?"

"Off the back porch." She frowned, wrinkles of concentration creasing her forehead. "Actually, just at the bottom of the steps."

"Did you get a look at him?"

"No. He was just outside the porch lights, and it was so dark. I just saw a shape, really."

"Did he appear large or small? Was he as tall as me?"

Her gaze flashed to him again, then she gazed down at her hands. "He seemed huge," she said, her voice small and tight. "But I don't really know. I was so frightened I couldn't think straight."

"I'll just put a question mark here on size, then."

"I'm probably imagining the whole thing. I'm so sorry I dragged you out here."

He thought of old Mrs. Lehman and her alien visitors. Sarah McKenzie seeing a dark stranger lurking on her back step didn't even compare. "Let me take a look around," he said. "If you think someone was trying to break in, I believe you."

At his words, her face softened and her eyes went dewy and huge as if she was going to cry. "Thank you," she said softly. "I'm still going to feel ridiculous when you don't find anything."

"Don't worry about it. Just relax, have a cup of tea or something, and I'll be back in a few moments."

She nodded. "Be careful, okay?"

Her concern for his safety climbed right in and settled in his heart. Just how was he supposed to keep a safe emotional distance between them when she said something like that, something that made this odd warmth steal through him?

He couldn't remember the last time somebody had worried about him. His family loved him, he knew that, but they had realized a long time ago that he could take care of himself.

Not at all sure whether he liked the feeling, he left Sarah sitting by her empty fireplace and walked out into the soggy night.

A cool drizzle settled in his hair and beaded on the oiled canvas of his coat. He barely noticed, narrowing his focus only on the job as he scoured the scene for any sign that someone had indeed been trying to break in to Sarah's house.

The gleam from his flashlight turned up little. All

looked normal on her cozy little back porch—no over-turned planters or dislodged cushions that he could tell.

Her backyard was fenced only on three sides. Anyone could sneak from the road around to the rear of the house. If someone wanted to break in, it made sense that he would go around to the back, where criminal activities wouldn't be as noticeable from the street.

He walked down the steps and down a small gravel pathway that curved around the house. There. There was something. He crouched, shining the beam of his flashlight into the flower garden between the walkway and the house. The light gleamed off the print of what looked like a man's work boot in the mud, as if someone had misstepped off the pathway.

It wasn't much to go on. It hadn't rained hard that day, so for all he knew, it could have been left earlier by a meter reader or Bob Jimenez, her landlord. But it was all he could see in the dark.

A careful look around the small house revealed little else, other than the interesting tidbit that Sarah McKenzie appeared to be an avid gardener, judging by all the upturned earth around the house.

She must spend every spare second she wasn't teaching outside with her hands in the dirt. The thought of the quiet, skittish schoolteacher pouring her heart and soul into creating beauty around her touched him in ways he couldn't explain.

He didn't know too many renters who would put such care and effort into beautifying a house they didn't own. Hell, he could barely manage to keep the grass mowed in the summertime around the place he'd bought after he made chief.

But Sarah was a nurturer. Plants, children, whatever.

Would she go for neat, ordered gardens, he wondered, where no flower would dare touch the next and all were arranged in some precise pattern according to shade, color or height?

Or would she prefer wild jumbles of color? Frenzied splotches of yellows and reds and purples growing every which way?

It seemed logical to assume a quiet schoolteacher would prefer a prim and proper garden. But some instinct told him that in a month or so the yard around her house would burst with lush, unrestrained beauty.

He had a feeling that for all her subdued reticence, there were hidden depths to Sarah that fairly begged to be discovered.

But not by him. He'd leave any exploring of Sarah McKenzie's deeper passions to some other man.

Some better man.

A guy who could give her happily-ever-after, a white picket fence and all the flowers and children she could ask for.

Why should that thought depress him so much?

It was none of his business. *She* was none of his business, other than one of the citizens of Salt River he was sworn to protect.

Keeping that firmly in mind, he forced his attention back to the investigation and finished walking the perimeter of her house. When he finished, he rapped hard on her door. She opened immediately, almost as if she'd been standing just inside watching and waiting for him.

She could tell instantly by the regretful look in his eyes that he hadn't found anything substantial.

Had she imagined the whole thing? Had she been

having another of those damn flashbacks again and somehow merged nightmare with reality?

She must have been. What other explanation could there be? She had been seeing things.

Anger at herself and an awful, painful embarrassment warred within her. After this and the way she'd freaked out the other day on her back porch, he probably thought she was the most ridiculous, paranoid schoolmarm who ever lived.

She had a fierce, painfully futile wish that Jesse Harte could have known her Before.

When she had been fun and adventurous and whole. When she drew people to her just like an ice-cream shop does on a warm summer day.

When she never saw strangers lurking in the shadows or panicked if a man touched her or had bouts where she stood in the shower for hours, scrubbing and scrubbing but somehow never coming clean.

"You didn't find anything," she said, a statement not a question.

"A bootprint in the mud. Other than that, nothing."

"I'm sorry." She clasped her hands together tightly, wishing she'd never called the police, wishing a different officer had responded, wishing she could sink right through the carpet and disappear. "You must think I'm the most foolish woman in town."

He grinned suddenly, looking impossibly gorgeous. "Not even close, sweetheart. You're not calling me to report seeing little green men in spaceships."

"No. Only bogeymen who don't exist."

"Sarah, if you think you saw a man out there, I believe you. Just because I can't see anything to prove it beyond a shadow of a doubt doesn't mean the guy wasn't there. It might have been a kid looking to steal some tools or just a peeping Tom hoping to get lucky and find an open curtain somewhere."

She couldn't help her instinctive shudder at the idea of someone watching her without her knowledge.

Jesse's cop eyes picked up on her reaction. "It's probably nothing for you to worry about," he assured her. "I'll cruise around the neighborhood and see if I can find any suspicious characters lurking around and I'll also put an extra patrol in this neighborhood for a while."

"Thank you. I… You've been very kind."

He gave her an inscrutable look. "Call me immediately if you see anything else suspicious. Try to get some sleep, okay?"

She nodded, then watched him walk back out into the drizzly night. A week ago, she never would have even considered the word *kind* in the same sentence as Jesse Harte. He was hard and dangerous and he scared the stuffing out of her. But something had changed in the past few days. She was coming to see there were facets to the man she wouldn't have guessed at before.

He believed her.

She pressed a hand to her chest, to the warmth that blossomed there despite the lingering anxiety. Another man might have shrugged off her concerns, especially after witnessing firsthand one of her wild panic attacks.

But Jesse believed her.

Sarah lifted her face to the gloriously warm afternoon sun, wishing she didn't have to go back into her classroom in another few moments.

She would have been tempted to sacrifice her entire

summer vacation if she could only spend the rest of the day right there on the playground with the sun on her face and that sweet-smelling breeze coyly teasing her hair and rustling her skirt around her legs.

She had spring fever as badly as her students. After a week of gloomy weather, she longed to be out in the garden, planting and pruning and fertilizing.

Who would have thought she would be so addicted to gardening? What had started out as a little thing earlier in the spring—a simple desire to plant a few flowers in the empty beds around the house—had quickly turned into an obsession.

It amazed her because it was so unexpected. She, who'd never even had a houseplant before, was turning into an avid gardener. She loved the whole process. Painstakingly selecting seeds or starts at the nursery, preparing the earth for them, watching the hesitant little green stalks slowly unfurl toward the sun.

There was an odd sense of power in the process. Though Mother Nature definitely played a heavy hand with her sun and rain, in all other respects Sarah was master of her little garden. She chose which seedlings belonged where, when and how many to plant, which to thin away and which would be given the chance to bloom.

She found it heady and intoxicating. At least in this one area of her life, she felt in control.

She rolled her eyes at herself—how pathetic was that?—then lifted her face to the sun.

On a day like this one, her panicked call to the police three nights earlier seemed unreal. Ridiculous. As far away as the few wispy clouds up there. She could only have been imagining that terrible moment when she thought she saw someone standing outside her back door. It was the only explanation that made any kind of sense.

This was Star Valley, a place that could practically be the poster child of peaceful, rural America.

Who here would want to lurk outside the house of a boring schoolteacher?

She sighed. No one. That's why she must have been imagining things.

Jesse had been very patient with her. He had been true to his word—several times each evening she had seen police vehicles drive past her house. She found their presence comforting. And if she carefully watched to see if a certain gorgeous police chief might be driving one of them, well, that was nobody's business but her own.

She glanced at her watch. Five more minutes before the bell. She hated to be a spoilsport, but she was going to have to start gathering her students. She glanced around the playground at the rope-jumping and the hop-scotching and the heated game of four-square in the corner. The children looked jubilant to be outside. Maybe she could just hold class out in the sunshine today.

She spied Corey under the spreading branches of a maple tree whose leaves were small and new, his back propped against the trunk. As usual, he sat by himself, and her heart twisted with sympathy for him.

He had a few friends, she knew, but none in their class. Her students were not cruel to him, but they were uneasy around a boy with such a hostile attitude toward everything.

He could use some company, she decided, and ducked under the low overhang of branches to join him.

As she neared the boy, she could tell instantly something was wrong. Corey's head was buried in his arms and he was shivering slightly in the cool shade.

"Corey? Honey? Are you all right?"

After a long moment he lifted his face slowly, as if the movement pained him. He was pale, she saw with concern, his flushed cheeks the only spots of color on his face.

"I don't feel too good," he whispered.

She knelt in the grass and touched his forehead with her fingers. "You do seem warm. What else is going on?"

"My throat and my head hurt and I itch."

For the first time she noticed ominously familiar red blisters creeping up his neck and covering his arms below his sleeves.

"Where do you itch?"

He looked positively miserable. "Everywhere. Especially my stomach and my back."

"Oh, dear," she murmured.

Corey finally met her gaze, worry darkening his eyes. "What's wrong with me?"

For all his cocky bravado most of the time, he was still just a boy, she reminded herself. And right now he was a very sick boy. "Sweetheart, have you ever had the chicken pox?"

"No," he mumbled. "I don't think so."

"You do now."

The boy's eyes widened, his features twisted with dismay. "I can't. I'm supposed to help Chief Harte. We're supposed to practice today after school."

"He'll just have to do his presentation without you or reschedule it until you're better. You need to be home in bed. I'm sure that's what's itching. Let's take a look at your back."

She reached for his T-shirt. Corey froze, then scrambled back against the tree, out of her reach. "No. No. That's okay."

"Just pull it up a little so I can see how bad the spots are on your back."

He batted halfheartedly at her hands, but she persisted and finally lifted his T-shirt up just enough so she could see.

The normal playground noises around them—the rattle of chains on the swings, the shrieks and laughter of children, the breeze rustling the new maple leaves above them—seemed to fade away.

All she could hear was her own horrified gasp.

Halfway down his back, red, puckered skin surrounded a sickly gray scar in a distinctive S shape at least three inches long. It looked like a brand, like the ownership mark she saw on cows all around Wyoming.

Bile swelled in her throat and her stomach heaved. Dear Lord. How could anyone do such a thing to a child?

"Who did this to you?" she asked when she could find her voice through the horror.

His lips clamped together and he looked away from her, avoiding both her gaze and her question. Her hand shook, but she reached out anyway and gripped his shoulder firmly. Fury made her voice hard, tight. "Corey, answer me. Who did this?"

She felt him tremble a little under her fingers and realized she was taking completely the wrong tack with him. If her fierceness didn't scare him, it would only make him more belligerent. She yanked her hand back and shoved it into the pocket of her cardigan.

"Sweetheart, you have to tell me. This is wrong. Who did this to you?"

"Nobody," he finally answered. His voice sounded thin and raspy, but she didn't know if it was from fear or from his illness. "I... I did it myself."

She stared at him. "What?"

"Yeah. I did it. Well, I had my friend help."

Could he be telling the truth? She had read of children with severe emotional or developmental problems being self-destructive. Pounding their heads repeatedly against the cement or pulling out clumps of their hair or shredding their skin. She knew that sometimes physical pain could be a release valve of sorts for children who didn't know how else to cope with their emotional pain.

Maybe Corey was far more troubled than anybody realized.

Merciful heavens. Nothing in her training had prepared her for anything like this. She wanted to gather him into her arms and hold him close, but she didn't want to make a wrong move here. Perhaps she should leave this to trained professionals. But she cared about Corey too much.

"Why would you hurt yourself this way?" she asked quietly.

"Didn't burn much."

He was lying. She could see it in his eyes. It must have been excruciatingly painful—the scar still looked red and sore.

"Why, Corey?"

He shrugged, looking down at the grass. "My mom wouldn't let me get a tattoo."

"A...a tattoo?"

"I wanted my name but she said no, so I did an *S* for Sylvester."

"How?" Her voice sounded as raspy as his. "How did you do it?"

Corey still continued looking down at the grass. She looked at him carefully but couldn't tell if he was being evasive because he was embarrassed or because he was being less than honest.

"Me and some guys heard about gangs branding themselves. It sounded cool so we, um, decided to see if we could do it. We bent a hanger into an *S* and heated it up. You won't tell my mom, will you?"

Another wave of nausea washed through her. Dear heavens. The child was only ten years old and he was scarring himself, mutilating himself, to look cool. And then he was worried about her snitching to his mother!

The bell rang. She could see her students lining up at the door waiting to go in. They would have to do without her for a few more minutes, at least while she called Ginny Garrett. She would see if one of the other teachers could take her class until Corey's mother could arrive for him.

"You need to see a doctor, Corey."

"For the chicken pox?"

"And for your...for what you did. It could be infected."

"Then my mom and Seth would have to know."

"I can't keep this a secret, Corey. I'm sorry. It's not right. I have to tell them."

His face crumpled and again he looked exactly his age, like a scared little boy, then his features hardened into familiar belligerent lines. He called her a harsh name a ten-year-old had no business even knowing, let alone repeating. "You act like you're my friend, but you're not. You're just like all the other stupid teachers. If you tell my mom, you'll be sorry."

He climbed to his feet and would have run away, but she held him in place and half dragged him to the office so she could place the call. By the time they got inside the building, Corey stopped struggling. He walked along beside her like a prisoner on the way to Old Sparky.

Maybe Star Valley wasn't so idyllic after all, she thought as they neared the office. Not if children could do such horrible things to each other.

She didn't even want to think about the alternative, that someone else—his stepfather, maybe—might have done this to Corey.

Jesse pulled up to the Salt River Medical Clinic and sat in his Bronco, studying the low-slung cedar building. Ginny and Corey were still here. He could see her silver Range Rover in the parking lot.

Since Sarah's call a half hour earlier, the beauty of the bright April day seemed to have dimmed. The sun still shone, but its glow seemed tarnished somehow.

He muttered an oath. He could hardly believe what she'd told him—that Corey and his friends had branded themselves as if they were no better than cattle.

Sarah had been distressed almost to tears as she'd told him the details of the scar on Corey's back.

"It was horrible, Jesse. You should have seen him so calmly describing how he did it. I can't understand why he would do such a thing."

"It's not against the law, Sarah. I'd say this is something Ginny and Seth are going to have to deal with."

"I know. I just… You're going to think I'm crazy again, but when he was talking about it, I got the distinct impression he was lying about the circumstances. What if he didn't get it willingly? Couldn't criminal charges be filed then?"

"You think whoever might have given him those black eyes and other injuries might be responsible for this, too?" Jesse had asked.

"I don't know. Maybe." There had been a long silence on the other end, then Sarah had spoken quietly. "I know you're busy, but will you please talk to him? Just see if you believe him. He's a child, Jesse. A boy who was squeamish last week when he skinned his knee on the playground. Why would he consent to do this to himself?"

In the end, what else could he do but agree to talk to the kid? Sarah trusted him to get to the bottom of the many mysteries surrounding the boy. How could he do anything else?

He blew out a breath and climbed out of the Bronco. Inside the clinic he found Ginny at the counter filling out insurance forms, bracing Maddie on her hip with one hand while she wrote with the other. She looked small and fragile.

Lost.

"Hey, Jesse," called Donna Jenkins, her red hair just a few shades lighter than her lipstick. The nurse gave him a flirtatious smile—the same one she always gave him—which he returned quickly before turning to Ginny.

"How did you find out?" she asked, and he frowned at the defeated look in her eyes.

"Sarah—Ms. McKenzie—called me. She's worried about Corey."

Ginny nodded, absently grabbing her baby's fingers before Maddie could steal the pen out of her hands.

"How is he?"

"He's in with Doc Wallace right now. He's definitely got the chicken pox, and the…the other thing is apparently infected. Doc Wallace is writing him a prescription for antibiotics."

"You mind if I talk to him?"

She shrugged. "You can try. He's not saying anything about it, but maybe you'll get more out of him than I can."

Doc Wallace was just closing the door to the examination room when Jesse walked down the hallway. He turned in surprise when he saw him. "Jesse Harte! What brings you here?"

Jesse could never see Salt River's crusty doctor without remembering that terrible night when he was seventeen and he'd been brought here right after the accident before being airlifted to the regional medical center in Salt Lake City. He had a flash of memory, of kind words and a comforting touch and teary blue eyes telling him without words that his parents hadn't made it.

He pushed the memory aside. "I just wanted to have a word with your patient."

"You really think this is a police matter? It seems to be just a boy doing something ridiculously stupid."

"I'd still like to talk to him just to make sure."

"I hope you've had the chicken pox, then. Just keep

in mind he's a sick kid who might not be up to answering a lot of questions."

Jesse nodded and pushed open the door. Corey was sitting on the exam table in a hospital robe, his scrawny legs dangling over the side. His eyes widened at the sight of Jesse, then narrowed in contempt and something else that looked like betrayal.

"She told you."

He played innocent. "Who?"

"Miss McKenzie. Why'd she have to go and tell you?"

"She was worried about you."

"The hell she is. She's just got it in for me like every other teacher."

"You know that's not true. She cares about you. If she didn't, I wouldn't be here."

"You gonna arrest me?"

"No. Nobody committed any crime here." He watched the boy carefully as he spoke. "Unless someone did this to you against your will. Do you know what that phrase means? Against your will?"

For just an instant, fear flashed through the boy's eyes, but he quickly looked down at his bare feet. "Yeah. It means if someone did something I didn't want them to do."

"Is that what happened?"

Corey's gaze darted around the examination room, to the sink and the door and the panda wallpaper. To anything but Jesse. "No," he finally said, his voice belligerent. "How many times do I have to say it? I wanted a tattoo and my mom wouldn't let me get one. I don't care what she says. I still think it's cool."

"What does your dad have to say about it?"

Again that fear tightened his features. "He...he didn't have anything to do with it."

For the first time, the boy's voice wavered and Jesse narrowed his eyes. Damn it. Could Sarah have been right about Seth all along? The thought made his stomach heave. "Corey, did your stepfather hurt you?"

Corey stared at him. "Seth? Hell, no. He wouldn't hurt me."

He looked so genuinely astonished at the suggestion that Jesse felt a vast relief. Seth was his friend. The idea that he might be involved in this was repugnant.

But if Seth didn't do it, who was hurting this child?

"I need some names, then."

That fear flashed across Corey's features again. "What names?"

"The other kids involved in this so I can make sure they get medical treatment if they need it."

Corey stuck out his chin. "I ain't tellin'."

"You don't want your friends getting sick, do you? You can die from a bad infection if it's not treated, did you know that? In the old days, before antibiotics, people died just from getting a cut in their finger."

He watched the wheels turning in the boy's head as he digested the information and considered his options. "The other guys chickened out," Corey finally said. "I was the only one with the stones to go through with it. Are you happy now?"

Not by a long shot. Sarah was right. There was far more to this than the boy was revealing in these crummy little bits and pieces.

"Why don't you give me their names anyway?" Jesse suggested. "Just so I can back up your story."

He crossed his arms and jutted his jaw. "No. I'm

not squealing on my friends. Nothing you do is gonna change my mind."

Before Jesse could pressure him on it, the door opened and Doc Wallace entered, Ginny and Maddie right behind him.

"Everything okay in here?" Doc Wallace asked.

Jesse nodded. "We're just finishing up. Corey, think about what I said. If you decide to tell me anything else, either for your own safety or your friends' safety, you know how to get in touch with me, right?"

The boy managed a smirk, even though Jesse could tell he was miserable and itchy. "Yeah. But don't sit by the phone, 'cause I won't be callin'."

Jesse thought he would probably fall right off his chair if he ever did hear from the kid.

Chapter 8

Corey was the first of what turned into a virtual chicken pox epidemic at Salt River Elementary. In Sarah's class alone, six other children besides him had been hit with the nasty virus.

She sympathized with them all. She could still vividly remember her own awful bout with chicken pox when she was eight—the itching and the sore, swollen throat and the unrelenting tedium of being quarantined at home for ten days.

Her professor parents had juggled their respective class loads so one of them could be home with her during the day, but even the rarity of being completely at the center of their attention hadn't been enough to make up for the misery.

The boredom had been the worst, she remembered. Knowing how energetic her students had been, she figured they were all going crazy being cooped up while spring exploded around them.

The night before, she had come up with the idea of delivering care packages for her poor students, complete with a few books, word puzzles and games to keep their minds off the torment.

She had to admit, a big part of her motivation for the visits to her students was a desire to make amends with Corey. She knew he still hadn't forgiven her for telling his mother and Jesse about the crude *S* branded onto his back.

Her peace offering had been in vain, though. He wouldn't even allow his mother to let Sarah into his bedroom, so she'd ended up dropping his package off with Ginny.

Corey was the first stop. The rest of her Saturday morning had been much more rewarding. The children had been as delighted to have a visit at home from their teacher as they were about the books and small gifts.

She smiled, remembering the joy on all their dearly familiar little faces. What would she have done if she'd given in to her impulse right after the attack and left teaching? She would have missed it beyond measure. She needed her students to bring laughter and innocence into her life.

Well, most of them were innocent. Her thoughts returned full circle to Corey. She had to find another way to reach him, but she didn't have the first clue where to start.

She pushed the troubling thoughts away and concentrated on the drive. What a lousy day to be sick, she thought again as she cruised along the winding road toward her last stop, the Diamond Harte—hit with the double whammy of both Dylan and Lucy coming down with the spots.

The day was sunny and warm, with only a few high, powder-puff clouds to break up the vast blue expanse of sky.

Springtime in the Rockies was glorious, she was discovering. Snow still capped the highest peaks, but everything else burst with lush, vibrant color. She loved seeing evidence of new life everywhere, from the lambs leaping in pastures to the new leaves on the trees to the buds erupting everywhere in her garden.

And the road to the Diamond Harte was among the prettiest she'd traveled in Star Valley. A creek tumbled beside it, full and swift from runoff. Lining the banks were sturdy cottonwoods, thick green undergrowth and the occasional stunning red stalks she'd learned were a western relative of the more common southern dogwood.

On the other side of the creek, in a pasture surrounded by gleaming white fences, a trio of horses raced against her trusty little Toyota as it climbed the last hill before the ranch house.

At the crest, she stopped for a moment to savor the view.

The Diamond Harte nestled in a small, verdant valley. At the center was the ranch house itself, a sprawling log-and-stone structure that looked as if it had been there forever.

It was flanked by a huge red barn and a half dozen other outbuildings. More of those beautiful, sleek horses grazed in pastures here and she remembered that Matt Harte, Jesse's brother, raised not only cattle but champion cutting horses.

This was where Jesse had grown to manhood. He had probably climbed those fences and raced bareback across those fields of green and floated twig boats down the creek.

She felt a strange little tug at her heart picturing the big, gorgeous man who both terrified and intrigued her as a mischievous boy with startling blue eyes and a devil's grin.

Drat. Couldn't she even go fifteen minutes without thinking of him? She hadn't talked to him since the week before, the day she had seen Corey's stomach, and she hated to admit that she missed him. The way those blue eyes crinkled at the corners when he smiled, the funny little flutter in her stomach whenever he looked at her, the way he somehow always managed to tease her out of her nervousness.

He was so vibrant and alive, he made her world seem much more drab in contrast.

She had to stop this. Firmly pushing thoughts of Jesse away, she drove the rest of the way to the ranch house, then carried her bags up the porch steps and rang the doorbell.

Ellie Webster Harte—Star Valley's busiest veterinarian—answered the door.

Ellie always seemed so beautiful and together whenever Sarah saw her. Today, though, her hair was slipping from a ponytail, she didn't have any makeup on and the T-shirt she wore had a streak of flour dusting one shoulder. She looked frazzled and worn-out.

"Sarah!" she exclaimed. "Matt told me you called and were on your way out. What a brave soul you are to face our miserable pair!"

Sarah smiled. She had come to know Ellie earlier in

the year when they'd worked together on a school fund-raising project and she genuinely liked the other woman.

Though they had arrived in Salt River at roughly the same time, that was about the only similarity between them.

Ellie was spunky and energetic and not at all afraid to go after what she wanted—everything Sarah used to be. She had often marveled at the courage Ellie must have had to uproot her daughter and move to Star Valley, away from everything that was familiar.

"How are the girls?" she asked.

Ellie made a face. "Awful. We've already given them each two oatmeal baths and smeared them with calamine and they're still itching like crazy. Give me a whole stable full of sick horses any day over two ten-year-olds with chicken pox. They're climbing the walls."

Sarah laughed and held up the gift bags she'd packed. "Maybe these will help entertain them, at least for an hour or so."

"You're an angel! I can't believe you went to so much trouble!"

"It was no trouble. I love the girls. I just wish I could do more to help them feel better."

Before the other woman could answer, the smell of burnt chocolate wafted out of the kitchen.

Ellie sniffed, then her face dropped. "Rats!" she moaned. "My cookies! I have to confess, I'm not much of a cook. That's Cassie's expertise. But the girls were craving chocolate chip, so I did my best. I swear, we'd all starve if Cassie wasn't bringing regular meals over from the Lost Creek."

"I'll run these up to the girls while you rescue your cookies, okay?"

"Thanks. Third door at the top of the stairs." Ellie rushed down the hall toward the kitchen, leaving Sarah standing alone in the entry.

Her knee burned a little by the time she made it up the long flight of stairs, but she ignored it as she counted doors. Even without Ellie's directions, she would have known the third door on the right belonged to the girls by the collage of teen idols whose faces plastered the door.

She smiled a little as she pushed it open, then her heart seemed to stutter in her chest and she stopped breathing.

Jesse Harte, the subject of way too many of her thoughts lately, sprawled at the foot of one of the two twin beds in the room. Dylan and Lucy sat together at the other end wearing matching flannel pajamas. All three of them held playing cards, and other cards were scattered across the bedspread.

Jesse obviously hadn't been expecting her, but his surprise quickly gave way to a grin of delighted welcome. He opened his mouth to greet her, but the girls had caught sight of her first and beat him to the punch.

As usual, Dylan was the first to speak. "Miss McKenzie!" she exclaimed. "What are you doing here?"

There was that flutter in her stomach again as Jesse grinned at her. Sarah tried fiercely to ignore it, just as she usually ignored the nagging ache in her knee. She held up the matching pink gift bags. "I brought treats."

The girls shrieked and dived over their uncle toward the bags.

"Oh, sure." He gave a rueful laugh that did funny little things to her nerve endings. "This is the thanks I get for spending two solid hours listening to your boy band music and letting you both whip my butt at crazy eights. The minute a pretty lady walks into the room carrying presents, you both forget all about me."

The girls looked back at their uncle, clearly torn about what was the most polite thing to do in this situation, until Jesse rolled his eyes at them. "I'm joking. Go ahead. I know you're dying to see what goodies Miz McKenzie brought for you."

They gleefully dived for the bags again and the next few moments were filled with ripping paper and exclamations of delight.

Their enthusiasm made her smile as she watched them, grateful for whatever impulse had given her the idea for the gift bags.

Out of the corner of her gaze, she sneaked a peek at Jesse. She expected him to be looking at his nieces, too, but to her astonishment, his attention was focused only on her.

"That was a very nice thing to do, Miz McKenzie," he murmured. The approval in his blue eyes slid through her like a caress, completely disarming her.

"It's not much. Nothing compared to two hours of crazy eights and all the pop music you can stand."

"I am feeling a little unhinged right about now. I never realized there were so many ways for teenage boys who can't even grow chest hair yet to sing about losing the loves of their pitiful young lives."

She listened to the sounds emanating from a small shelf CD player and had to smile. "I heard this particular group is coming in concert to Idaho Falls next month," she teased. "Since you love their music so much, maybe you should take the girls."

She hadn't meant Dylan and Lucy to overhear, but

unfortunately the chicken pox hadn't affected their hearing at all.

"Yes!" Lucy gasped with astonished joy. "Oh, Uncle Jess, that would be so awesome! Please, please, please?"

He glared at Sarah. "Thank you very much. Now how am I supposed to get out of it?"

She fought the urge to clamp a hand over her mouth, dismayed that her teasing Jesse had begun to spiral out of control. It would have been too late, anyway. The damage was already done.

"Sorry," she whispered to Jesse.

"If I have to go, you're coming with me," he growled back.

Although he sounded disgruntled, she could see by the glint in his blue eyes that he wasn't really upset. Relief washed over her. She wasn't sure she could handle having this man angry with her.

"I'm sure I probably have plans that day," she assured him.

"Break them. You're not getting out of this that easily—you're coming with us."

"Does that mean we're really going?" Lucy asked gleefully.

"I guess you both do have birthdays coming up. I'll have to see if I can swing tickets for the four of us," he answered, with a pointed look at Sarah.

For the next few moments the girls could talk of nothing else but their favorite group, until Sarah felt her eyes begin to glaze over. She was out of her depth here.

But even though she knew she had no real excuse for staying, Sarah couldn't make herself walk out the door, too busy watching and listening to the camaraderie between Jesse and his nieces.

The girls obviously adored him. Sarah was ashamed to discover she was jealous of their bond. The glaring contrast between Jesse's boisterous family and her own solitary life depressed her, made her feel even more alone.

She was just about to make her excuses and leave when Ellie walked into the room in time to catch the girls yawning in tandem.

"I saw that," Ellie said with a frown. "Ladies, it appears your uncle and Miss McKenzie have tired you right out."

"It's exhausting business whipping me at every hand. Isn't that right?"

Even tired, Dylan could still serve up a cheeky grin. "Not really. We're used to it by now."

"Be that as it may," her mother said sternly, "I think you'll both feel better after you rest for a while."

The girls groaned as Jesse climbed to his feet. "Well, Miz McKenzie, I believe that's our cue to leave these two card sharks to their beds."

"Matt said you planned to ride the Piñon trail this afternoon," Ellie said to him as she tucked the girls in. "How far do you think you'll make it? Before he took off for Afton this morning, your brother said to warn you the snow levels were still pretty deep a few weeks ago when he was up there and you might not make it very high."

Jesse's grin was every bit as cheeky as Dylan's. "Doesn't matter, as long as I'm far enough to get out of range of the cell phone. It's my day off, but Lou doesn't seem to know what that means. She still calls me a dozen times a day."

"Didn't it ever occur to you to simply turn your phone off?" Sarah asked.

"What's the challenge in that? Besides, I could never lie to Lou if she asked why she couldn't reach me. This way I don't have to."

He glanced at her, a considering look in his blue eyes. "Do you ride?"

"Um, horses?"

"No. African elephants. Of course, horses."

The girls giggled and Sarah smiled, amazed that she enjoyed his teasing so much. "Not really. I know the front end of a horse from the back, but that's about it. I think the last time I rode was probably at summer camp the year I turned twelve."

"Doesn't matter. We can give you one of the more gentle horses and take it slow."

She didn't like the sound of that "we" business. "I don't really think…"

"What a great idea!" Ellie exclaimed. "Sarah, you have to go with him. It's such a gorgeous day, you'd be crazy not to."

"You can take my horse or Dylan's," Lucy chimed in. "Dandy and Speck are both really gentle."

Confronted with four Harte faces watching her with the same eager expression, Sarah knew she was well and truly trapped. She tried in vain to come up with a polite way to decline the invitation without disappointing them all.

She couldn't very well tell them the prospect terrified her. Not riding a horse up a mountain trail on a beautiful spring day—she had to admit she found that idea thrilling and adventurous, in keeping with the way she was trying to repair her life.

Riding that horse alone with Jesse Harte was another story, though.

She had come a long way in conquering her nervousness around him, but the idea of spending an hour or two alone in his company was as daunting as skydiving with her bum knee.

"You're completely outnumbered," Jesse finally said with that same devastating grin. "Only way you'll get out of it now is to come down with the chicken pox yourself."

"Unfortunately, I've already had them, so I'm immune," she murmured.

"Too bad. Guess that means you'll have to go with me, then." His grin just about took her breath away.

With a resigned sigh, she followed him out into the hallway, wishing fiercely that she'd been smart enough to build up an immunity to a certain police chief she could name.

He shouldn't have railroaded her into this.

Jesse watched Sarah duck her head to ride under a thick, fringy pine branch spreading over the trail. A few drops of rain from the quick shower the night before still nestled among the needles. As she brushed under it and emerged on the other side, glistening droplets clung to her thick blond hair like stars.

No, he definitely shouldn't have brought her. Not because she wasn't enjoying it. On the contrary. Her eyes shone as brightly as the water droplets in the sunlight and her face beamed with excitement.

He shouldn't have brought her because he didn't need to see this side of her. He didn't *want* to see it. It was tough enough fighting this completely inappropriate attraction to her in town, when she was shy and nervous around him. This smiling, glowing woman was damn near impossible to resist.

But he would resist her. He had to.

He had already worked hard to convince himself that he had to keep a safe, casual distance between them. She wasn't his type. He had a strict policy against becoming involved with breakable women and he had the feeling Sarah was more fragile than most.

On the other side of the trees, the trail widened enough for two horses. He dug his heels into his horse's side and caught up with her.

"You're doing great. How's your knee?"

"A little achy, but nothing out of the ordinary."

He wondered again how she had injured it. A car accident? A sports injury, maybe? Somehow he didn't think so. Call it cop's intuition, but he had a feeling her injured knee had some connection with whatever put those shadows in her pretty green eyes.

He also knew she wasn't about to share that information with him.

"Maybe we better not push it. We can stop just up ahead. There's a spot up there where you can see the whole valley."

They climbed one last rise in the trail, to a wide plateau covered in meadow grass and piles of melting snow. He helped her dismount and the two of them walked closer to the edge, toward a handful of large granite rocks. She perched on one and wrapped her arms around her knees as she gazed in wonder at the panoramic view.

"This is incredible! I didn't realize we were climbing so high. I swear, you can see clear to Jackson Hole!"

He leaned a hip against the boulder. "Not quite. If we went all the way to the top of the trail, we could."

"It's so gorgeous, it almost makes me want to cry."

He smiled at her awestruck expression. "Please don't! I'm not very good with crying women."

"I imagine you're probably good with any kind of women," she muttered under her breath, so low he thought he must have been mistaken.

He decided he would probably be wise to change the subject. "There's the Diamond Harte." He pointed to the ranch. "Prettiest spot in the valley, isn't it?"

"How big is the ranch?"

"About ten thousand acres, give or take a few. Then we have grazing rights to about that same number on Forest Service land above the ranch. In a month or so when the snow melts a little more, I'll be taking a couple days off to help Matt and his men drive them up there. It's a great time. If you're around, you ought to come out and watch."

He turned and found her watching him, her eyes soft and a small smile lifting the edges of her mouth the way the breeze fluttered the ends of her hair. "You love the ranch, don't you?"

She was so beautiful. He swallowed hard, fighting down the sudden fierce urge to reach for her. Finally he had to look away from her and back down at the place he'd been raised.

"Yeah," he finally said. "Yeah, I do love it."

"Why didn't you stay?"

How could he answer that? Jesse gazed down at the ranch and then over at the town sprawled just a few miles away from it, acutely aware of the wind rattling the aspens and the quiet fluttering of insects around them and the vast, beautiful silence of the mountainside.

He thought of several things at the same time. His parents' deaths, the reckless, selfish choices he'd made in the intervening years. The debt he owed to the people of Star Valley who had been willing to forgive.

Finally he shrugged. "Ranching was Matt's dream, not mine. I was too restless to be happy at it for long."

"What was your dream?"

He smiled ruefully. It had taken him years to figure that out. "I wanted to be on the right side of the law for a change. I love putting on that badge every morning and knowing today might be the day I save someone's life or return someone's property or help someone find lost hope again."

She was watching him again with that warm light in her eyes. Damn, he wished she wouldn't do that. "You're a good person, Jesse Harte."

"Don't kid yourself, Miz McKenzie," he murmured.

Badge or not, he was still the bad boy of Salt River and always would be. There was one sure way to prove it, he thought, and leaned across the space between them, toward that softly curving mouth.

He shouldn't be doing this. The thought registered briefly, but he didn't heed it. He had been itching to kiss her for too long. He wasn't about to give up this chance, even though he knew it was a mistake.

An instant later, his mouth brushed hers and he forgot everything but her.

Sarah froze. Her breath lodged somewhere in the vicinity of her throat and she was vaguely aware of a wild fluttering of her pulse.

He was going to kiss her. She could tell by the way he angled his head, by the sudden glittery light in his eyes.

She wanted to tell him to stop. She wanted to cry out that he shouldn't waste his time kissing her.

That she was broken.

But she couldn't hang on to any of those thoughts fluttering through her head like drab moths. Not when his beautiful, rugged features were only inches away, when she could feel the soft caress of his breath on her cheek.

She wanted him to kiss her, she realized with shock. She wanted to feel those hard, beautiful lips on hers, to taste his mouth, to know the sweet edge of passion once again.

Was that the fragile sensation sparkling to life inside her? Desire? She barely recognized the feeling, it had been so very long since she'd experienced it. She had begun to fear maybe that was just one more part of her that had shriveled up and blown away after the attack.

But no. Desire was definitely seeping through her bones, settling in all the deep, empty hollows inside her.

She wanted Jesse Harte to kiss her. Wanted it fiercely, so fiercely it was stronger even than the thin sliver of fear curling through her.

He paused for just an instant and watched her out of those incredible blue eyes, and then his mouth dipped to hers.

Please don't let me panic. Please don't let me panic, she prayed.

Her heart stuttered briefly, but the instant his mouth brushed hers, she forgot all about being afraid.

He had obviously kissed a lot of women. He knew

just the right way to skim his lips against hers, to make her feel wanted and needed, not overpowered.

She sighed into his mouth and closed her eyes to savor every moment. The masculine smell of him—a heady, woodsy mix of pine and sage and leather—his warm mouth that tasted like chocolate peppermints, the slight rasp of stubble against her skin.

Sensation after sensation poured over her and she wanted it to go on forever. Her position on the boulder put them at about the same height and she found it easy for her hands to creep around his neck, for her to draw him closer so she could continue to lose herself to the wonder of his mouth.

She wanted this man. Those first trickles of tentative desire swelled and surged with each touch of his mouth, until they rushed through her like spring runoff, pooling in her womb, between her thighs, in her heart. Until she wanted to weep with a vast, wonderful relief.

She wanted him! It seemed like a miracle, like rediscovering a part of herself she'd thought was lost forever.

His tongue licked at the corners of her mouth and she parted her lips, welcoming him inside. The kiss deepened and she could feel heat emanating from him like a sun-warmed rock.

She wanted everything, wanted those hard arms around her and his hair under her fingers and his hands on her skin. She made a soft noise in her throat and pulled him closer.

At the sound she made, Jesse froze and pulled back. Talk about a plan backfiring. He tried fiercely to catch his breath, to hang on to the last shreds of control.

He'd meant to show her he was too wild for a woman

like her. Maybe scare her a little so she'd stop looking at him with those damn stars in her eyes.

So much for that idea.

She had stunned him.

That was the only word for it. He couldn't remember ever feeling as completely undone by a woman, by the torrent of emotions that single kiss had sent tumbling through him—tenderness and protectiveness and a raw, hot need.

He wanted to pull her close, to safeguard her from whatever sometimes put that lost look in her eyes, to keep her safe and warm and loved.

Now he was the one who was scared to death. Breathing hard, he shoved his hands into his pockets and was amazed—and even more terrified—to realize they were shaking slightly.

It was just a kiss.

He'd kissed plenty of women before, tasted their mouths, touched their skin. Too many, according to Matt and Cassie. They liked to teasingly accuse him of leaving a long string of bruised and broken hearts across western Wyoming.

They were wrong. He had hurt a few women, he hated to admit it, but not on purpose. He had always made it abundantly clear up front to the women he dated that he wasn't looking for anything permanent.

Most of the time, that's all they wanted, too—he was careful to make sure of that—but one or two had started to take things too seriously.

When he could see them getting that light in their eyes that warned him they were starting to dream of wedding cakes and flower girls, he knew it was time to break things off.

He liked party girls. He wasn't ashamed to admit it. Big hair, big smiles, big breasts. Maybe it was a holdover from his wild younger days. He didn't drink anymore, didn't smoke, didn't swear much, but he still liked to date women who knew how to have a good time. Women who were there only for the short term.

So what was he thinking to kiss Sarah McKenzie— a very long-term kind of woman—as if he meant it?

And why, if it was just a kiss, did he feel as if that boulder she was sitting on had just rolled right over him?

He blew out a breath and sneaked a look at her. Big mistake. Her eyes were all soft and dewy and she almost looked as if she was going to tear up any minute now.

Panic ripped through him. He couldn't bear it when women cried.

What the hell was he supposed to do now?

He'd blown it big-time and now he was going to have to work even harder to keep away from her. A soft, fragile, forever kind of woman like Sarah McKenzie deserved far better than a rough lawman with wild blood running through his veins.

Trouble was, he didn't *want* to stay away from her. He liked her, respected her and—damn his hide—still wanted her.

He cleared his throat. "Should we keep going up the trail or are you ready to head back?"

She blinked at him, looking more vulnerable than a tiny kitten in the middle of a pack of junkyard dogs, and he watched her trying to gather her composure. Little by little, that glowing color began to fade from her face. He told himself he was relieved, but a hard kernel of regret dug into his heart as he watched it disappear.

"I...maybe we'd better head back," she murmured. "It's later than I realized and I have some things to do back in town."

He nodded and brought the horses over, then tried to make as little contact with her as possible while helping her into the saddle, afraid that if he touched any more of that soft skin, he might pull her into his arms and not let go.

The ride down the trail was uncomfortable, stiff and quiet. The birds were still singing, the mountains still bright and cheerful with spring, but much of the joy seemed to have gone out of the day.

All too soon, they arrived back at the Diamond Harte. He reined in near the ranch house, then went to help her dismount. She felt small and fragile in his hands—his fingers almost touched around her waist.

He released her quickly before he could pull her back into his arms. Maybe he moved *too* quickly. When he helped her to the ground, she stumbled a little and he had to reach for her again to steady her.

"I'm okay," she assured him, stepping away. "Just a little wobbly."

"Are you sure?"

"Yes. Thank you for taking me," she said brightly. Too brightly. "I didn't realize how much I've missed riding."

He had hurt her. He could tell by the brittleness in her voice and the distance in her eyes. Damn. That's what he'd been afraid of.

"I'm sure Matt would let you ride his horses anytime you'd like. There are dozens of trails above the ranch that are perfect for an hour or two trail ride. I'll talk to him about it for you if you'd like."

Her smile looked as if one of the girls had stuck it on her face with glue, but missed the corners somehow. "I appreciate the offer, but when I want to ride again, I'll talk to him. Thanks anyway. Do you need help putting the horses up?"

They were talking like polite strangers, like distant, formal acquaintances, and he hated it. "No. I've got it."

"Well, goodbye then. Thank you again."

"Sarah…" *I'm sorry,* he started to say. She looked at him expectantly but he wasn't sure exactly what he was apologizing for. For kissing her? Or for stopping?

"Never mind," he mumbled.

She pursed her lips, gave him one more of those terrible imitations of her smile, then walked to her car with her limp just a little more pronounced than usual.

What had she been thinking?

She should never have climbed on the back of that horse the day before, should never have gone riding with Jesse.

With every muscle in her body aching, Sarah stepped away from the bulletin board she was redecorating in her classroom Sunday evening. She gingerly eased onto the softest chair she could find in the room—one of the rolling computer chairs that, to her everlasting relief, possessed a comfortably padded seat.

She was going to be here all night trying to finish this thing if she had to continue taking these breaks every ten minutes.

The breaks had become a necessity, though. She stretched her knee out carefully and winced at the hot ache that forcefully reminded her of her folly. Unfortunately, her knee wasn't the only sore part of her body, but it seemed to have borne the worst of it.

She refused to acknowledge the other, not-so-physical ache that had settled somewhere in the vicinity of her heart after her afternoon spent with Jesse Harte.

She refused to regret their kiss, her aching heart notwithstanding. It had been warm and soft and sexy, and had made her feel wonderfully alive for the first time in months.

What she *did* regret—no matter how much time she spent castigating herself for the futility of it—was that she would never have the chance to kiss him again.

Jesse had made it clear he wouldn't be kissing her again anytime soon. He had ridden down the mountainside as if he had a snarling grizzly at his back.

The irony had not escaped her. For so long she had believed she would never feel desire again, never want to be with any man again.

And when she suddenly discovered that part of her hadn't died, had only been lurking somewhere deep inside, the man she wanted was obviously not interested.

She had to stop thinking about him. Mooning over the man wasn't helping her finish the job here.

She sighed and forced her attention back to the bulletin board, with its border of smiling suns wearing dark glasses, a not-so-subtle reminder that summer was just around the corner.

This would be her last bulletin board of the school year, since the term ended in just a few weeks.

Would she be here in the fall to take this one down and put up a new one, to greet a new crowd of fourth graders with their shiny notebooks and stiff new blue jeans and unsharpened pencils?

She hadn't decided yet. When she came to Star Valley, she had signed only a one-year contract, subject to renegotiation at the end of the school year. She had yet to make up her mind about signing a new one and teaching here another year.

On the one hand, Star Valley had provided exactly what she had needed the past nine months. Peace and safety. A place to regroup, to find the strength to survive.

A place to heal.

On the other hand, she feared she was becoming too comfortable here. Was she hiding out from the realities of the world in this place where she lived most of her life alone?

Maybe it was time to go back to Chicago. Maybe she would never really feel herself again—or at least finally begin to like the woman she had become—until she returned to face her friends and her family and her nightmare.

She didn't have to decide this tonight. She stapled the last smiling sun on the border, then stepped back to admire her work. Perfect. Now she could go home and soak her loudly complaining muscles in a nice hot bath.

She was cleaning up the mess she had made when she heard it.

A scratching, skittery sound that didn't belong in the quiet of her classroom.

Her heart gave a couple of hard knocks in her chest and she couldn't move. She could feel the flashback hovering on the edge of her consciousness. Broken glass. Hurtful hands. Choking, paralyzing terror.

Just before it claimed her, she realized with a vast, painful relief what had made the sound. Only a branch from the maple tree outside her window dancing in the cool spring breeze.

The problem was, she'd seen entirely too many horror movies when she was younger, too many shows where a scratching at the window turned out to be something far less benign than the wind.

"Scaredy-cat," she chided herself, breathing hard to force oxygen back into her bloodstream.

Being alone in the school had always spooked her a little, even before Tommy DeSilva. Sometimes she could swear she heard the distant echo of children's laughter, the rapping of a ruler on a desk.

And, thanks to him, now she heard phantom attackers lurking around every corner.

She hated being afraid.

Maybe that's why she forced herself to come to her classroom so often on the weekend or in the evening. To demystify it. Maybe if she spent enough time here, she would eventually become inured to the bumps and squeaks, to the branches scraping against her window.

Or maybe she just wanted to torture herself.

Whatever the reason, her psyche had had quite enough for tonight. Sarah shrugged into her fleece jacket, then turned off her light and quickly walked outside.

She felt instantly better out in the fresh air. The night was crisp, the breeze sweet and clean. A perfect spring night to follow two beautiful days. Above the lights of town, moonlight gleamed on the snow-covered peaks of the Salt River range standing solid and firm.

How could she leave here? She had come to love everything about Star Valley, through all the changing seasons.

She couldn't leave, despite her suddenly awkward relationship with Jesse Harte. She wanted to be here in August when the students came back, she wanted to take up Nordic skiing next winter if her knee would allow it, she wanted to ride the Piñon trail again and feel the cool mountain air on her face.

She would tell Chuck Hendricks on Monday that she would sign the contract and return for another year. She wasn't hiding away here. She was building a new life for herself.

She was smiling—and favoring her knee only a little, she was pleased to discover—when she turned onto Spruce Street and passed old Mrs. Jensen's cow-shaped mailbox.

The riot of tulips lining her neighbor's wrought-iron fence swayed in the breeze, their colors ghostly pale under the soft moonlight, and Sarah stopped for a moment to admire them.

She would bury tulip bulbs this fall, she decided. Masses of them, in every conceivable color. Reds, pinks, yellows, purples. And next spring she would wait eagerly for them to poke through the earth.

Already sketching out in her mind where she would plant them all—and daffodils, too—she was still smiling as she reached her own mailbox and started up the walk.

She was halfway to the porch when she lifted her head and saw it.

The porch light was still burning—she had turned it on when she left, as she always did when she expected to be home after dark—and its glow illuminated a scene that looked as if it belonged in one of those horror movies she'd been thinking about earlier.

Chapter 9

Jesse's cellular phone bleated just as the Utah Jazz basketball team tied the score at the end of the fourth quarter, pushing the critical postseason game into overtime.

So much for enjoying the last few hours of his time off.

He groaned and glared at the phone. His efforts to convince some of his officers they could handle all but the most urgent crises without him didn't seem to be working. They still called to check with him before making almost any kind of decision, from whether to give tickets or warnings to first-time traffic offenders to what kind of coffee filters worked best in the machine.

He'd have to work a little harder, apparently.

"This better be good," he growled into the phone.

Silence met his snarl, then a small, ragged-sounding voice spoke. "Jesse? Is that you?"

He forgot the basketball game in an instant as cold fear clawed at him. "Sarah! What's wrong?" He knew instinctively that she wouldn't have used this number unless absolutely necessary, especially not after the awkwardness of the day before on the mountain.

"Can you… Do you think you could come over?"

He shoved into his boots, not taking the time to bother with socks. "I'm already heading for the door."

"I'm sorry to bother you. I didn't know who else to call."

She sounded strange, disoriented, almost as if she was high on something, but he knew that was impossible. She couldn't be using. Not sweet, fragile Sarah McKenzie.

He remembered the day she had freaked out on her back porch when her knee gave out and he'd reached to keep her from falling. That's the way she seemed now—like someone on the verge of a full-blown panic attack.

"What's going on?" he asked, trying to tamp down on his own panic.

"I don't know. There's blood everywhere. Please hurry."

Blood. Everywhere. Those were the only words that registered.

"Sarah?" he called into the phone, but the line went dead. In an instant, he yanked his sidearm from the closet and raced for his Bronco, calling for an ambulance and backup as he went.

He drove the six blocks to her house with all his lights flashing and siren blaring, and broke just about every traffic law on the Salt River books—and a few the city council hadn't had a chance to come up with yet.

On Spruce Street he braked hard and the Bronco

shuddered to a stop just a few feet from where she stood in the middle of the road, clutching a cell phone and rocking back and forth on her heels.

He jumped from the truck and rushed to her, pulling her into his arms. "Sarah! What happened? Sit down. Where are you hurt?"

"No. It's not me."

He was so completely focused on her—on trying to visually assess her injuries—that he wasn't aware of anything else until she pointed toward her house. "There."

Reluctant to take his eyes off her for even a moment, he turned with impatience in the direction she was pointing. At first he didn't know what he was seeing. It just looked like dark shadows where there shouldn't be any, smears of muddy black.

Then his gaze sharpened and he realized what he was seeing.

His jaw sagged and he hissed a disbelieving curse, horrified by the scene. The dark shadows weren't shadows at all but blood. And, as she had whispered into the phone, it was everywhere.

On her porch pillars, on the door, pooled on her steps. Quarts of it. Buckets. It looked as if someone had butchered a cow right at her front door.

What in the world?

He stared, trying to comprehend it. He'd been a cop for a dozen years, had investigated everything from car accidents to bar fights to spouse abuse—and even a murder a few years back when one ranch hand had shot another over a woman.

But he couldn't remember ever seeing anything this grisly.

It couldn't possibly be hers. She wouldn't still be standing if it were. As if on cue, at just that moment she seemed to wobble in his arms. Even if she wasn't injured, he realized, she was shocky. Her face was pale as death in the moonlight, she was shaking uncontrollably and she looked as if she would fall over at the first stiff wind.

"Let's get you into the Bronco." He picked her up, struck by how delicate she felt in his arms, then settled her into the passenger seat. He had a wool blanket in the back in case of emergencies, although in his wildest dreams he would never have come up with this kind of scenario. He reached for it and tucked it around her.

"Can you tell me what happened?" he asked.

She shrugged helplessly. "I don't know. I was at the school working...."

"This late? By yourself?"

At the fierceness of his voice, her eyes went a little wild and unfocused, and he tempered his expression. The last thing she needed after a shock like this was an interrogation from him. "Sorry. Go on."

"I came home just before I called you and...and saw it like this. I don't know what happened."

Another siren cut through the night before he could ask her anything more. His backup pulled in behind him and Chris Hernandez climbed out of the squad car, her eyes wide and astonished.

"Sweet Almighty. What happened here?"

"I don't know," he said grimly. "But I'm sure as hell going to find out."

He was suddenly glad Chris was the responding officer. She was a good cop, one of his best. Beyond that, the fact that she was a woman might help make Sarah a little more at ease.

"Can you stay here in the Bronco with Miss McKenzie until the ambulance arrives?"

Sarah made a small, distressed sound and grabbed his arm. "I don't need an ambulance. I'm fine."

"Sweetheart, you're more pale than that moon up there."

"Please, Jesse. I feel foolish enough as it is. I don't need an ambulance. Honestly."

After a moment of indecision, he instructed Chris to cancel the ambulance but to stay with Sarah while he looked around. "Call in the county crime scene unit, too," he added. "I'm afraid this is a bigger job than we can handle alone"

"Sure, Chief."

He walked toward the house, noting that neighbors had already been drawn to the sirens like flies to a corpse. With the prurient interest of the uninvolved, they stood on their front porches, craning their necks to see what was happening.

At least they were keeping their distance. Nobody else should have to see this.

Up close, Jesse was even more sickened by the mess. The blood or whatever it was hadn't just been randomly splashed around. Whoever had done this wanted to destroy—the bastard had set out to do the most damage possible. Dark stains covered everything. The trim of the porch, the windowsill, a white wicker planter full of cheerful pink flowers.

Worse, words had been painted on the white of her door. Terrible, vile obscenities—names that shouldn't be used against anyone, especially not a woman like Sarah McKenzie.

He dipped a finger into one of the puddles of red and brought it to his nose. Definitely blood, judging by the metallic tang. Where the hell had so much blood come from? It would have to be an animal, he decided. Or a couple of animals, even. The forensics lab could have that information to him in just a few hours.

Whatever it came from, the blood was still wet, which meant the vandal had finished up probably no longer than twenty minutes ago. What if Sarah had come home and caught him in the act?

His stomach churned at the thought. Anyone capable of this kind of viciousness would be capable of anything.

He suddenly noticed something even more worrisome, something he had overlooked in the shock of seeing all that blood. The blood wasn't the worst of the damage. Every single window he could see had been systematically shattered.

The raw savagery of it shocked him. This hadn't been a random act, but something aimed specifically at her. What could she possibly have done to make someone this angry at her?

A quick look around her house showed that most of the damage was confined to the front where it would have the most shock value. He was just about to head back to the Bronco and wait for the sheriff's crime scene unit when he spotted something on the porch, something he'd missed the first time through.

A men's baseball-type cap with an embroidered logo of an olive nymph dry fly on it was lying in a puddle of blood. The cap was dirty, as all good fishing caps are, but the only blood he could see on it was underneath, where it rested in the puddle, which likely meant it had landed there after the vandal had done his work.

As a clue, it wasn't much. Half the men in town probably owned a similar kind of cap. But maybe forensics could lift prints off it. He used a pen to pick it up, then walked back toward the flashing lights.

Hernandez slipped out of the Bronco to talk to him, closing the door behind her so Sarah couldn't hear their conversation.

"How is she?" he asked the officer.

She shrugged. "Pretty shook up. I keep trying to talk to her, you know, just to make conversation, but she acts like she doesn't even know I'm there. What's her story?"

"She's just a nice lady who doesn't deserve to have something like this happen to her."

"It's more than that. You haven't been sitting there with her, Chief. It's spooky, if you ask me. I've seen it before with crime victims. It's almost like she's not here, like she's gone somewhere else inside her head. Something's definitely weird with her."

"This would be a shock for anyone to come home and find on their doorstep."

"Maybe. And maybe she knows who it is. Maybe that's why she's so scared."

He didn't like the implications of that idea at all, that Sarah had reason to know who might be terrorizing her.

"You find anything up there besides a nasty mess and words that would get my mouth washed out with soap every day for the rest of my life if my mama saw them?" Chris asked.

"Just this." He held up the baseball cap. "I want to see if she recognizes it, then you can bag it and hand it over to CSI. Why don't you start canvasing the neighbors and see if anybody saw or heard anything?"

Inside the Bronco he found Sarah staring through the passenger window with wide, unblinking eyes. He wanted to pull her into his arms, to tuck her head under his chin and hold that trembling body against him until his heat warmed her skin, warmed her soul.

He couldn't do any of those things, though. All he could do was try his best to find the sick animal who had done this.

He held up the baseball cap. "Do you recognize this?"

She blinked several times, as if sliding back into the present. "I... I don't think so. Do you believe it belongs to the person who..." Her voice trailed off as if she couldn't quite find the right words.

It didn't matter. He knew what she meant. "Seems likely. I found it on the porch. It doesn't have any splatters on it, which makes me think it wasn't there when most of the blood was spilled."

She drew a ragged-sounding breath. "So it *is* blood. I thought... I was hoping it might be paint."

"No. Definitely blood. Probably from an animal, maybe a cow or something."

She said nothing for several moments, mulling over the information, then she turned to him again. "How much longer before I can begin cleaning it up? Mr. Jimenez will be angry if it stains."

"Forget Bob. I'll send someone to clean it up in the morning after the crime scene investigators are done."

"I have to do it tonight, Jesse. I won't be able to sleep inside there, knowing all this is out here."

At the tremble in her voice, he again fought the urge

to pull her into his arms. "Sweetheart, I don't know if you noticed, but most of your windows are shattered. We can put boards up tonight, but it's going to take time to order replacements for them."

She looked at the house once more and seemed to crumple. This time he lost the internal battle he was waging and reached for her. She came to him willingly, as if she had been waiting just for this, and settled her head against his chest.

"If you think for one second that I'm letting you stay there alone tonight, you're crazy," Jesse murmured against her hair. "You're coming home with me."

After a moment she pulled away. "I can take care of myself."

She said the words firmly, and he knew she was trying to convince herself as much as him. A soft, aching tenderness settled in his heart.

"I know you can take care of yourself. But you shouldn't have to. Not after this. I'm sorry, but you're going to have to stay with me. I would take you out to the ranch, but with the girls sick, I think Ellie has all she can handle right now."

"I don't want to impose. I could stay at a hotel until the windows are fixed."

"Let me do this, Sarah. Please?"

She looked at the carnage outside her house for a long time, then finally nodded.

Both of them knew she didn't have much choice.

She stood under Jesse Harte's shower for a long time, long after her skin was red and puckered from the heat, long after her aching knee couldn't hold her upright anymore and she had sunk to the tile with her arms wrapped around herself, huddling there and trembling.

But still she couldn't seem to get clean.

He had found her. It was the only explanation she could come up with.

Somehow Tommy DeSilva had escaped from prison and come to find her.

Who else would have reason to hate her so badly? She couldn't think of a soul. Surely no one in Star Valley would do such a thing.

Ever since she had seen what had been done to her house, she had teetered back and forth on the thin line between flashback and reality. She felt as if she had spent the past eighteen months trying to wake up from a horrible nightmare, only to have it sneak up on her again when she least expected it.

Just the thought of being in the same state with Tommy DeSilva sent panic churning through her veins.

When she realized who must have vandalized her house, her first instinct had been to flee, to pack up her car and leave Star Valley behind. But she was afraid if she started running, she would never be able to stop. She would spend the rest of her life looking over her shoulder, always waiting for him to find her.

Still shivering, she wrapped herself in the warm towel Jesse had provided, then reached for the robe he had been thoughtful enough to instruct that kind female officer—Officer Hernandez, wasn't it?—to pack for her, along with a few of her other possessions.

She would have to tell him.

All of it. The awful, sordid details of what had happened in Chicago. He would have to know so that he could start looking for DeSilva.

Dear heavens, she didn't want to tell him. She stared at her reflection in the mirror, a hot, heavy ache welling up in her throat. When she told him, he would never be able to look at her the same way again. He would see the same stranger she saw staring back at her in the mirror right now.

A victim.

As much as she wanted to stay silent, she knew to-night's events had taken that choice out of her hands. She had to tell Jesse everything. He had to know the ugliness she had somehow unleashed on his town, how-ever unwittingly.

She tied her robe tightly and went to find him.

The first creature she met outside the bathroom was the huge golden retriever he had introduced as Daisy. The dog was lying in the hall, chin on her paws, as if waiting for Sarah. Sarah found great comfort in her presence, like having a big shaggy guardian angel.

At the sight of her, the dog wagged her long tail and rose gracefully to her feet, then led the way down the hall.

Jesse was in his kitchen, a surprisingly efficient nook with pine cupboards and wood floors that opened to a larger, carpeted living area. He was barefoot, she saw, and couldn't for the life of her figure out why she found that so appealing.

"How was your shower? Did you have enough hot water?"

There probably wasn't enough hot water in the whole town to keep her warm. "Yes," she lied. "Plenty."

"Good. I was just brewing you some tea. My sister, Cass, swears it's the cure for everything, from hangnails to PMS. Why don't you sit down and I'll bring you a cup?"

She nodded and, with her retriever shadow, walked to the sitting area next to the kitchen.

Even though the night was mild, Jesse had lit a small fire in the stone fireplace, and tears stung her eyes at his thoughtfulness. The warmth washed over, enfolded her like a thick quilt, seeping into her chilled bones as she sat down on a couch covered in fabric of dark blues and greens.

Daisy immediately settled into what looked like her customary spot, atop a braided oval rug in front of the fireplace.

"Here we go." Jesse brought her tea in a mug with a leaping trout on the side. "Can I get you anything else? I can make you a sandwich if you would like."

The thought of food made her stomach churn greasily. "No. I…no. Tea is fine."

He took a seat in the wide recliner that was obviously *his* customary spot and watched until she took a sip of the strong herbal tea. To her surprise, it did make her feel somewhat better. She could feel the panic recede just a little further.

"It's good," she murmured. "Thank you."

They talked for a few moments about innocuous things—the weather, the sports team he liked, his sister, Cassie, who had decorated the house for him when he bought it the year before. He was trying his best to put her at ease, she realized, touched by his efforts.

She was almost tempted to just stay there sipping tea, savoring the hiss and crackle of the fire, blocking out any of the ugliness of the evening or of that morning so many months ago in Chicago.

But she couldn't put it off. She had to tell him.

It was so much harder than she thought it would be. Like the story she read her class of squeezing water from stone.

"Jesse, I have to tell you something," she finally just blurted out.

He frowned at her tone. "What's wrong?"

"I... I lied to you earlier."

His frown deepened. "You what?"

"I lied. I told you I don't know who might have been responsible for vandalizing my house."

"But you do?"

She took a deep, shuddering breath for strength. "His name is Tommy DeSilva. I don't know how it's possible, but I think he must have found me somehow and followed me from Chicago."

"Why would he do that?"

She couldn't look at him. She couldn't watch the pity and revulsion she knew would appear on those strong, masculine features.

She felt a quick, sharp pang of loss, knowing that after she told him, he would definitely never kiss her again as he had the day before on the mountainside.

Not that she expected him to, but this would definitely make such a likelihood impossible.

"Because my testimony sent him to prison for rape and attempted murder," she answered.

He was quiet for a long time and when he finally spoke, his voice sounded strained. "Who was his victim?"

He knows, she thought. She could hear it in his voice, that thin thread of pity and shock already filtering through. But still he needed to hear the words. She needed to *say* the words.

She looked at her tightly laced fingers, at the glossy fabric of her robe, at the oatmeal weave of his carpet.

At anything but him.

"Me," she finally whispered. "Eighteen months ago, Tommy DeSilva attacked me and…and raped me and left me to die."

Chapter 10

At her stark words, Jesse froze, his breath a tight and heavy ache in his chest.

A million emotions surged through him: shock, dismay, sorrow. Most of all, a fierce, overriding fury at the son of a bitch who had hurt her.

He should have guessed her secrets before. A fine cop he was. She had thrown out enough clues to stop a damn train.

Maybe he had suspected it, deep in his subconscious. He'd seen enough crime victims over the years that he must have picked up at least some of the signs.

But maybe he hadn't wanted to see what was right in front of him, to face the grim reality that someone as good and decent as Sarah could suffer such brutality.

So many things about her now made sense. Those dark shadows in her eyes, her skittishness around him and just about every other man he had ever seen her with. That slight, subtle limp.

He started to speak and had to clear the raw choke-hold of emotion from his throat before he could get the words out. "Is your knee injury from the attack?"

Her head barely moved when she nodded.

She watched him out of those serious green eyes and he knew she was waiting for some kind of reaction from him. What the hell was he supposed to say to her after a bombshell like that?

I'm sorry? She had to know he was.

I wish it had never happened to you? The words were a vast understatement.

I'd like to find the bastard who hurt you and rip him apart with my bare hands? He sensed the ragged feroc-ity of his emotions would only upset her more.

So what was he supposed to say? To do? He wanted to go to her and pull her from the couch and into his arms. He wanted to hold her close and whisper soft kisses into her hair and promise he wouldn't let any-body ever hurt her again.

But he didn't have the right to promise her anything.

"Do you want to know about it?" she asked quietly at his continued silence.

Did he? No. He wanted to pretend it had never hap-pened, that something so ugly had never even touched her. Every instinct in him wanted to urge her to stay quiet.

Somehow he knew that the telling would change both of them.

But he couldn't give in to those strident voices. It *had* happened. She had been brutally attacked. And she had survived. It seemed small and selfish of him to want to pretend it had never happened, just because he wasn't sure *he* could handle hearing about it.

Besides that, he sensed she needed to tell him.

"It might help us in our investigation, if this guy is really in town." He tried to keep his voice even, hoping like hell the jumble of fury and reluctance and heartache he was feeling didn't filter through.

She was quiet for a moment, her hands wound tightly in her lap. The only sound in the house was Daisy's snuffly breathing and the snapping fire on the grate. Then she finally spoke.

"I taught third grade in Chicago," she began. "Eight-and nine-year-olds. It was a poor, inner-city school, in quite a rough area. My parents couldn't understand why I didn't take a job in Evanston closer to Northwestern, where they both are professors, but I loved my job. The children were so eager to learn, just fascinated by everything I taught them." Her soft smile damn near broke his heart.

She paused for several seconds and he sensed she was trying to gather her courage to reach the crux of the story. "I... I had a student named Beatriz DeSilva. I know teachers aren't supposed to have favorites, but I have to confess, she was always one of mine. She had these beautiful long, glossy braids and the sweetest smile."

That soft smile of remembrance teased at her mouth again, but quickly fluttered away. She swallowed hard. "One day out on the playground, I told her to put on her mittens. It was a really awful day, with a bitter wind blowing off the lake. Other than that, it seemed like just a normal day."

Her voice took on a faraway quality. "It seemed as

if everything moved in slow motion. Bea reached into her pocket for her mittens, just as I had asked her to do, but when she pulled her hands out, something else fell out as well and landed on the blacktop. A small bundle containing several packets of dirty white powder."

"Cocaine?"

She shook her head. "Heroin. With a street value of nearly two thousand dollars."

Children in third grade shouldn't even know what heroin looked like, let alone carry it in their pockets along with their mittens. He was disgusted, but not really surprised. Unfortunately, he had seen and heard much worse. "What did you do?"

"Bea was wailing and shaking, terrified out of her wits that I had seen the drugs. I pulled her into the classroom and made her tell me everything. I've never seen a child so frightened." Sarah folded her hands together tightly. "She finally broke down and told me that her older brother Tommy fancied himself a big-time dealer in the area. He was all of eighteen. He sometimes used her to drop small shipments for his clientele, forcing her to do it with threats that he would hurt their baby brother if she didn't."

She cleared her throat before continuing. "Bea was supposed to have delivered the drugs that morning before school, but for some reason she didn't. We were having a special assembly first thing that morning and she didn't want to be late for it. I never would have found out what her brother was putting her through if not for that."

She clamped her lips together and he watched her pulse quiver in her throat. "I was so furious. She was only a child. Just a sweet little girl doing what she was told to protect her baby brother. I immediately called the police. Bea and her little brother were turned over to social services while officers went looking for Tommy."

"They didn't find him?"

"Oh, they did." Her bitter smile held no mirth. "He was arrested and charged, but released on bail six hours later."

"And he came looking for you." A statement, not a question. He knew enough about the criminal mind to know that sometimes vengeance came before anything else. Food, drugs, sex. They all paled in comparison to getting even.

Beneath her robe, her shoulders trembled just a little with her shudder. "He broke a window into my classroom and was waiting for me the next morning when I arrived at school."

His retriever whimpered at the distress in Sarah's voice, then rose from her spot by the fire and padded to her. Jesse was about to order her down, but he stopped, sensing Sarah was drawing a comfort from the dog he wasn't sure he could provide.

Daisy rested her chin on Sarah's knee and she patted her absently, her fingers working through the long yellow fur like worry beads.

"I was there early to catch up with some work," she finally continued. "If I had been a half hour later, the other classrooms in that hall would have been filled with teachers and I could have called for help. But there was no one else there."

"What happened?" The words felt like tiny sharp stones in his raw throat.

"I think he was more upset at losing the drugs than anything else. He kept saying he owed people and now

I owed him. Stupid me, I was more angry than scared at first. I told him he was worse than an animal for endangering a child."

She blew out a breath. "I shouldn't have baited him. That's when he hit me. He—he had a gun and he hit me on the side of the head with it. The impact stunned me and I fell to the floor, and I can remember lying there on that faded, dirty tile, thinking I was going to die. That this punk—this stupid, hopped-up gangbanger— was going to kill me."

He couldn't even begin to imagine the horror or the courage it must be taking her to tell him about it. "He didn't fire the gun?"

"No. I'm not sure why. I guess he must have realized that would have brought people running. He used it to hit me, though. He just kept hitting me and hitting me with whatever he could find. The gun, a chair, a stapler, a chair, his fists."

Stop. Enough. He couldn't stand hearing any more. He growled a harsh oath, intending to beg her to stop this grim recital, but she didn't seem to hear him, lost in the past.

"It seemed like it lasted forever, but it was probably only a few moments. Eventually I stopped fighting and came close to passing out. That's when he…he raped me, then he left. I was terrified he would come back, but after a few minutes I somehow managed to crawl out into the hall and the custodian found me."

She paused. "I remember feeling so grateful that at least my students didn't have to see me that way."

This time her tiny smile did break his heart. He felt it shatter into jagged shards.

"Oh, Sarah. I'm so sorry." He couldn't keep silent any longer, whether he said the wrong words or not.

She blinked at him and he watched her click back into the present. Color soaked her cheeks and she became suddenly fascinated with Daisy's fur. "DeSilva must be in Star Valley. He's the only one I know who... who hates me enough to do something like that to my home."

"Can you describe him so I can tell my officers what they might be looking for?"

She closed her eyes as if picturing him in her mind, and he was struck again by her delicate features, by soft skin stretching over the hollows and curves of her face. He wanted to skim his fingers over that face, to trace the dark smudge of her lashes and the thin bridge of her nose.

How could a woman who seemed so vulnerable have survived such an ordeal? Maybe that was the reason for her fragility, because she *had* survived and was still trying to find her way in the aftermath.

"He was big for eighteen," she said. "Probably your height, muscled like a body builder. He had a small beard back then, just a little fuzz on his chin. I remember thinking he barely seemed old enough for facial hair. He might have shaved it off by now."

He hated making her relive any more details, but the more information his officers had, the better the chances of finding the bastard if he was indeed in Star Valley. He almost hoped DeSilva was dumb enough to come after her. If he was here, Jesse would find him.

"Any other defining characteristics? A tattoo or anything?"

"Nothing very original. He had a snake twining

around his arm and a four-lettered obscenity tattooed across his knuckles."

"That will help. That kind of thing is pretty rare around here." He rose, grateful to be able to take some action, no matter how small. "I'll call this description in to my officers and the sheriff's department and also get someone on the phone to Chicago so they can fax us a mug. Are you okay here for a few moments while I do that?"

She nodded, and watched him cross the room toward the phone with quick, restless movements. He was like a dark storm cloud, simmering with barely contained energy.

What was he thinking? She wished she could read his emotions better. She knew he was upset. By the time she'd finished giving him the ugly details, he had been barely breathing, as motionless—and dangerous—as a rattlesnake poised to strike. But she couldn't read much more into his features than that.

Everything would be different now. He knew the truth and they could never go back to the casual, friendly place they had been before.

She could hear him on the phone describing Tommy DeSilva to his officers, a hardness to his voice she seldom heard. She found it oddly comforting.

Jesse would keep her safe.

No matter what wild creatures clawed at her subconscious, he would hold them at bay.

Daisy settled a little deeper into sleep, her weight heavy on Sarah's bare feet like one huge furry slipper. Despite the tumult of her emotions, she had to smile. Apparently Jesse wasn't her only self-appointed protector. Anyone who wanted to get to her would have to make it past not just one very large and dangerous man but his ferociously amiable golden retriever, as well.

Jesse ended the call a few moments later and returned to the sitting area. "I put out the word that we're looking for any suspicious strangers in town. It's a little too early in the season for many tourists to be passing through on their way to Jackson Hole or Yellowstone, so if this DeSilva is anywhere around, he'll stand out like a Christmas tree in July."

"Thank you."

He shrugged. "For what? I'm just doing my job."

"For that and for letting me stay here. I'll try to get out of your hair as soon as I can."

He narrowed his gaze. "You're not going anywhere until we catch whoever did a number on your house tonight, so you might as well just accept it."

Her spine stiffened, vertebra by vertebra. She appreciated his protectiveness—it warmed a small, cold place inside her. But she had been a victim long enough.

She refused to completely surrender her life.

If DeSilva wanted her badly enough, she knew he would find her, whether here or at her own place.

"I'll stay until I can get someone to clean up the mess and replace the windows. When the house is ready again, I'll move back."

He opened his mouth as if he were gearing up for a fierce argument, then closed it again. "If we're no further along in the investigation by that time, we can talk about it."

"All right." She was suddenly exhausted. So tired she could hardly move, and her knee throbbed viciously.

Jesse picked up on it instantly. "Why don't you get

some rest? You can sleep in tomorrow. I can have Cassie come over, if you'd like."

"No. I have school."

"Seems to me you have a good excuse to find a substitute and take the day off."

Chuck Hendricks would just love that. "No. I need to be there. We're having a test in math later."

He sighed at her stubbornness. "Come on, then. I'll show you to the guest room."

Sarah tried to stand, but having seventy-five pounds of dog sleeping on her feet made it a challenge.

"What's wrong?" Jesse asked when she didn't follow him down the hall, then he realized her predicament. "Sorry. Daisy. Come," he ordered. His retriever creaked sadly to her feet but spoiled the effect by bounding over to him like a puppy.

He led the way down the hall and opened a door across from the bathroom where she had showered. He held the door open for her, wide enough for three of her to pass him without even brushing against his shirt.

She noticed the careful distance he maintained between them—as if he were afraid to touch her—and her heart wept a little.

"Are you sure you'll be all right?"

She nodded, not trusting her voice. Everything was different, just as she knew it would be. What would he say if she could somehow find the words to tell him how badly she needed the warmth and safety of his arms around her just then?

She couldn't ask. She wasn't sure she could bear it if he held her with stiff awkwardness, like some fragile piece of glass.

"Good night," she finally said, then closed the door between them.

The guest room was large with an inviting, queen-size pine bed covered with a log-cabin quilt in rich plums and greens. A small lamp graced a matching table next to the bed and she fought the urge to turn it on. She wasn't afraid of the dark. She wouldn't allow herself to be. The thin spear of moonlight shining through the window would have to be enough.

She climbed into bed and pulled the quilt to her chin, focusing on that ribbon of light, on the soft texture of the cotton sheets, on the low murmur of his voice on the telephone, probably checking on the investigation. The smell of him lingered in the room—laundry soap mingled with the woodsy cedar scent of his aftershave.

The exhaustion was still there weighing down her muscles, but she knew sleep would be a long time coming. Despite her weariness, her body still seethed with tension, her mind still raced.

She supposed she would have found it shocking if she *had* been able to drift off easily after the stress of the evening. Not when she had just been forced to re-live in graphic detail the nightmare she had been desperately trying to forget for the past eighteen months.

She thought of the shock on Jesse's hard, beautiful features as she had told him. That subtle withdrawal she knew he probably wasn't even aware of. She had seen it, though. The distance still hurt, even though she had been expecting nothing less.

She had seen variations on the same theme with everyone in Chicago after her attack.

Her friends hadn't known what to say. They wanted

to pretend it had never happened, wanted her to just get over it and go back to the old Sarah.

Her parents had been devastated. Her mother had wept for days, her father had retreated into his study. They had insisted she come to their quiet home after the two weeks she spent in the hospital, and had babied her as if she were four years old again.

Underlying their reaction had been subtle, unspoken accusation. If she hadn't stubbornly insisted on teaching at an inner-city school, if she'd been in Evanston, where she belonged, it never would have happened.

And there was Andrew. The man she had been prepared to spend the rest of her life with. She should have been able to turn to him for comfort after the attack, but she hadn't even been able to face him when he came to the hospital.

She knew she was more to blame for the collapse of their relationship after the rape than he was. She also knew it couldn't have been very solid to begin with if it couldn't survive this test. That didn't stop the harsh sting of failure.

It felt strange to speak of her attack. She hadn't told anyone but Jesse in the nine months since she'd come to Salt River. Not a word. If she didn't speak of it, she could try her best to pretend it never happened to her—that it was some other poor woman who had endured those terrible moments in that dingy, tired classroom.

Besides, it wasn't exactly the sort of thing she could bring up in casual conversation with the other teachers. *May I use the copy machine after you? Oh, by the way, did I mention I was brutally beaten and raped at my previous school?*

She sighed and rolled to her side, toward the window and that pale, comforting slice of moon.

She could still hear Jesse moving around in the other part of the house and she was suddenly struck by the realization that this was the first night she had spent in the same house with another person since she had moved out of her parents' big house and come to Salt River.

So why did she feel more alone than ever?

She absolutely did not want to go back in there.

Friday afternoon, Sarah sat in her car trying to find enough strength somewhere deep inside her that would carry her up those steps and into Jesse's house.

She wasn't sure she could survive this another night. For five days she had smiled and made small talk and tried to pretend she was comfortable living in his house, that she didn't notice the tension simmering between them.

The effort was exhausting her.

One more night. That's all she had to get through. The company making the custom windows for her rental had promised they would send workmen to install them in the morning, even though it was Saturday.

She just had to get through another evening trying to pretend her feelings for Jesse weren't growing stronger with every passing moment.

He wouldn't be home for another hour or two. In the few days she had been staying there, they had fallen into a routine of sorts—awkward though it was.

She would stop at the grocery store on the way to his house after school and start dinner, then play out in the yard with Daisy for a while.

When his shift ended, Jesse would come home and

they would discuss their respective days while they shared a meal. She told him of her students and school politics and her inevitable end-of-the-school-year blues. He would talk about his officers and the calls he'd gone on that day and his inevitable pain-in-the-neck paperwork.

After dinner he would wash up, then stretch out in his favorite chair with the newspaper or a book or the remote while she sat at his kitchen table grading papers. A few torturous hours later, she would eventually give up this test of endurance and retire to the guest room for another sleepless night.

She knew entirely too many things about Jesse Harte after sharing such close quarters with him for nearly a week.

She knew he woke early to run or lift weights, and that when he worked up a sweat, his hair clung to his neck in thick dark spikes.

She knew he laughed at silly jokes his nieces told him over the phone, and that the sound of it—rich and full and generous—could work itself down her spine and leave her breathless.

She knew he was passionate about his job, and considered any crime that took place in his town a personal affront.

And she knew she was teetering precariously close to falling in love with him.

That was why she sat in her car like the craven coward that she was, trying to summon the courage to make it through one more night. Each moment she spent with him, she slipped a little further down that dangerous slope, and it scared her senseless.

It was completely ridiculous, she knew that. Pathetic,

even. The shy, skittish schoolteacher pining over the most gorgeous man in town. It was even more pathetic when the man in question couldn't bring himself to touch her in even the most casual of ways.

She sighed. And there was the truth of the matter. That's why she dreaded going inside—because every night, she came closer and closer to begging him to touch her again, to kiss her as he had the day they went riding together.

Only one more night. She could be strong for one more night, couldn't she? She would go home in the morning, whether the dratted windows were installed or not. Heaven knew, she dreaded making a fool of herself over him far more than she feared going back to her house.

A rap on her car window suddenly startled her out of her thoughts. Her heart jumped until she recognized Jesse's younger sister standing outside her car, her short dark hair ruffled in the breeze and her blue eyes clouded with worry.

"Is everything okay?" Cassie Harte asked, her voice muffled by the layer of glass.

Sarah nodded, aware of the heat soaking her cheeks. She must look like an idiot, sitting out here in her car staring at his house. She opened the door and climbed out. "Everything's fine. I was just unwinding for a moment before I went inside."

"I'm sorry to disturb you, then."

Sarah laughed ruefully. "I'm glad you did. Daisy's probably going crazy wondering why I'm just sitting out here."

A pang of discomfort settled in her stomach as she used the key Jesse had given her to unlock his door.

She knew she was probably being silly, but it seemed so presumptuous to act as if she belonged here in the house of this woman's brother.

She knew Cassie, but only casually. Early in the school year she had seen quite a bit of her at school functions with Lucy, and had heard from one of the other mothers that Cassie had basically raised her niece until Matt Harte married Ellie Webster over a month before.

She wasn't sure what had happened to Lucy's mother, but by a few of the whisperings she'd heard, apparently she'd disappeared in the midst of some kind of horrible scandal involving Cassie's ex-fiancé.

Sarah also knew Cassie had moved away from the family ranch after her brother's wedding and now had a job cooking at the Lost Creek dude ranch north of town.

She didn't know much about her, but she did know she liked Cassie. From the time she first moved to Star Valley, the other woman had gone out of her way to make Sarah feel welcome.

Cassie followed her up the stairs and into the house, loaded with boxes and bags. "Nobody in this family tells me anything," she said. "I swear, I would probably still believe in Santa Claus if I had to rely on my big brothers to fill me in. I didn't have a clue what had happened to your house or that you were staying here, until this morning when I ran into Ellie at the grocery store. How are you doing?"

"Fine. Anxious for things to get back to normal, but fine."

"I can understand that. I love him dearly, but I'll be the first to admit Jesse's not always the easiest person to live with. I also know he's not much of a cook—

believe me, I know—so I brought a few ready-to-heat dinners. That's why I dropped by. I hope you don't mind."

Ah. So that explained the mystery of her packages. "That's very sweet of you, but I'm going home tomorrow."

Cassie's shrug looked elegantly feminine, despite her T-shirt. "You can take some food back to your house with you or Jesse can always freeze them for another time."

Cassie set a box down on the counter between the kitchen and family room and began removing foil-covered containers. "Hope you like spicy food. Since I wasn't sure of your tastes, I went by Jesse's. The hotter the better for him."

She thought of the Thai food she used to devour by the cartonful in Chicago. She hadn't realized she missed it until right this second. "Spicy is fine."

"Good. This one is plain old lasagna and this one is artichoke heart enchiladas. Two of his favorites. I've written cooking instructions on each one, but basically you just have to throw them in the oven. Oh, and here's a couple of salads and some bread sticks and turtle pie for dessert."

Sarah laughed helplessly. "Whoa. Slow down. This is more food than I could eat in a week."

"If you were alone, maybe, but if I know my brother, you'll be lucky to get seconds of any of it. Now, which one would you like tonight, lasagna or enchiladas? Just choose and I'll get it started for you."

"Um, which would you say is your brother's favorite?"

"That's a tough one. He loves them both, but I'd

probably have to say the lasagna would squeak ahead, just barely."

"Lasagna it is, then."

Cassie turned on the oven, then began working in the kitchen with quick, efficient movements that made Sarah feel like a complete incompetent.

"You know, you really don't have to do this," she said. "I can probably follow directions."

Cassie's smile lit up her whole pixie face. "I know. But cooking is what I do best, so don't spoil it for me."

While Cassie put the foil tray in the oven and began to transfer the rest of the food to the refrigerator, Sarah went to work preparing the salad.

"So tell me," Cassie said while they worked, "is Jesse any closer to finding out who vandalized your place?"

Sarah shook her head. "He had a couple of leads, but neither one amounted to much."

If anything, he and his officers were further than ever from finding who had made such a mess at her house. Jesse had learned the vandal had used cow's blood—apparently from a cow that was killed and mutilated in a pasture near the Diamond Harte.

Monday morning he had also called Chicago and learned Tommy DeSilva was still in a maximum-security facility in Joliet. DeSilva might have sent someone after her, but Jesse didn't seem to think it was very likely. It seemed an unusually long time to wait for revenge, when he could have more easily sent someone after her when she was still in Evanston staying with her parents.

Which left the terrifying conclusion that she had an unknown enemy somewhere in Star Valley. She couldn't even begin to figure out who it might be.

"Well, I hope he finds him fast," Cassie said fiercely. "It makes me sick that someone could terrorize you that way. And I can promise you that when Jesse does find whoever it is, he's going to make the creep very, very sorry. One time in school when I was about seven, he found out that Kip Burton used to tie my shoelaces together every day on the school bus so I'd fall on my face. Kip was a year older than Jesse and twice as big, but that didn't stop my brother."

"What did he do?" Sarah knew she shouldn't be so intrigued by the image of Jesse as a boy.

"He tied Kip's shoelaces together with Wally Martin's, who was even bigger and meaner than Kip. Wally wasn't happy about it, I can tell you that. By the time Wally was through with him, Kip could barely even tie his own shoes. I think he still holds a grudge to this day."

Sarah's laugh was the first genuine one she had enjoyed in a week. When the sound of it faded, the kitchen fell silent except for Daisy slurping at her water bowl. She glanced at Cassie and found the other woman watching her closely, a strange light in her eyes.

"I think you're really wonderful for Jesse," his sister said quietly.

Sarah flushed. "Oh, no. We don't… I mean, we're not… You've got it all wrong."

Cassie didn't look convinced. "That's too bad. He needs someone like you in his life."

"What do you mean?"

Cassie was silent for a long moment, and Sarah felt her scrutiny and wondered at it. After a moment, she spoke.

"Our parents were killed in a car accident when Jesse was seventeen. Did you know that?"

She had wondered about the elder Hartes, but no one had ever told her their fate and she'd never dared ask. "I'm sorry," she said softly. "That must have been horrible for all of you. How old were you?"

"I was twelve. Matt was twenty-one. It *was* hard on Matt and me, but I think their deaths hit Jesse the hardest. He was the only one in the truck with them when Dad hit a patch of ice in the canyon between here and Jackson. The truck rolled about a hundred feet down a steep embankment and almost into the Snake River."

Sarah made a soft sound of distress and wondered why Cassie was telling her this.

"Mom and Dad weren't wearing seat belts," she went on, "and they had massive injuries. I think Jesse knew they were dying, but that didn't stop him from going for help."

Sorrow for what he must have gone through squeezed her insides. "Was he injured?"

Cassie nodded, a faraway look in those startling blue eyes so much like her brothers'. "His leg was broken in a couple places, his wrist was shattered and his shoulder was dislocated. I can't imagine the kind of pain he must have been in, but he still managed to claw his way through snow and ice, up that steep hill toward the highway. It took him more than an hour. By the time he made it to the top and flagged down help, Mom and Dad were gone."

The kitchen fell silent again as Sarah tried to come up with an adequate response that didn't exist. Before she could say anything, Cassie continued.

"An experience like that changes a person. Jesse was

always a little wild, but after Mom and Dad died, he spiraled out of control. Drinking, partying, fighting with anybody who even looked at him wrong. Matt must have bailed him out of jail a dozen times."

"He must have been hurting so badly." She wanted to cry just thinking about it.

She wasn't sure what she'd said that made Cassie smile so unexpectedly or look at her with that funny light in her eyes again.

"Even worse than the fighting were the women. I swear, he dated every bimbo between here and Cheyenne. It's about time he realized he deserves better than that. He deserves a woman like you. Someone warm and smart and decent."

If Cassie only knew how far off the mark she was! The last thing Jesse needed in his life was a woman with the kind of problems Sarah had.

"Well, as I said, you have the wrong idea about us. I'm only staying here because Jesse wouldn't let me check in to a hotel and I didn't know where else to go. Your brother and I are only friends."

They were, she realized with surprise. She genuinely liked and respected him. She had told him things no one else in Star Valley knew about and she trusted completely that he would keep her secrets.

"Well, you can't blame a sister for hoping."

The door opened before Sarah could come up with a suitable reply. An instant later, the subject of their conversation loomed in the doorway, looking big and dark and gorgeous in his uniform.

Cassidy chuckled—at what, Sarah wasn't exactly sure, but she suspected it had something to do with the sudden blush scorching her cheeks.

"Hey, brat," he greeted his sister, but there was clear affection in his expression and in his voice. "I thought you were too busy with those fancy rich cowboy wannabes you're cooking for now at the Lost Creek to bother hanging around us lesser mortals. What are you doing here?"

She sniffed. "I brought food. But if you're going to make fun of my new gig, maybe I'll just take my lasagna and leave."

His face brightened like a kid waiting outside the gates of Disneyland for the park to open for the day. "You brought lasagna? And bread sticks, too? Sarah, sweetheart, did I ever tell you my baby sister is a goddess in the kitchen?"

Sarah swallowed hard at that devastating grin.

"It should be ready as soon as the timer goes off." Cassie gathered up the boxes she had carried the food in. "Since you already tossed the salad, all you need to do is heat the bread sticks in the microwave for just a few seconds."

"You're leaving?"

"You know me. Always on the run."

"Why don't you stay and eat dinner with us?" Sarah asked. It was such a brilliant idea she was amazed she hadn't thought of it earlier. Cassie could provide a much-needed buffer between her and Jesse and maybe ease some of the tension that always churned between them.

"Another time. I've got things to do. Sarah, I enjoyed talking with you. It was very educational."

Cassie kissed her brother's cheek, then surprised Sarah by pulling her into an embrace and kissing her cheek.

As she watched her walk out the door, Sarah experienced a brief, fierce moment of regret that there really wasn't anything more between her and Jesse. Not only because of her growing feelings for him, but because she had always wanted a sister. She suddenly knew without question that Cassie Harte would have been perfect.

Jesse leaned his hip on the countertop, enjoying the sight of Sarah busying herself in the kitchen. He loved watching her. She always looked so pretty and flustered, and she blushed whenever she caught him at it.

"You have a nice visit with Cassidy Jane?"

She looked up, a startled look in her eyes. Just as he'd hoped, that appealing color crept over her cheeks. "I had no idea Cassie was short for Cassidy."

He snagged an olive out of the salad and popped it in his mouth. "Yep. Just like Butch Cassidy. We're all named for outlaws."

"I knew you were. Jesse James, right?"

He smiled his best bandito smile. "Exactly."

"I get the Cassidy and the Jesse James but what about Matt? I admit, I'm not the world's best Wild West historian, but I'm not familiar with any outlaws named Matt."

"Matt's the one who started it all. My dad was the great-grandson of Matt Warner, who rode with Butch and Sundance in the Wild Bunch. Dad was fascinated with stories of the old West that had been handed down in his family and he wanted to name his firstborn after his ancestor. The rest of us just followed the theme."

"Your mother must have been a very understanding woman."

He smiled. "She used to call us her own little wild bunch. Living out on the ranch away from most neighbors, we had to learn to entertain ourselves. We used to play hide and seek, and Mom would pretend she was the sheriff rounding us all up to take us to the lockup. We even made this star out of glitter and construction paper that said Sheriff Mom, and she always kept it on the fridge. She'd pin it on and come looking for us."

He hadn't thought about that star in years. What had happened to the silly thing? It had probably disintegrated years ago. The memory made him smile and a little sad at the same time.

His folks had been gone a long time—sixteen years this winter—but sometimes he still missed them so much, he felt it fill his lungs until he couldn't breathe around it. The grief and the guilt always hit him at the same time.

He looked up and found Sarah watching him out of soft, sorrowful green eyes that saw too damn much.

"Cassie told me about the accident," she said quietly. "I'm so sorry. They sound like they were wonderful people. They would have to be in order to produce such fine children."

"I wish they had lived long enough to see that I'm the one chasing the bad guys now."

"I'm sure they would both be very proud of you," she said, and her soft smile was like a shot of pure mountain air, chasing away the thickness in his lungs.

"You remind me a lot of my mom. She was a teacher, too. Taught seventh-grade English."

"I'm sure that must have put quite a crimp in your junior high school social life, to have your mother always watching over your shoulder."

He laughed. "I don't remember it being too much of

a detriment. Somehow I always found a way to keep the worst of my rabble-rousing out of her line of sight."

Sarah looked doubtful. "She probably knew much more than you're giving her credit for. Mothers—and teachers—usually know exactly what you're up to."

"I really hope not," he said vehemently.

Her low laugh slid right to his gut. "I know. I know. You were the bad boy of Salt River, Wyoming, right?"

"You don't believe the hype?"

She shrugged, a rare, teasing light in her eyes that sent need uncoiling inside him like barbed wire. "Sorry, Jesse, but all I've seen is the reformed version."

Now, there was a challenge if he'd ever heard one. "There's still a little bad boy left in me, I can promise you that," he murmured, and stepped a little closer to her.

Wariness flickered in her gaze—and something else that he couldn't quite recognize—but she didn't retreat. Not even when he took another step forward and another, then leaned in to back up his words with action.

Chapter 11

He knew he shouldn't be doing this. He could come up with a dozen reasons not to kiss Sarah McKenzie. Hell, a hundred, if he really put his mind to it.

All those excuses might be fine in the abstract, but none of them meant a damn thing in reality. Not when she smelled like a summer garden after a rain shower and when she lifted her face for his kiss with the same trusting beauty of one of those rain-soaked flowers turning toward the sun.

And when his subconscious had spent the past week torturing him with fantasies of doing exactly this.

Just a quick kiss, he vowed to himself, just to taste the sweetness there, to tease her a little, then he would back away and return to his side of the friendly, casual distance they had worked so hard this week to maintain between them.

At the first touch of her mouth under his, silken and warm and welcoming, he forgot about keeping that frustratingly safe chasm between them. Forgot about treating her with polite, casual restraint.

All he could focus on was the slick heat of her mouth against his and the way her slender body bowed so perfectly in his arms and the way she kissed him back with an enthusiasm that would have startled him if he'd been capable of rational thought.

He wasn't consciously aware of undoing the clip that restrained all that luxurious hair, but somebody did it. He figured it must have been him, since he was the one whose fingers tangled in it, raked through the long, silky strands, tugged it gently so her head fell back to give him better access to her incredible mouth.

She moaned against his mouth. At the sound of it, low and aroused, he lost the last tenuous hold on his control. He deepened the kiss, molding her body to him, letting her feel the strength of his arousal.

Her arms slid around his neck and the movement pressed her small, firm breasts against the muscles of his chest.

Heat rushed to his groin and he pressed one thigh between hers. She wore a skirt and another of those short-sleeved sweater sets, demure and sweet, that somehow still always managed to conjure up all manner of wicked thoughts in his head. This one was pale lavender, and he had no trouble slipping a hand underneath it to caress the achingly soft skin at her waist.

She rewarded him with another of those sexy noises she made, so he pressed his advantage and ventured higher along that expanse of skin, toward the lace covering her breasts. When he was nearly there, she gasped his name, and a small, delicate shudder racked her frame.

He froze, breathing harder than a rookie on his first call, his hand still under her sweater.

What the *hell* was he doing?

He was about to feel up Sarah McKenzie like some kind of randy teenager hoping to get lucky in the back seat of his dad's sedan—even knowing what he did about her past and the scars that had been carved in her soul.

She must be scared to death to have him mauling her like this, after what she'd been through.

Self-disgust roiled through him, sick and hot and greasy. She had trusted him and this is how he repaid her?

It made him feel even worse to realize that even now—when he was fully aware of the gross inappropriateness of groping her while she was a guest in his home—part of him didn't want to stop.

Somehow he mustered strength enough to edge away, though his body groaned in protest.

He shoved his hands into his back pockets. "That was unforgivable, Sarah. I'm so sorry."

Her breathing was as ragged and shallow as his, her eyes dark with confusion. "You're sorry for what?"

"I shouldn't have kissed you. Touched you. I was way out of line."

"No, you weren't. I wanted you to kiss me." She cleared her throat. "And to, um, to touch me."

Her voice was strong and determined even though color coated her cheeks like autumn brushed on leaves. Still, her words did nothing to ease the guilt writhing around inside him.

He raked a hand through his hair. "I promised you would be safe here, and you are. Even from me. *Especially* from me."

"I wanted you to kiss me, Jesse," she repeated. "I've been wanting you to kiss me again since that day on the mountain."

He stared, hearing the exasperation in her voice. "You have?"

"Why do you sound so surprised? If I took a poll, I imagine I'd find that half the women in town probably want you to kiss them."

This time he was amazed to find that *he* was the one blushing. "That's ridiculous," he mumbled.

"It is not. Half the women in town and probably a vastly higher percentage of the women who hang out at the Renegade would stand in line for a chance to be right here."

"That's different. *You're* different."

"Why? I'm still a woman."

Same equipment, maybe, but he could come up with very few other similarities between her and the kind of wild party girls who hung out at the local honky-tonk. "Trust me. You're different. I should never have kissed you."

She was quiet for a moment, then lifted her chin. "Because of what Tommy DeSilva did to me?"

He couldn't lie to her. "That's part of it."

At his words, the color faded from her face and her features seemed as frozen as a mountain lake in January. "I see," she murmured.

But he could tell she didn't. How could she possibly understand, when he wasn't sure he did? She probably was thinking some nonsense about how he didn't find her desirable or that he couldn't get past the fact that she had been raped.

That was so far from the truth, he wanted to laugh. Every moment she spent living in the same house with him, breathing the same air, he only wanted her more. From the moment he walked in the door after work until he somehow made it through the torturous hours until he left again in the morning, he had to fight like hell to keep from touching her, from kissing her, from doing exactly what he'd just done.

She didn't have a clue.

He had worked hard to make sure of it, to conceal as best he could the effect she had on him. The hunger eating away at him. If she'd caught even a glimmer of it, he had no doubts she would have moved back into her shell of a house in a second, broken windows or not.

How would she react if she knew he spent every damn night tossing and turning in his bed, listening for her down the hall, cursing the fact that she was so tantalizingly close but completely out of his reach?

He wanted her with a fierceness that stunned him, but he knew he couldn't act on it. She needed tenderness, gentleness—a delicate, careful touch. How the hell was he supposed to provide those things when he lost control with just a simple kiss?

The plain truth was that he didn't trust himself. He wasn't sure he could give her all those things he knew she needed after what that bastard had done to her.

Yeah, part of the reason he had stopped had to do with Tommy DeSilva. Whenever he thought about her attack, a hot, savage spear of rage lodged in his chest. He had never experienced such mindless fury in his life.

And even though he hadn't known her at the time—

even though her attack had happened a thousand miles away—he couldn't shake this strange sense of responsibility, as if the system of justice he believed in so strongly and worked so fiercely to uphold had failed her.

He was a cop, and a damn good one. He should be used to seeing the darker side of society. He was, even in a small town like Salt River. But somehow knowing that a sweet, innocent woman like Sarah had been the victim of something so terrible hit him in the gut like a cannonball whenever he thought about it.

He ached to make everything better for her. It was impossible, he knew that. He couldn't change what had happened to her—hell, he couldn't even find the words to tell her how very sorry he was—and the knowledge made him helpless with frustration.

The timer on the oven went off before he could look for those elusive words once more.

"That's your lasagna." Avoiding both his touch and his gaze, Sarah crossed to the oven and removed the casserole dish with oven mitts. "Shall we eat here at the bar or in the dining room?"

He didn't want to eat. Cassie's lasagna appealed to him about as much as gnawing on cement right about now. Not when the air between them still hummed and sparked with tension.

"Sarah—" he began, but she cut him off.

"Let's eat in the dining room, shall we?"

Her abrupt tone and her cool body language told him she wanted the subject dropped.

He huffed out a breath. As much as he needed to clear the air between them, he refused to force a heated discussion that she would obviously prefer not to have.

Frustration churning through him, he jerked his chair out and sat down.

They went through the motions of eating in silence for several minutes. Finally, just around the time he was ready to climb the walls, she rose from the table. "You know, I'm really not hungry after all. I have a PTA meeting at seven, so I think I'll just run over to the school a little early and try to finish some work in my classroom."

He slid his chair back, noting with a frown that she had barely picked at her food. "I'll go with you."

"That's not necessary."

"I don't want you going out at night by yourself. Not when we still haven't caught the vandal who redecorated your house."

That stubborn chin tilted in the air once more. "It's not necessary," she repeated.

"It is to me."

"Look, Jesse, it's bad enough for my reputation that I have been staying here alone with you all week. If you insist on following me all over town, people might start to get the wrong idea about us. And neither of us would want that, would we?"

Let them get the wrong idea. Maybe then she'd let him past this cool reserve. "Do you really think anybody cares where you're staying?"

"This is a small town with conservative values. I'm a single woman teaching impressionable children. Like it or not, I'm under a microscope. If enough parents complained to Chuck Hendricks about me staying with you, he wouldn't hesitate to fire me."

"I won't go in, then. I'll just drive over behind you

to make sure you arrive safely, then I'll come back in a few hours when the meeting's over to see you home."

She opened her mouth to argue, but he cut her off with a glare, all his frustration simmering back. If she wanted him to shut up, he would, but he wasn't going to back down about this. Not when her safety was concerned. "Damn it, Sarah, I care about you. I don't want anything to happen to you. Just let me do this, all right?"

She blinked at his vehemence, then shrugged. "Fine. I'll be ready in a few moments."

She should be paying attention.

Sarah stretched her knee out, wiggled around on her folding metal chair in a vain effort to find a more comfortable position, and tried to focus on the twangy voice of Nancy Larsen.

The PTA president was saying something about next year's fund-raising projects, but she might as well have been speaking pig Latin. Sarah couldn't seem to focus on anything but a certain frustrating, sexy, aggravating police chief.

She had replayed that scene in his kitchen at least a dozen times in the hour since the PTA meeting started. Every touch, every texture, every scent was imprinted on her mind, burned into it like the mark on Corey Sylvester's skin.

Just remembering his mouth on hers—the heat of his body pressed against hers, his hard, callused hands on her skin—turned her insides hollow and weak, her breasts achy and full.

She had wanted the kiss to go on forever. Hours, days, weeks. Forget food, forget sleep, forget anything but Jesse and his incredible mouth and clever, clever hands.

While she was being honest with herself, she might as well admit that she wanted much more than stolen kisses in his kitchen. She wanted to explore the hard muscles of his chest she could see bunch and play under his shirts. She wanted to glide her hands and her mouth over his skin.

She wanted to feel his hard strength inside her.

She shifted on her cold metal chair as color washed over her cheeks. She shouldn't be thinking about this in the middle of a PTA meeting, for heaven's sake!

She couldn't help it, though. It still seemed like some kind of wondrous miracle that she could want him that way, after eighteen months of believing she would never be able to feel the hot pull of desire again.

Unfortunately, what she wanted wasn't important. The reawakening of these long-dormant needs and desires inside her didn't matter. Not when Jesse admitted he couldn't get past what had happened in Chicago.

Telling him had changed everything, just as she had known it would. Just as it had with Andrew.

Like Andrew, Jesse couldn't look at her without remembering what had been done to her. She had seen it in his eyes. He was afraid to touch her, fearful that he would put his hands in the wrong place or say the wrong thing.

That he couldn't be gentle enough.

The hollow yearning in her stomach changed to something else. Something wistful and sorrowful and angry at the same time.

It was always there on the edge of her consciousness, that terrible October morning. Always lurking like some huge, hideous, wild creature, just waiting for her guard to slip so it could stick its vicious claws into her once more.

Since she had come here, she had tried to cope by not telling anyone. If people didn't know, then her attack didn't exist. It wasn't real. It couldn't *possibly* be real.

But Jesse knew now. She had been forced to tell him and now he couldn't touch her without also touching the rabid creature that followed her everywhere.

The young, frizzy-haired rape counselor who had visited her in the hospital right after the attack had given her a thick packet of information. Booklets and hotline numbers and support group schedules, to try to help her process what had happened.

During those long days in the hospital she had forced herself to at least skim through the information, but she hadn't been able to absorb much from it. No one could possibly understand what she was going through, so what was the point in reading about other people's experiences?

Actually, she found it surprising that she remembered anything from that time.

She had been barely there, aware on one level of all the specialists and nurses and therapists checking this monitor and adjusting that medication, coming and going endlessly.

They existed on the periphery, though.

Mostly, she had been cushioned in some merciful limbo, wrapped in a protective cocoon of lethargy where no one could reach her. Where no one could hurt her.

One of the few things she remembered from that barrage of information was one article where the author, herself a victim, had eloquently discussed the culture of isolating silence surrounding women who had been raped.

No one wants to talk about or to hear about it. The crime itself is often considered so unspeakable, so shameful, that its victims are rendered mute, she remembered reading. Their names are omitted from newspaper articles as if they no longer exist, their faces become a blurred, vacant circle on the television.

The loved ones of rape victims especially don't want to talk about it, uncomfortable with the complex ferocity of their own emotions and ravaged by the victim's.

She had seen that in her family and friends. Her mother's tears. Her father's devastated rage. The shock and pity of her friends—and the guilty relief that it had happened to her instead of to them.

And so she had slipped willingly into that silence everyone seemed to expect of her.

She hadn't minded. Not really. She had wanted it that way. Needed it that way. The last thing she wanted to do was rehash the morning that had changed her life, to relive every detail of the attack whenever she looked into the faces of everyone around her.

But now Jesse knew, and he wouldn't touch her because of it.

Sometimes the injustice of it made her want to scream and weep at the same time. She had done nothing to deserve what had happened to her, yet she was still being punished.

Most of all, she hated that her rape hadn't ended when Tommy DeSilva climbed back through that jagged glass of her classroom window. It was not a static, isolated moment, but sometimes seemed to go on and on and on, sucking any color and joy from her life.

She closed her eyes, suddenly exhausted.

She couldn't bear the idea of going back to Jesse's house, to the thick, constant tension between them. She wanted her own space, her soothing, peaceful gardens, the scent of her own pillow.

One more night. She could make it through a few more hours at his house.

And then she would wrap herself once more in her safe, protective, suffocating cloak of silence.

Jesse looked at the clock on the wall of his office, hanging above a framed print of a moose hip-deep in the Snake River, moss dripping from his antlers.

The kid wasn't going to show.

Corey was nearly an hour late for their last run-through of the anticrime presentation they were scheduled to give the next week.

It shouldn't surprise him, since the day seemed to be rapidly changing from bad to worse, starting first thing when he had walked out of his bedroom before his shift that morning to find Sarah headed for the front door, her bags in tow.

He had talked until his teeth ached, trying to convince her to stay at his house a few more days, but she had been adamant.

He knew why she was eager to leave, and he couldn't say he blamed her. The tension between them had become unbearable.

Even though he knew why she wanted to go, he sure as hell didn't have to like it. The idea of her living alone, unprotected, on that dark street with whoever had targeted her still on the loose appealed to him about as much as sticking his hand in a meat grinder.

He had argued fiercely, but she had stood firm. He had seen a completely unexpected stubborn light in her soft green eyes and had recognized the futility of pushing any harder.

The window installers were coming that day and she itched to get back to her gardens on her day off, she said. What did he expect her to do all day at his house alone?

He blew out a breath. He should have tried harder, but she had been right—what difference would it make if she spent the day alone at his house or alone at her own?

Finally he'd decided to let it ride, as long as she agreed to take Daisy with her for protection. The big dog could stand guard until the end of his shift, when he would take over. Though, of course, he neglected to fill Sarah in on that little detail of his plan.

Daisy was as gentle as a lamb, but her sheer size alone might deter any attacker and she also had moments of fierceness when the people she loved were threatened. One day the summer before, she had faced off against an angry bull at the Diamond Harte when Lucy had wandered into the wrong pasture by mistake. Since the dog had immediately taken Sarah into her big heart, he had no doubt she'd protect her any way she could.

Even with Daisy on guard duty, though, he couldn't shake his uneasiness.

Only part of this itch between his shoulder blades had to do with any hypothetical danger Sarah might be in. He had faced a few things in the middle of yet another night stirring and pacing down the hall from her. Things that scared him far more than punks who scrawled graffiti on her door.

He cared about Sarah McKenzie, in a way he never had about any other woman. Somehow her gentleness and her courage and her quiet beauty had reached right in and wrapped themselves around his heart.

He'd been hoping Corey would help take his mind off Sarah and these new terrifying feelings, but now he didn't even have that.

His stomach grumbled, reminding him he'd been too busy arguing with her—and trying to fight the urge to quiet that soft mouth the very best way he could come up with—that he hadn't had time to grab anything to eat for breakfast.

There were usually bagels out by the coffeemaker, the healthier alternative to that old cop cliché, doughnuts. He walked out to check out his options and found Chris Hernandez standing at the desk talking through the security window to someone in the small waiting room.

The officer turned when she heard him approach. "Chief, the mayor's wife is here. For some reason, she seems to think she's supposed to be picking her son up here. Do you know anything about it?"

He frowned. So Corey had ditched him without his mother's knowledge. The little rascal. "I'll take care of it, Chris."

He walked up to the window to greet Ginny. She smiled brightly when she saw him and hitched Maddie higher on her hip. She was wearing one of those designer nylon workout suits and looked cool and stylish, except for the mushy crumbs on her shoulder from the cookie Maddie was flailing around in her chubby little hands.

Even with the crumbs, Ginny looked worlds away from the scared, defeated woman who had lived on Elk Mountain with Hob Sylvester.

"Hi, Jess. I'm here for Corey, but if the two of you aren't done, I'm happy to wait."

He hated having to pop that cheerful mood of hers, but her scamp of a son hadn't left him with much choice. "Corey's not here, Gin. He never showed."

Her bright smile trickled away like petals blown on a hard wind. "What do you mean, he never showed? I dropped him off right in front of the police station more than an hour ago. I watched him walk in."

"He must have waited until you drove away, then snuck right back out again. I'm sorry."

She seemed to shrink, to crumple right in front of his eyes. "I don't understand this. I thought he was really looking forward to your presentation. Why would he run off?"

"It's a nice day. Maybe he just wanted to go fishing or something."

"Maybe." She didn't look convinced. Instead, she looked about ready to burst into tears any minute now.

Aw, hell. Just what he needed. He wasn't any good with crying women. "Come on back and we can talk about it." He thumbed the security button for the door, then held it open for her. "Here, let me take the rug rat."

The baby felt soft and light in his arms, despite her chubby arms. She grinned at him, proudly displaying all four of her little teeth, and handed him her cookie.

"No, thanks," he said. "Maybe later, sweetheart."

Maddie seemed to think that was the most hilarious

thing she'd ever heard. She let out a piercing squeal and bucked her whole body back and forth, forcing him to hold on tight so she didn't slip out of his arms.

"Whoa there, partner." He laughed and Maddie responded to it by giving another James Brown-like squeal and patting his cheeks with her sticky fingers.

"I'm sorry. She's such a mess." Now Ginny looked embarrassed *and* defeated.

"I'll wash."

He didn't mind. Maddie was a doll, with her chubby cheeks and that curly blond hair and huge blue eyes. A quick memory of his niece Lucy when she was this age flitted through his mind—how she used to curl up on his lap with her thumb in her mouth and let him rock her to sleep.

He'd forgotten that. Lucy hadn't cared that he was a wild hell-raiser in those days—she had given him unconditional love anyway. To her, he was probably just the big, funny-looking guy who told silly jokes and tickled her cheeks with his razor stubble.

What would it be like to have one of these of his own?

The thought came out of the blue, just about knocking him on his butt. He had a sudden image of a giggly little girl with Sarah's honey-blond hair and big green eyes.

Yikes. Slow down. That kind of thinking could get a man in serious trouble.

"I'm so sorry about the mix-up," Ginny said when they reached his office. "I'm sure you had a million better things to do than sit here waiting for Corey to show."

He jerked his mind away from the weird, terrifying fantasies that had suddenly taken over. "It's no big deal. I'm just worried about him. Any clue where he might have gone?"

"No. How terrible is that for a mother to say? I have no idea where my son might be." Misery coated her voice. "Probably the same place he's been sneaking off to for the last few months."

"He's been doing a lot of this?"

"Two nights ago he climbed out his bedroom window and took off somewhere until after two in the morning. The only reason we knew he'd been gone is that Maddie woke up. When I got her settled back to sleep, I went to check on Corey and caught him climbing back through the window."

"Did he say where he'd been?"

"Just hanging out with his friends. That's what he says, anyway. I don't know what to do anymore. We've taken away his bike and his scooter and his roller blades. He hasn't had TV or computer privileges in a month. Nothing we do is working. He's still sneaking out. Seth is talking about sending him to military school—this whole brand thing has been the last straw. Can you imagine a child doing such a thing to himself?"

"Maybe military school would be the best thing for him, just for a while. Until he straightens himself out."

Tears welled up in her eyes. "He's just a baby, Jess. Ten years old. It's a terrible thing to feel like you're losing your child."

He passed her his handkerchief and shifted Maddie in his arms, guilt tugging at him. He sure hadn't done a very good job of finding out what was happening with the kid. He'd thought they were making progress the few times they'd rehearsed, but Corey still clammed up every time Jesse tried to talk about anything other than their presentation.

"We'll find him, Gin. I've got two officers out in the field right now. I'll have them both keep an eye out for him and I'll hunt for him, too." They could look between their hourly patrols past Sarah's house. "We'll get to the bottom of it, I promise."

She sniffled into the handkerchief. "Thank you, Jess. Why do I always seem to end up dumping my problems on you?"

"I just wish you didn't have so many to deal with. You deserve to be happy."

Her chin wobbled a little. "Do I?"

"Yes. Of course! You've been through some rough times, but you've survived. You've made a great life for yourself, with a good, decent man. Hang in there. Corey will settle down. Look at me. I was a whole lot more wild than he could ever dream of being and I turned out okay."

She managed a watery grin. "That's a matter of opinion."

Maddie apparently thought that was the second funniest thing she'd ever heard. She let loose with another round of squealing giggles, showing off her tiny little teeth.

"See? She agrees with me."

This time Ginny's smile looked a little more natural, he was relieved to see. "I'd better take the little urchin home and get her washed up," she said. "Thanks Jess, for everything. I don't know what I'd do without you."

He rose along with her. "I'll carry Maddie out for you."

"You don't have to do that. I'm used to carrying her."

"Let me. I don't get to hold a sweet little thing like this very often."

"You need a family of your own. I've always thought you'd make a wonderful father."

He thought of that little girl he'd just imagined with Sarah's eyes and smile. The funny tug in the pit of his stomach just about made him break into a cold sweat.

He hid his reaction behind a casual grin. "No, thanks. I see Lucy and Dylan and all the mischief they get into, and then the grief that Corey's giving you right now, and it convinces me maybe I'm better off sticking with Daisy. At least she doesn't talk back to me much."

Ginny's smile was bittersweet. "Oh, Jess. Children might break your heart sometimes, but they bring far more joy than sorrow, even in the worst of times."

"I'll have to take your word for that."

They walked out of his office into the squad room and were nearly to the door when Ginny stopped behind him.

"Hey, why do you have Seth's favorite fishing cap? Did he leave it here? I swear, that husband of mine would lose his head if it wasn't screwed on."

He froze, Maddie still squirming in his arms, and turned back to her. Ginny was holding the evidence bag containing the only link they had to the suspect in the vandalism at Sarah's house.

He thought of smeared blood and vicious messages and shattered windows. "That hat belongs to Seth?" he asked carefully, his heart pounding in a thick and sluggish away.

"Believe me, I wouldn't make a mistake about something like that. I've tried to burn the blasted thing several times. You'd think it was solid gold, for all the fuss

Seth makes whenever I threaten to throw it away. He about pitched a fit when he couldn't find it last week. He'll be so glad to have it back." She reached to open the bag.

"Wait!"

His loud command made Ginny jump and Maddie giggle. His mind raced as he tried to process the information and figure out what to tell Ginny about the ugly suspicions that had suddenly taken root.

"Do you mind if I hang on to it for a while longer? I'd like to see his face when he gets it back. My officers would enjoy playing a little joke on the mayor. You know. Wrap it up and give it to him as a gift for, um, giving us such a hard time about our budget."

She shrugged. "Sure. Anything to keep that stinky, dirty old thing out of my house a little longer."

He could think of nothing but the implications of that cap belonging to Seth as he walked Ginny to her Range Rover and buckled Maddie into her car seat in the back.

He gave the little girl a distracted kiss, then kissed Ginny on the forehead. "I'll let you know if we find Corey. If he comes home before you hear from me, give me a buzz so I can call off my officers."

"Thanks, Jess." Some of her cheerfulness had returned and she smiled and waved as she backed out of the parking space and drove away.

He watched her go, his mind still racing. Could Seth really have been involved with the vandalism at Sarah's house? He thought about how upset the mayor had been when he'd been accused of abusing Corey. Could he have somehow found out Sarah was behind the accusation? Was this a payback of some kind?

It didn't make sense. He had known Seth most of his

life, gone to Scout camp with him, double-dated in high school. The man he knew couldn't possibly be capable of such viciousness, could he?

But what other explanation could there be for his cap being on the scene?

Somehow Corey was the link. He needed to find the kid, sit him down and have a good long talk.

He was just sliding into his Bronco when his radio buzzed with static. "Chief, do you copy?" Jim Lovell's voice came over the airwaves along with a big dose of static.

He reached for the mike. "Yeah, Jim. What's up?"

"You might want to get over here. Ron Atkins just found a body on his ranch. A woman's body."

His heart stopped beating, his vision dimmed around the edges. All he could think of was Sarah, alone at her house with just a dog for protection.

Sarah hummed along with the country song on the radio as she tore pieces of lettuce for her salad. It was a little late for lunch—after three—but she'd been too busy earlier in the day to eat.

Daisy sat at her feet, looking up every few minutes with a hopeful look in her big brown eyes.

"I don't think you'd like the salad, sweetie," she assured the dog, but slipped her a few pieces of cold chicken anyway. They disappeared with one big gulp and a plea for more, making her laugh.

She had spent a great morning puttering around in her garden. She had needed it after the night before, desperately craved the peace she found there. Having Daisy's gentle, uncomplicated company had only made the morning that much sweeter.

Maybe she ought to get a dog. A big, furry retriever just like Daisy to share her secrets with and talk to and draw comfort from on cold winter nights when she had no one else.

She sighed. She sounded pathetic, but she couldn't deny she felt much better today after pouring out her woes to the dog.

It's a good thing Daisy couldn't talk, or she would have an earful to give to Jesse about the silly woman who was afraid she might be falling in love with him.

She gave a rueful laugh. She wasn't kidding anybody, not even Daisy. She wasn't afraid, she was terrified. What's worse, there was no *maybe* about it. She was already there, head over heels in love with a man who wouldn't even touch her.

The doorbell rang suddenly, sounding unnaturally loud in the quiet house. Her heart jumped into her throat, no doubt in her mind as to who stood on her doorstep. Daisy had given it away, uttering just one excited bark then leaping for the front door, only to stand there with her tail wagging like a metronome on steroids.

Okay. Calm down, she ordered herself, and swung open the door. She could be cool and composed.

She wasn't at all prepared for the fury on his face, blazing at her like a furnace blast.

"Where the hell have you been?" He brushed past her and into the house, hand on his gun butt as if expecting a whole platoon of criminals to be sharing her Caesar salad.

She stiffened her spine at his tone. "I've been here all day, exactly as you ordered me this morning."

His glower turned even more forbidding. "Haven't

you ever heard of answering the phone? I've been calling the whole damn afternoon."

"I've been outside in the yard. You wouldn't believe the weeds that took over in just a week…"

He cut her off with an oath far more pungent than the fertilizer she'd just finished spreading on her fledgling vegetables.

"You mean to tell me you didn't take a cordless phone outside with you?"

Her mouth pursed into a tight line. She wasn't about to let him stand here in her house and yell at her as if she were a fractious child. "I don't recall that being among the lengthy list of commands you left me with this morning. Did I miss one?"

"It's called common sense."

Her eyes widened. "Excuse me?"

"Until we know who's nursing one serious grudge against you, I don't want to take any chances with your safety."

"I was perfectly safe. I kept Daisy with me the entire time."

"How was I supposed to know that when you didn't answer the damn phone? You have any idea how worried I've been?"

Now that she looked more closely, she could see the lines of strain around his mouth, the dark shadows in his eyes. *He was worried about her.* Most of her annoyance at his sharp tone began to fade away, replaced by a slow, steady warmth that leapt to life in her chest.

"I'm sorry," she murmured. "But as you can see, you worried for nothing. I'm perfectly fine. Great, even."

He pulled his brown police-issue Stetson off and raked a hand through his dark hair. "Small consolation that is when I haven't been able to concentrate on anything but you all afternoon. If I could have broken away from the crime scene any earlier, I would have been here hours ago to check on you."

"Crime scene?"

He shrugged. "A rancher found some bones on a remote area of his property, just inside the city limits. We called in the Wyoming State Police and they'll do most of the investigative work, but I still had to secure the scene."

"Do they think it was murder?"

"Too early to say until the state forensics lab has a chance to do its thing. All we know is that it was a woman, judging by the clothing found on the scene, and she's been there a while. Other than that, we don't have much to go on."

He paused for a moment, then narrowed his gaze dangerously. "And you're not going to distract me that easily. You wouldn't believe the kinds of things that raced through my head when I couldn't get through. Don't scare me like that again."

The concern in his voice, in those glittering blue eyes, made her suddenly, abashedly, weepy. "I'm sorry. I didn't think. I was just so happy to be out in the garden again."

He continued watching her, a strange light in his eyes. "Your nose is sunburned."

That's where the sting must be coming from. She touched a finger to it, then felt a matching blush take over the rest of her skin. Why was he looking at her like that?

"Um, I was just making a salad. Chicken Caesar. There's more than enough for two if you'd like to stay."

"I'd rather kiss you again."

She froze in place, her gaze darting to his as she felt her face flame even hotter.

"Don't look so surprised." He parroted her words of the day before. "I'm sure half the men in town would love to do the same."

"But not you, obviously," she muttered, then stopped, mortified that she'd given voice to her thoughts.

His laugh was short and held little amusement. "You've got to be kidding. I haven't been able to think about anything else for days."

"You don't have to lie, Jesse." She dug her fists into Daisy's fur, refusing to meet that blue gaze. "I don't blame you for not finding me attractive after learning what…what happened in Chicago."

"Not finding you attractive?" He growled an oath. "You don't have a clue, do you?"

"About what?"

"I could be crude and show you exactly what happens to me just being in the same room as you, but I'll refrain."

She stared at him, stunned, and he blew out a ragged-sounding breath. "Sarah, I think you are without question the most beautiful, courageous, incredible woman I've ever met. You're like a soft, slender willow, bowed by the wind but not broken by it, and I've been *attracted* to you—as you so mildly put it—since the day you moved to Star Valley."

A slow heat began to blossom inside her at his words. She felt shaky and aroused and very, very touched. So touched that she had to swallow hard twice before she could get the words out. "Why did you stop last night, then?"

He stepped forward and traced a thumb down her cheek. The tenderness of it brought tears to her eyes. "Oh, sweetheart. Not because I didn't want you. It took every ounce of strength I could find to step away."

"But you did step away."

"Because I knew that if I touched you again, kissed you again, I would make love to you."

"I wanted you to." She swallowed hard once more, trying to gather that courage he claimed she had. At last she managed to summon enough to meet his gaze. "I still want you to."

Chapter 12

He closed his eyes, her words slicing through him like a hot blade, and dropped his hand from her skin. He couldn't touch her right now. Not when his control teetered on a razor-thin edge.

"Sarah, I can't."

He heard her shaky intake of air and opened his eyes to find her features had become a still, fragile mask.

"Okay. I guess we know where we stand." She stepped away from him, and his heart broke a little.

He wouldn't let her retreat. Not like this. He gripped her hands in his and found them cool and trembling.

"Listen to me, sweetheart. Stopping the other night was the hardest thing I've ever done in my life, but I had no choice. I was too close to losing control. Too hungry for you. If it scared the hell out of me, I could only imagine what it would do to you. I couldn't take the risk of frightening you."

"Because I was raped."

She said it as a statement, not a question. He blew out a breath. "I hate that it happened to you. I would give anything I own to change the past, to be able to go back and protect you from it somehow."

"You can't, though," she said. "It *did* happen to me and it's part of who I am now."

Her hands grew still in his and she met his gaze. He was stunned by the jumbled mix of emotions swimming there, but he also recognized desire when he saw it.

"I'm so tired of being afraid. Tired of feeling numb and timid and half-dead all the time. I feel alive with you, Jesse. Wonderfully alive. And very, very safe."

How was he supposed to find the strength to walk away after she said a thing like that? "Sarah—"

"You won't hurt me, Jess. I know you would die before you would ever hurt me." Her low voice strummed along his spine and he suddenly couldn't seem to draw enough air into his lungs.

He couldn't walk away. Not after this.

He murmured her name again, then cupped her sweet, beautiful face in his hands and kissed her gently.

She sighed against his mouth and settled in his arms as if she belonged nowhere else.

This was what she wanted. Dear heavens, this was exactly what she wanted. Sarah nestled against him, loving the strength of his arms around her, the solid expanse of chest beneath her hands. This hard, dangerous man cared about her—she had seen the truth in his eyes. How could she ever be frightened of that?

She loved him. Loved him and wanted to be here with him, with every shimmering, buzzing cell in her body.

"You'll tell me if I do anything you don't like," he commanded. "If I touch you wrong or startle you or anything at all."

Laughter bubbled up in her chest. Who would have believed it? The heartbreaker of Star Valley was more nervous about this than she was! "I swear," she said, managing to choke down her giggle. "You'll be the first to know."

He kissed her again, long and hard and full of promise, until she just about melted all over the floor of her living room.

"We're not doing this here." He drew back, his voice hoarse. "I don't need a damn audience."

She glanced down and found Daisy watching them with interest, her tail wagging as she moved her head back and forth between the two of them like an observer at a Ping-Pong tournament.

Sarah laughed out loud this time, full of joy and tenderness and that wondrous thrum of anticipation. "My bedroom. Through the hall, second door on the right."

Her laughter changed to a gasp when he effortlessly lifted her into his arms and carried her through the house to her room, closed the door with his boot and set her gently on the bed.

"Promise me, Sarah. Promise you'll tell me if you're at all uncomfortable."

She nodded slowly, their gazes locked together. "As long as you promise you won't hold back."

He stood watching her for a long time, until hot color soaked her skin in a slow glide from cheeks to neck to breasts. Then he leaned down and kissed her with soft, aching tenderness.

"I promise." He whispered the vow against her mouth and she breathed it inside her.

She wrapped her arms around him, pulling him closer, and he deepened the kiss, explored her mouth until she was wet and weak and trembling. She gasped when his lips slid away from hers and began trailing kisses down the column of her neck.

"You taste like sunlight." He nipped another taste. "Sunlight and flowers."

She watched him, breathless and aroused and suddenly embarrassed. "I've been out working in the garden all day. It's probably more like sweat and fertilizer."

"Let's see." He glided his mouth down the column of her throat, to the buttons of her faded denim work shirt. She found it unbearably sexy watching his hands—broad and strong and masculine—as he worked each button. And even more sexy when his mouth followed the pathway of those hands, pressing soft, barely there kisses in a long trail down the strip of skin revealed by each undone button.

After dipping his tongue into her navel, he slid up and caught her mouth with his again. "Nope. Definitely flowers," he murmured.

He slid aside the edges of her shirt, then worked the front clasp of her bra with a skill she might have teased him about under other circumstances. Now she could only watch him, her breath tangled in her throat as he freed her breasts from the lacy cups.

She wasn't very well endowed in that area. He was probably used to chesty women who knew how to flaunt their advantages, she thought glumly. Before she could come up with some kind of dismissive joke about it, her gaze met his and the stunned masculine appreciation in those dark blue depths sent her pulse rate skyrocketing.

He whispered a prayer or an oath—she wasn't sure which—then pressed his mouth reverently first to one slope then the other.

She made a low, strangled noise in her throat and he quickly looked up. "Everything okay?"

She couldn't talk just now. Not with this aching tenderness in her throat, this heavy ache in her breasts, in her womb. She decided this was one of those times when words weren't necessary anyway, so she gripped his hair tightly and drew his head back to her.

His laugh sounded rough against her breasts, but his mouth was gentle. His lips settled over one jutting peak, drawing it slowly into his mouth. She still hadn't found her breath when he began removing the rest of her clothing, then his own.

Distracted by the slow, heated magic of his mouth on her skin, she was hardly aware of it until he stood before her.

She blinked, stunned. He was beautiful. Ruggedly, unashamedly male, with a sculpted chest tapering to a lean waist, skin stretched taut over hard muscles. Her eyes dipped lower and she blushed bright red at the evidence of his desire.

"Don't look at me like that," he ordered roughly.

"Like what?"

"Like I'm the big bad wolf about to gobble you up."

"Promises, promises," she murmured, and had the very distinct pleasure of seeing his eyes go wide and unfocused with desire.

He joined her on the bed again and she had to close

her eyes as sensation after sensation washed over her at the intimacy of being there with him.

He kissed her again, his mouth gentle as his hands explored her skin with slow, sensual movements. She sighed against his mouth. She loved the way he was touching her, but something was wrong. It took her a moment to figure out what. He was treating her like some kind of fragile porcelain doll, not like a woman.

She wanted more. She wanted to taste that wildness in him. Wanted heat and strength and passion, not this careful deference.

Frustrated, yearning, she reached between their bodies and closed her fingers around him. He froze with a harsh intake of breath, impaling her with his gaze. The raw desire there was everything she could have asked for and more.

"Be careful," he warned, sending shivers of anticipation rippling down her spine.

"I'm tired of being careful. I won't break, Jesse. I promise."

Her words seemed to unlock some kind of dam inside him. His movements became urgent, hurried. He licked, nipped, tasted her skin, while his long fingers played at the apex of her thighs.

She was more than ready for him, wet and slick and eager. She wanted him, wanted this. Still, she tensed when she felt his hard strength *there* preparing to enter her. A thin edge of nerves suddenly crackled through her like heat lightning and she jerked back.

She muttered a curse, furious with herself. She wasn't afraid. Damn it, she wouldn't be nervous. This was Jesse, and she trusted him completely.

"Sarah, look at me," he ordered. She obeyed, her breath coming hard and fast as she tried to stay in control.

The tenderness in his blue eyes, on those gorgeous hard features, almost made her weep. He framed her face with his hands. "It's okay. We'll take things slow for now. There's plenty of time for more later if you want to. And if you don't—if you're not ready—that's okay, too."

"No. Please, Jess. I want this."

He studied her for a moment, looking for any indication her words held more bravado than she was really feeling. Apparently satisfied, he slid between her legs again and entered her slowly, carefully.

She held her breath and kept her eyes open, her gaze locked with his. This was right. Oh, sweet heaven, this was right. She felt as if she were floating along on a sweet, warm river of need and it was wonderful.

Exercising great care and restraint, he moved inside her subtly, just enough that she gasped. The easy current of desire eddying around her churned a little faster, a little wilder, and she clutched at him.

He kissed her, blue eyes still wide open and burning into hers. "It's okay," he murmured against her mouth. "Don't be afraid. I promise, I'll stop if you want me to."

If he stopped, she would drown. She knew it as surely as she knew she loved him. These warm, erotic waves would change to the icy sea where she usually floated and she would sink below the frigid depths.

She couldn't find the words to tell him, so she used her mouth, her hands, her body.

She saw the need haze his eyes, felt his movements become more urgent. Finally, when she thought she wouldn't be able to bear this sweet tension another instant, he reached between their bodies and touched her.

Slick heat poured through her as she gasped his name and together they plunged over the edge of a churning, sparkling, beautiful waterfall.

Then he held her while she gave in to the tears of relief and amazement and sweet, healing peace.

She was officially a fallen woman.

Sarah smiled a little as she turned the lights off in her classroom late Monday afternoon.

All day, through math and spelling and social studies, she had been able to think of nothing but Jesse and waking this morning in his strong arms.

They had shared an incredible weekend, much of it in bed. After a quick trip back to his house Sunday morning for clothes and food for poor, hungry Daisy, they had cooked breakfast together in her little kitchen, laughing like a pair of kids making mud pies even as they paused frequently for more of those long, intoxicating kisses that turned her knees to spaghetti.

They ate breakfast in her bed and barely made it through the omelettes before she was in his arms once more. The kisses had led to touches, the touches to more.

Later she put him to work in her backyard, digging and pruning and hauling. She had this idea for a goldfish pond in the corner and had roped him into helping. It was no real hardship, she had to admit, watching him wield a shovel with those powerful muscles flexing under his shirt.

Jesse had a standing command performance for Sunday dinner at the Diamond Harte when he wasn't on duty. Despite her protests, he had insisted on taking her along.

She smiled a little, remembering the reaction of his family. She had feared it might be awkward for them to have her as an unexpected guest, but the girls had been ecstatic at the prospect of sharing dinner with their teacher.

She had the feeling Jesse didn't usually bring someone to the family gatherings—Ellie and Jesse's older brother, Matt, hadn't managed to conceal their surprise—but they had been warm and welcoming.

Cassie had just grinned at her.

It had been wonderful to see the easy, teasing affection in the family. She had missed this growing up as an only child, the banter and the stories and the easy, loving familiarity.

Though she knew the danger of it, she couldn't help wondering what it would be like to belong, to be a part of this tight-knit family.

She wasn't stupid enough to think what she and Jesse shared could ever be a forever kind of thing. What could she—a dowdy mouse of a schoolteacher, afraid of her own shadow—hope to offer a man as vibrant and alive as Jesse Harte?

For some mysterious reason, he was attracted to her. Any doubts she might have entertained about that had been dispelled about the seventh or eighth time he had reached hungrily for her over the weekend.

But she knew it wouldn't last.

She hadn't told him she loved him. A few times she had come close to whispering it as she had rested beside him with her cheek against his warm skin, listening to the steady comfort of his heartbeat. But she had swallowed the words down, knowing he wouldn't want them. Knowing they would only make him uncomfortable.

Her sigh stirred the air. She had gone into this with her eyes wide open. She knew from the beginning Jesse wasn't a forever kind of man, so she had determined to squeeze every ounce of joy from this time and store it up in her heart.

For this moment, he was hers. She wasn't going to spoil it by regretting the impossible.

Besides, how could she be depressed when a man like Jesse Harte—with his hands and his strength and his devastating smile—would be on his way to meet her within the hour?

She reached the outside door of the school and unfurled her umbrella, with its print of one of Monet's water lily series.

It had started to rain the night before, a wild, noisy, flashing storm that battered the new windows of her little cottage. She and Jesse hadn't minded. They'd been snug inside, tangled together under her thick comforter.

By morning, the violent weather had changed to a soft, steady rain that hadn't eased all day. Her class had been forced to endure all three recesses inside, and she had done her best to keep her restless, ready-for-summer students entertained with seven-up and desk baseball and computer games.

Only a few more weeks and the school term would end. Every year she promised herself she wouldn't get emotional at the end of the year and every year she did. She would miss her students when they moved on to fifth grade. The only consolation she could find was that in a few months she would have thirty more children to love.

Her shoes were soaked by the time she reached her car. She unlocked her door, shook the water off her umbrella and started to close it when she heard the low rumble of an approaching vehicle.

Somebody else working late, she thought. Or maybe Jesse coming to check on her. The thought warmed her deep inside and she turned with a ready smile. It slid away at the sight of a dilapidated, mud-splattered pickup truck.

The driver was a stranger, a man around Jesse's age. Through the rain sluicing down his windshield she could see a long, drooping mustache and dirty blond hair receding off a high forehead.

He definitely wasn't a teacher. Maybe he was a new custodian or a parent looking for a late student.

She gave a quick, impersonal smile, and was about to slide into her car when he opened his door and called her name on a question.

With a sudden vague foreboding she stood with the door of her own car open and one foot inside. Her upholstery would be drenched in this rain, but she didn't care. Even though she knew it was silly, she suddenly needed the security of her vehicle.

"Yes," she said, with a calmness she didn't feel. "I'm Sarah McKenzie."

"I'd like to talk to you about my kid. He's in your class."

She frowned, even more uneasy. After an entire school term, she thought she knew the parents of every single student in her class, but she definitely didn't remember this man. "I'm sorry. I think you're mistaken. Are you sure I'm your child's teacher?"

"Yeah." He climbed out of the truck and walked over to her, his hand outstretched. He had thick, beefy fingers and a build to match. Definitely someone she didn't want to mess with. "Name's Hob Sylvester. My boy, Corey, has been in your class for a few months."

Corey Sylvester? She knew Seth was the boy's stepfather, but she had no idea Corey's real father even lived in Wyoming, let alone in Star Valley. This was the first she'd ever heard of him.

Knowing his identity should have allayed her misgivings, but she still felt an icy prickle under her skin that had nothing to do with the rain. "It's terrible weather out here and the school is closed, Mr. Sylvester. Why don't we make an appointment tomorrow right after school to talk?"

He studied her for a moment, then twisted his lips into a cold smile. "No. I'd rather talk now."

Her uneasiness blossomed into full-fledged panic. Her gaze skittered around the virtually empty parking lot, to the darkened school. A few people might still be inside, but they would never hear her call for help from clear out here.

They were completely alone and the knowledge suddenly terrified her.

"We can talk tomorrow." She slid into her car, heedless at how rude she might appear to a parent of one of her students, or how foolish she would probably feel later, when she was safe and warm and dry in her own house, in Jesse's arms.

All she could focus on now was the sudden panic spurting through her. Adrenaline surged in her veins and she yanked the door closed behind her and fumbled with the locks.

She wasn't fast enough. Before she could engage them, the man yanked the door open.

"Don't you want to talk to me?" His voice was more like a snarl now. "I thought teachers were always complaining about parents not being interested in their kids' education. Well, I'm interested, so let's talk."

He loomed over her, large and menacing. All he wanted to do was talk, she assured herself. Just talk. What was the harm in that? It helped her regain control a little.

"I'm sorry, Mr. Sylvester. I'm late for an appointment," she lied. "Please come to school tomorrow." She heard the pleading note in her voice and hated it, but couldn't manage to keep it out.

"My daddy always said, why do tomorrow what you can do today?"

His eyes looked wild, something she hadn't noticed before, and she picked up the strong, fiery smell of hard liquor on his breath. Five in the afternoon and the man was stinking drunk.

Without warning, he suddenly grabbed her arm and tugged her from the car with one hand. In his other, a stubby black handgun appeared out of nowhere.

At the sight of it, her mind went completely blank, like a vast field of blinding new snow.

No. Please, God. No.

This couldn't be happening to her again.

"Come on, teacher. You and me are gonna take a little ride."

His grip on her arm tightened and her vision grayed

around the edges. The flashback punched her hard in the stomach.

Suddenly she wasn't in the parking lot of Salt River Elementary anymore, with the comforting mountains around her and the rain drizzling steadily down. She was once more in her classroom in Chicago, with Tommy DeSilva hitting her, ripping at her clothes, on top of her.

The scream built in her throat, died there. No. She blinked hard, using every ounce of strength she possessed to choke down the memories. She had to stay in control, stay focused.

Jesse would find her. When she wasn't at home as he expected, he would come to the school and see her car. He would immediately know something was wrong, and he would find her.

She had to help him. To send some kind of message, a clue where to start looking for her.

She took a deep breath, again fighting down the panic that crouched like a snarling beast inside her. Think, she ordered herself, clutching her bag more tightly in her hand.

Her bag! She had been taking home a stack of reports on the California gold rush to grade, and Corey's paper was right at the front of the stack. She remembered, because she'd been so pleased and surprised that he had actually bothered to turn in an assignment.

While the man yanked her toward the truck, she managed to hitch the bag to her shoulder so she could use her free hand to reach inside. Her fist closed over the report she had to pray was Corey's. As Hob Sylvester struggled to shove her into the truck, he didn't notice at all when she dropped the report and her bag where she hoped Jesse would find them.

As a clue, it wasn't much—obscure, at best—but she would have to trust that Jesse would understand.

Inside the old pickup she nearly gagged at the stench, of stale sweat and spoiled milk and the sick, yeasty scent of old beer. It was filthy, covered in fast-food wrappers and crushed beer cans and used tissues. On the passenger seat was a pile of empty paper coin rolls and what looked suspiciously like a pair of women's underwear.

Hob Sylvester swept them all to the floor, then shoved her in.

The only way she would get through this was to keep her wits about her. "What did you want to talk to me about?" she asked woodenly, as if this were just another parent-teacher conference.

He chortled as he elbowed the floor gearshift. The truck lurched obediently forward. "We can talk about anything you want, darlin'. We could talk about Corey's grades or the damn price of tea in China or how you're gonna help me get back what's mine."

He smiled and she had the strange thought that with those striking green eyes he had probably been handsome once. Now the eyes were bloodshot, his mouth hard.

In the side mirror she could see the school building recede into the distance as they drove through the rain. Panic began to chew at her again, but she pushed it away.

"You know this is kidnapping, don't you? You're taking me against my will."

He snorted. "I might not be a smart schoolteacher

like you, but I'm not completely stupid. I know exactly what I'm doing."

"This is a serious offense, Mr. Sylvester. Why don't you let me go and we can pretend this never happened? I won't tell anyone."

"Because I've got plans for you, teacher. Big plans."

She drew a deep, shuddering breath. She couldn't think about it. Jesse would find her. She knew he would. He had to.

Corey's father picked up a bottle still in the paper bag and took a long swig, then wiped at his mouth. If he were drunk, he might be careless. She would have to pray she could find a way to escape.

"Where are we going?" she asked, striving with everything she had to keep her voice casual.

"A place where nobody can hear what I'm gonna do to you."

His smile didn't come close to reaching his eyes. This time she could no longer keep the panic at bay. It snarled once, then lunged for her and swallowed her whole.

Man, he had it bad.

He hated to admit it, but Matt had been right. After dinner the night before, his know-it-all big brother had taken him outside on the pretext of showing off one of his new mares.

Eventually—as he realized now Matt intended all along—the conversation had drifted to what the hell he thought he was doing messing around with a nice woman like Sarah McKenzie.

Before he could get huffy about his big brother's insulting tone, Matt had taken one look at him and ended up poleaxing Jesse with the truth.

Jesse James Harte, the bad boy of Salt River, Wyoming, was head over heels in love with a sweet, quiet schoolteacher.

He'd damn near punched his brother in the face at the time. It couldn't be true. He cared about her—wanted to keep her safe and make her smile—and he was definitely attracted to her gentle, willowy beauty, but he couldn't be in love with her.

Throughout a day spent chewing it over, though, he'd been chagrined to realize Matt had been right. It burned his gut worse than Cassie's hot chili to admit that his nosy older brother had recognized Jesse's feelings for Sarah before he did.

But how could he have realized it when he didn't have any kind of frame of reference to measure his feelings against? He'd never been in love before. Never even come close.

He'd always figured there was something lacking in him, some cold empty place inside where something good must have died the day his parents did. Or maybe it had just shriveled away in those wild, rowdy years after.

But now that he'd been knocked over the head with the truth, he couldn't deny it. He was in love with Sarah McKenzie. He had a feeling he'd been on his way there since the day she came to Salt River.

Now, as he drove toward the school to meet her, he was amazed at the anticipation thrumming through him. It hadn't even been twelve hours since he'd left her warm, flower-scented bed and he couldn't wait to see her again. To touch that soft skin. To watch her eyes go hazy with need, to see that smile sneak out of no-where—that sweet smile that always seemed to reach right into his chest and yank out his heart.

He was in love with her. Now, what the hell was he supposed to do about it?

For the first time in his life, he was thinking about more than just having a good time. He was thinking about forever kinds of things—happily-ever-after kinds of things. Marriage, kids, the whole works.

And trying to ignore the snide little voice inside him that he couldn't seem to make shut up, the voice reminding him that he didn't even come close to deserving a woman as good and decent as Sarah.

He gripped the steering wheel a little tighter, eyes straight ahead. He didn't want to think about that now. About his past and the things he'd done. He didn't want any of that touching her, ever.

A few blocks from the school, an older rattletrap of a pickup passed him, its huge gas-guzzling engine growling through the late afternoon. He didn't recognize the truck and couldn't see much of the driver through the rain, but he waved anyway. This was Salt River. It would have been rude not to.

A few moments later, he pulled into the school parking area and saw with relief that Sarah's sage Toyota was one of only a handful of cars in the parking lot. Good. Looked as if his hunch was right, to come here instead of her house. Even with the school year winding down, Sarah still put in long, hard hours at her job.

He admired her dedication and wondered again where he would have been if one of his teachers had taken the interest in him that she did with all her pupils.

Though it was still an hour or so from sunset, the

gunmetal-gray storm clouds made it seem much darker and later. He looked for Sarah's classroom windows, but didn't see any lights on inside. That didn't mean anything. Maybe she had a faculty meeting or was busy in the library.

He didn't mind waiting. It would give him a chance to figure out how to deal with this tangle of emotions twisting through him.

He started to pull in next to her car when his headlights caught on something lying in a puddle a few feet away. Some kid had probably dropped his backpack in a hurry to catch the bus and get home to his Nintendo. He should pick it up before the rain ruined it, if he wasn't too late.

With his engine still running, he climbed out to retrieve the thing. It wasn't a backpack, he discovered as he neared the puddle. He crouched and reached for it, then stopped when he recognized the tapestry floral print.

He'd seen Sarah walking out the door with this very bag earlier that morning.

What would her tote be doing out here in the rain? He frowned, unease suddenly crawling down his spine like a furry spider. She wouldn't have left it out in the rain. Not a chance. She was much too careful for that.

Leaving the bag, he walked to her car, and that one little prickle of unease became a whole damn nest of spiders skittering all over him at what he found. Her umbrella, the fancy flowery one he'd kissed her beneath that morning before she left her house, lay closed but not snapped on the ground.

Even more ominous, the car wasn't locked and he could see her keys in a jumbled heap on the seat.

What was going on here? The bag, the umbrella, the keys. They were here, but where the hell was Sarah?

Maybe she'd forgotten something and gone back into the school. But why would she leave her keys and her umbrella out here in the middle of a downpour, especially when he knew the school was always locked at this time of the afternoon?

He was about to bang on the door and scour the building for her when he spied something else in the puddle, a glimmer of white underneath her bag that he'd missed before. He lifted the sopping mess, which turned out to be some kind of homework assignment.

As soon as he read the student's name scrawled in uneven letters at the top, he knew instinctively that Sarah hadn't left this paper separate from the rest by accident. It was a clue to tell him where to find her.

She was in trouble, and it was somehow linked to Corey Sylvester.

Cold, stinging fear clutched his stomach. Could Seth have gotten to her somehow? Damn. He should have put some kind of protection on her. He'd thought they'd have more time before Garrett found out he was under investigation for the shattered windows at her house, the bloody warnings to mind her own business, the attempted break-in a few weeks earlier.

He hadn't arranged protection for her, though, mainly because he was still having a tough time believing Seth could be involved. He had a possible motive—anger at her for accusing him of hurting Corey—but Jesse wasn't convinced he had the personality for revenge.

He'd been working hard to come up with an alternative theory that made sense to explain why the mayor's favorite fishing cap had been found at the scene of a pretty sick crime. Coincidence? Mistake? A plant of some kind?

But how could he argue with this paper staring right back at him? Sarah was in trouble, he could feel it like a deep ache in his bones. What kind of trouble, he didn't know, but the trail led him right back to Seth Garrett.

What would the son of a bitch hope to gain? He didn't know and he couldn't wait around here to figure it out. His heart pounded out a fierce rhythm as he rushed to the Bronco and sped off through the gathering darkness. On the way to the Garretts, he radioed for an officer to search the school grounds and double-check her house, just in case he was wrong and she was safe and sound somewhere.

Even as he gave the order, he knew she wasn't.

Something was wrong. She needed him and this time he couldn't fail.

He didn't bother knocking at the Garretts', just shoved open the unlocked door.

Seth stood poised at the base of the stairs, as if he were just on his way up. Surprise flickered on his face at the intrusion, but Jesse didn't give him a chance to say a word. With adrenaline pumping through him like an uncapped oil well, he grabbed two fistfuls of beige golf shirt and rammed the other man against the wall so hard Seth's head connected with an ugly-sounding crack.

"You son of a bitch. Where is she?" Jesse barely recognized the rough, feral voice coming from his throat

In contrast, Seth's voice came out strangled. "Who? Ginny? She's in the kitchen."

He gave the man another hard shake. "Where's Sarah? What have you done to her?"

Seth's eyes widened. "Sarah McKenzie? Corey's teacher? I barely know the woman."

"You know her enough to stalk her. To lurk outside her house and smash in her windows and leave nasty notes on the door." He shook again. "I know you took her. Now, where is she?"

"You're crazy! I don't know what you're talking about, Jesse. I swear it."

Drawn by the raised voices, Ginny rushed into the entry. "Jesse! What is going on? Let him go!"

"Stay out of this, Gin."

"No. Good heavens, Jesse. What's gotten into you?"

"Is she here at the house? Are you hiding her in your garage?"

"Hiding who?" Ginny fluttered her hands. "This is ridiculous!"

"Sarah McKenzie is missing. And the only one I know in Salt River who might have a grudge against her is your husband."

"You're nuts." Seth's voice came out raspy. "What kind of grudge would I have against her? Corey's done better in just a few weeks spent in her class than he has all year!"

"How about retaliation for having your good name smeared by allegations of child abuse? You found out she's the one who made the accusation, didn't you?"

Seth's astonishment was either completely genuine or he had a lock on winning best actor of the century. "I had no idea who made the complaint until you just said it. I wouldn't have cared anyway, since it was completely false. I would never hurt Corey or Sarah McKenzie. Come on, Jess. You know me! You know I couldn't do any of this!"

The stunned sincerity in his expression, in his voice, gave Jesse the first flickers of doubt since he'd seen that soggy piece of paper with Corey's name on it. He suddenly realized he was a few moments away from strangling one of his oldest friends.

Could he have made a mistake?

He could barely see through the black haze of rage and worry consuming him at the thought of the nightmare Sarah must be going through. But he considered himself fairly good at reading people, and right now Seth looked stunned.

Jesse reluctantly released his hold and Seth slumped to a pine bench against the wall, rubbing his throat. "What's this about, Jess? Why would you think I'm involved?"

He raked a hand through his hair. What was he supposed to do now? He had to find her and couldn't afford to waste time here with explanations if Seth wasn't involved. What had she been trying to tell him by leaving that damn paper out of her bag?

"You heard about the vandalism at her house?"

"Yes. Betty Ann, my secretary, told me. She heard it from her sister Janie, who works with Sarah at the school. It sounded like a real mess."

"We found something of yours on the scene. We have reason to believe it was left there by whoever did the dirty work. I had a theory that it might be some kind of twisted revenge thing, but maybe it was just a plant. Something to throw us off."

"It wasn't me, I swear it."

Frustration prowled through him, gnawed at him. He wanted to pound his fist against the wall, to smash every single one of Ginny's pretty little knickknacks in the room.

Where was Sarah?

"Somehow her disappearance is linked to Corey. I can feel it in my bones. She left one of his homework assignments out of her bag. It was the only one she pulled out and I know she had to mean something by that. But what? Where the hell can she be?"

He heard a small sound above his head, like the mew of a tiny kitten, and Jesse jerked his gaze to the stairs. Corey stood halfway down, his hand on the railing and his face so pale his freckles stood out in sharp relief.

Ginny stepped forward. "Corey, do you know something about this?"

"Maybe." His usual screw-you attitude was nowhere in sight. Instead, he just looked like exactly what he was, a young boy—and a frightened one at that.

"What do you know?" his mother asked, when he didn't say anything more.

He swallowed hard and gripped the railing. "You'll be mad if I tell you."

Seth started up the stairs and laid a hand on the boy's shoulder. "Son, you have to tell what you know. Ms. McKenzie might be in danger."

Tears welled up in his eyes. "I didn't think he'd hurt her."

"Who, Corey?" Jesse pounced on him. "Where is she?"

"You could try Elk Mountain," he whispered.

They all stared at him. "What?" Jesse growled.

"The trailer on Elk Mountain. Where we used to live."

Ginny hissed in a breath, her face going as pale as

her son's. "What are you talking about? That trailer's abandoned. It's just a pile of junk. Why would Sarah possibly go there?"

"I don't know. But if she's missing, I think maybe my dad might have taken her there. That's where he's been living." Tears welled up in the boy's frightened eyes. "I'm sorry I didn't tell you he was back, Mom. He made me promise not to. Said he'd hurt Maddie or you if I told."

Hob Sylvester. Son of a bitch. Suddenly Corey's mysterious injuries these past few weeks made a whole lot more sense. "Why would Hob want to hurt Sarah? He doesn't even know her."

Corey sniffled. "I don't know. He was real mad at her, though. Said she should mind her own business after she had to go and tell 'bout the, um, the thing on my back."

"He…your father did that to you?" Ginny asked weakly.

Corey looked guilty and miserable at the same time. "When I told him about Seth wanting to adopt me, he got real mad. Said I was a Sylvester and he wouldn't let me ever forget it."

Jesse didn't wait to hear the rest. He was already heading for the door, a ragged curse on his tongue. Hob Sylvester. He thought of all the calls he'd responded to over the years on Elk Mountain, back when Ginny and Corey lived there. The bruises and the broken bones and the wounds that went far deeper than flesh.

Hob was a crazy, vindictive bully who was capable of anything. Just thinking about his sweet Sarah in the hands of a man like that sent a hot, greasy ball of fear slicking through him.

He had to hurry.

This time—please, God, this time—he wouldn't be too late.

"Here we are. End of the road, Teach."

Sarah tried not to listen to the voice. She was in a safe, warm place where no one could touch her—no one could scare her—and she couldn't let anyone disturb her.

She breathed deeply, shoving the entire weight of her psyche against the door to the terrifying world outside. If only she tried hard enough, she could keep that door closed tightly and could stay right here in this nice, safe, blank nothingness.

"Come on. I ain't got all day." Someone on the outside grabbed her arm and yanked her out of both the truck and her safe, private haven.

She wobbled a little at the impact of her abrupt return to earth.

"Come on," Corey's father said, his voice harsh and ugly.

He gripped her arm and started dragging her toward the only structure in sight among the towering trees, a dilapidated trailer with peeling aluminum skin of some nondescript color.

No. This wasn't right. She was supposed to be at her safe little cottage right now with Jesse, not at some junk heap in the middle of nowhere.

"I want to go home," she muttered.

"Tough," he snapped. He shoved her hard up the wooden steps. They were wet from the rain and she stumbled on a loose board. She reached a hand to the rickety railing to steady herself, then gasped as splinters drove into her skin.

The sharp pain brought her fully back to the grim reality of her situation. She was on an isolated mountainside with a man who appeared to be drunk at best, completely crazy at worst. Even if Jesse somehow miraculously managed to figure out where they'd gone, it still could be hours before he arrived for her.

She was going to have to save herself.

The idea just about sent her scurrying back to the safe place inside her head.

The flimsy door to the structure wasn't locked and Sylvester shoved her inside. Could he actually live here? It was little better than one of those cardboard boxes the homeless used back in Chicago.

It looked as if someone had tried to make the trailer a home at one time, but the wallpaper was stained with water, the lace curtains tattered and ripped.

Her gaze landed on something familiar. It appeared she'd just solved the mystery of the school's missing coins. The shattered jar lay in a corner in thick broken shards amid a pile of coins.

So Chuck Hendricks had been right—Corey had been involved in the theft. Or at least his father had been.

She didn't have time to dwell on it. Sylvester shoved her toward a blue-and-gold couch missing most of its stuffing.

Still holding the gun, he immediately reached for yet another bottle on the counter, this one already half-empty, and carried it to the only other piece of furniture in the room, a chair of the same ugly print.

For a few moments he drank and muttered, some

disjointed soliloquy about Seth and Ginny and Corey, about how Seth was going to pay for taking from Hob Sylvester. About how the stupid bitch was still his wife, no matter what any judge had to say about it.

She thought she heard Jesse's name in there, but she was only half listening, her nerves quivering as she tried to figure out how she could make it out of there in one piece.

The man obviously wanted revenge, but she wasn't quite sure how she fit into the whole picture. Though she didn't really want to know, she figured the more information she had to rely on, the better her chances of surviving.

She thought of Jesse and the weekend they'd shared, the bright color he had brought to her cold, gray world. She wanted to be in his arms again, to feel wonderfully, miraculously whole again. To tell him how very much she loved him.

She was going to have to survive, no matter what.

"What are you planning to do with me?" She interrupted Sylvester's rambling with a calmness that belied the panic surging through her veins.

He blinked at her in surprise—just as if the chair he was sitting on had suddenly started carrying on a conversation—then suddenly smirked at her over the lip of the nearly empty Jack Daniel's bottle. "You're gonna help me, Teach."

"How?"

"See this?" He held up the gun with a broad smile. "This here belongs to Seth Son-of-a-Bitch Garrett. Registered and everything. Who do you think's gonna get blamed when it happens to be used to commit a crime?"

"Seth?"

"Give the teacher an A-plus." He saluted her with the bottle.

Keep him talking. Talking and drinking, until Jesse had time to get there or until he passed out, so she could escape.

"How did you get the gun?"

Sylvester grinned at his own cleverness. "Wasn't hard. I made my boy give me the key to their fancy house so I could get in whenever I wanted. They never even knew I'd been there. Not like at your house. I didn't even get close before you saw me and called the police."

She thought of the intruder, that dark, menacing shape outside her window. "That was you?"

He snickered but didn't answer.

"Why me?"

"You dropped right into my lap, sugar." He seemed to have a little trouble getting the words out and she prayed he was too drunk to notice as she casually stretched her leg out and pretended to shift positions while she carefully slid a thick, five-inch-long shard of glass from the shattered coin jar closer, hiding it under her shoe.

"My kid said you and our pretty-boy police chief were close. Thought I'd see if he was tellin' me more lies. For once he was right. The minute you saw me, you called him, didn't you?"

"He's the police chief. Of course I called him."

"Aw, come on. You don't have to fool ol' Hob Sylvester. You're doin' him, aren't you?"

She flushed at his crudeness. *Keep him talking. Even if you don't like what he's saying.* "What does that have to do with anything?"

"When I saw you, I came up with a great idea. Kill

two birds with one stone, you know, and make them both pay for screwing up my life. While I'm setting up that son of a bitch Garrett to take the fall when you're found shot to death with his gun, I can also make Jesse Harte bleed by taking away something of his. It's the least I can do for my old football buddy." His cold smile oozed hatred.

"What did Jesse do to you?"

"Ruined my life, that's what he did!" He threw the empty bottle against the wall suddenly and she shuddered at the crash. "If it wasn't for him, I would have played college ball and maybe even the pros. I was one hell of a wide receiver. Had colleges knockin' down my door. University of Wyoming, Colorado. UNLV. They all wanted Hob Sylvester on their roster, I'll tell you what. Then Jesse Harte had to go and ruin it for me."

"How?" she whispered.

"Last game of the regular season, scouts in the stands, and QB hotshot Harte decides to blow off the game. He didn't even show up! How was I supposed to let the scouts see what I could do when I had that wussy Troy Smoot throwing for me?"

She didn't understand half of what he was saying. Football wasn't exactly one of her areas of expertise, but besides that, his words began to slur.

She cursed her stupid knee. If not for that, she could probably easily outrun a man who was more than half-drunk, even down a slippery mountainside.

Jesse, please hurry.

"Him and Garrett and that bitch I married are in it together. And now they have to pay. That's all. You just made the mistake of getting messed up with the wrong guy, sugar."

He was crazy. He had to be if he thought this ridiculous plan would actually work, that anyone would blame Seth Garrett for her death.

"Guess we might as well get to it, right?" He lifted the gun and she couldn't help flinching.

"Here? You're going to kill me here, now?"

"Why not?"

She drew a shaky breath, scrambling for an answer. In the end, she decided to play to his ego. "Seems to me a smart man like you would realize the police would never believe Seth would bring me out here to kill me," she pointed out. "All the clues except the gun will point to you. Your fingerprints have to be all over this place."

He scratched his head. "So where should we go?"

She had the sudden, hysterical urge to laugh. Was the man actually drunk—or insane—enough to think she was going to give him a blueprint for her own murder? "Where would Mayor Garrett do it?"

His big, dissipated face suddenly brightened. "I know. The courthouse. The sumbitch practically lives there. Come on, let's go."

He gestured with the gun toward the door. Her time was running out.

Sarah pretended to stumble as she rose, and staggered to her knees. While still down, she quickly closed her fist around the thick glass shard, heedless of it slicing through her skin.

As her fingers folded around the sharp, cold glass, a strange, empowering strength flowed through her. She might go down in the end, but this time she would go down fighting, damn it.

She stayed on the ground for several seconds, until

Sylvester turned toward her, snarling impatiently. "Come on. Hurry up."

It wasn't hard to make a distressed noise. "My knee. I have problems with it sometimes. I don't think I can get up."

He muttered a harsh curse. "You better not be faking," he warned, but stretched a hand out to help her up.

He brushed her breast as he reached for her. If not for that, she might not have had the courage, but in that moment he became Tommy DeSilva. All her hatred toward what had been done to her focused on him.

With a grunt of rage, she drew her hand back and aimed for his eyes with all her strength.

With a scream of pain, Sylvester backed away, clutching at his face. Bile rose in her throat at the sight of him, like something out of a horror movie—the glass shard sticking out of one eye, blood pouring everywhere.

She nearly collapsed right then as the past jerked back to the present, but she knew she wasn't safe. Not while he still had a gun. With one hand she snagged the keys to the truck off the counter where he'd left them and raced out the door as fast as her knee would allow.

Half skidding, half jumping, she made her way down the slippery steps and was almost to the truck when a wild shot rang out behind her. She didn't take time to look, just leapt for the cab of the truck, then fumbled with both locks.

She wasted a few scary moments trying to figure out which key would start the truck, then she jammed the right one in. It worked! The truck rumbled to life just as another shot rang out, shattering the passenger window. Sarah didn't wait around anymore. She muscled the truck into gear, thanking heaven her father had bothered to teach her how to drive a manual, then roared through the darkness.

She was halfway down the mountain, trying her best to drive with shaking hands and tears of shock running down her face, when she heard the first siren.

Chapter 13

"Okay. Twelve stitches down, just a few more to go. Can you hang in there?"

Sarah nodded at the short, competent doctor with the steel-gray buzz cut and kind blue eyes behind wire-rimmed glasses. She had never been treated by a doctor wearing a bolo tie before.

"Good girl." He smiled and hunched back over her palm to continue repairing the damage she had done to herself by wielding a broken shard of glass with her bare hand.

"How's the pain?" the nurse asked.

Numb. Just like the rest of her. She had novocaine where her emotions, where her soul, were supposed to be. "Fine." She mustered a smile. "Can't feel a thing."

"Let me know when it starts to wear off," Dr. Wallace said. "We can give you another shot."

She nodded. All she wanted to do was close her eyes for a while and pretend the past two hours had never happened. But the white-coated professionals at the Salt River Health Clinic wouldn't give her that luxury. Not when there was poking and prodding and bandaging to be done.

It didn't really matter. She doubted if she would be able to forget, even for a moment. Lucky her—she now had a lovely assortment of nightmares to choose from each night.

Besides, what she *really* wanted was Jesse's arms around her once more, for him to gather her up against that broad, hard chest and hold her there forever.

The few fleeting moments after he yanked her out of Hob Sylvester's battered pickup and into his arms had been the only time she'd felt completely safe since she had walked out to her car after school.

She had sobbed with relief as he held her fiercely. It was over. Jesse was there and everything would be okay.

But the embrace had been brief. After making sure she wasn't seriously injured, he had handed her off to Officer Hernandez with terse instructions to take Sarah to the clinic while he dealt with Sylvester.

The doctor stopped stitching at her sudden frown. "Are the shots wearing off? Are you regaining feeling?"

"No. I was just… I was wondering how he is. Sylvester."

The kindness vanished from the doctor's eyes. Instead they looked flinty, angry. Not at her, she realized, but at the man who had wreaked such havoc in her life and others.

"Last report I had, the chopper crew had him stabilized," he answered. "The doctors at the University of Utah will take care of him. Who knows, they might even be able to save the sight in that eye. Won't do him much good in prison, though, and that's exactly where the sleazebag is headed."

As Chris Hernandez drove her to the clinic, the police radio in her vehicle had squawked the entire time. Through the crisp communications, Sarah learned that Hob Sylvester had surrendered to Jesse and county sheriff's deputies without a fight, in too much agony from his injury to stage much of the fuss she suspected Jesse had been hoping for.

She closed her eyes, trying to block the memory of that terrible moment when she had lunged toward him with that glass shard. Another nightmare to add to her list.

She wouldn't regret it, though. She had only been protecting herself, had done what she had to. If she ever did have a twinge of guilt at possibly causing a man to lose the sight in one eye, all she had to do was remember Corey and his bruises and the gruesome, obscene mark of ownership his own father had left scarred into his back.

"Okay." Dr. Wallace tied off the last stitch. "We're all done here."

"May I go home now?"

"I don't have any reason to keep you any longer. Do you have a ride home?"

"Yes. I'll take her."

At that deep, rough voice, Sarah's gaze flew to the door of the exam room. Jesse filled the doorway. An ugly smear of blood on the shoulder of his uniform gave her a bad moment, until she realized it was her own, from that brief time he had held her.

She almost flew into his arms right then, but checked the impulse. She could hang on for a few more minutes, just until they were alone.

If she hadn't already restrained herself, the look in his eyes would have done the job.

He looked wild. As if fierce violence seethed just under his skin. In another man, she might have found that raw energy terrifying, but not with Jesse. In him, it was only unsettling.

"Are there any precautions she needs to take once she's out of here?" he asked the doctor.

"Just use common sense. Keep the bandage dry and change it a few times every day."

"What about something for the pain?"

Sarah shook her head. "I don't want anything. I'll be fine."

The doctor shrugged. "You heard the lady. She can take over-the-counter pain relief if necessary, or if the pain intensifies, give me a call and I'll write out a scrip."

The doctor and nurse walked out of the exam room, leaving the two of them alone. Sarah waited for Jesse to pull her into his arms at last. Instead he stood by the door, his features stony and hard. "Are you ready?" he asked gruffly.

"I…yes. Please, take me home."

A few moments later, Jesse had bundled her up and ushered her out to his waiting patrol vehicle, all without touching her once.

Baffled and hurt by his distance, she sat quietly in the passenger seat, listening to the tires humming on the wet road and the staticky voices on the scanner. What was wrong? What had she done to make him so angry?

"I'm going to have to ask you some questions," he finally said when they were a few blocks from her house. "Do you want to answer them tonight or in the morning?"

She frowned at his formal tone and wrapped her hands tightly around herself, trying to contain the chill spreading through her. What was wrong? What had she done?

"Tonight," she murmured. "I have school tomorrow."

"Don't you ever get a substitute?"

"When I need it. I won't need one tomorrow. I'm sure I'll be fine in the morning."

He was quiet for several moments, his mouth in a tight line. "I didn't think you would want to be alone," he finally said, "so I arranged for Cassie to stay the night with you. She's probably at your house now."

I wouldn't be alone if you stayed with me, she almost said. *If you stay and hold me and keep me warm.* She choked down the words. How could she say them when he obviously had gone to a great deal of trouble to fix things so he wouldn't have to stay with her?

He didn't want to be alone with her. She might still feel shocky and rattled, but she could figure out that much.

Where was the sexy, laughing man who had spent the night with her? Who couldn't seem to touch her enough over the two days? Who had awakened her by blowing raspberries on her stomach and had explored every inch of her skin with his powerful hands? Who had looked at her with a soft, aching tenderness glinting in his blue eyes?

Somehow between this morning when she had left his arms and tonight, that man had disappeared. This Jesse was a stranger, abrupt and distant and withdrawn.

"It was nice of Cassie to agree to stay," she murmured, staring out the windshield at the wet road glistening in the headlights.

"She's worried about you. I'm sure she could stay a few nights or more if you need her to."

He pulled into her driveway and turned off the engine but made no move to climb out. For the first time she saw the lines of strain around his mouth, the muscle clenching in his jaw, the wildness that turned his blue eyes dark and murky. He looked like a man just barely holding on to control.

She swallowed hard and gathered courage. If she could take on a man with a gun, surely she could confront the man she loved. "Jesse, what is it? Why are you so upset?"

Some of his fury bubbled out and the look he aimed at her was razor sharp. "Why the hell do you think I'm upset? You could have been killed tonight!"

She drew a deep, shuddering breath, remembering those terrible moments when she thought she would never see him again. "But I wasn't. I survived, Jesse."

"No thanks to me. I should have been able to protect you. It was my job to keep you safe and I let Sylvester waltz right in and take you. Hell, I practically handed you to him on a silver platter."

"Your job? Is that all it was?"

He didn't answer. In the dim moonlight she saw that muscle clench in his jaw again, but he didn't say anything. In the awful, drawn-out silence, she wondered if he was able to hear the crack and shatter of her heart.

She was a fool. She had begun to build stupid, silly fantasies of forever with a man who didn't know the meaning of the word. Who had probably slept with her out of pity and obligation, only because she had practically begged him to.

"I changed my mind," she said quietly, opening the door of the Bronco. "I don't think I want to answer any questions tonight. Now I think I would just like to go inside and sleep."

"Sarah—"

She shook her head. *Go away. Go away before I break apart.* "Good night, Jess."

Clutching her bandaged hand against her heart, she walked slowly, carefully into her house on old, tired bones.

Sometimes being clean and sober really sucked.

Right about now, Jesse would give just about anything for a good, stiff drink. Or two or three or ten. And it was only eight-frigging-thirty in the morning.

He had one mother of a headache squeezing his skull like a junkyard compactor. That's what happened when he tried to keep going for twenty-four hours on no sleep and way too much coffee.

The words and spaces on the incident forms in front of him all blurred together into one big gray mess and he blinked, trying to focus. It was a futile effort. How was he supposed to fill out the necessary paperwork of Sylvester's arrest when he couldn't concentrate on anything but fragmented, tortured images from the evening before?

The cold clutch of terror in his stomach at finding out Hob Sylvester had taken Sarah.

That terrible moment when he had pulled her, bleeding and sobbing, from that ratty pickup truck and into his arms.

Finding out from a ranting Sylvester that Jesse couldn't live down his past, that it was an intrinsic part of his present—that one of the reasons Hob had targeted her, put her through a hell Jesse couldn't even begin to imagine, was because of him. Twisted revenge for some stupid thing he'd done sixteen years ago, in those awful, reckless months after his parents died.

The last image in his mind was the worst—the shattered hurt in Sarah's big green eyes right before she walked away from him.

He had wounded her. She had needed things from him the night before that he had been unable to offer.

He hadn't meant to hurt her, hadn't wanted to, but on some level he supposed it had been inevitable. Sooner or later she would figure out she deserved better.

His sweet Sarah.

His chest ached suddenly and the words swam before his eyes. Not his. She had never been his. He had been fooling himself to think a man with a hell-raising past could hold on to something so good.

He scrubbed his hands over his face and forced himself to turn back to the paperwork. He was on a short clock here—he would have to leave soon if he was going to make the five-hour drive to Salt Lake City to interrogate Sylvester in the hospital.

And wouldn't it be a treat trying to spend five minutes in the same room with the bastard without breaking him into tiny little pieces?

There had been more than a few moments the night before when he'd been tempted to indulge in a little police brutality while he arrested the son of a bitch. For Sarah. For Ginny. For Corey. The only thing stopping him had been the honor of his badge and the very real fear that if he started, he wouldn't be able to stop.

His phone suddenly buzzed and Lou's gravelly voice gritted over his intercom. "Boss, you have company coming in."

"Not now, Lou. I'm busy. Just tell 'em I'm not here."

"Too late." His little sister stalked into his office, her eyes a dark, stormy blue and a fierce scowl on her face.

"You're an idiot," Cassie snapped. "Did I ever tell you that?"

He did not need a confrontation with her today. He leaned back in his chair. "Good to see you, too, sis. And yes, I believe you've mentioned that a time or two."

"What the hell is wrong with you?"

I need a drink. And a woman I can't have. "What *isn't* wrong?" he murmured.

She shook her head in disgust. "Would you like me to round up a few puppies you can drop-kick, too, just for laughs? Because that's exactly what you did to Sarah last night."

"I didn't do anything!"

"Yeah, that's the point, isn't it? She needed comfort. She needed to feel safe. She needed you, you big idiot! And you just ditched her like you were some kind of cabbie dropping off a fare."

"It wasn't like that," he muttered.

"What was it like?" His little sister didn't get mad very often. She had always been the calm one in the family, the peacemaker, but right now she churned with fury, like some vast, storm-tossed ocean.

At his continued silence, she shook her head in disgust. "You don't get it, do you? For some mysterious reason the woman is crazy in love with you, Jess. I've seen the two of you together, I've seen the way you look at her and I know her feelings are not one-sided."

"You don't know anything about this."

"Maybe not. But I have seen you with plenty of women over the years. Too damn many, if you ask me."

"I didn't ask you," he muttered.

She went on as if she hadn't heard him. "And never once have you looked at any of them the same way you look at Sarah. You want to tell me why, then, you ran off when she needed you more last night than she's probably ever needed anyone in her life?"

"I had things to do. Loose ends to tie up, just like I do now," he said, with a pointed look at the paperwork scattered across his desk.

"And those loose ends were more important than Sarah?"

"No. But I had a job to do. If I had focused on that job in the first place, none of it would have happened."

He hadn't meant to say that. Not to Cassie, who knew him too damn well. She stared at him, then her eyes narrowed. "This is why you didn't stay when she needed you last night? Because you think it's your fault Sylvester got to her?"

He didn't answer. He didn't need to.

"You're an even bigger idiot than I thought," she snapped.

"Just back off, Cass. This is none of your business."

"It is my business when two people I care about are hurting. You're not responsible for what Hob Sylvester did, Jess."

"No. But I was responsible for keeping Sarah safe, and I failed."

She came around to his side of the desk and perched

on the edge of it. After a moment spent studying him, she sighed. "This is about what happened with Mom and Dad, isn't it?"

He opened his mouth to argue, then closed it again. The night before, he had experienced the same grim helplessness he had felt climbing up the mountainside after the accident. Knowing his parents were down there dying while he tried to claw his way to help. Knowing his father probably would have seen that patch of black ice and been able to avoid it if he hadn't been arguing with him at the time.

Knowing he couldn't fix this, that he would have to live with the harsh guilt of failure for the rest of his life.

All those feelings and more had plowed through him the night before as he had rushed after Sarah.

Once more he had failed to save someone he loved.

"Oh, Jess." Cassie must have read all those things in his face. She touched his cheek tenderly and he had to fight the urge to wrap his arms around his little sister and cry like a baby.

After a moment, she cleared her throat. "None of it was your fault. Not Mom and Dad's accident and not what happened to Sarah."

"I should have been able to keep her safe."

Cassie shook her head. "You can't save the whole world, Jess."

"I didn't need to save the whole world. Just Sarah."

Cassie was quiet for a moment, then she spoke softly. "Did it ever occur to you that maybe this time she needed to rescue herself? If only to prove to herself that she could?"

He stared at her, struck speechless by her words. By her wisdom.

Why hadn't he seen it? He had been so consumed with guilt at not saving Sarah, at letting Sylvester get to her, that he hadn't thought about how empowering it must have been for Sarah to fight back against Sylvester when she was threatened this time.

To fight back and to win.

He thought of her attack in Chicago. Where on earth had she found the kind of courage to defend herself against Sylvester, especially when she knew the consequences better than anyone else? When she had lived through those very consequences and still had the scars to prove it, both physical and emotional.

A hot, fierce pride settled in his heart. His brave Sarah.

"I'm no expert in this area," Cassie went on. "Heaven knows, I've made a mess of my own life. But I have the feeling the two of you could share something special. Something rare and precious. Don't let the past get in the way of your future."

She was right. That was exactly what he was doing. He was throwing away the best thing that had ever happened to him because he was afraid. If Sarah could be brave enough to fight for her life, couldn't he be brave enough to fight for his?

Yes. Hell, yes.

"Thanks, brat." He kissed her forehead, then headed for the door.

"Where are you going?" she asked.

He grinned, his first smile since the afternoon before, when he had seen Sarah's empty car. "School. It looks like I still have a few things to learn."

Chapter 14

She had a feeling it was going to be a very difficult day. School had been in session for only an hour and she already felt exhausted, as wrung out as a wet, soapy dishrag.

Maybe she should have found a substitute today. With only another two weeks of school before summer vacation, her students were wired, wriggling around in their seats and chattering incessantly.

After the trauma of the day before and a night spent staring at the ceiling—longing for something she couldn't have—she wasn't sure she had the energy to keep up with them.

On the other hand, she had only a few more days with her class and she hated to miss a minute of it.

Right now their restlessness had been moderately contained while they painted watercolors under Janie

Parker's instruction, but she feared the brief respite wouldn't last.

"Miss McKenzie?"

She glanced up to find Corey standing at her desk, shifting from foot to foot. The boy had been wary around her since school started, giving her furtive, watchful looks all morning.

She knew she would have to talk to him at some point about what had happened the day before, about what his father had done to both of them, but she didn't want to push him. He would talk to her when he was ready.

And it looked as if the time was now. "Hi," she said softly.

He swallowed hard. "I, um, I made you a picture." He held it out. "The paint's still a little wet."

"Thank you, Corey!" Touched beyond words, she took it carefully, treating it like the treasured prize it was. "This is really lovely."

"I know you like flowers and stuff. That's what it is."

Her heart crested, overflowed, and she felt the hot sting of tears. "I can see. You're very good, Corey. When it dries, I'll have it framed and hang it on my wall so I can look at it and be in a garden anytime I want. Even in the middle of winter."

He gave her a small, pleased smile, but she could tell he was still troubled. He stood there chewing on his lip for several moments. She waited patiently, knowing he would get around to it sooner or later.

"I'm real sorry about what happened to you, Miz McKenzie." He finally blurted out the words all in a rush.

Tears shimmered in his eyes. "It's my fault he took

you. I should have told someone he was back. He told me not to, but I shouldn't have listened. If I had told, Chief Harte might have found him before he hurt you."

He sniffled, then one tear slid down through his freckles, then another and another. She couldn't bear his distress any longer. Teary herself, she gathered him against her. "Shhh. Sweetheart, it's okay. None of it was your fault. I know it wasn't your fault."

"I didn't want to see him anymore, but he made me. Said I was a Sylvester, too, and I needed to spend time with my old man. I thought he would hurt my mom or Maddie if I didn't go."

"I know."

He swiped at his eyes with his sleeve and she handed him a tissue. "Do you hate me now because I was too chicken to tell and lied about everything? About Hob taking the school quarters and the mark on my back and everything else?"

"Oh, Corey. No. Of course not." How could she tell him she knew all too well what it was to share your life with the snarling creature fear could be? "On the contrary. I'm very proud of you. Even though you were afraid of your father, you finally did the right thing last night and told Chief Harte where to find me. It was a very brave thing to do."

He colored and looked down at her desk, mumbling a denial. She smiled at the top of his head. She had been right about Corey. Inside this troubled, rebellious child lurked a sweet boy who painted flowers for his teacher because he knew she liked them.

"So we're still friends?" Corey asked.

"The best," she assured him. "Now, why don't you take your seat again for the rest of art class?"

He nodded. With a watery smile he turned and started to return to his seat, then froze, his head turned toward the doorway of the class. Sarah followed his gaze and her heart began a fierce, slow rhythm.

Jesse's broad shoulders filled the door frame. He wore his police uniform, complete with Stetson and sidearm, and he looked big and masculine and wonderful. Her love for him was a thick, heavy ache in her chest.

He was watching Corey and she held her breath, praying Jesse wouldn't ruin the progress she had just made with the boy, that he wouldn't be angry with him for the secrets he had been forced to keep.

She should have known better. Jesse's expression held no condemnation. Though he said nothing, the look he shared with Corey was warm and approving. The boy basked in it. As he walked the rest of the way to his desk, his shoulders were a little bit straighter, his head a little higher.

Jesse's gaze returned to her and Sarah felt heat crawl up her cheekbones. She thought of the vast chasm between them the night before, the cold distance he had placed between them. Her emotions were already so ragged she wasn't sure she could endure more this morning.

He opened his mouth to speak to her, but before he could, Dylan and Lucy spied their uncle. They rushed to him, chattering eagerly. He returned their hugs, but his gaze never left Sarah's face as he bent his head to speak to the girls.

From her desk at the other side of the room, she couldn't hear more than the murmur of his low voice, but the girls' eyes widened. They looked at him, then back at their teacher with such amazed expressions that she could only wonder with a little clutch of apprehension what he had said to them.

The girls rushed back to their seats and Jesse straightened. The noisy bustle of her classroom seemed to fade into a dull murmur, leaving just the two of them.

"Miz McKenzie, may I speak with you out in the hall?"

Please. She couldn't break down in the middle of class. She cast her eyes around the classroom looking for an excuse and found Janie watching them both, her expression filled with avid curiosity.

"Go, Sarah," the art teacher said. "I've got everything covered in here."

Thanks for nothing. Left with no alternative, she rose slowly from her desk and followed him out into the hall, steeling her heart against more of this painful reserve.

"This really isn't a good time for me to give a statement," she said when the door was closed firmly behind her. "Could we do it after school?"

"I'm not here to take your statement."

"No?"

He shook his head but didn't elaborate, just watched her out of those blue eyes that saw entirely too much. Could he tell she had stayed up most of the night silently weeping over him? Over her own foolishness in offering her heart to a man who didn't want it?

She sincerely hoped not.

"How's your hand?" he asked.

Whatever she thought he might say, she hadn't expected that. "I…fine. Showering was a little tricky, but I managed. It's a little sore, but nothing I can't handle."

"I know. Have I ever told you how your ability to

cope with anything life throws at you never ceases to amaze?"

How was she supposed to answer that? Flustered, she looked down at her bandaged hand, then back into his blue eyes that watched her so steadily. "I'm sorry, Jesse. Art class will be over in a few moments and I have to get back to my class. If you're not here for a statement, how can I help you?"

"By forgiving me."

She blinked at him, stunned by the intensity of his words. "There's nothing to forgive."

"As my baby sister so bluntly informed me this morning, I was an idiot last night."

Had Cassie heard her weeping last night from the guest room? She must have, even though Sarah had tried fiercely to muffle her sobs with her pillow. Mortified heat soaked her cheeks and she swallowed hard, focusing her gaze on the brown carpet. "It doesn't matter."

"It matters to me. I hurt you. I would give anything to take it back, but I can't."

He was quiet for a long time, until she finally had to look up, to meet his glittering blue gaze. He reached for her hand, the bandaged one, and held it tenderly. "My only excuse is that I've never been in love before."

She stared at him. "What did you say?"

"I said I've never been in love before."

"And you...you are now?"

He smiled. "Don't sound so shocked, sweetheart. Why do you think I've been acting like an idiot? A certain schoolteacher I know is tying me up in knots inside."

She looked so astonished by the idea—then so intrigued—that if he hadn't already realized he loved her, he would have tumbled headfirst right then.

"I love you, Sarah," he murmured.

There. That wasn't so bad. Would her face go all soft, her eyes all bright, every time he said it? He couldn't wait to find out.

She sniffled. "You do?"

"Completely."

"Why?"

He laughed outright. "You're not supposed to ask me why. You're just supposed to accept it."

"How would you know? You said you've never done this before."

She had a point there. "Okay. Why do I love you? Because you're sweet and brave and wonderful and you make me feel like a better person when I'm with you."

There were stars in her eyes when she murmured his name, and he couldn't stand it any more. He had to kiss her.

"Wait," she said when he bent his head.

Jesse groaned and rested his forehead against hers. "You're killing me here, sweetheart. Do you need more reasons why I love you? There's plenty more where those came from. It just might take me a minute. I'm afraid I'm not thinking too clearly right now."

She shook her head, laughing a little at his disgruntled tone. "Later, maybe. I just wanted you to know that I… I feel the same way."

"Good," he said, reaching for her again.

No. She couldn't get away that easily, she had to say the words. "I love you, Jesse Harte. Because you're kind and strong and wonderful, and you made me laugh when I didn't think I ever could again."

He gazed at her, his blue eyes dark with emotion, then he cleared his throat. "Now can I kiss you?"

She smiled and wrapped her arms around his neck. He swept her to him, then that hard, beautiful mouth was on hers, full of love and joy and promise. She forgot where they were, forgot the aching loss of the night before, forgot everything but the wonder of being in his arms.

"What is the meaning of this?"

She gasped at the interruption and would have pulled away, but Jesse held her tight, looking over her head at the principal. She watched that devil's smile take over and he spoke in the slow drawl he sometimes used. "Well, see, Chuck, it's called kissing and it can be a real kick when you're doing it with the right person."

He turned that slow, sexy smile in her direction and Sarah forgot to breathe.

The principal glared at both of them. "Yes, Chief Harte, I believe I know what kissing is. I also know it doesn't belong in the classroom."

Jesse just shrugged. "I guess that's why we're out in the hall, then, Chuck."

It took every ounce of control to hold on to her laughter while the principal tried to figure out how to answer that. Eventually he gave up, just returned to his office with a grunt, and her laughter bubbled out. "You are a troublemaker, Jesse Harte."

"I've been trying to tell you, I'm reformed. Haven't you been listening?" After a moment, his grin faded and a hint of uncertainty appeared in his eyes. "I've had a pretty wild past, Sarah. Done plenty of things I'm not proud of. I want you to know that up front."

And she had been to hell and back. And survived.

"The past doesn't matter," she said. "It's where we go from here that's important."

He swept her into his arms again. When he finally broke the kiss this time, they were both breathless.

"Um, looks like we've drawn a crowd." His voice came out strangled.

She glanced back at her classroom door and found most of her students peering at them through the small window. Lucy and Dylan were right in the front, their eyes huge and their mouths hanging open.

"I guess Chuck is right," Jesse muttered. "This really isn't the place for this."

She stared at him in astonishment. "You're blushing! I can't believe you're blushing!"

"Look what a terrible influence you are already!"

She laughed. "Don't change too much. See, I've got this thing for bad boys…"

For this one, anyway.

* * * * *

**Don't miss *An Amish Wife for Christmas*,
coming November 2018 from Love Inspired.**

Visit the Author Profile page
at Harlequin.com for more titles.

LOVE THINE ENEMY

Patricia Davids

A time to weep, and a time to laugh;
a time to mourn, and a time to dance.
—*Ecclesiastes* 3:4

With endless thanks to my critique partners,
Deborah and Theresa. You girls rock!
So many words—so little paper.

Chapter 1

Cheryl Steele planted her hands on her hips. "Angie, in order to attend your wedding, I have endured the wrath of my director, risked losing the best role of my career and traveled miles out of my way. At this moment, I'm very close to regretting all that effort."

In the small dressing room at the back of an old stone church on the outskirts of Wichita, Kansas, Cheryl's sister ignored her ire. "You will go out to the ranch, won't you? For me?" Angie coaxed again. "It's practically on your way."

"It's fifty miles *out* of my way." Exasperated by her younger sibling's persistence, Cheryl tried changing the subject. "Your veil isn't straight. Let me fix it."

"My veil is fine. You didn't answer my question."

"Yes, I did. Two dozen times in the past two days. The answer is, *no!* Now, hush." Cheryl adjusted the veil then stepped back and gazed in poignant wonder at the vision in satin and lace before her.

"Well?" Angie demanded.

"You look...radiant...beautiful.... I don't think I

can find the right words. Jeff is a lucky man. I hope he knows it."

A mischievous grin curved Angie's lips. "He does. I tell him every chance I get."

Cheryl chuckled. "I bet you do."

Angie's smile faded. "Please say you will go out to the ranch before you leave the state. For me. Consider it a wedding present."

Cheryl sighed. "You don't give up, do you?"

"Not when it's important."

"There's nothing important about a few acres of grass and some rundown buildings in the middle of nowhere."

"It was our home. Our family is there."

"No! It was never a home after Mom died!" Cheryl shouted, then realized she was overreacting. She drew a deep breath and tried for a calmer tone. "I'm sorry. That ranch was the place we were stuck at until Cousin Harriet took us away. *She* gave us a home, and *you* are all the family I have left."

Irritated by her sister's persistence, Cheryl turned away and busied herself with the satin ribbons of Angie's bouquet of fragrant yellow roses. "I don't know why you keep harping on the subject."

"Harriet wanted you to go back, Cheryl. It was the last thing she asked of you before she died."

"I know." Cheryl's anger drained away replaced with an aching sense of loss. She owed everything to Harriet Steele.

The day their mother's cousin had descended like a whirlwind to defy their grandmother and whisk both girls away from the ranch had been like something out of a fairytale. At first, Cheryl had been terrified their grandmother would come and take them back. But after a month in Philadelphia, Harriet had called Cheryl and Angie into her study and told them they were to live with her for as long as they liked. She had granted them an opportunity of a lifetime—a chance to live where no one knew them—where no one looked down on them—where no one hit them ever again.

And she gave Cheryl an even greater gift—the opportunity to study ballet. Harriet had passed away five years ago, a month before Cheryl debuted in her first major role, but Cheryl knew that every step she danced, every triumph she achieved in her career, she owed directly to that staunch, remarkable woman. Knowing that she had failed to honor the woman's last request left a bruised place in her heart.

Cheryl glanced at her sister's troubled face. This was Angie's wedding day. She should be happy today. She deserved that and much more.

"Why is it so important to you?"

"Because I see that you need closure, even if you won't admit it. You're still hiding. You're still afraid, and it isn't healthy."

"I'm not afraid." Somehow, her words didn't carry the conviction she had hoped for.

"Then you'll go?"

"No."

"Not even for me?"

With her sister's disappointment so painfully clear, Cheryl found herself wavering. "It's not like Doris would welcome me with open arms. Besides, if she didn't care enough to come to your wedding, why should I make an effort to see her?"

"Grandma Doris is stuck in the past. She can't…

or won't…move on with her life. Seeing you, perhaps gaining your forgiveness, it could help. As for Jake—"

"Stop it!" Cheryl's anger came roaring back to life and she cut her sister off with a raised hand. "I don't want to hear another word about those people. Not one word!"

Angie caught Cheryl in an unexpected quick hug. "Oh, Cheryl, where we come from is part of what makes us who we are. Changing your name didn't change that."

"Now you sound like a psychologist."

Drawing back with a little laugh, Angie said, "That's because I'm studying to become one, remember?"

"I thought you were going to treat kids. I'm twenty-six years old, sis. Four years older than you."

Sadness settled over Angie's features. "You may be older, but in some ways you are still a hurting little girl. I would go back and change things if I could. So much of it was my fault."

Cheryl took her sister's face between her hands. "Don't ever say that. The blame belongs to Dad and Jake and Doris. They were the adults. You were a child."

"You were a child, too."

"I was old enough to know what I was doing. I don't regret anything."

"If that were true, you wouldn't have cut yourself off from Grandma Doris and Jake after Dad died. You can't let unresolved issues from the past ruin your life."

Cheryl looked at Angie in amazement. "Are you kidding? My life isn't ruined. I'm the lead ballerina in a fabulous dance company. What more could I want?"

"But are you happy?"

Was she? She was happy when she danced, but after the lights went down…when she went home to an empty apartment alone… Cheryl shook off the troubling thoughts. "Hey, I'm supposed to be asking you that question. You're the one getting married."

Angie's expression softened. "I'm very happy. God has blessed me in more ways than I can count. I give thanks to Him every day. He brought me a man of faith who is my true love."

Cheryl swallowed her bitter retort. Angie was entitled to her beliefs. As far as Cheryl was concerned, God, if there was one, hadn't bothered to intervene when He had been needed most. Cheryl didn't believe. Not anymore. It was another topic she decided to ignore.

Determined to sidetrack Angie's questions, Cheryl said, "I do wish you and Jeff could come see me dance. It's a wonderful production of *Alice in Wonderland,* and I *love* the role of Alice. Our performance tonight is a special one for disadvantaged children. That was one reason I really wanted the role. Most of the cities on our tour have at least one performance especially for children. You know I believe kids everywhere should have a chance to see how beautiful ballet is."

"I wish we could have worked it out, too. But that silly man of mine wants to take me to Hawaii for our honeymoon. Who am I to argue with a romantic like that?"

"All right. If I can't talk you out of marrying the fool, then let's get started so I can get on the road. The forecast is calling for snow. Snow in April! I'd almost forgotten how unpredictable the weather is out here. I'll never understand why you moved back."

"I came back because this is where my roots are. Yours are here, too."

"No, mine have been transplanted to New York, and they're thriving, thank you very much."

Angie studied Cheryl's face for a long second. "I wish I believed that."

"Enough with the analyzing."

"You can't keep avoiding the subject forever."

"I can, and I will. Drop it, Angela. I mean it. I don't have any family except you. That's the way it is."

"What if Jake asked to see you?"

"I'd say, 'Jake who?'"

"He's your brother."

"Half brother."

Angie reached out and took hold of Cheryl's hand. "Can't you consider forgiving him?"

"No. He got what he deserved and Eldorado Prison is *not* on my itinerary—so don't even ask."

Angie's shoulders slumped and she nodded in resignation. A knock sounded at the door and she went to open it. One of the ushers stood on the other side.

"Everything's ready," he said. "The guitarist wants to know if he should start playing or if you wanted to see him first."

Angie looked at Cheryl and sighed. She turned back to the usher. "Tell him to start playing, please."

Cheryl didn't understand the sorrow in her sister's voice. "What's the matter, honey?"

Angie held out her hand. "Why is it that the people I love are all so stubborn? Never mind. Let's go get me married."

Hours later, hunched over the steering wheel of her rental car, Cheryl peered through snowflakes the size of goose feathers as they filled the beams of her headlights. She was driving into a storm and into the middle of nowhere, and for what? Because she couldn't bear to remember the look of disappointment on her sister's face.

Tightening her grip on the wheel, Cheryl marveled at her own folly in leaving the turnpike for this deserted stretch of rural highway. She had a major performance later tonight. She should be resting in her hotel room by now. But when the exit sign for Highway 77 had appeared, she had taken it—almost against her will. That had been an hour ago—long enough to regret her decision a hundred times. Still, she had to be close now. She fought down the feeling of dread that rose with the thought. Seconds later, the gray shape of a rural mailbox loomed out of the snowy night.

She braked, feeling the car slide on the slick road as she turned into the barely discernable country lane and stopped.

At least the snow and the darkness hid the desolate landscape of the rolling Flint Hills from her sight. Only a dim gleam, from a porch light or perhaps a window, showed her where the old ranch house stood out on the prairie. She was home.

No sense of nostalgia filled her—only bitterness— a bitterness buried so deep she hadn't realized she still carried it until this moment. Staring at the flickering light in the distance, she suddenly understood why she had come.

She hadn't come because of Angie's pleadings. She had come to prove that nothing remained of the frightened girl who had left so many years ago.

"You can't hurt me anymore!" She wanted to shout those words in the old woman's face, but she didn't move. Her fingers grew ice-cold where she gripped the wheel as the old shame and fears crawled back to replace her bravado.

Coming here had been a mistake. She shifted the car into Reverse. She couldn't change the past. No one could. Cheryl Thatcher had effectively buried that past. Cheryl Steele didn't intend to resurrect it. Angie might believe in forgiveness, in healing old wounds, but Cheryl didn't. There was no forgiveness in this bleak land.

The tires whined as they spun in the snow, then suddenly they caught and the car lurched out of the lane and onto the pavement. Cheryl shifted into Drive, then stepped on the gas and didn't look back as she headed down the winding two-lane highway that would take her away. This time, forever.

Half an hour later, she raged at her own stupidity and bad luck. The snow came down faster and thicker with every mile. Her side trip had turned into a major mistake. A glance at the clock on her dash showed it was already half-past six. It would be close, but she could still make it. She *had* to. Her position was too important to risk by missing a performance. She would have to let Damon know she was running late. She dreaded placing the call. He wasn't an easy man to deal with at the best of times. Reaching down, she fumbled in her purse for her cell phone.

"Dumb cow," Sam Hardin muttered under his breath. "I try to do you a favor and this is the thanks I get. You make me ride home in the dark."

He glanced across the corral to the long, low shed where his cattle huddled together out of the wind. One stubborn heifer had refused to join the herd and had kept Sam searching for her long after the others were rounded up. He swung the metal gate shut with a clang after she ambled through. Now all his expectant cows and those with newborn calves at their sides were safe from the approaching storm. He dismounted to make sure the gate was secure, then leaned his arms on the top panel.

The truth was he didn't mind the ride or the time alone. He didn't have a reason to hurry home tonight. No one would be missing him. His grandfather might be up pretending to watch television while he dozed in his chair, but the twins were spending the night with Sam's mother, and without the girls' constant activity and chattering voices, the big house felt empty and lonely. As empty as his heart had felt since Natalie left him.

Beside him, his bay gelding snorted and shook his head. Drops of melting snow flew from his long mane, and his bridle jingled faintly in the cold air. Sam left off his somber musing and gathered the reins as he cast a worried look at the sky.

"I guess that stockman's advisory is going to be right on the money, tonight, Dusty," he said in disgust. "When was the last time it snowed like this in April?"

Mounting, Sam turned his horse for home. It was dark and snowing heavily by the time he reached the main pasture gate. He dismounted, opened it and led Dusty out, then he stretched the barbed wire strands taut and lowered the wire hoop over the gatepost. He turned his coat collar up against the rising wind and settled his hat more firmly on his head.

Remounting, he patted Dusty's neck and spoke to

the patient cow pony. "Only a little longer, fella. Then you can bed down in a warm stall with an extra ration of oats—you've earned it."

Dusty's ears perked at the mention of oats, and Sam laughed softly as he set his horse into a trot along the wide shoulder of the highway and headed for the ranch house. Suddenly, the glare of headlights blinded him as a car sped out of the snowy night and came straight at him.

At the last second, the car swerved, then pitched into a skid on the icy roadway. From the corner of his eye, Sam saw the vehicle fly past as his horse leapt sideways. It missed them by inches as it spun off the road, plunged down an embankment and slammed to a stop in a small group of trees.

Sam reined in his terrified horse. It had been a close call—too close. The thought of his daughters losing another parent sent a chill up his spine that had nothing to do with the temperature. *Thank You, dear Lord, for sparing me.*

With his heart still hammering wildly, Sam dismounted and stared at the car in the ditch. *Please, let everyone be okay.*

He left his horse at the edge of the road and made his way down the steep slope to the wrecked car. His boots slipped in the wet snow, and he skidded the last few feet to the bottom. He saw the driver's door was crushed against a cedar tree, so Sam made his way to the opposite side. What kind of idiot drove at such breakneck speed in this weather, anyway? He yanked open the passenger door and the dome light came on.

The idiot was a woman. Her blond head rested against the high seat back with her pale face half turned toward him. A thin line of blood trickled from her left temple, slipped down the slender column of her throat and disappeared beneath the scooped neckline of her red sweater.

Was she dead? The grim thought sent a curl of dread through him. He jerked off his gloves and leaned in to check for a pulse. He found one, strong and steady beneath his fingers. Relieved, he let out a breath he hadn't realized he was holding. Her eyes fluttered opened, and she blinked in the light.

"Lady, are you okay?" he asked, trying to sound calm.

She lifted a shaky hand to her head. "I don't think so."

Bitter-cold air swept around Sam and into the car as he held the door open. Her trembling was probably due to shock and not the freezing temperature, but he wasn't helping. Easing onto the slanting front seat, he closed the door. The interior light shut off, and the only illumination came from the headlights reflecting off the snow outside. He began to unknot the bandanna at his throat. "Where are you hurt?"

"I'm going to be so late," she muttered and closed her eyes.

Fright and cold made his fingers clumsy. With a jerk, the bandanna finally came loose. He pressed it to her bleeding temple. "Late for your own funeral, maybe. You're crazy to be driving so fast in this weather."

She pushed his hand away and turned a fierce scowl in his direction. "I'm not the crazy one here! You were riding a horse in the middle of a highway—at night—in a snowstorm! Do you have a death wish?" she shouted, then winced.

"Lady, I wasn't in the middle of the highway. I was on the shoulder when you came barreling at me. The road curves here, but I guess you didn't notice. You were over the center line and speeding toward the ditch. I just happened to be in your way."

She stared at him a long moment. "Oh."

"Yeah, oh!"

"Well, I missed you, didn't I?"

The last of his tension evaporated. "You did. You and the good Lord have my sincere thanks for that."

"I don't think He did me any favors."

"I wouldn't be too sure about that. If you'd gone off the other side of this curve at the speed you were traveling you might be dead now. There's a steep drop and a stone wall on that side."

He offered the bandanna again. "Are you hurt anywhere besides that cut on your forehead?"

"I'm not sure." Taking the cloth from him, she held it to her head and gave a hiss of pain. After a second, she focused on him again. Sudden tears welled up in her eyes. "I'm so sorry. Are you sure you're okay? Is your horse all right?"

"Dusty and I are fine, honest."

"It all happened so fast. I almost killed you." A sob escaped as a tear slipped down her pale cheek.

"Almost doesn't count except in horseshoes and hand grenades. Hey, yelling I can take, but tears—don't even go there," he warned.

She managed a trembling half smile. "I'll try."

Sam shot a quick look at the windshield. The wipers had stopped with the engine, and snow already covered the glass.

"We need to get out of this weather, and this car isn't

going anywhere. My ranch isn't far, but we should get going before this storm gets any worse. Can you move?"

"I think so." She shifted in the seat, then gave a sharp cry as she grabbed her left thigh with both hands.

"What's wrong?"

"My foot is caught," she answered through clenched teeth.

He saw a tremor race through her body. The temperature inside the car was dropping rapidly. He needed to get her someplace warm and soon.

"Here, take my coat while I have a look." He shrugged out of his sheepskin jacket and tucked it around her shoulders. They felt slender and fragile under his large, work-hardened hands. Her hair swept across the back of his wrist in a soft whisper stirring an unexpected awareness of her as a woman. He forced the thought to the back of his mind. He needed to concentrate on getting her out of here.

She bit her lip as she tried again to move. "My foot's wedged under something. I can't move it, and it hurts when I try."

Reaching over the steering column, he turned on the interior light. "Hold still while I check it out." Leaning down, he peered under the dash. "I'm Sam Hardin, by the way."

Cheryl's breath caught in a sharp gasp of surprise. He was one of the high-and-mighty Hardins. Her pulse began to pound. Feelings of shame and guilt rose like bile in the back of her throat. This couldn't be happening. Not now, not after all this time.

She glanced fearfully at the man beside her. Did he know who she was? Had he seen her family's pictures plastered across the local papers? Had he been at the trial that had sent her father and brother to prison? Did he know she had been her father's accomplice and that she'd done time for her crime?

Chapter 2

Cheryl drew a shaky breath and forced herself to calm down. Of course Sam Hardin didn't know who she was. How could he? It had all happened nearly fifteen years ago. She wasn't a child anymore; she was an adult now. Driving by the old ranch had dredged up painful feelings and the accident had unnerved her, that was all.

"I'm pleased to meet you, Mr. Hardin. My name is Cheryl Steele," she said at last, watching his reaction. She'd changed her name when she was old enough, wanting to be rid of even that reminder of her childhood. Only a handful of people knew she had once been Cheryl Thatcher.

"Pleased to meet you, Cheryl Steele, and you can call me Sam. So where are you from? That's an east-coast accent I hear, isn't it?"

"Manhattan," she confirmed, relaxing even more. It was true. The city had been her home for the past six years.

"You're from Manhattan, Kansas?" he asked from under the dash.

"No, Manhattan, New York," she said quickly. Something was wrong, seriously wrong. She tried but still couldn't budge her foot. Fiery agony shot up her leg. "The pain's getting worse."

"Okay, hold still while I see if I can move this metal."

"Hurry, please."

"You're a long way from home, New York. What are you doing way out here?"

"I thought I was taking a shortcut to Manhattan."

"You were taking a shortcut to New York City on this road?" he asked, his amusement evident.

"Very funny," she muttered in annoyance. "No, not a shortcut to *the* Manhattan. I'm trying to get *your* Manhattan. I need to be at the University Theater by seven at the latest. It's very important."

Her whole foot throbbed painfully now. She had to perform in less than an hour. She couldn't be trapped out here.

He grunted with effort as he tried to move the crumpled metal. "It gave a little. Try now."

Her foot wouldn't budge. Panic swelled in her and she struggled against the confining metal. "Please, get me out of here!"

"I will. Take it easy."

"I'm a ballet dancer," she whispered. What if her injury was serious? What if she couldn't dance? Didn't he understand how frightened she was?

He sat up beside her. Softly, he cupped her cheek with one hand and wiped a tear away with his thumb. "You'll be dancing again in no time, New York. Right now we have to keep our heads. Your foot is caught between the floor and the side wall where it's caved in. I'll get you out, but it may take a bit."

She managed a nod. "Okay. I understand."

"Thatta girl."

Cheryl worked to regain control of her emotions. He was right. She had to keep her head. She needed to focus on something besides the fear and the pain. She had learned that trick early in life and used it often in her grueling career. She chose his face.

His rugged features softened when he smiled. It made the creases in his lean cheeks deepen and small crinkles appear at the corner of his eyes. His mouth lifted a little higher on one side, giving his smile a roguish charm.

Suddenly, she was grateful to have him in the dimness beside her. His hand was gentle when he'd touched her face. His voice was calm and steady. He inspired trust, and that thought surprised her. For most of her life she had considered ranchers to be the enemy—something else she had learned early on.

He said, "I need to find a way to pry this metal apart."

"There should be a jack in the trunk," she volunteered.

"Good thinking." He flashed her a big, heart-stopping, crooked grin. "Kinda smart for a city girl, aren't you?"

His teasing comment amused her even though she suspected he was simply trying to distract her from the seriousness of the situation. Well, she could play city-girl versus country-boy, too. After all, she was a rising star with the New York Theater Ballet. She had performed far more difficult roles.

"I don't imagine you keep a jack in your saddle-bags, cowboy. Or do you?" she quipped.

"No, ma'am, I don't." He slipped into an exaggerated drawl that would have done a Texan proud. "My ol' hoss has gone lame, but he ain't never gone flat."

Cheryl tried not to smile at his poor joke.

Pulling the keys from the ignition, he grinned as he opened the car door. "I'll be back in a jiffy."

She nodded, but she had to fight another wave of panic as the door closed behind him, leaving her alone. She took several deep breaths until she felt in control of her emotions. A glance out the windshield told her what she already knew. She was going to miss tonight's performance.

Her understudy would be able to dance the part, but Damon Sands, their director, was going to be furious. He'd already been unhappy about Cheryl's plans to leave the company during their short break to travel to her sister's wedding. Only her repeated assurances that she'd be back in plenty of time for the production had mollified him. Now, she'd be lucky if she didn't lose her position after this fiasco. Damon had an unforgiving nature, especially when it came to his work.

She searched around for her cell phone but couldn't find it. Moments before the wreck she had tried to use her phone only to see that it displayed No Signal. Chances were it wouldn't work even if she had it in her hand. She was stuck with no way of letting Damon know where she was.

Stuck in the middle of nowhere, that's where she was. No, worse. She was stuck in the middle of the Flint Hills. Until two months ago, nothing could have induced her to return here. Nothing, that was, until the call from Angie. Even as she'd listened to her sister's deliriously happy voice begging her to come for the wedding, Cheryl had hesitated. She'd given in to her sister's pleading only because the wedding would be in Wichita. A hundred miles seemed far enough away from their old home to let her feel safe about a brief visit.

Yet, even with this catastrophe, Cheryl was glad she had come. She smiled as she remembered the beautiful ceremony in the tiny church decorated with ivy and deep yellow roses. The strains of a classical guitar floating down from the choir loft had filled the air with the sounds of love transformed into music.

A blast of cold air jerked her back to the present as Sam opened the car door and slipped in beside her. Working quickly, he positioned the jack and after several turns, the metal pinning her began to spread. He eased her foot loose and she bit her lip to keep from crying out at the pain.

"I'm sorry if I hurt you," he said.

Unable to speak, she nodded. Her foot throbbed wildly.

"At least you're free." His bright tone made her want to hit him.

"Can you ride a horse, New York?"

Her gaze flew to his. "You're kidding, right?" One look told her he wasn't. She nearly groaned at the idea of hanging her leg over a horse.

"Of course I can ride," she answered with more confidence than she felt. She hadn't been near a horse in fifteen years.

"Good, I'd hate for this to be your first lesson. Do you have a coat or something to keep you warm? The wind is bitter outside."

"It's on the backseat."

He retrieved it for her. After returning his coat,

Cheryl slipped into her own, then located her purse on the floor. She gritted her teeth as she prepared to leave the relative safety of the car.

Sam stepped out and pulled on his coat, glad of its retained warmth. Thick snow swirled past his face. Glancing up, he saw Dusty standing at the edge of the road with his head down and his rump to the wind. A whistle brought the horse to him, and Sam turned to Cheryl. He grinned at the expression on her face as she stared at Dusty. "Don't worry, New York, I won't let you fall off."

"I'm not worried about falling off, cowboy. I'm worried about freezing solid up there," she shot back.

"Freeze on the horse, be home in thirty minutes and thaw out in a hot bath, or freeze in the car and wait for the next taxi to come by. It's your choice."

"When you put it that way…" She sent him a suspicious look. "A hot bath—you promise?"

"Yup. Cross my heart."

He swung up into the saddle and offered her his hand. She jumped as he lifted her and swung her up behind him. To his surprise, she made the move with ease and grace. He glanced back at her face and saw her lips pressed into a hard, tight line, but she didn't complain. Miss New York had guts, all right. She settled her hands at his hips, but he pulled her arms tight around his waist.

It felt good. It felt right. It had been a long time since a woman had held him.

He turned the horse toward home, glad he had two long snow-covered miles to remind himself she was an injured woman who needed his care, nothing more. She was only passing through.

The elegant dancer behind him might stir his senses,

but he wasn't foolish enough to act on that attraction. He certainly wasn't looking to get involved with any woman again. Not after Natalie. He would never give another woman the power to hurt him or his children the way his ex-wife had.

Cheryl clung to Sam and kept her face pressed to his back, but soon, even his large, powerful frame offered little comfort. Her head and her leg throbbed with every step the horse took. The wind chilled her to the bone, and there was nothing she could do except endure it. That was how she remembered this country. As something to be endured.

"How much farther?" she yelled over the wind. Her purse strap slipped off her shoulder and slid down her arm to bump against the horse's side, but she didn't loosen her grip to pull it up as she huddled behind Sam.

"Not much. Less than half a mile," he shouted back.

In spite of his encouragement, it seemed like hours before the horse finally stopped. Lifting her aching head, Cheryl saw they stood in front of a small porch surrounded by a wooden railing already piled high with snow. Snow-laden cedars stood on either side of the porch hiding most of the pale, native limestone house from her view, but the warm glow of the porch light was as welcome as all the bright lights of Broadway.

She released her frozen grip on Sam. He swung his leg forward over the horse's neck and slid down. Turning, he lifted her off the horse and lowered her gently to the ground. Balancing on one foot, she clung to his shoulders. Then, without a word, he swept her up into his arms.

She wrapped her hands around his neck, and her gaze moved to his face. She became aware of the strength in the arms that held her and the intensity of his gaze as he studied her in return. Suddenly, she felt warm and breathless.

An echo of that awareness flared in his eyes. Then, just as quickly, his gaze cooled. "Let's get you inside."

Sam forced his attention away from the sweet, soft curve of her lips. He quickly climbed the steps, wrestled one-handed with the door, then stepped inside. After setting his guest gently on the high-backed bench in the entry, he took in her battered appearance.

She was as pale as the snow outside. Streaks of dried blood ran from a bruised cut on her temple down the left side of her face and neck. Blond hair, slightly longer than shoulder length, framed her face in soft waves. Her eyes were a startling sapphire-blue surrounded by thick, dark blond lashes. But when she looked up at him, he saw pain and exhaustion filling them. The total sum of her fragile beauty stunned him like the kick of a horse.

"Are you okay?" he managed to ask.

She nodded. "I just need to warm up."

"Rest here. I have to put Dusty away. I'll be back in a few minutes." He started out the door, then turned. "Oh, watch out for the cat. He's Bonkers."

She glanced around, then closed her eyes with a grimace as she leaned her head back. "Crazy cowboy owns an insane cat. Why doesn't that surprise me?"

Chuckling, Sam left the house and quickly led Dusty to the barn. He unsaddled the horse, fed him a measure of grain and gave him a fast rubdown.

"So, what do you think of her?" he asked. Dusty kept his nose buried in his oats. Sam paused in his brushing. "What, no comment? It's not every day an ugly old cow pony gets to give a real ballerina a ride. Me—I think she's drop-dead gorgeous."

Dusty snorted once. Sam grinned and resumed the quick, short strokes of his brush. "You're right, looks aren't everything. For whatever reason, the good Lord has placed her in my care. I'll put her up for the night, then get her out of here first thing tomorrow." He gave the horse a final pat and left.

Pausing outside the barn door, Sam turned up the collar of his coat. The blowing snow piled in growing drifts around the barn. If this storm didn't let up soon, he could be stuck with his unexpected guest for more than one night. The idea didn't annoy him the way it should have. Instead, a strange feeling of anticipation grew as he started toward the house.

The sound of the door opening and a gust of frigid air announced Sam's return. Cheryl eyed her rescuer closely as he paused inside the entry to hang up his coat and hat. As he raked a hand though his dark brown hair, curls flattened by his hat sprang back to life, and she noticed a touch of gray at his temples. He was older than she'd first thought. Perhaps somewhere in his early thirties.

As he turned toward her, she guessed he had to be six feet two at least. He towered over her, but he wasn't intimidating. His eyes were warm and friendly. A rich hazel color, they were framed with thick, dark lashes any woman would envy. He didn't have a classically handsome face, she thought, yet there was something appealing about it.

She gave herself a swift mental shake. What on earth was wrong with her? She had more sense than to be moonstruck by a handsome man with a pair of smiling eyes. Plus, he was a rancher. *And* a Hardin. She'd seen

enough of that judgmental and unforgiving lot in her
youth to last her two lifetimes. The chiming of a clock
sent her thoughts back to her real problem.

"Thanks for the rescue, cowboy, but I can't stay."

"My granddad lives with me if you're worried about
your reputation."

"It's not that. I have to get to Manhattan."

"You aren't going anywhere tonight."

"It's important."

"Unless you can change the weather or sprout wings
and fly, you're stuck."

She sighed in defeat. "May I use a telephone? I lost
my cell phone in the car. I have to let someone know
what's happened to me."

"There's a phone in the living room," he said, stoop-
ing to gather her in his arms again.

"I can make it on my own," she protested.

"Not till I see how bad that leg is." He swept her up
effortlessly, carried her into the living room, and set
her gently on the sofa. Bending over her leg, he eased
off her shoe and sock.

A hiss of pain escaped Cheryl's clenched lips, and
her hands grew white-knuckled as she gripped the sofa
cushions.

He let out a slow whistle. "Lady, you aren't going be
dancing on this any time soon. You need X-rays, maybe
even a cast. I'll get some ice for it. That may keep some
of the swelling down."

Cheryl opened her eyes when the pain receded and
stole a quick peek at her throbbing foot. Her ankle, dis-
colored and swollen, looked as bad as it felt, but she'd
danced on worse. Her art demanded it.

With her career in mind, she glanced around for

the phone, then paused as she caught sight of her sur-
roundings. For a moment, she felt as Alice might have
when she stepped through the looking glass. The small
porch flanked by cedars had given her the wrong impression. Instead of an old farmhouse, she found herself in a home that looked like a color layout for *Better
Homes and Gardens*. A series of floor-to-ceiling windows made up one entire wall of the huge room. To her
right, a wide staircase led down to a lower level, and to
her left was an open, airy country kitchen.

A bold Indian-blanket pattern covered the sofa she
rested on. Its brick red, hunter-green and royal-blue
tones were reflected in the room's brightly colored ac-
cents. Matching love seats flanked the sofa and formed
a cozy seating area arranged at the edge of a large, patterned rug. Polished wooden floors and a rough beam
ceiling lent added warmth to the room.

Looking over the open counter into the kitchen, she
watched Sam move deftly, getting ice, a plastic bag and
a towel. He seemed at home in the kitchen. That didn't
exactly fit the rugged cowboy images she remembered.

He returned and handed her a small ice bag. "For
that bump on your head."

"Thank you." Cheryl took the bag and held it to her
temple. He placed a second pack carefully around her
ankle.

For such a big man, he had gentle hands. She shivered when he touched her bare skin. Abruptly, she
pulled her foot away. "I can manage."

Her rapid heart rate had to be from the pain and
nothing else. "You have a fabulous home," she said to
distract him when he shot her a puzzled look.

"You were expecting a dilapidated log cabin?" An engaging sparkle glinted in the depths of his eyes.

"Oh, not in Kansas," her reply was quick and flippant. "Everyone knows there aren't any trees out here. I was expecting a soddy."

"A soddy?" His eyebrows shot up in surprise. "I'm impressed you know the term. Sorry to disappoint you, New York. We don't live in sod houses anymore."

"Don't tell me you have electricity and indoor plumbing, too?" she asked in mock amazement.

He stood and grinned at her. "Smart aleck. Make your phone calls. I'll let Granddad know we have a guest for the night."

Cheryl worried briefly that his grandfather might be someone who would recognize her, but her other concerns pushed the worry aside. She had more pressing problems. She picked up the phone and punched in Damon's cell phone number. When he finally answered, he had little sympathy for her dilemma.

"This tour is a showcase of my work. A second-rate dancer can make it look second rate. How can you do this to me?"

"I'm sorry, Damon. It was an accident. I'll catch up with you as soon as I can get another rental car."

"How bad is your foot?" he asked with grudging concern.

"Only a sprain. It'll be fine in a few days."

"I hope so. I don't need to remind you that good reviews mean good attendance, and good attendance means better funding for the company. If this tour doesn't go well, we'll all be looking for work."

"I know. I'll be there as soon as I can."

"Two days! We open in Kansas City in two days.

Don't let me down, Cheryl. Work is hard to find when word gets out that a dancer is unreliable."

It was a threat—one she didn't dare ignore. She was on her way up in her career, but Damon Sands could make things hard for her if he chose.

"I'll be there," she promised. Nothing was going to keep her from finishing this tour.

"You'd better be," he snapped and hung up.

The last call she placed went to the rental car company. They weren't happy with her either. She'd just finished that conversation when Sam walked back into the room.

"You're looking kind of glum, New York. Is your boyfriend mad at you for standing him up?"

She pressed her fingers to her throbbing temples. "My boss, not my boyfriend, and, yes, he's angry. This tour is important to him, and to me."

"Tour?" he asked, clearly puzzled.

"I dance, remember? My ballet company is on an eight-city tour for the spring. We've been performing in Tulsa for the past two weeks. We were scheduled to give a one-night-only performance at the University Theater in Manhattan tonight. From there, we go on to Kansas City for a week, then two weeks in Denver, two weeks in Salt Lake City, then Reno, Fresno and San Francisco."

"How'd you get separated from your company?"

"That is a long story."

"I'm not going anywhere and neither are you," he said, sitting beside her.

He was right. She tried to keep the bitterness out of her voice as she recounted the tale that had landed her almost in his lap. Literally.

"My sister called a few months ago to tell me she was getting married. She knew I'd be on this tour, so we planned her wedding to coincide with a break in my itinerary. The wedding was today."

"Your sister lives near here?"

"In Wichita. We had it all planned," Cheryl said with a shake of her head. "I flew from Tulsa to Wichita for the wedding. I couldn't get a flight into Manhattan today so I rented a car. The rest you know."

She pushed back a strand of hair and sighed. "My company will travel to Kansas City tomorrow with or without me."

She wouldn't think about what would happen if she couldn't join them—if her foot was broken, not just sprained, and she couldn't work for weeks.

"We can't do anything about it tonight," Sam said.

He was right. She would simply have to make the best of it.

"I doubt the road to Manhattan is even open now," Sam continued. "Soon as the weather clears, I'll get you to Kansas City even if we have to ride Dusty all the way."

The twinkle in his eyes proved he was trying to cheer her. She held up her hands clasped together and begged, "Not that! Please! Not another ride on Dusty."

"Now, that will hurt his feelings."

"Not as much as he hurt my behind."

Cheryl gazed at Sam's amused face feeling oddly happy in spite of her predicament. It was easy to trade banter with him. Why was that? He was everything that she had loathed, once upon a time.

Still smiling, he stood and held out his hand. "Come

on. I've got the perfect answer for your saddle sores. I ran a bath for you while you were on the phone."

She brightened. "That's right. You did promise me a hot bath to get me to come home with you."

"And you accepted, cheap date that you are." He picked her up, and she circled his neck with her arms.

Her pulse began to race once more, and she didn't try to delude herself—it wasn't due to the pain in her foot. She tried for a nonchalant tone. "Obviously, I need to raise my standards. Next time you'll have to promise me chocolate and roses."

His gaze met hers for a long instant. "It's a deal," he said softly. She looked away first.

He carried her through a doorway beyond the kitchen and through a huge bedroom to the bath. The room, tiled in stark black and white, held a large, black whirlpool tub in one corner, while a separate shower area took up the opposite wall. Inviting steam rose from the tub.

She stared in amazement. "Wow! This is awesome."

"Compliments can go to my ex-wife. It's her design."

"She has great taste."

"So she told me. In everything except husbands."

"Your bathroom is bigger than the living room of my apartment in Manhattan. Your wife let you keep a house like this after a divorce? What'd she get?"

When he didn't answer, Cheryl glanced at his face. The smiling, teasing cowboy had vanished. It was as if his face had turned to stone.

"She got her freedom," he said at last.

Chapter 3

Sam turned away, but not before Cheryl glimpsed the pain in his eyes. Instantly, she regretted prying into his private life. She knew what it was to carry around things too painful to talk about.

He indicated some clothes on a small wicker stool beside the tub. "I've left you a robe and some sweats you can use when you're done. Call me if you need anything."

He was gone before she could think of a way to apologize. Feeling like a heel, she pulled off her sweater and noticed the bloodstains on her clothes. One more thing ruined—rental car, job, favorite sweater—what next? Determined to salvage her clothes, she hopped to the sink and began filling the basin with cold water. She glanced into the mirror and nearly screamed at her gruesome reflection. With shaky hands, she began to wash away the blood from her face.

Suddenly, her lip started to tremble as hot tears stung her eyelids. She dashed them away with the heels of her hands. She would not cry. Hopping back to the tub, she tried to stifle the sobs building inside her. She sat on the rim and discovered another problem. She couldn't get her tight-legged pants off over her swollen ankle. It was the last straw.

Outside Sam had rested his head against the bathroom door as his anger ebbed away. Three years, and he still couldn't talk about Natalie's cheating and desertion without feeling a bitterness that nearly choked him. When she'd left him with their two small daughters to raise alone, the hurt had gone bone-deep. The old saying, *Love is blind,* was no joke. It had been all too true for him.

I've tried to forgive her, Lord, but I still can't find that in my heart. Grant me Your grace. Help me heal the wounds she left behind and keep me from making such a mistake again. For my children's sake, I beseech You.

If he ever became involved with another woman, it'd be with someone who wanted to be a mother to his children. Someone who'd put the twins first, before anything else, and give them the love they deserved. In spite of his surprising attraction to the woman he had rescued tonight, he knew that a New York ballerina didn't fit that bill.

Lord, I once let my emotion rule my head and I made a mistake that I'm still paying for. I know that with Your guidance I am wiser now.

He might be wiser, but that didn't stop him from feeling attracted to his visitor. He appreciated Cheryl's sharp wit and quick sense of humor. And he couldn't help but notice that she made a pleasant armful when he held her. He reproached himself for the foolish thought. She was injured, and she needed his help. He turned away from the door, but paused when he heard a noise from inside.

He didn't want to intrude on her privacy, but he wanted to be sure she was okay. He pressed his ear to the door and heard her muffled sobbing. His heart gave a queer little tug at the sound.

She had every right to a good cry. A night like to-night would have taken the stuffing out of anyone. When she called his name, it had surprised him. He took a deep breath, entered the room and stopped short.

She sat on the edge of the tub wrapped in his large robe. Her injured ankle rested on the tub edge with her dark pants bunched around it.

"What's wrong?" he asked.

"I c-can't get m-my pants off o-over my f-foot."

Each hiccuping sob tore at his heart. He watched her struggle to regain control. She didn't like to cry in front of him—he could tell by the way she scrubbed at her tears as they fell. He wanted to offer some comfort but sensed that she would rather recover her composure on her own. He turned to the problem at hand, or rather, at foot.

She was right. Her pant leg wouldn't come off over her swollen ankle. He found a pair of scissors, sat on the tub rim, and began to slit her pant leg up one side.

"The last time I had to do this was when Kayla got a big splinter in her knee. Kayla's one of my daughters. Lindy is her twin. They turned five last October.

"Anyway, Kayla had a long wooden sliver through her jeans. I had to cut them off before I could see how badly she was hurt. Fortunately, it wasn't deep. I thought I was doing fine until I put a bandage on Kayla's knee. Soon as I did, Lindy started wailing."

"Wh-Why?"

He glanced at Cheryl and grinned. "She said because she and Kayla weren't ''dentical' anymore. So I had to cut off *her* jeans and put a bandage on her knee too."

Cheryl smiled. "Identical twin girls. I'll bet that's a handful."

"Yes, they are, but I wouldn't have them any other way." He slipped her pants gently over her foot. "There you go."

"Th-thanks for your help."

"Don't mention it. Mom was a teacher, and she taught me to be gallant at all costs."

Startled, Cheryl looked up. Her fingers grew icy-cold, and she pushed them into the deep pockets of his robe as fear tightened the muscles in the back of her neck.

"Does your mother teach near here?" she asked, trying to sound as if she was making polite conversation and not desperate to know the answer.

"No, she's retired."

Eleanor Hardin had been her junior-high principal. Could Sam be Eleanor's son? How old had her principal been? Cheryl tried to think, but she could only recall the woman with a child's vision. "What about your father?" she asked casually.

"He passed away a few years ago. My grandfather lives here with the twins and I. Nobody knows cattle like Gramps does. You'd never know he was seventy-five. He rides almost every day. Well, I should leave you to finish your bath instead of standing here babbling while the water gets cold." He all but bolted out the door, closing it behind him with a bang.

Relieved at being left alone, Cheryl shed Sam's robe

and sank into the whirlpool, leaving her foot with its ice pack propped on the rim. After all the time she'd spent trying to forget the past, why had she ended up so close to it all again?

Was this what Angie had wanted: to see her big sister exposed and shamed? No, Cheryl didn't believe that. Angie's heart was in the right place, and her intentions were good. Cheryl knew she had only herself to blame. She had chosen the road that led to this disaster.

She kneaded her temples trying to ease the headache pounding away inside her skull. She had to think.

Even if Sam was Eleanor's son, he still had no idea who she was. As long as he continued to think of her as a New York dancer, she'd be safe. And what if he did find out? It wasn't as if she were wanted for a crime. But people out here had long memories and unforgiving natures; she knew that from personal experience. A lot of them would remember that Hank Thatcher's oldest daughter had been in reform school for helping her father steal cattle.

If anyone discovered who she really was, the old story would be out in a flash. Her juvenile records might be sealed, but that wouldn't stop the press from having a field day with the story. No doubt, Grandma Doris would be happy to tell the tale of how her rebellious granddaughter had ended up behind bars. The thought of reliving those painful days made Cheryl feel ill.

It didn't matter what Angie thought, or what Harriet Steele had intended, Cheryl knew she would never go back to the ranch again. It wasn't worth the risk. She had worked too long and too hard to let anything jeopardize the career she loved. She rubbed a weary hand over her face. She had to get away from here.

The soothing hot water began to ease her aches and pains. Slowly she relaxed, and her feeling of panic faded. She was safe for tonight. The storm might keep her here, but it would also keep everyone else away. First thing tomorrow, Sam would drive her to Kansas City, and she could leave Flint Hills behind forever.

Feeling somewhat better, she finished her bath and washed her hair, being careful of the lump on her temple. After that, she climbed out of the tub and pulled on the gray sweatpants and sweatshirt Sam had left for her. They were big, but comfortable. A search through his medicine cabinet turned up a roll of wide tape, and she expertly wrapped her foot and ankle. It hurt, but she knew it would feel better once she had it taped.

With that done, she washed out her sweater and was pleasantly surprised to find the bloodstains had come out. She hung it to dry on the towel rack and left the room.

Sam came up the stairs in time to see her crossing his living room. Dressed in his old sweats with a towel wrapped turban-style around her head, he could only marvel that anyone could look so graceful and appealing while she hopped on one foot.

He shook his head in resignation. So much for his stern lecture to himself about caring for helpless, injured women. He headed to the bathroom and rummaged in the medicine cabinet until he found a small bottle of pain pills left over from his last run-in with a moody bull.

She was reclining on the sofa when he entered the living room again. Her face looked freshly scrubbed, not a trace of tears anywhere. In his sweats with the sleeves rolled back and a towel around her hair, she looked comfortably at home—as though she belonged here. He dismissed that crazy thought and offered her the pills. "Are you allergic to any medications?"

"Not that I know of. Why?"

"I called the hospital while you were in the tub. They said you could take these if you weren't on any medication or allergic to them."

She took the bottle and read the label. "I've taken these before. They make me sleepy, though."

"That might not be a bad thing. You did a good job wrapping that ankle." The professional-looking bandage impressed him.

"Injuries are a fact of life in my profession. You have to get good at taping joints."

He brought her a glass of water, and she took two of the tablets. "Are you hungry?" he asked.

"A little," she admitted.

"How about a bowl of homemade chicken soup? It'll only take me a minute to heat it up."

She arched one eyebrow. "Don't tell me you know how to make soup from scratch? My image of cowboys may never be the same."

"Good. I haven't had a gun fight in ages, and I never sing to my horse," he said, heading into the kitchen.

"I'll bet that makes Dusty happy. Anything else I need to know to completely destroy my concept of macho Western men?"

"I can use a vacuum cleaner, and I'm an architect."

"An architect—really?" She glanced around. "Is this one of your designs? It's beautiful."

"Natalie and I collaborated on it."

"Natalie?"

"My ex-wife." For some reason, he suddenly felt the

need to explain. "We split up about three years ago. We met in college, two budding architects hot to leave our mark on the world. We seemed to have a lot in common. As it turned out, we didn't. We lived in Kansas City for a while, but after Dad died, I gave up the business and came back to ranch full-time. She didn't care for life out here. She met someone else and that was that."

"I'm sorry. Do you see your children often?"

"The twins live with me, not with their mother." He looked up with a brittle smile. "She's in China, the last we heard."

"That's a long way from Kansas. What does she do?"

"She's the International Design Director for some big-shot hotel over there."

"Sounds important."

"I'm sure she thinks so."

"Where are your children?" She looked toward the stairs.

"Fortunately for you, they're spending the night with my mother."

Her head snapped around. "Why is that fortunate for me?" she asked, her tone oddly sharp.

Out in the kitchen, Sam laughed. "Let me see if I can enlighten you. 'Why is the sky blue? What holds the clouds up? Why do rocks come in different sizes? Why can't we eat grass like the cows? Why does the sun always come up in the east? Why do we call it *east?*' They never stop talking."

Cheryl smiled, but her mind was racing. How was she going to avoid meeting more of Sam's family? Even if his mother wasn't Eleanor, there had been other Hardins at Jake's and her father's trial. Cheryl was dying to ask specific questions, but she didn't want to arouse Sam's suspicions.

"They sound charming. Do you think they'll be back before I leave?"

"No. Believe me, you do not want to ride in a car with them all the way to Kansas City."

"And your grandfather, will he be joining us? I'm not exactly dressed for company."

"Gramps was asleep when I looked in." Sam carried in two steaming bowls of soup and two glasses of milk on a tray and set it on the coffee table beside her. "I'll pick the girls up on my way back from Kansas City. What about you? Do you have a husband, children?"

Cheryl relaxed once she realized she wasn't going to meet more of his family. "No, no ball and chain or rug rats for me. I can't even take care of a parakeet." She took a bowl of soup from the tray.

Looking up, she realized he wasn't amused by her flippant remark. She had made it sound as though she didn't like children.

"My work comes first," she explained. "I don't have room in my life for anything but dancing. Ballerinas don't usually have long careers. A husband and children will have to wait. Besides, while I was in school I earned money by working at a daycare center. That was enough kid-time to last me for a several more years."

"What about other family?" he asked.

Briefly, she considered how to answer. When in doubt, tell the truth—just not all of it. "There's only my sister. I have a half brother somewhere, but we've never kept in touch. My parents are both dead."

A *half brother somewhere* was partly true. As far as

she knew, Jake was still in prison. Harriet had kept in touch with him, but she was gone now.

"I always wanted a brother but all I got was a little sister. Becky lives in Denver. I don't get to see her as much as I would like."

To change the subject, Cheryl said, "This is good soup, cowboy."

"Thanks, but you don't have to sound so surprised."

There was a lot about the man that was surprising to Cheryl. She only hoped that his good cooking was the last shock in store for her tonight.

They ate in companionable silence and listened to the sound of the storm outside as the driving snow hissed softly against the tall windows. When she finished, he gathered up her tray and carried it into the kitchen. She tried to hide a yawn, but he saw it.

Walking back to the sofa, he held out his hand. "Come on, New York, it's time you went to bed. You can barely keep your eyes open."

"I thought I would sleep here." She patted the sofa and looked away, uncomfortable with his intense scrutiny.

"Take my bed. You'll be more comfortable, and the bathroom is only a hop away. The guestroom is on the lower level, and I don't think you should tackle the stairs. I'll sleep down there."

He made sense, and it wasn't as if she were throwing him out of his bed to sleep on the floor or something. Another yawn convinced her she'd probably fall asleep standing on one foot when the pain pills really kicked in.

"Okay, but I can get there by myself."

"At least lean on me so you don't fall."

She hung on to his arm as they made their way to his bedroom. At the edge of the bed, she sat down just as a yowling, hissing ball of fur erupted from underneath it and attacked her good foot. Cheryl shrieked in surprise and jerked her legs up on the bed.

Sam reached down and scooped up the snarling fury. "Hey, is that any way to treat a guest? Behave yourself. Cheryl, I'd like you to meet Bonkers."

Draped over Sam's arm, the fat, yellow feline turned to stare at her. He wore a smirk remarkably like the Cheshire Cat mask one of her fellow dancers wore in the ballet.

"We call him Bonkers," Sam explained, "because normally he's very sedate, but every once in a while—"

"He just goes bonkers," Cheryl finished. "I get it." She studied the man who held the cat and said, "This tendency runs in the family?"

His grin widened. "Occasionally."

Cheryl massaged her foot. "I was down to only one good foot and now that's full of claw marks."

Sam turned instantly contrite. "Did he hurt you? Bonkers is usually careful not to break the skin. Let me take a look."

"No. I'm fine." She pointed toward the door. "Take the menace and leave."

With a brief salute, Sam did as he was told, taking the cat with him. Cheryl watched the door close, then flopped back and stared at the ceiling fan over the bed.

What was it about Sam Hardin that she found so attractive? They'd met under dramatic circumstances, that could be part of it. She admitted he was good-looking in a rugged sort of way. He was also kind and funny, but it was something more that. Something she couldn't put her finger on, something she didn't want to examine too closely.

In the end, she decided it was a combination of too much excitement and the strong pain pills. Knowing that she would feel more like her old, sensible self in the morning, she crawled under the thick quilt and settled in. For a while, the painful throbbing in her foot kept sleep at bay, but soon the pain pills did their work, and she drifted off.

Sam fed the cat and retreated to the guestroom downstairs. As he lay in the unfamiliar bed, sleep eluded him, and he spent a long time staring at the ceiling. She was sleeping above him.

He berated himself for acting like a fool, but it didn't help. The woman was dangerous to his peace of mind. Why did she have to be the first one to interest him since Natalie? Why did it have to be a woman who belonged somewhere else?

Come on, Sam, you're thirty-three years old. You're not some kid. You've been there—done that. You don't need her kind of trouble no matter how attractive she is.

He punched his pillow into shape for the tenth time. This was nothing more than the excitement of the night. After all, it wasn't as if he made a habit of rescuing beautiful, intriguing women. Tomorrow he'd drive her to Kansas City and deposit her with her dancing friends, and that would be the end of it.

The sound of the wind finally lulled him to sleep, but Cheryl's face played in and out of his dreams leaving him feeling restless. In the morning, he woke feeling anything but refreshed. He climbed out of bed,

302   Love Thine Enemy

dressed and went out to work off his sour mood with chores and shoveling snow.

An incessant ringing woke Cheryl from her drug-induced sleep. She fumbled for the phone on her bedside stand without opening her eyes.

"Hello?" she mumbled into the receiver with her face still pressed into the pillow.

Silence answered her. She tried again a little louder. "Hello?"

"Is Sam there?" a sharp, feminine voice asked.

"Ah—Sam who?" Cheryl muttered, wishing she could just go back to sleep.

"Samuel Hardin. My son."

Cheryl's eyes snapped open. Quickly, she took in the unfamiliar room. In a flash, memory returned.

"Let me speak to Samuel. This is his mother, Eleanor Hardin," the demanding voice hammered in Cheryl's ear.

It *was* her! Cheryl sat up with her heart lodged in her throat.

Chapter 4

Cheryl ran a hand through her tangled hair and winced when she hit the bump on her temple. Sam's mother *was* Eleanor Hardin—former principal of Herington Junior High—and one person who was sure to recognize Cheryl Steele as Cheryl Thatcher.

"You must have the wrong number." Cheryl tried to stay calm.

"Really?" came the unamused reply. "It's rather hard to misdial a number on speed dial, don't you think?"

"Oh, you mean Sam. I'm sorry. I'm still a bit groggy from the drugs he gave me."

"Drugs?" His mother's voice shot up an octave.

"Oh—not those kind of drugs."

"Exactly where is my son?"

"I'm not sure. He said something about staying in the guestroom."

"I'm relieved to hear that, at least. Have him call me right away. I don't believe I caught your name."

Cheryl relaxed a tiny bit. Thanks to her acquired

New York accent or plain good luck, Sam's mother hadn't recognized her voice.

"It's Cheri," she replied cautiously. It wasn't actually a lie. Some of her friends called her that.

"Thank you, Cheri. Have Sam call me."

The line went dead in Cheryl's hand. She stared at the phone stupidly for a second, then hung up.

Things were rapidly moving from bad to worse. Cheryl had spent too many hours facing Eleanor Hardin across the principal's desk at school for the woman not to recognize her. Those memories were painful to recall, but not as painful as the memory of Mrs. Hardin's testimony before the judge at Cheryl's juvenile hearing. Eleanor had read Cheryl's own words to the judge. Words from a diary that detailed a troubled girl's desire to lash out at others and to gloat about the crimes she'd gotten away with. Those words had been enough to send Cheryl to a juvenile detention center for nine months.

If only she hadn't written those things. If only Angie hadn't found the diary and taken it to school. If only the book hadn't ended up in Mrs. Hardin's hands. For Cheryl, having her private thoughts exposed to others had been bad enough, but knowing her words had helped send her father and brother to prison had been almost more than she could bear. She didn't want to relive any part of those times.

Snatching up the phone again, she dialed information for the number of the Highway Patrol. She had to find out if the roads were open. She had to get out of here.

Sam entered the front door feeling pleased with himself. He'd fed the stock, the stalls were mucked out and he'd found an old pair of crutches in the tool-shed where he kept the snow shovels. He carried them into the house like a trophy. The aroma of fresh coffee greeted him.

New York was in the kitchen. She'd traded in his sweats for her red sweater and black corduroy pants with one leg slit up to the knee. She looked as if she'd slept better than he had.

She was buttering a piece of toast as the coffee-maker sputtered the last drops of coffee into the pot. He glanced around and realized she'd washed the dishes he'd left piled in the sink and put them away. She de-layed meeting his gaze when he walked into the kitchen.

He said, "Thanks for cleaning up. You didn't have to do that."

She kept her eyes down, staring at her toast. "It was the least I could do."

Her voice sounded strained, but he couldn't see her eyes. Was she was all right? "You'll do dishes in ex-change for a place to sleep? Marry me, baby, you're my kind of woman," he teased.

She shot him a look of disdain. "They don't make that kind of woman anymore, cowboy."

"A guy can hope, can't he?" All right, she was upset about something, but what? "Is your foot worse?" he tried.

"Looks bad—feels the same." She set her toast and knife down on the counter. "Your mother called this morning. Early."

"So?" Now he was confused.

She arched an eyebrow. "Do strange women often answer your phone at 7:00 a.m. and tell your mother they're still groggy from the drugs you gave them?"

"You didn't."

"I did. You have some explaining to do. She wants you to call her."

"I'm sorry if she embarrassed you. I'll explain, don't worry. She always calls to check on Gramps before we go out to do morning chores. Oh, I found these for you. They may be too tall. If they are, I can shorten them." He handed her the crutches and started for the stairs

When he came up half an hour later, she saw he wasn't alone. An elderly man with snow-white hair and piercing dark eyes behind thick glasses accompanied him. His slightly stooped frame was clad in blue jeans, a plaid shirt and worn cowboy boots.

She watched the older Hardin's expression intently as Sam introduced them, expecting to be denounced on the spot.

"Pleased to make your acquaintance," Walter Hardin said as he sank down on the sofa beside her. "Sam tells me you're from New York City."

"I am." Her knees went weak as she sensed a reprieve.

"I took a trip to New York once. It was crowded, but folks were a lot nicer than I'd been led to expect."

She smiled, almost giddy with relief. She didn't recognize Walter Hardin and saw little to indicate that he might recognize her. Maybe the trial of her father and brother hadn't attracted as much attention as she imagined. Or maybe it had simply been so long ago that people had forgotten it.

She said, "I called the Highway Patrol this morning. Everything south of I-70 and east of US 77 is closed."

"I figured as much," Walter said. "Hope you don't mind spending a little time with us."

"You and your grandson have been very kind, but I really need to get to Kansas City."

Sam took a seat across from them. "The snow has stopped, but until this wind lets up, the roads will drift shut as fast as the crews can open them. The forecast is calling for warmer temperatures tomorrow. It'll melt fast once that happens."

She finally asked the question that had been burning on the tip of her tongue. "Will your mother be bringing your children home soon?" She had to be gone before Eleanor Hardin showed up.

Sam shook his head. "No, they're snowed in, too. The girls want to stay a few days, and Mom doesn't mind. I'll pick them up after we find a way to get you to Kansas City."

Cheryl relaxed. It seemed a little good luck had finally come her way.

Walter pushed himself up from the sofa. "That coffee smells good. I think I'll fix myself a cup. You want one, Sammy?"

"Sure, Gramps."

As the elder Hardin made his way to the kitchen, Sam turned to Cheryl. "Do the crutches fit you?"

"They're too tall, Sammy. But the autograph is priceless."

"What?"

"They're signed, To Sammy, with all my love, Merci."

He chuckled and took the crutch from her to read the faded writing along the edge. "I'd forgotten about that. She said she didn't want to sign my cast, she wanted to sign my crutches because then her name would be closer to my heart."

"How romantic."

He shook his head. "We were in high school."

"That must have been hard. With your mother as a teacher, I mean."

"Mom taught over in the next school district. Believe me, I think I would have transferred schools before I became one of her pupils. She was strict as they come. I hear they called her Hard-as-Nails Hardin over in Herington."

Cheryl bit her lip to keep from making a comment. The kids at school *had* called her that, and worse. "Tell me about your old flame."

"She's a friend."

"'With all my love?' That's more than friendly, Sammy."

"Okay, we were an item in high school. Now, we're just—good friends."

By his hesitation, Cheryl wondered if the fires of this particular high-school flame weren't entirely dead. "You still see each other?"

"Occasionally. How much shorter do these need to be?"

Cheryl remained curious about the woman who lingered in Sam's affections, but let the subject drop. After he'd adjusted the crutches, she tried them out again. Swinging herself across the room, she said, "This is much better. Thank you." Turning around, she headed toward the front door.

"Where do you think you're going?" he demanded.

"To get my purse. I think I left it out in the entryway last night."

It was still lying on the bench where she had left it, but when she picked it up, she had an unpleasant surprise. It felt too light. A quick check showed her wallet was missing. She was on her knees looking under the bench when Sam came up behind her.

"What's wrong?" he asked.

"My wallet is gone."

"Are you sure?"

She rolled her eyes and gave him a don't-be-stupid look. "Of course, I'm sure. It must have fallen out of my purse during the accident last night." A sudden thought hit her, and she looked at him sharply. "Unless you have it."

He helped her to her feet. "Why would I take your wallet?" Clearly, he seemed puzzled by her accusation.

To check up on me? To see if I'm really who I claim to be?

Paranoia seemed to be leaking out her pores. If she wasn't careful she would give him a reason to do just that. "I meant, maybe you found it and forgot to give it to me," she finished lamely.

"I haven't seen it," he said.

She gave him a bright smile. "Then it's still in my car."

"In this weather, it'll be safe enough."

"True, but I'd feel better if I had it. My credit cards, checkbook, driver's license, everything is in it."

"I have to ride out and check on some cows that are due to calve. I'll look for it on my way home. Can I bring back anything else from your car?"

She sat down on the bench. "If you think you could manage my suitcase, that would be great. So you really are a cattle rancher, not simply an architect who lives in the country?"

"Yes, ma'am. You're looking at the breeder of some

of the finest Charolais cattle in the Midwest. That's what I was doing out last night. Moving cattle into the barns. Most of the calves have already been born, but I still have a few cows that are due to calve soon. I didn't want the little critters to be born out in a snowdrift."

Cheryl burst out laughing at the image.

"What's so funny?" he demanded.

"That paints such a great picture. You trying to round up white cows and their little white calves in a snowstorm." Her laughter died away when she saw the speculative look on his face. Suddenly, she knew she'd made a mistake.

"How does a girl from New York City know what color Charolais cattle are?"

She raised a hand to her temple to ease the sudden pain in her head. How could she answer? She couldn't lie to him, but she didn't want Sam to know who she really was. Cheryl Steele from New York was talented, self-assured and witty. Cheryl Thatcher had been a sad, pitiful creature. It would be best if she never came back.

The cat chose that moment to leap into her lap. Cheryl jumped, startled by the animal. "Bonkers, you scared me to death. Don't you get tired of attacking people?"

"Hardly ever," Walter supplied as he came in with a steaming mug in each hand. He gave one to Sam.

Cheryl avoided looking at Sam or his grandfather. "I have such a headache this morning. I think I'll go lie down for a while."

"Is there anything we can do?" Walter asked, his concern evident.

"No, thank you." She pushed the cat off her lap and left the room moving slowly on her crutches.

Sam watched her go and realized she hadn't answered his question. And what had caused the dark pain that filled her eyes so briefly? Maybe it had been her headache, but he had the feeling there was more to it than that. She presented an interesting puzzle. One minute she was smiling and laughing, the next minute she looked like a scared, lost waif.

She's not your puzzle to solve, Sam reminded himself. Don't forget that fact.

After discussing his plans for the day with Gramps, Sam headed downstairs to his office, but he couldn't get his mind off his houseguest. He admitted he was attracted to Cheryl, intrigued by her even, but he wasn't a fool. For his own peace of mind, it would be best to remember she'd be gone soon.

He busied himself in his office for the remainder of the morning and worked on his latest project. He loved designing homes almost as much as he loved ranching, and he'd missed it since he came back to take over the homestead. In spite of his father's and grandfather's experience, years of poor cattle markets, dry weather and bad investments had left the ranch on the verge of ruin.

It'd taken every scrap of Sam's time and most of his money to get the place back on its feet. This year, with the income from his breeding program, he stood to make a real profit for the first time in years. Enough to let the ranch survive.

That time might have come sooner if he hadn't spent so much money building this house. He had used the construction to try to keep Natalie happy. And she had used it to dupe him.

Every trip she'd taken to Kansas City for the best glass, the right tile, the most unique rugs, had only

been a cover to meet her lover, and Sam had never suspected anything until it was too late. It had been a bitter lesson to learn.

He turned his attention back to his design. Thanks
to his former partner in Kansas City, he now had the
chance to work for the firm again. The added income
would provide a much-needed cushion for the ranch.
A lot hinged on the home he was designing here. If all
went well, construction would begin on the massive
stone house on a hillside outside of Kansas City within
the month. The only drawback was that it meant he'd
need to travel to Kansas City frequently over the next
few weeks.

A little after one o'clock, he put his plans away and
headed upstairs. There was no sign of Cheryl, so he
fixed a tray of toasted cheese sandwiches and a salad,
then knocked on her door.

"Come in," her groggy voice called.

He opened the door and carried the tray inside. "I
thought you might like some lunch."

"Um, sounds great." She raised up on one elbow
and pushed her hair out of her face. "What time is it?"

"One-thirty. The wind's died down, and I'm going
to ride over and check the cattle. I wanted to let you
know I was leaving."

"Be careful out there." Worry tinged her voice and
put a small frown between her beautiful blue eyes.

"I will. Besides, Dusty always comes straight home
after work."

"Make sure you're on him."

She looked adorable with her hair mussed and her
eyes still cloudy with sleep. He deposited the tray and
quickly turned to leave. Bonkers made a dash inside as

Sam started to close the door. The cat jumped on the bed and began to butt his head against her side for attention.

She ran a hand down his back and he purred loudly. "I think your cat is beginning to like me."

"I think you're beginning to like my cat."

"He's persistent. I admire that." She picked Bonkers up and rubbed a knuckle under his chin. A look of bliss crossed the big cat's face.

Sam turned and stomped out of the room feeling ridiculous. He couldn't be jealous of a cat. What he needed was a long, cold ride in the snow to take his mind off his very charming visitor.

Hours later, Cheryl sat in Sam's living room waiting with his grandfather. Both of them anxiously watched the clock. Sam had been gone far longer than he should have been. It was almost dark. At the sound of the door opening, she and Walter hurried out to the entryway. Sam paused inside the doorway and set her suitcase down. He looked cold, tired and worried.

"Is everything okay?" she asked.

"I've got some bad news, New York."

"Did we lose some calves?" Walter asked.

She crossed her arms over her chest and shivered in the cold draft. She knew the loss of even a few head could spell financial disaster for some ranchers. How many ranchers had been put in financial jeopardy by her family? She hated to think about it.

"The cattle are all okay, but your wallet wasn't in the car, Cheryl."

"What? Are you sure?"

"I'm sure."

Walter said, "You look terrible, Son. Cheryl made

hot cocoa earlier. Would you like some? I could make coffee if you'd rather."

"Cocoa sounds great."

Cheryl hobbled to the kitchen with them. Sam shed his coat with a weary sigh. Walter filled a thick, white mug with the steaming drink and held it out to Sam. He took the cup and sipped it. "Man, this hits the spot."

He sank into a chair at the table. "I searched all through your car. There weren't any tracks in the snow, so no one else had been in it since the snow stopped. Is it possible it fell out on the ride back?"

"I guess it's possible—my purse was unzipped. Did you look around the outside of the car?"

"I tried, but there's too much snow yet. Hey, we know we only rode along the highway and down my lane, so it's out there somewhere. We'll find it when the snow melts."

"When the snow melts! When might that be?" Cheryl snapped. She couldn't wait for the snow to melt. The longer she stayed, the more likely it was that Sam would find out who she really was. The daughter of a felon, one of those "thieving Thatchers," as people in the community had labeled her family. Someone who had spent time in reform school instead of prison only because of her age.

It wasn't fair. She wasn't that person anymore. She was the "Steel Ballerina," the darling of New York's young ballet set. How would her fans or the press react when they heard she had been convicted of cattle rustling and assaulting a sheriff's deputy? At best, she'd become a laughingstock. At worst, her career would suffer. All because she'd taken this stupid side trip.

"I can't believe my rotten luck!" She shuffled to the

far side of the room, narrowly missing the cat's tail with her crutches when she swung around. Bonkers scrambled out of her way.

"Take it easy," Sam cautioned. "You're making me feel like I should take cover with the cat."

"This is serious, Sam!"

"I know, but don't worry. We'll find it. Have a little faith."

"Don't worry? I need my driver's license, my money and my credit cards. I need to catch up with my company before they leave Kansas City. If I'm not dancing by then, I'm out of a job for the entire spring. Don't worry? I can't even go back to New York. I sublet my apartment until the end of June because I was going to be on this tour."

She was tired, her foot ached like a bad tooth and all he could say was, "Don't worry."

"What about your sister? Can you stay with her?"

"Yesterday was my sister's wedding, remember? She's on her honeymoon in Hawaii. I doubt the happy couple booked an extra room for me."

"Okay, calm down. Things will work out, you'll see. The snow can't last more than a few days."

"Oh, that's just like a man. Calm down and wait till the snow melts! I can't believe this! Nothing has gone right since I set foot in this stupid state!" She hobbled out of the room slamming the bedroom door behind her.

Walter stared after her. "There's something about that gal that seems familiar."

"She has a temper like Natalie's. That's what makes her seem familiar. Women like her don't have any understanding or patience for the forces of nature. They want the world to jump for them when they snap their fingers."

"You're wrong to judge all women using Natalie as a yardstick, Sam."

"I know, but I can't help it. Once burned—twice shy." What he didn't admit was how attracted he was to Cheryl and how it scared him. He couldn't explain it or reason it away. In his head he knew she was a woman every bit as wrong for him as his ex-wife had been. *Lord, help me to remember that.*

Chapter 5

Cheryl opened the bedroom door early the next morning and peeked out. There was no sign of Sam or Walter. Bonkers came to weave around her legs and meow at her. She picked him up and rubbed her chin on his head. The blinds on the glass wall were open. Now that the driving snow had stopped, early-morning sunshine poured through the tall windows. She put the cat down and crossed the room on her crutches to take a closer look at the spectacular view spread before her.

Sam's home sat on the very edge of a steep bluff. The balcony that ran the full length of the house outside the windows gave the illusion of a house suspended in midair. In the valley below, frosted trees outlined the winding course of a small creek. Beyond them the prairie rose again to flat-topped, snow-covered bluffs and sparkling rounded hills that rolled away as far as she could see. Overhead, the brilliant blue sky arched like an azure bowl over a dazzling, glittering world. Her mother would have loved this view.

Cheryl laid her forehead against the cool window

glass. Her mother had loved every rock and blade of these vast grasslands. Even after her friends and neighbors had turned against her. Cheryl had never understood it. And she'd never understood why her gentle mother had stayed with Hank Thatcher.

A womanizer, a bully and a drunk, her father was always angry. Her earliest memory was of hiding behind the sofa and listening to the sounds of her mother weeping. The only happy times in her childhood had been when her father wasn't home.

Mira Thatcher had been Hank's second wife. As she grew older, Cheryl suspected that her mother stayed because of Hank's son. Jake, Cheryl's half brother, was eight years her senior, and Mira loved him like one of her own.

Cheryl was nine the first time her father and Jake were arrested and convicted of stealing cattle. The condemnation of the ranching community, the pitying looks, the whispers behind their backs made life hard for Mira and her daughters, but at least Hank had been out of the picture. When Cheryl turned eleven, her father and brother came home, but things only got worse. That summer, her mother died.

Drunk as usual, Cheryl's father had been driving when the accident happened, yet he survived with barely a scratch. The day after her mother's funeral, Grandma Doris moved in with them. That year was the worst year of Cheryl's life.

A hard and bitter woman, Doris Thatcher wielded her strict discipline with a heavy hand. No one was exempt from the sharp edge of her tongue. She harped endlessly at her son to stop drinking, straighten up, get some work done—the list went on and on. Hank ignored her, and Jake had simply moved out, leaving Cheryl and Angie to bear the brunt of her harsh lessons punctuated with blows from a leather strap.

At school, Cheryl had been equally miserable, but she hid her feelings behind a wall of anger. Protective of Angie and sensitive about her family, she made an easy target for the taunts of the other kids. She never backed away from a fight—even the ones she knew she couldn't win. For that reason, she often wound up in the principal's office facing Eleanor Hardin.

Eleanor had been one of Mira Thatcher's few friends. Maybe that was why her disappointment in Cheryl's behavior had been so blatantly obvious. In the face of it all, Cheryl had remained stubbornly silent about her treatment at home. When pressed, she resorted to belligerence, and that attitude made it easy for people to believe the worst of her later. "Like father, like daughter," they said. After a while, Cheryl stopped caring about what they thought.

But it had all happened so long ago.

Cheryl turned away from the window. She had changed more than her name since then; she had changed who she was inside. At least, she had believed that until she found herself back in Kansas.

She worried her lower lip between her teeth. From the time she had driven away from her grandmother's ranch, Cheryl had found herself hiding from and skirting around the truth the way she had done as a child.

Determined not to dwell on the uncomfortable thought, she donned her leotard and spent the next hour performing the exercises and stretches that kept her body flexible and graceful for the dance. It was hard work, awkward and painful with her swollen foot, but she welcomed the pain as a distraction from her unsettling thoughts.

Finally, when she finished her morning routine, she flopped down on the sofa and put her aching foot up on a pillow. A moment later she heard the front door open. She looked up and a tingle of anticipation fluttered in the pit of her stomach.

Sam entered the living room and stopped short when he caught sight of Cheryl lying on his sofa. Her hair was pulled back into a ponytail, but a few wisps had escaped and the sweat-dampened curls clung to her sculptured cheeks and the slender column of her neck. She wore a black leotard, hot pink, calf-length Spandex pants and only one shoe with white ribbons that crisscrossed her delicate ankle. Her other foot lay propped on a pillow, and he saw the blue-black bruising and swelling extending above and below the edges of the tape she had wrapped it with.

"You shouldn't be using that foot." His admonishment came out sounding gruffer than he intended.

Clearly miffed at his scolding, her lips pressed into a tight line. Would they soften if he kissed her? Where had that thought come from?

"I know what I'm doing," she said.

He was saved from making a reply by the ringing of the phone. As he answered it, Cheryl picked up her crutches and went to busy herself in the kitchen until he joined her a short while later.

Glancing up from her coffee mug, she saw the worried look on his face. "What's the matter?"

"That was my mother. My sister was taken to the hospital last night."

"Oh, Sam, I'm so sorry. Is it serious?"

"Becky is pregnant, but she's not due for another ten weeks. She started into early labor. The doctors were able to stop it, but she has to stay on strict bed rest."

"Can you get to the hospital? Are the roads open?"

"Becky and Michael live in Colorado."

"I see." Cheryl poured him a cup of coffee. "Is it her first baby?"

"No, they have three. That's part of the reason Mom called. She'll be on her way to Denver as soon as the roads are open to help Michael take care of the kids." He sipped the coffee she'd given him.

"Three kids would be a handful for a man with his wife in the hospital."

"Yeah, well, two kids will be a handful for me with the ranch work and a house going up in Kansas City. Mom takes care of the twins while I'm working."

"What will you do?" she asked in concern.

"I guess I'll have to start looking for a temporary nanny. I hope, for Becky's sake as well as my own, that she gets out of the hospital soon." He lifted his mug in a small salute. "You make a good cup of coffee, New York."

"Thanks, cowboy." She stared into the dark liquid of her own cup. "Sam, I want to apologize for taking my foul temper out on you last night. You've been more than kind to me, and I'm sorry I repaid you by acting like a spoiled child."

"Apology accepted. As much as I like that outfit, I think you should change into something warmer."

She frowned at him. "Why?"

"The snow's melting fast. I think I can get you into Council Grove and have a doctor look at that foot."

Cheryl bit her lip in indecision. She needed to see

a doctor, she suspected there was more wrong with her foot than a sprain, but could she risk running into someone in Council Grove who might recognize her?

"Can't you get me to Manhattan or Kansas City?" she asked hopefully. "I could see a doctor there."

He shook his head. "Sorry. They had more snow north of here. The roads aren't open in that direction yet."

"I hate to put you to more trouble, Sam. I'll be fine for another day."

"No, you won't. You need to get that foot looked at. I'm taking you and that's final."

She couldn't think of a good reason to argue with him.

Thirty minutes later, they were bumping along the lane and out onto the highway. The ride was rough, but Sam handled the truck with a skill she had to admire. They arrived in Council Grove a little battered but none the worse for the trip.

She reluctantly agreed to let Sam cover the cost of the ER visit until she found her wallet and could send the hospital a copy of her insurance card. It was not an arrangement she liked, but she couldn't see any alternative.

Through her wide, round sunglasses, she studied the occupants of the small hospital's waiting room as she waited for her turn to see the doctor, noting thankfully that none of the faces looked familiar. Cowboys, farmers and housewives discussed cattle, crop losses and sick kids. The weather dominated the conversations going on around her. Nothing had changed much in the years she'd been gone.

She studied the worn linoleum on the floor and tried

to decide what she would do if her foot were broken. She reviewed the list of friends she could stay with until her apartment was available again, but it was a pretty short list. Even getting back to New York would be difficult without money or credit cards. Her sister would be home in a few weeks. Cheryl didn't want to impose on the newlyweds, but her savings wouldn't pay the bills and the cost of a motel for a month or more. All in all, things looked pretty bleak.

"Why, Sam! What are you doing here? You're not sick, I hope? Is something wrong with the girls?"

Cheryl looked up to see a tall redhead eyeing Sam as if he was a free lunch and she hadn't had a bite all week. The woman sauntered across the room and stopped in front of him, but her gaze pinned Cheryl like a hawk.

Cheryl knew the look—she'd been subjected to it more than once. She was being assessed as a potential rival. The redhead definitely had her sights set on Sam.

"The girls are fine," Sam said. "I'm here with a friend. You're looking well, Merci. How's the new job going?"

"Good, thanks. We're busier today than usual." The woman turned her gaze on Cheryl. "I don't believe we've met. I'm Merci Slader. I'm a unit clerk here at the hospital."

So this was Merci, Sam's old flame. "Cheryl Steele," she offered her hand.

Merci took it in a limp grip. Her smile was definitely frosty. "I don't recall Sam mentioning you before."

"We've only just met. I'm sure he'll have a lot to say about me later. Won't you, cowboy?" Cheryl patted his knee.

"What happened to your leg, dear? Did you trip and fall?" Merci's voice was more than a little catty.

Cheryl laughed, "No, I had a car accident in the storm. Fortunately, Sam came along in time to rescue me, and we got—stuck together!"

"Miss Steele, the doctor can see you now," a plump gray-haired nurse called from the doorway.

Cheryl rose gracefully and leaned on her crutches. "It was so nice talking to you. Do keep Sam company while the doctor looks at my foot, won't you? I know how he likes to visit with *old* friends." She cast Sam an innocent smile and swung across the room.

Half an hour later, Cheryl had lost her cheeky attitude. She sat on the exam table while Dr. Carlton pointed out the two fractured bones that put an end to her income and plans for the entire spring.

"I've spoken to your physician in New York. He has made a few recommendations, but I'm not sure I can carry them out." The middle-aged doctor was a comical figure, short, bald and rotund, but he spoke with professional politeness.

Cheryl chewed her lip a moment. "What did Dr. Fuller have to say?"

"He recommended I put you in an extra-heavy cast, then add a ball and chain to see if that'd slow you down." He peered at her from over the edge of his reading glasses. "Seems he's had a mite of trouble keeping you off an injury in the past."

Cheryl had the grace to look shamefaced.

"I see evidence of an old fracture here, but it's healed well." He pointed it out on the black-and-white X-ray film as he held it up to the light.

"Isn't there something else we can do besides cast it, Dr. Carlton? I've got to be able to work again soon."

He lowered the film and faced her. "I think you know the answer to that. Do you want to continue to dance?"

"More than I want to breathe."

"I believe that. Now, if you want to dance the way Dr. Fuller tells me you can, you will let me set these bones, cast your foot and you'll keep off it for six to eight weeks."

"But—"

"No, don't interrupt me, young lady. You have had a crushing injury. Your tendons and muscles, as well as your bones, need time to heal. Your other choice is surgery to pin the bones. I'd send you back to Dr. Fuller for that, but you would still be off that foot for at least six weeks."

"Those are my choices?"

"If you want this foot to heal well enough to continue your career, yes."

She nodded in resignation.

"Good. By the way, Dr. Fuller is having his office fax over your insurance information. At least that will be one less worry for you." He stood and opened the door of the small room, then paused. "Have we met before? You look familiar somehow."

She glanced up in surprise. Why would he think that? She was sure she'd never met him. Her infrequent visits to the doctor as a child had been to an elderly physician in the neighboring town of Herington more than thirty miles away.

"No, I don't believe we have," she said. "Unless you've been to New York lately."

He shook his head. "It'll come to me. I never forget

a face. I'll have the nurse give you a sedative before I set that foot. I'm afraid this won't be fun."

Dr. Carlton was a master at understatements. It was not fun.

An hour later, Sam half carried her to his truck and settled her with care on the seat. "Are you all right?"

"Everything's spinning like a top. My foot's throbbing like a wild thing. This cast weighs a ton, and whatever medicine they gave me is making me sick. Other than that, cowboy, I'm peachy."

She sat up straight, determined to prove she was all right. She noticed Merci Slader watching them from the front of the hospital. The woman didn't look happy. Merci shouldn't worry. Cheryl had no designs on Sam.

Someone else was watching them. Cheryl could just make out a face in the frost-covered window beside the door. There was something familiar about it. A chill ran up her spine.

"Are you ready to go?"

Sam was beside her waiting to close the truck door. She glanced at him, then back to the hospital. The face in the window was gone.

Had she imagined it? The painkillers the doctor had given her were certainly making her feel weird. She closed her eyes, leaned her head back. "I'm ready. I think."

Sam kept a close eye on her as they bounced along the highway through deep tire ruts in the snow. He could see she was in pain, but she wasn't one to complain.

"Sam, stop the truck," she insisted suddenly.

"What for?"

"Stop now!"

He stepped on the brake and the pickup slid to an abrupt halt. She opened the door, stepped out and was thoroughly sick at the side of the road.

Sam hurried around the truck, dropped to one knee at her side, and held her as she retched. Carefully, he gathered her hair back and held it away from her face. It felt like soft strands of the finest silk as it curled around his hand.

What was there about this woman that got under his skin so easily? She could talk and act like the most independent woman in the world, but he couldn't shake the feeling she needed someone to take care of her. Someone like him.

He marveled at his own foolishness. He was in deep trouble if holding a woman while she was being sick struck him as romantic. The realization that she would be gone from his life in a day or two brought a sharp twist of regret.

He continued to hold her, talking soothing nonsense until her spasms passed. After a few minutes he was able to get her back in the truck, but she was shaking like a leaf, and her face was pasty pale.

"I'm sorry," she moaned.

Sam wet his bandanna in the melting snow and used it to wipe her face. Her eyes flew open at the touch of the cold cloth. She gave him a limp little half smile, but it didn't ease his mind.

"Do I need to take you back to the hospital?" he asked.

"No, I'll live. That cold cloth feels wonderful. I've always wondered why cowboys wore bandannas, now I know. They're great for first aid."

Her voice sounded so forlorn Sam couldn't help himself. He leaned in and kissed her forehead. "You women gave up wearing petticoats, so someone had to carry the bandages. Are you ready to go?"

She nodded, leaned her head back and closed her eyes. She was asleep before Sam got around to the driver's seat. He shifted her until she was lying along the seat with her head on his leg. He sat for a moment and let his fingers linger on her cheek. Yes, he would be sorry to see her go. He put the truck in gear and drove slowly home.

At the ranch, she stirred as he lifted her out of the pickup, but she didn't wake. He carried her into the house and laid her gently on his bed, then he stood back and watched her as she slept. She was a tough little character. He reached down to smooth a lock of hair from her face, and she smiled in her sleep at his touch.

He liked her, Sam realized. He liked this tough, sassy, graceful-as-a-willow young woman. She stirred him in so many ways. She was beautiful, true, but her quick mind drew him more than her pretty face. She made him laugh, but at the same time she made him feel strong and protective. He tried to be objective about his feelings toward her, but she gave a soft snore, and it chased his objectivity away. He smiled but it was touched with sadness. She wasn't for him.

She wouldn't stay, he knew that even as he found himself wishing for a way to keep her here longer. He wanted time to sort out his feelings. To see if this was an infatuation or something deeper. He'd tried to harden his heart against her, but in spite of his best efforts, she'd hobbled right into the one spot that had been lonely and empty too long.

Why had God brought her here? To test him, or to

heal him? He might never learn the answer. He simply had to have faith in God's plan for him. He closed the bedroom door and headed for his office.

Bonkers lay stretched out along the back of the sofa in his favorite spot, but suddenly, he jumped up and took off for the front door. An explosion of sound came from the entryway. Squeals, giggles and the sound of running feet.

A pair of identical five-year-old girls flew into the room and wrapped themselves around Sam's legs.

"Did you—" one girl began.

"—miss us?" the other finished.

Sam shook his head. "Nope."

"Yes, you did."

"You missed us."

Sam looked up to see his mother smiling indulgently from the doorway. "Okay, maybe a little."

"We had lots of fun at Grandma's," Lindy said, clearly excited by her time away from home.

"Can we go outside and play now?" Kayla asked.

"Can we get—" Lindy began.

"—our sled out?" Kayla finished her sister's sentence as the twins often did, much to the bemusement of those who knew them.

Sam lifted them up, one in each arm, and looked into the two most important faces in his life. "Kisses first," he said. Two sturdy sets of arms circled his neck, and smacking kisses covered his cheeks. His heart expanded in his chest until he thought it might burst. God had been good to him.

Eleanor Hardin walked in and began pulling off her gloves. "If I had known they were going to be snowed in with me, I would have been busy when you called and asked me to watch them."

He smiled and shook his head. "No, you wouldn't have. You loved every minute of it. Come in."

"I can't stay. I've got to get on the road."

"You're driving to Denver now? Is I-70 open already?"

"Yes, to both questions."

He could see her searching the room with her eyes. "Cheryl is resting right now," he said. "The doctor set her broken foot this morning, and she's sleeping off the sedation."

Eleanor looked perplexed. "I thought her name was Cheri."

"Who's Cheri?" the twins asked simultaneously.

"It's Cheryl," Sam answered.

"Her foot really is broken? The poor dear." A slender woman with a short gray bob, Eleanor was dressed in jeans and a bulky green sweater. She swooped in and took charge as usual.

She plucked the girls out of his arms and set them down. "Go change into your snowsuits. Daddy will take you outside, but not until you're dressed, including mittens."

"Who's Cheryl?" the twins insisted, jumping up and down.

"Girls, listen," Sam said sternly. "Cheryl is our guest and she's sleeping in my room, so you'll have to be quiet."

An identical mulish look appeared on their faces so he knelt in front of them. "You can't wake her up. Understand?"

"Yes, Daddy," they replied together.

"Good. Now, go get dressed for sledding while I walk Grandma out to the car."

The twins took off for the stairs. Picking up Bonkers, Kayla said, "You can ride—"

"—on the sled, too," Lindy told the cat.

Eleanor turned back to Sam. "Bonkers doesn't look thrilled, does he? Son, I'm sorry to leave you in such a fix."

He could see she was genuinely torn about leaving. He draped his arm over her shoulder and gave her a squeeze. "Now, Mom, Becky needs you. Tell her the girls and I will keep her in our prayers. Go. Don't worry about us. We'll be okay."

She reached up and pulled his head down to give him a quick peck on the cheek. "I know you will—you always are. I wish I could meet your Cheri."

"Cheryl, Mom, and she isn't mine. I told you, she's a ballet dancer touring the country with her company. She's been stranded here for a couple of days by the storm, that's all. If I-70's open, she'll be able to get to Kansas City tomorrow and rejoin her friends."

"If her foot is broken, she certainly can't dance."

"I know. I've been thinking about that. Maybe she could stay and help take care of the girls until you get back? If she can't work, she might be happy to take the job."

"Are you certain you want to ask a stranger to watch the girls, Sam? That isn't like you. What do you know about her?"

Not as much as he would like to know, he realized. "It was just an idea."

"I'm not sure someone on crutches would be able to keep up with your two little whirlwinds."

"The girls can entertain themselves. Even with her leg in a cast, she should be able to manage them with Gramps to help."

"I know I'm leaving you in a lurch, but please think this over carefully."

"I will. You know me, I never do anything without a lot of thought."

"True. Now, walk me out to my car. There are some things I'll need you to take care of while I'm gone. I have a small list of things for you to do."

"Small? Knowing you, it's as long as my leg."

"Nonsense. It's only as long as your arm."

With a laugh, Sam followed his mother out the door.

At the stairwell, two little girls stuck their heads up and checked to see if the coast was clear, then they crossed to their father's bedroom still lugging the enormous cat.

Chapter 6

Cheryl woke to a nagging ache in her foot and trouble breathing. It felt like a twenty-pound weight pressing down on her chest. She opened her eyes and found herself staring into the cat's broad face. A yellow twenty-pound, fur-covered weight.

"Bonkers, get off." She gave him a not-so-gentle shove.

She was in Sam's room again, she realized, yet she couldn't remember how she'd gotten here. A slight noise caught her attention, and she turned her head.

Two identical little girls peered at her over the edge of the mattress. Their chins were propped on chubby hands and their elbows rested on the bed. The cat sat between them watching her with an unblinking stare.

Cheryl closed her eyes. "Let me guess. Tweedledee and Tweedledum?"

She opened one eye slowly. The pair remained. They watched her with solemn brown eyes, much darker than their father's, but their short chestnut hair held a multitude of curls like his. It seemed she was going to meet Sam's children, after all.

"Hi." Cheryl spoke slowly—her mouth felt as if it had been stuffed with cotton. "You must be Lindy and Kayla."

They nodded.

"I'm Cheryl." Coming fully awake, she sat up and cast a fearful glance toward the door. "Is your grandmother here?"

"She went to see—" the one on the right started.

"—Aunt Becky in Denver," the one on the left finished.

Lightheaded with relief, Cheryl leaned back on her elbows. Her luck had held. The Queen of Hearts wasn't going to come running in and demand her head.

Cheryl eyed the bulky white cast on her leg. Her foot was broken, she was out of a job and she had no place to live. Some luck.

"Did Bonkers—" began the one on the right.

"—wake you up?" finished the one on the left.

Cheryl smiled to reassure them. "He did, but that's okay."

The twins looked at each other silently for a long moment. Cheryl detected a twinkle, very much like their father's, sparkling in the depths of their brown eyes. Bonkers lifted a paw and gave it a lick.

"Daddy said—"

"—we can't wake you up, but—"

"—he didn't say, Bonkers—"

"—couldn't wake you up."

Cheryl followed the twisted logic, but she was having trouble following the single conversation coming from the two children. She scooted up in bed and leaned against the headboard, gritting her teeth as a stab of pain shot up her leg. "Do you always do that?"

"Do what?" they asked together.

"Finish each other's sentences."

Again, that look flashed between them. "Not always," they replied together again.

"I know your names are Lindy and Kayla, but which one is which?"

"You have to guess."

"How'd you hurt your foot?"

"How'd the doctor get that cast on?"

"Can you still—"

"—wiggle your toes?"

Cheryl smiled. "I think your father tried to warn me about you and your questions."

"Daddy likes you," remarked the child on the right.

"Yes, he does," the girl on the left added. She picked up the cat, draped him over her shoulder, and they all trooped out of the room. Cheryl eyed the bedroom door for a while, but the Mad Hatter and the White Rabbit didn't show.

She left the bed an hour later still feeling unsteady, but she managed the crutches well enough. The pain in her foot was bearable if she didn't move too fast or bump it. There was no one in the kitchen or the living room, and Cheryl toyed with the idea of going back to bed until she heard the sound of shouting outside.

She crossed to the sliding glass door that led to the balcony and eased it open. A crisp, cold breeze blew in, lifting the ends of her hair and chasing the last of the cobwebs from her mind as it carried the sound of children's laughter to her.

Leaning a shoulder against the doorframe, Cheryl

watched the sledding party in progress on the slope of the opposite hillside. Sam stood behind the twins as they piled on a red sled. He steadied it, then gave a shove that sent them squealing and shrieking to the bottom of the hill. They tumbled out of the sled, trudged back to the top and started all over again.

Cheryl smiled with amusement as Bonkers crept up to investigate the sled. The twins picked him up and settled him in between them. Sam gave them a push, and they flew down the hill again. Halfway down, Bonkers apparently decided he didn't care for the ride. He jumped out but went rolling and sliding down the snowy slope. The twins shrieked in alarm as they hurried toward the snow-covered cat.

Bonkers didn't wait for help. He picked himself up with wounded dignity and stalked off, shaking his paws with every other step. Cheryl laughed aloud at the cat's antics. She saw Sam laughing, too.

He must have heard her because he looked up and gave her a brief wave. She waved back. A warm glow settled in the center of her chest as she watched him playing with his children. This was a new side of him. It couldn't be easy raising two small daughters, but he seemed up to the job. He was certainly enjoying himself now. He even took a turn on the sled as the girls shouted encouragement.

Cheryl covered her smile with one hand. What a comical figure he made when he sat on the small sled. His long legs were bent with his knees drawn up almost to his ears. With one hand, he kept his hat jammed on his head. The other hand he held high in the air like a bronc rider as the twins pushed him off the hilltop. His grin was as big as all outdoors, and Cheryl had no trouble imagining the boy he'd once been as he flew down the hill and tipped over at the bottom.

An unexpected stab of jealousy pierced her as she watched Sam and his girls. Her father had never played with her and her sister; he had never smiled and laughed with them. A sudden, fierce longing to go out and join the fun came over her. Instead, she gave a rueful glance at the cast on her foot. With her luck, she'd end up breaking another bone, more than likely in her neck this time.

The sledding halted when a snowball fight broke out. It quickly became father against daughters, and it was a pretty even fight as the snowballs flew fast and furious between them. Suddenly, a cry of pain brought the game to a halt. Sam quickly crossed to where one of the girls sat in the snow with her sister bending over her.

Sam pulled off his gloves and knelt in front of her. He pushed the brim of his hat back with one finger. "What's wrong, Lindy?"

"I hurt my eye," Lindy answered with a pout on her lips and one fist balled up against her face.

"Let me look." He tilted her face up and carefully brushed the snow from her cheek. "I see it. There's an ouch-maker right here." He touched his lips in a gentle kiss to her eyelid. "Is that better?"

"No."

"It's not?" he asked in surprise. "I must be out of practice. My ouch-remover always works. Let me try again." He planted a second kiss on her cheek. "How's that?"

"That got it." She rubbed her eye and smiled at him.

"I think my eye hurts, too," Kayla said in a wistful voice.

"It does? Well, come here and let me see." Sam examined Kayla's eye critically and planted a kiss on her cheek as well. "Better now?" he asked, and she nodded. "Good! Ready to fight some more?"

"No, we want to make snow angels."

"Grandma showed us how."

"Did she? You know what? She showed me how when I was about your age, too. Let me see if I remember." He flopped backward into the snow and began to swing his arms and legs and the twins quickly joined him.

Cheryl watched the scene from the balcony door, and her heart warmed at the sight of Sam's tenderness. She remembered her own mother kissing her cheek to make the tears go away. It was a startling, clear and treasured memory of her mother, and Cheryl couldn't believe she'd forgotten it until now.

She stepped back and closed the door. Just for a moment, as she watched Sam and his children on the hillside, Cheryl wondered what her life would have been like if her father had been more like Sam. His children were very lucky, indeed.

Back in the bedroom, she sat down on the edge of the bed and picked up the phone. After dialing Damon's cell phone, she braced herself to give him the bad news.

He answered on the second ring. "Sands here."

"Damon, this is Cheryl."

"It's about time. Where are you?"

"Still stranded."

"What? Are you kidding?"

"No, and it only gets worse. I'm afraid my foot is broken. I'm not going to be able to rejoin you for a few weeks."

"Don't tell me that! Geoffrey is already complaining because Miranda is taking your place in rehearsals. He says she outweighs you by ten pounds and his back is killing him from trying to lift her."

"He complains about my weight, too."

"I know, but you don't miss your jumps."

Cheryl cringed. "Did she?"

"The jeté entrelacé, twice! Fortunately, she recovered well. You understand I have to terminate your contract."

"Damon, please. I'll be back in a few weeks at most."

"Maybe! I can't hold your place. I'm sorry, Cheryl."

"But I need this job."

"It's too bad. You had potential."

It was the highest praise Damon had ever given her. She knew she wouldn't get anywhere by arguing with him. She was fired. The least she could do was take it with dignity. "I hope I have the honor of working with you again someday."

"We'll see. I've got to go. Give me your address so I can have your last check forwarded to you."

She gave him Sam's address then hung up the phone and stared at it for a long time. The best role of her career had just gone down the drain. She knew there would be other roles, other chances to shine, but they seemed very far away at the moment. Now, what was she going to do in the meantime?

Several hours later, the tantalizing smell of roast beef drew her out of the book she'd been trying to read and out of the bedroom into the kitchen.

The twins were setting the table. One laid down the dishes, and the other followed arranging the flatware carefully beside each plate. Sam, wearing oversized orange oven mitts, removed a cookie sheet of golden-brown biscuits from the oven.

"Something smells wonderful," she said, maneuvering into the kitchen. The cast was heavy and her pain medicine left her feeling lightheaded and groggy. She joined Walter at the kitchen table, happy to have made it without falling.

Sam set the biscuits on a plate in the center of the table. "Are you feeling better? I could have brought you something to eat in bed. You didn't have to get up."

She smiled wanly. "I'm a little better, thank you. I wanted to get up. I'm not used to lying around."

"At least let me get that leg elevated. The doctor said you need to keep it up."

"Did he? I don't remember much after he set it."

Sam brought another chair and padded it with pillows, then gently lifted her foot onto it. The twins eyed them intently. He introduced them, and Cheryl had the feeling they hadn't told their father about meeting her earlier. She decided to keep mum as well and was rewarded with a grin from each of them. They came and sat on either side of her at the table.

Sam introduced the child on her left as Lindy, and the one on her right as Kayla. Cheryl tried to find some way to tell them apart, but she couldn't. They were dressed identically in blue jeans and green shirts.

Walter led the family in saying grace. Cheryl bowed her head with the others, but felt awkward and uncomfortable with her pretense of piety. The meal started out quietly, but the twins soon opened up and regaled her with stories of their stay at their grandmother's during the storm and of playing in the snow.

Eating at a tennis match would be easier, Cheryl decided. They continued to start and finish each other's sentences on some hidden cue. She found she couldn't turn her head fast enough to keep up with them. Finally, she looked at Walter. "How do they do that?"

He shrugged. "Beats me."

"What do you do?" Lindy asked Cheryl.

"I'm a classical ballet dancer. A ballerina."

"Do you dance on your toes?" This time Kayla popped up with a question.

"Sometimes, but only when the steps of the dance call for it. Not all ballet is danced on your toes. There are lots of different steps."

"Do you wear a tutu?" Sam asked with a smirk.

Lifting her chin, she replied with a haughty air, "I wear many different costumes when I dance. Yes, I wear a tutu, but I have even worn a cowboy hat."

"Not in a ballet," Lindy jeered in disbelief.

Cheryl grew serious as she studied the girls' faces. "You've never been to a ballet, have you?"

Of course they hadn't. Neither had she at their age, and if it hadn't been for one special woman, Cheryl would have spent her whole life never knowing the beauty or her love of dancing. She glanced at Sam and Walter and wondered what they thought about her career. Did they consider it frivolous? And why should it matter what Sam or anyone else thought? It shouldn't, but for some reason, it did.

Focusing on the children, she began to explain her art. "Some ballets are written to express the joy of the dancing, and some tell a story, like *Cinderella* or *Peter and the Wolf.* In that ballet, I was the duck," she confided, and the girls giggled.

She stared at their father a long moment. "There is

even a ballet about a lonely, clumsy cowgirl who wins
the heart of the most handsome cowboy on the ranch.
It's called *Rodeo*."

She'd never had the role, but she knew exactly how
the character would feel. Lonely and left out, sad and
filled with a longing to be loved for who she was inside. Afraid no one could ever love her.

"Can you show us?" asked Kayla.

"What?" Momentarily lost in thought, Cheryl stared
at the child.

"How to dance on our toes?" Lindy added.

Shaking her head, Cheryl said, "I'm afraid I can't.
Not with my foot in a cast. Perhaps your father will
take you to Kansas City someday and you can see a
ballet there. There are several good companies there."

Kayla leaned forward. "Is that where you dance?"

"Cheryl is from New York, girls. That's much farther away than Kansas City. No, we can't go there and
don't ask," Sam told them. "Enough questions. Eat!"

Cheryl, surprised to find her appetite returning, did
justice to Sam's meal, including his light and fluffy biscuits. She sighed inwardly as she glanced across the
table at him. He was a good cook, a devoted father and
a Christian. None of those were things she expected to
find attractive in a man. Especially not a rancher. Somehow, she'd always thought that men who lived this life
were hard and bitter. Like her father.

Instead, she was the one with bitterness in her heart.
She didn't like deceiving Sam. He'd done so much for
her already. Would he have been as helpful if he'd
known who she really was? Maybe. Still, she should
tell him. He deserved to know the truth. He looked up
and their eyes met.

The air around her seemed to hum with a sudden intimacy.

Tell him who you are. Maybe he won't care.

As she stared at him, the friendliness of his gaze lightened her heart. Then she remembered the way other people had looked at her once they realized she was a Thatcher. The looks of condemnation—the looks of pity. Years of knowing people laughed at her behind her back, made fun of her, distrusted her, those feeling didn't go away simply because she wanted them to.

She looked away from Sam's gaze and struggled to quell the longings he kindled. She couldn't bear to see any of those emotions in his eyes.

She would be leaving soon. She would take her secrets with her and go back where no one knew anything about her past—a past she desperately wanted to forget.

To avoid Sam's scrutiny, she focused her attention on his children. As the meal progressed, she started to think she could detect a slight difference in mannerism between Lindy and Kayla. Lindy seemed more outgoing, a little brasher than her sister. Lindy's face was a little thinner, too. Cheryl directed several comments to the girls, and Lindy usually answered first.

Suddenly, Kayla dropped her spoon, and both girls piped up, "I'll get it!" They dived under the table together.

She heard giggling, but the children didn't reappear until Walter spoke. "Enough playing. Get up here and finish your meal."

They popped up and sat down in their chairs, but they continued to giggle. Sam tried to hide a grin, as well.

"What's going on here?" Cheryl asked with growing

amusement. "If I had two shoes on, I would be looking to see if you'd tied my laces together."

"Oh, we wouldn't—" Kayla started.

"—do that," Lindy finished.

They ate the rest of their meal between giggles and grins, and as Cheryl studied their faces, she decided she had been mistaken. Kayla's face was slightly thinner.

When the meal was done, Sam stood and consulted a list posted on the refrigerator door. "Lindy, it's your turn to load the dishwasher tonight."

With a small groan, the girl on Cheryl's right got up and began to clear the table. Bewildered, Cheryl said, "I thought you were Kayla?"

That brought a fresh outburst of laughter from the twins, and Cheryl looked at Sam. He couldn't keep a straight face.

"Oh, I get it, now," she said. "You two switched places under the table, didn't you?"

They nodded, and Cheryl shot Sam and Walter a stern look, but she couldn't maintain her stoic face either. They all dissolved into laughter.

The rest of the evening she spent answering dozens of questions from the twins—about dancing, about her career and about New York City. Cheryl sat on the sofa with her foot propped up and answered their rapid-fire questions as best she could.

Walter had gone to his room, but Sam remained and looked on with an indulgent smile as they grilled her. He said, "Don't say I didn't warn you."

Cheryl didn't mind. She loved talking about the city and about her work. "These two should work for CNN. How many questions can they ask in an hour?"

"Enough to fill an encyclopedia. By the end of the night, I'll know everything there is to know about you."

Cheryl's grin faded. Not everything, she hoped.

"Do you have kids?" Lindy asked her.

"No, I don't."

The twins exchanged a knowing look, and Kayla said, "Are you married?"

"No."

Kayla glanced at her father and smiled in spite of the stern look he leveled at her. "Our dad's not married either."

Cheryl sensed where they were going. She propped her elbow on the arm of the sofa and settled her chin on her hand. "I heard that."

Lindy grew serious. "Don't you think he's handsome?"

Cheryl tapped her fingers against her cheek and struggled not to laugh as Sam rolled his eyes. "He's sort of handsome."

"Would you like to have some kids?" They both looked at her with hopeful faces.

That threw her. The focus of her life had been dancing, to the exclusion of everything else. And yet, when she'd watched these two and Sam playing in the snow, she'd been filled with a longing to join in the fun, to become a part of something she didn't really understand—part of a family.

"I'm afraid I don't have time for a husband or for kids," she said at last. "I'm much too busy with my career."

The twins exchanged downcast looks.

Lindy recovered first from their setback. "Is it fun to be a dancer?"

Cheryl pondered the question. "It's very hard work. I have to practice for hours every day. Sometimes I even get hurt, and I still have to make myself go on. My boss—he's a choreographer, a person who designs a dance—he can be very tough. He's seldom happy with how our group performs, and he will make us do it over and over until he thinks it's right. But yes, it is fun."

She closed her eyes. "Sometimes when I'm dancing, the music catches me up and carries me along like a bit of thistledown on the wind. I can't describe it, really, but dancers call it *the float.* When I'm there, I forget how hard it is, and I only think about how much I love it."

Sam found his gaze riveted to Cheryl's face. She was an elegant, sophisticated woman. She glowed with excitement and happiness when she talked about her craft. "You've been blessed with a great gift—to love the work you do."

She met his eyes. "Blessed with a gift. I've never thought of it that way. Maybe that's true."

Sam cleared his throat. "Girls, it's bedtime."

"Not yet!" they pleaded.

"Yes, it is. You've had a long day."

"Can Cheryl read us a story?"

"And listen to our prayers? Please, Daddy?" Lindy pleaded.

"I'd love to, if it's okay with you, Sam?"

"Please, Daddy?" Kayla added a soulful look.

"Okay." Sam watched as the twins gathered up the cat and headed for their room. "Can you make it down the stairs?" he asked Cheryl with a glance at her cast.

"Yes, cowboy. I can manage a few stairs."

"I was going to be gallant and offer to carry you."

"No. I think I'll be safer on my one good foot."

"Okay, but don't sue me if you fall."

The elegant, sophisticated woman stuck her tongue out, then followed the twins downstairs.

He would give anything to see her dance, Sam thought. The idea sobered him. She had devoted years of her life to the study and performance of an art he had barely acknowledged. He was attracted to her, yes, but it was useless to think it could lead to anything more. They didn't have anything in common.

He'd chosen the wrong kind of woman once. He wouldn't make that mistake again.

Cheryl managed the stairs without a mishap. The lower level of Sam's house was similar to the upper one, except the long room was a recreation room complete with a television, a billiard table and an assortment of games and toys for the children. Brown, overstuffed leather chairs sat grouped around a game table where a chess set waited for someone to finish a game.

The twins headed for one of the four doors along the back wall. "Here's our room," one of them announced.

It was Lindy who spoke, Cheryl decided, as she followed her into the room. Twin beds covered in spreads depicting rodeo scenes sat side by side. A pair of rocking horses stood stabled in one corner, decorated with carelessly thrown clothes, and an assortment of horse figurines lined up on the top of a bookshelf. Cheryl barely had time to glance around before the children urged her to see the next room.

"This is Gramps' room." Lindy held her fingers to her lips. "He says he goes to sleep early so he can get up with the chickens."

"That's funny 'cause we don't have any chickens," Kayla confessed.

Cheryl hid her grin with a hand to her mouth.

"This is the guestroom," Kayla supplied, opening the next door. The room was decorated in the same Indian prints and bold patterns as the living room upstairs. The bed, neatly made, showed no sign that Sam had spent the night there.

The final door turned out to be Sam's office. Photographs of buildings both old and new as well as pictures of the twins decorated the walls. A large computer occupied a wide desk and rolled sheets of blueprints were neatly stored in deep bins. A drafting table held sketches of a beautiful stone and glass house. She had only a moment to admire the clean lines of the structure and to wonder what else he'd designed before the twins hurried her away.

They quickly got themselves ready for bed. After dressing in matching pajamas, they knelt beside their beds and folded their hands.

"God bless Daddy—"

"—and Great-Grandpa Walter."

"God bless Grandma Eleanor—"

"—and Aunt Becky and her baby—"

"—and God bless Bonkers and our new friend, Cheryl."

Cheryl was moved by the sincerity of their small voices even if she had been lumped in with the cat. When was the last time anyone had prayed for her?

Before her mother passed away Cheryl had believed in God. But when her mother died, what little goodness Cheryl knew died with her. Grandma Doris hadn't liked the local preacher. She stopped taking Cheryl and Angie to church. Their father was proud of the fact that he'd never set foot inside one.

Cheryl had knelt beside her little sister in those early days and listened to Angie's prayers. God hadn't answered those prayers and Cheryl had given up believing in Him. But what if she had been wrong? What if God answered Angie's prayers in His own time? Angie was happy now with a man who loved her. She said her tough childhood gave her a special insight into the children she wanted to help.

Cheryl found it disturbing to think that the bad things in her life might have happened for a reason. Sam and his family were making her think about things she had ignored for years.

After their prayers were finished, the girls presented Cheryl with a book. She read them their favorite story of Cinderella from the dog-eared copy. When she had finished, she tucked them in, wished them good-night and turned to leave.

"Wait." Lindy sat up in bed.

"Daddy always gives us a kiss," Kayla finished with a yawn.

"Like this?" Cheryl kissed the top of each head.

"Yup."

"Like that."

"I'm glad I got it right." Cheryl smiled softly as she turned off the light and left the room. Sam was waiting outside the door.

"I should be jealous." His voice, little more than a whisper, caused her pulse to take an erratic leap.

"Why?"

"They never go to bed that easily for me."

"I think you wore them out playing this afternoon."

"You might be right," he conceded with a grin.

"You have beautiful children, Sam. You're a lucky man."

"I think so, too. I've been blessed," he answered quietly.

Suddenly, she realized how close he stood. His eyes roved over her face as though he were trying to memorize each feature. She stared for a long moment into his dark eyes. If only things were different. Why wish for such a foolish thing?

"We think she's beautiful, Daddy," a little voice said. "Don't you think she is?"

Cheryl felt the heat of a blush steal up her cheeks.

Sam looked down at the big eyes of his daughters as they peeked out the crack of their bedroom door. He tried for a stern, fatherly tone but didn't quite make it.

"I think she's very pretty." His mouth twitched as he tried not to smile. "What are you doing out of bed?"

"You didn't kiss us good-night," Lindy reminded him.

"Back to bed, both of you. I'll be in soon."

"After you kiss Cheryl good-night?"

"Close the door, now!"

It snapped shut. He stepped back a pace and shoved his hands in his pockets. "I'm sorry about that."

"It's okay. They mean well. Good night, Sam."

"Before you go, I wanted to invite you to attend church with us in the morning. The service starts at nine if you'd like to come."

"I'm not the church-going type, but thanks," she said with a shake of her head.

"If you change your mind, the invite will stay open."

"I won't." She didn't meet his eyes as she turned away.

Sam pushed a hand through his hair as he watched

her climb the stairs. He'd always considered himself a smart man, but he sure wasn't acting like it where she was concerned. He knew better than to get involved with her. By her own admission, her career was more important than a husband or a family. Now, it seemed she didn't share his faith.

He glanced toward the closed bedroom door. Silently, he vowed to remember that his children were the most important people in his life. They needed good examples, good role models to follow. As much as he felt drawn to Cheryl, she wasn't what he or his girls needed.

Chapter 7

Cheryl tried to concentrate on the book she was reading, but it was useless. She prided herself on being levelheaded, on her ability to stay focused on her career. She had never let a man interfere with her desire to be a successful dancer. Yet, her career was something that seemed to slip to the back of her mind when Sam Hardin was around. He scrambled her common sense without even trying. One glimpse of his endearing, lopsided grin, and her insides turned to jelly.

Glancing out the window, she watched low gray clouds scuttle across the prairie sky. The wind that drove them today was a warm south wind and the snow was melting rapidly. Soon, she'd be able to disappear as fast. The thought brought an ache to her heart as real as the ache in her broken foot.

Sam had pleaded work as his excuse and vanished downstairs after the family returned from church. He'd been down there most of the afternoon. Supposedly, he was working on finding a nanny to take care of the children while his mother was gone.

The twins were playing downstairs, and occasionally the sound of their voices floated up the stairwell. Their happy chatter filled the house with a pleasant hubbub.

Cheryl picked up her book and tried to concentrate again, but when she found herself reading the same page over for the third time, she put it down with disgust. From the corner of her eye, she spied Bonkers walking around the end of the sofa, and she did a double-take.

The cat strolled through the living room dressed in a pink, ruffled, baby dress with little puffy sleeves. His outfit was complete with ruffled underpants that had a hole cut out for his tail. A pink bonnet tied in a lopsided bow beneath his chin was the crowning touch. Cheryl couldn't help herself—she burst out laughing.

Bonkers paused in his trek across the room, gave her a malevolent stare, then slipped beneath the sofa. A moment later, the twins came pounding up the stairs and piled to a stop in front of Cheryl. She still wasn't sure which one was which.

"Our baby is missing."

"Have you seen him?"

Cheryl pointed downward. "I believe he's under the sofa, girls."

They dropped to the floor and peered beneath it.

"Yup, he's under there."

"I think he's mad at us."

"I told you he didn't want baby lotion on his tail, Lindy." Kayla's scolding clued Cheryl into which one was speaking.

"You did not."

"Did too!"

"Did not!"

"All right, now," Cheryl intervened. "Bonkers will come out when he's ready."

The twins climbed on the sofa beside her.

"I was only trying to be a good mommy. I didn't know it would make him mad," Lindy confessed with a long face.

"I'm sure he won't stay mad, sweetheart. And I think you will be a great mommy," Cheryl tried to console her.

"Our mommy was a bad mommy," Lindy said.

Dumbfounded, Cheryl stared at her. "What do you mean?"

"Our mommy didn't want us," Kayla answered sadly.

"She gave us away," Lindy added with a dramatic sigh.

"Just like kittens stuffed in a sack."

"Who said that?" Cheryl demanded.

Kayla exchanged a glance with her sister. "Jimmy Slader's mom, after church today."

"When she didn't think we were listening," Lindy added.

"Merci Slader?" Cheryl asked in disbelief.

Both girls nodded.

Cheryl hesitated, uncertain of how to proceed. Having a serious conversation with two five-year-olds was a little out of her league. More than that, she felt she shouldn't be prying into Sam's private life.

"What has your father told you about why your mother doesn't live with you?" she asked gently.

"He said they both loved us," Kayla volunteered.

"But they didn't want to be married anymore," Lindy added.

"Mommy wanted to marry someone else and live far away."

"And Daddy wanted to live on the ranch."

"So they chose the bestest place for us to live."

"Here with Daddy," Lindy concluded.

A simplified answer for a marital breakup, but Cheryl wasn't about to delve into anything more complicated. "I think your dad would tell you the truth."

"I think so, too," Lindy declared.

"Besides, I don't remember being in a sack," Kayla added.

Lindy crossed her arms. "Me neither!"

Cheryl fought back a smile. "I think Jimmy Slader's mom may be full of hot air."

The twins giggled, but Kayla grew somber again. "Is it okay if I still love Mommy, even if she didn't want us?"

"No, you can't!" Lindy shouted. "I told you that!"

Cheryl gathered them close in a quick, impulsive hug. "Yes, you can, darling. It's okay to love her."

She struggled to find the right words. "When someone you love does something bad, you don't have to like what they've done, but you can still love that person." Her father's and her brother's faces came to mind, and she realized the truth of what she was saying. She knew her dad hadn't been much of a father, but she'd never stopped loving him, never stopped trying to earn his love in return, even though she knew the things he did were wrong. And she'd never stopped loving Jake even after all this time.

She gazed down at the children. "Do you understand what I'm trying to say?"

"I think so," Kayla said.

"Maybe." Lindy sounded reluctant to agree.

Cheryl smiled softly. "I'll bet Jimmy Slader loves his mother, even though she's full of hot air."

They both grinned, then Lindy said, "Daddy says she wants to take care of us when he can't be here."

Kayla crossed her arms and looked sullen. "Until Grandma comes back."

"'Cause he has to go to Kansas City, and we can't go with him."

"But we don't want her. So he's gonna find—"

"—a ninny to take care of us."

Cheryl struggled to keep a straight face with difficulty. "I think you mean a nanny."

Kayla gave a sharp nod. "Yup, that's what we said."

Cheryl caught a quick look that flashed between the two of them. Suddenly, she had the feeling she was being set up.

Lindy looked at her with beseeching brown eyes. "Why don't you stay and take care of us until Grandma comes back?"

"We like you," Kayla added sincerely.

Cheryl discovered something new about children then. Even when you knew you were being wheedled, it didn't keep you from wanting to give in. It tugged at her heart that they would ask her to stay, and she felt like a heel for rejecting their offer.

"I can't. The only reason I haven't left already is because I haven't been able to find my wallet. I lost it out in the snow after my accident, but the snow is almost gone now, and your father will be able to find it soon, and then I have to leave."

"But you can't dance with your foot broken. You said so," Lindy argued.

"I know, but if I'm lucky, I can get a job helping take care of costumes or the sets. Ballet is what I do." She stroked a hand through each set of downy curls. "Like your dad takes care of the ranch and builds houses. It's my job."

"But why?" they pleaded.

Cheryl didn't quite know how to convey the meaning of the word *career* to them. "When you dress Bonkers up in baby clothes, that doesn't make him a real baby, does it? He's still a cat."

She paused to see if they understood what she was saying. "Right now I may not seem like a ballerina, but inside I am. It's all I've ever wanted to be."

The two faces watching her grew sadder with each word she spoke. Their solemn eyes filled with tears.

"You just don't like us," Kayla said mournfully.

"That's not true," Cheryl insisted.

Bonkers sprang up beside them on the sofa. His bonnet hung from his neck by a shredded ribbon. Lindy gathered up her make-believe baby, and the girls climbed down. Cheryl reached out to stop them, but Bonkers flattened his ears and hissed at her, and she snatched her hand back.

Sam stood at the top of the stairs as the somber-faced pair marched around him without a word. Cheryl cast him a pleading glance, but he shook his head. "You have only known them for two days. I've had to cope with them for five years, and they still do it to me. Welcome to the Giant Rat Fink Club."

"If those two don't end up on the stage, the world will be denied the presence of great actresses," Cheryl said in awe.

"I hate to tell you this, New York, but they're just getting started."

He walked over and sat beside her on the sofa. "I have to admit, it's a good idea. I'm sure I can't pay you what a ballerina earns. In spite of appearances, ranching isn't always a prosperous business, but I think I can pay you what a ninny would make."

They exchanged amused glances. "I think you have an exaggerated idea of what a ballerina pulls down," she said. "It's a tempting offer, Sam, but no."

"You said yourself that you can't dance. This way you have a place to stay and a little money coming in until your foot is healed."

"Sam, I can't. I adore your kids, but I have to rejoin my company."

He grew serious as he studied her face. He reached out and brushed a wisp of hair back from the edge of her jaw, then dropped his hand. He stood and smiled at her. "I hate to think you're leaving us for a bunch of guys in pink tights."

A grin struggled through her sadness. Trust Sam to find a way to make her smile.

He gave a nod in the direction of the stairs. "I've got to get back to work now. Is there anything I can do for you?"

"No, I'm fine."

"Do you think you could stay until Friday at least? I really do need to go to Kansas City on Thursday. If I can convince these clients to go with my design, it'll mean a lot. It seems the girls aren't crazy about Merci's offer to let them stay with her. Walter thinks he can handle them, but the truth is, I'd feel better if I had someone to look after all of them."

"I'll stay until then," she conceded. "It's the least I can do after all you've done for me. Besides, I can't go anywhere until I have my wallet back, or until I know for sure I need to report everything as lost."

"Thanks. Most of the snow is gone. I'll go look for it again this afternoon," he offered, turning to leave.

"Thanks, Sam." Cheryl watched him walk back to the staircase. His broad shoulders slumped as he thrust his hands deep in his pockets. Watching him walk away, she had the strangest feeling that she'd just lost something very valuable, and it wasn't her wallet.

Sam checked on the twins, but they weren't in their room. It wasn't unusual for them to retreat to the barn or the garden when they were unhappy. He'd talk to them about Cheryl's leaving later.

Back in his office, he sat down at his desk, dropped his head onto both hands and raked his fingers through his hair. All he had to do was find a way to tell the twins they couldn't have what he wanted, too. For Cheryl to stay.

He reminded himself once again that this attraction couldn't go anywhere. She was the exact opposite of what he needed. He needed a woman who wanted to be a mother to his children. Cheryl was beautiful, funny and intelligent, but she wasn't interested in being a mother, or in living on a ranch. She had a life planned that was far different. A life he and his children could have no part in.

An hour later, he heard the twins return. He opened their bedroom door to find two muddy and tired girls. They nodded quietly when he told them Cheryl wouldn't be staying. The arguments he expected didn't materialize. He left their room feeling a little worried and more than a bit suspicious of such cooperative behavior.

The weather warmed up to its normal springtime high the next day. By afternoon, the snow was gone except for a few drifts that lingered in the shade of the buildings and trees.

By mutual and unspoken consent, Sam and Cheryl avoided any talk of her leaving. Cheryl expected the time to pass awkwardly but was surprised to find that she enjoyed a growing friendship with Sam. If her smiles were too bright, or her humor a little forced, no one seemed to notice. When she found herself longing for something more, she ruthlessly pushed those feelings aside. And if she wasn't sleeping well, she put it down to her aching foot.

The twins were treating her like royalty, she noted, as they carefully carried her lunch tray out onto the balcony for an impromptu picnic on the second day of beautiful weather. The snow was gone from the hillside where she had watched them sledding. Here and there, hardy spring flowers that had been hidden by the snow were putting in an appearance.

Cheryl was enjoying her time with the girls when the sound of footsteps caused her heart to flutter and skip a beat. Sam came up the stairs that led to the balcony from a walk at the side of the house.

"Am I too late for lunch?" he asked.

"Nope, you're just in time." Lindy presented him with a messy version of a peanut butter and jelly sandwich. "I made it myself," she announced proudly.

Cheryl had already sampled hers. She watched Sam take a seat and tip his hat back.

"This is what I like," he stated cheerfully.

"Peanut butter and jelly?" Cheryl inquired with a raised eyebrow.

"Nope. Having lunch with three pretty ladies." He drew smiles from all the ladies with his blatant flattery and took a hearty bite of his sandwich. He had a little jelly left on the side of his mouth when he finished, and Cheryl found herself holding his chin steady to wipe it off with her napkin. His teasing grin faded, and his eyes darkened. She let her hand fall back to the table and looked away.

Across from them the twins glanced at each other and smiled slyly. "Can we go play?"

"Sure," Sam answered absently, and they took off.

Easy, Sam, he cautioned himself. You can be friends, but nothing more. He tried to concentrate on something besides the way she made him wish she wasn't the wrong woman for him.

"The girls really like you," he said. "Not many people can learn to tell them apart as quickly as you have."

"I adore them. They're as bright as new pennies. You've done a fine job with them, Sam."

"Thanks. You should have kids of your own. You're great with them." He dropped his gaze to his plate. That was a stupid thing to say. He must be as transparent as glass, but what would it hurt to put the idea out and see how she reacted? He held his breath as he waited for her reply.

"Maybe I will. Someday. Who knows?"

Sam's hope rose. It wasn't a flat no. If only they had more time.

She smiled at him brightly. "I'd just have to meet the right man first."

"And what would the right man be like?"

"Oh, someone who loves ballet and hot pretzels with mustard and New York City even in the summer when it's muggy and clogged with smog."

"I thought maybe it would be a guy who brought you chocolate and roses?"

She looked away and didn't answer. Sam rose to his feet. He had to stop kidding himself, she'd never be happy here.

"I've got a council member meeting at church tonight and Walter has his weekly checkers game with one of our neighbors. Do you think you can handle the terrible twosome by yourself for an evening?"

She smiled and nodded. "No problem, cowboy. Just leave me the phone number where you'll be, the hospital's number…" she began to count off on her fingers, "…the sheriff's number, poison control, the fire department, ah, your insurance agent's number, the number for your next of kin, the vet's number…"

"The vet?"

"In case anything happens to Bonkers."

"Aren't we being a little paranoid?"

"Good idea. Leave me your therapist's number."

"I don't have a therapist. But I'm beginning to think I may need one. Oh, I almost forgot. This letter came for you today." He pulled a folded white envelope from his shirt pocket and handed it to her.

"That must be my last paycheck." Cheryl took it and tucked it in her shirt pocket. She would look at it later. That way if she burst into tears at the tiny amount no one would see her.

Later that day, as she watched Sam let his daughters help with the housework, she realized that he loved being a father. He was endlessly patient with the girls' less-than-perfect efforts, and Cheryl found herself admiring his kindness and the gentle way he helped tiny hands perform eager tasks.

For ten years Cheryl had been consumed by her work. Now, everything she'd denied she needed was suddenly spread out before her, and she was disturbed to feel she'd been missing out on something equally as important as her dancing.

Her evening alone with the twins went smoothly. Later that night, she remembered her paycheck and pulled it out of her pocket. When she opened the envelope there wasn't a check. There was only a single sheet of paper without a signature. On it in bold block print was written,

Go away. You aren't wanted here. Go away.

The terse missive made Cheryl's skin crawl. Who had sent it? Who wanted her gone? She picked up the envelope, but there was no return address. It seemed that she had made someone angry. Merci perhaps? Who else could it be?

The troubling letter kept her awake long after she lay in bed. Sleep eluded her as she listened for the sound of Sam coming home and wondered what she should do about the note. There really was nothing to do, she realized. She would be leaving soon. Only she didn't like the idea that someone would think she had turned tail and run away after a sick prank like this.

It was after midnight when she finally heard Sam's truck in the driveway, followed by his quiet footsteps across the hardwood floor in the living room. She turned over and settled his pillow under her face, but sleep was a long time in coming.

The following day, between the insistent twins and the lure of the warm sunshine, Cheryl decided to venture out and explore some of the ranch. Once outside, the twins headed for the large red barn and white painted corrals across the gravel yard. A windmill twirled gaily beside the barn. The breeze that spun it brought the loamy scent of spring to her, and Cheryl was surprised to discover how much she'd missed the enticing freshness and smells of a Kansas spring.

Sam stood saddling a tall, roan horse beside the barn. He wore a light blue denim shirt, jeans and leather chaps. His high-heeled boots sported blunt silver spurs. The fringe of his chaps fluttered softly as he moved. The man was a cowgirl's dream come to life, she thought, as she watched him lift the heavy saddle with ease. He spoke softly to the big roan as he bent to reach under the horse's belly for the girth. Too bad she wasn't a cowgirl.

Sam lowered the stirrup after he'd finished tightening the cinch and patted the roan's shoulder. The horse, meanwhile, had his head down allowing the twins to scratch enthusiastically behind his ears.

"Come on, Cheryl, come see our new baby calf," Kayla insisted. The girls took off toward a second, smaller corral.

Cheryl smiled at Sam and willed her heart to stop its wild fluttering as she followed the pair to where a little Charolais was busy suckling lunch from his patient mother. His stubby tail was twirling nearly as fast as the windmill. Every now and then, he gave his mother's udder an impatient butt with his snowy head.

"Wait a minute," Sam called. He mounted and rode up beside them. "Grandpa Walter has gone into town for feed, so you girls will be on your own while I'm gone. It's okay if you want to pet Henrietta's new calf, she won't mind, but don't go into the other corral. I opened the barn door so Harvey can come out now that the weather's getting warmer. You stay out of his corral. Is that understood?" His tone was stern.

"Yes, sir!" rang out from all three of them.

"Good." He grinned at Cheryl's mock salute.

"Who's Harvey?" she asked.

"Possibly the salvation of this ranch."

"I don't understand."

"He's one of those pedigreed cattle I was talking about. Harvey is our three-time-grand-champion Charolais show bull and the backbone of our advanced breeding program. There are cows lined up as far away as Canada who are just waiting to have one of his calves."

Cheryl wrinkled her nose. "He's going to be busy, isn't he?"

"Very busy, I hope." Sam grinned at her, touched the brim of his hat, then whirled his horse and rode away.

She watched him ride out of the yard. It wasn't fair. The man looked even better on horseback.

The twins leaned through the fence and began petting the calf's wooly head when he paused in his eating to investigate these potential new playmates. He frisked away from the twins, and the girls slipped through the fence to follow him in an impromptu game of tag.

Cheryl glanced toward the barn. A small white cat, followed by a trio of black-and-white kittens intent on catching their mother's twitching tail, emerged to sit in a patch of sunshine. Cheryl looked for a bull but didn't see him.

It was foolish to worry about a cat that obviously lived in the barn, but she didn't want the kittens playing in harm's way.

"Here kitty, kitty," she called, extending her hand. The next instant, the bull's massive head appeared in the doorway. He dwarfed the kittens clustered beneath him. Cheryl held her breath, certain she was about to see them trampled.

She checked quickly for the twins. They were still in the adjacent pen. They stood looking into a large round stock tank. It extended under both sides of the corral fence so animals in both enclosures could drink from it. Cheryl didn't think they could see the kittens.

She looked back at the gigantic white bull. He snorted once over the kittens, but the silly things didn't have the sense to run. Then, he put his muzzle down and snorted again. One kitten merely arched its back and rubbed against the giant's nose. With a gentle push Cheryl wouldn't have believed if she hadn't seen it, the bull moved the kittens out of his way, stepped out into the sunshine and lumbered across the corral.

He was a magnificent animal. Dense white ringlets covered his head and thick neck, and his snowy coat gleamed in the sunlight. Powerful muscles moved smoothly as he trotted around the perimeter of the corral.

"Cheryl, look what we can do," Lindy called.

The twins had climbed to the top of the fence and begun to walk along it with their arms outstretched like tightrope walkers. It was a game Cheryl and her sister had played often as children. The object was to see who could walk the thick wooden rail the farthest without falling.

The bull took an interest in their activity and moved to stand beside the tank as the girls walked over the top of it. With the huge animal standing so close, suddenly, the children's game didn't look so safe. Cheryl moved down the fence toward them. She wanted to call out, but she was afraid to startle the girls.

Lindy reached the far side of the tank and jumped down with a laugh. Cheryl let out a sigh of relief, then everything happened at once.

Lindy's jump startled the bull. He swung his head against the boards with a blow that shook the entire fence. Kayla lost her balance, uttering a short, bitten-off scream as she fell. Her head struck the steel rim of the tank as her body disappeared with a splash.

Cheryl screamed Kayla's name and lunged to grip the fence in front of her. Lindy's scream echoed her own.

Sam was headed down the lane when he heard the screams. He turned in the saddle in time to see Cheryl throw her crutch over the corral fence and vault over after it.

He couldn't believe his eyes. She fell once, came up with her crutch and continued to charge across the muddy pen sending the cow and calf bolting out of her way. Sam searched for the twins, but he saw only one child standing beside the stock tank screaming.

He ruthlessly hauled his horse's head around and spurred for the corrals.

Chapter 8

Cheryl reached the stock tank and gripped the cold metal rim. There was no sign of Kayla. Quickly, she stepped into the icy, hip-deep water and began searching by feel under the murky surface.

"Kayla, where are you, baby? Please, God, help me find her!" Cheryl heard the panic in her own voice. After years of ignoring God why would He answer her? She had stopped praying, stopped believing, yet her heart cried out to Him now. *Save this child.*

Unable to locate Kayla on the side where she had fallen, Cheryl took a deep breath and ducked under the fence that divided the tank. Her fingers touched a small hand. Quickly, she pulled the child to her and stood. Water streamed down her face as she gasped for air, but she cradled Kayla's limp body against her chest.

Sam galloped into the yard and reined his horse to a sliding stop beside the corral. He kicked free of the stirrups, vaulted out of the saddle and over the fence in a single movement and hit the ground running.

Cheryl slogged through the water and handed Kayla

into his reaching arms. He took the child and gently laid her on the ground.

"She was on the fence," Cheryl panted. "She fell and hit her head."

Stepping out of the water, she knelt beside him. "I couldn't find her, Sam. It took so long."

Kayla's lips were blue, her skin translucent and pale as marble.

Cheryl felt for a pulse in the child's neck. *Please, God, let her be okay.* To her relief, she found one, strong and steady beneath her fingers. The faint rise and fall of her little chest confirmed she was breathing. "She has a good pulse."

Sam's own heart began to beat again. "Thank You, Dear God, thank You," he uttered weakly. "Kayla, wake up, kitten. Can you hear me?"

Kayla's eyelids fluttered open, and she slowly focused on his face. "Daddy?" she whispered.

It was the sweetest sound he'd ever heard. He lifted her small body and cradled her close. "Yes, baby, Daddy's here." His voice broke, and he rocked her gently.

Wiping the tears from his face, he looked at Cheryl. "Thank you." He stretched out his hand. She grasped it firmly.

"Daddy, is Kayla okay?"

Sam took one look at Lindy's frightened face and pulled her close to her sister in his arms.

Cheryl said, "She hit her head pretty hard when she fell, Sam. I think we should get her to the hospital."

She was right. Reluctantly, he handed his daughter to her and stood. He was surprised to find his knees wouldn't hold him, and he staggered slightly as his head spun. Bending over, he braced his hands on his thighs and took several deep breaths. When his head stopped spinning, he tried to marshal his thoughts. "I'll go get the truck."

"Get a blanket first. She's freezing."

"So are you." He turned and hurried toward the house. As he set one boot on the fence, he paused and looked back. Cheryl knelt on the muddy ground with Kayla cradled across her lap, her soft voice reassuring both girls.

The cow and its calf had came up behind her and watched the proceedings with bovine inquisitiveness. Lowering her head, the cow sniffed at Kayla's face. Cheryl pushed the animal aside with an indifferent shove, as if she'd handled cattle all her life. Sam wasn't sure why, but the sight triggered a touch of unease in his mind. There was more to Cheryl Steele than she let on.

Sitting wrapped in a blanket in Sam's pickup, Cheryl held Kayla on her lap as they sped toward the hospital. Kayla lay pale and quiet, but her breathing was regular. Cheryl kept one hand inside the blanket just to make sure. She'd known these children only a few days, but already they'd wormed their way firmly into her heart.

Lindy sat between the adults on the seat. "I think God got me and Kayla mixed up," she said in a faltering voice.

Puzzled, Cheryl glanced at Sam, but he seemed bewildered as well. Cheryl slipped an arm around Lindy's shoulders and drew her close. "What do you mean, honey?"

"When you do something bad, God punishes you. But I think he got me and Kayla mixed up."

"Sweetheart," Sam said. "God is the one fellow who

can never get you mixed up. He isn't punishing you or Kayla. It was an accident."

"Even if we did something bad?"

"Your daddy is right, Lindy. It was a scary accident, that's all. Will it make you feel better to tell us what you think you did?"

Lindy nodded. "We found your wallet, and we hid it so you couldn't go away," her voice tapered off into a little whisper.

Cheryl was speechless.

Sam shook his head. "I should have known you two were up to something.

Wiggling free of Cheryl's hold, Lindy snuggled up against him. "Are you mad? It was my idea," she confessed with more resolve.

Draping an arm over her shoulder, he pulled her against him. "I'm disappointed that you thought you could make Cheryl stay by keeping something that belonged to her, but I'm not angry with you. I love you. Do you understand?"

Lindy nodded, "Cheryl told us you can love somebody even if they do bad things."

Sam met Cheryl's gaze over his daughter's head. "Did she?"

"Yup," Lindy answered.

"She's a smart lady."

Cheryl basked in the glow of his praise for only a moment. Then the reality of what had happened sank in. She should have been watching the girls more closely. She should have made them get down the second she saw what they were doing. This was her fault. At least God had answered her prayers.

Why hadn't He saved her mother the way He'd saved

Kayla? Was one life less valuable than the other? She had no answers for the questions that spun through her mind. She rode the rest of the way in silence.

In the ER, Sam stayed with Kayla while Cheryl was taken to have her foot looked at. Her cast was a water-logged mass of plaster. Dr. Carlton proceeded to scold her for using her foot, X-rayed it and applied a new cast. When he was finished, he held open the door of the exam room, and Cheryl maneuvered herself out on her crutches.

"There doesn't seem to be any damage to the healing bones," he informed her. "This is a walking cast I've put on. It is not a running, jumping or dancing cast, understood? I don't want you putting your full weight on that foot yet. Use the crutches for another two weeks, then a cane if it's comfortable."

She listened with only half an ear as he gave instructions to a petite, dark-haired nurse. When he turned back, he said, "I wish I could place where I know you from, young lady."

"Maybe she just looks like someone you know," his nurse suggested.

Cheryl tensed. She'd been told she looked like her mother. Could he have known Mira?

"Maybe. It'll come to me," he said.

"Where's Kayla now?" Cheryl asked, eager to see her.

"I'll find out for you," the nurse answered.

Cheryl was given the room number, then made her way down the hospital corridor. At Kayla's door, she paused. A sign said visitors were limited to family only. Should she go in?

Family or not, she needed to know for herself that Kayla was okay. She put her hand on the door.

"You can't go in there."

Cheryl turned to see Merci Slader coming down the hall.

"Hospital policy—family only," Merci said, stopping beside Cheryl. "Kayla is fine. I just checked with her nurse. Actually, I'm a bit surprised that you're still here. I thought you'd be on your way by now."

"I'll leave when I'm ready, Merci." She considered confronting the woman about the letter, but decided against it. There were more important things to think about. Like Kayla.

"I think the sooner you move on the better it will be for everyone. I know Sam thought you could help watch the girls, but obviously you can't do that in your condition. Isn't this terrible accident proof of that?" With a smug parting smile, she left.

Cheryl watched Merci go, then squared her shoulders. She needed to see Kayla, and she wasn't about to let Merci Slader or a few puny hospital rules stop her. She pushed open the door.

Inside, she found Sam seated beside Kayla's bed with Lindy curled up in his lap. He had one arm stretched over the metal rail, and he stroked Kayla's dark curls as she lay on the pristine sheets. She looked terribly small and helpless.

Sam spoke as Cheryl came and stood beside him. "Kayla, baby. Cheryl's here."

Kayla opened sleepy eyes and smiled up at Cheryl. "Hi."

"Hi yourself, Tweedledee. How are you feeling?"

"Okay."

Lindy leaned toward the bed and touched her sister's face. "I told them," she whispered.

Kayla's lip quivered and tears filled her eyes as she focused on Cheryl. "Are you gonna leave now? Please, don't go. We want you to take care of us!"

Sam tried to comfort her, but she continued to cry and plead. He sent Cheryl an imploring look and she understood. Kayla needed to stay calm and to rest.

"I'll stay as long as you need me." Planting a kiss on Kayla's brow, she added, "Why don't you try and sleep now?"

Kayla sniffled. "You won't leave until I'm asleep, will you?"

"No. I promise."

"Okay. Daddy, can Lindy sleep with me?"

"Sure." Sam settled Lindy in the bed with her sister. They snuggled together and Kayla slept at last.

Cheryl moved away from the bed and spoke in a low voice. "I'm so sorry, Sam. I should have been keeping a better eye on them."

"Hush. It wasn't your fault. I've told them a dozen times not to walk on the top of the fences. Besides, you saved her life." Sam drew her into his arms and settled his chin on top of her head as he held her close.

She relished the strength and the feeling of safety his embrace gave her. She rested against his tall, strong body, gathering comfort from his arms around her. It felt so right. She had promised to stay as long as Kayla needed her, but what on earth was she getting herself into?

Sam held her away and looked into her eyes. "Have I said thank-you?"

"You're welcome," she whispered, gazing at him.

He was everything her heart needed. His touch sent her senses singing with happiness. Before she knew what to expect, he bent his head and kissed her. The warmth of his lips spread to the center of her chest and sent her heart racing with delight.

A knock on the door brought her back to earth, and she quickly stepped away as Walter poked his head in.

Sam let Cheryl go reluctantly. He wanted her back in his arms, but instead, he spoke to his obviously worried grandfather. "Come in, Gramps."

"I got your message and came as quick as I could. How is she?" He moved to the bedside and reached a trembling hand down to caress Kayla's hair.

"The doctor wants to keep her overnight for observation. Her lungs are clear. She's got a goose-egg-size lump on the back of her head, but nothing's broken."

"The Lord be praised."

"Amen to that. It could have been so much worse."

"I've outlived my wife and my son. I sure don't want to outlive my great-granddaughter."

Cheryl laid a comforting hand on the old man's arm. He squeezed it in return, then wiped at his eyes. "What do you need me to do, Sammy?"

Sam rubbed a weary hand over his face. "I'll spend the night here. Could you drive Cheryl back to the ranch?"

"No. Let me stay," Cheryl pleaded.

"Look, why don't we do this," Walter suggested. "I'll stay with the girls while you take Cheryl home, and you can change." He gave Sam a wry smile as he looked him up and down. "I hate to bring it up, but you smell a bit ripe."

Sam looked down at his boots and jeans. Gramps

was right. He hadn't paid the least bit of attention to what he knelt in when he'd laid Kayla down in the corral. He grimaced and said, "You always said it's the smell of money."

Walter gave him a little push to get him started toward the door. "Every rancher says that. Go home and come back when you smell broke. I'll be here if the girls need anything."

"Okay, you win. Thanks." With a glance at the sleeping twins, he allowed Cheryl and himself to be herded out the door.

Cheryl paused as she entered the quiet house. It echoed with emptiness. The children added the life that made it home. The thought brought her up short. When had she started thinking of this place as home? It wasn't. It could never be. Not for her.

She changed while Sam went to shower, then she retrieved her wallet from under Lindy's pillow. Slowly, she made her way upstairs, sat on the sofa and laid her head back with a weary sigh. She had been a fool to promise Kayla she would stay longer. Every day she remained here she risked being exposed. She didn't want her past laid bare before Sam and his family. She cared about them. She wasn't the same angry, foolhardy girl who had caused so much harm all those years ago.

Raising her fingertips to her temples, she tried to massage away her dull headache. What was she doing getting more involved with this family? It didn't take a genius to see that Sam and the children were growing fond of her. That she returned their regard didn't change things. She wasn't being fair to them by building up their hopes that she would stay.

Her conscience nagged her. God had answered her prayers today and spared Kayla's life. What did He want from her in return?

Feeling tired but restless, she rose and opened the sliding glass door to the balcony and took a deep breath of fresh air. The soft evening breeze toyed with her hair as she stepped out and sat on the glider. Quietly, she rocked and watched as the sunset colored the timeless hills in shades of rose, lavender and gold.

She wasn't given much to introspection, Cheryl realized. She looked forward—never back. The past was too painful. She'd spent her whole life being ashamed of what her father and her half brother had done, what they'd made her a part of. She came to hate this land— the treeless, windswept hills where her mother and her childhood had both died painful deaths.

Gazing out at hills rolling away to the horizon, Cheryl slowly understood it had been the events that she hated, not this place.

These hills were a part of her. She knew the call of the meadowlark and the cry of the hawk that rode the wind in lazy circles across a flawless blue sky. She knew the ceaseless wind that sent the long grasses bowing before it in undulating waves. Her soul heard the music the wind played in the grass just as surely as she heard it when she danced.

The balcony door opened, but she didn't turn around. Dusk was fading and the evening stars began to shine in the darkening heavens. These hills may have been her home once, but not anymore. She wasn't strong enough to face the prejudice and shame all over again. The thought of Sam finding out what she had done sent a chill racing down her spine.

He sat beside her and slipped an arm around her shoulder. She wanted to lean against him, to draw comfort from his strength and warmth, but she didn't. Silently, she watched the stars come out, one by one.

She was so close to falling in love with this man. The earthy, masculine scent of him filled her with hopes and dreams she didn't fully understand. The tender way he stroked her hair left her feeling strangely content. It would be so easy to let herself love him.

She was already half in love with his daughters. Lindy and Kayla had crept into her heart when she wasn't looking. Somewhere between trading places under the table and the near tragedy today, they had opened her eyes to the joys of having children be a part of her life.

Until today, she had believed that to dance was all she needed. The grueling work, the pain and the joy of the dance was what she lived for. It was an all-consuming life because she wanted it that way. On the stage, people admired her for what she could do, for her talent, not for who she was inside. She didn't believe that she deserved someone to love and to be loved by in return.

Now, Sam and the children were showing her a different kind of life. A life where God and family came first. Where people worked together because they loved each other, not because they had to. But that life shimmered just beyond her reach—because she couldn't stay.

She was risking discovery, but more than that, she was risking a terrible heartache. Staying was out of the question. She would remain until she was certain Kayla was all right, then she'd leave. Sam's arm tightened around her shoulders

"Are you okay?" he asked.

"Just tired," she said quickly. Somehow, she had to find the strength to harden her heart against this longing to stay in his arms.

She moved out of his embrace, stood and pushed her hair back as she tried for a nonchalant tone. "I must say, cowboy, this place has supplied me with more excitement in one week than I've had in the last ten years. I don't know how you stand it."

He cleared his throat. "Yeah. It's been one tough day. Are you sure you're okay?"

She nodded as she moved away from him to stand at the balcony rail.

Sam felt empty and cold without her warmth against his side. He wanted her back in his arms. She had saved his child's life, and he was indebted to her, but it wasn't gratitude he felt when he held her. It was much more, yet he found it hard to trust his feelings. It was harder still to put them into words. He'd been wrong about a woman once before. What if he was wrong again?

How did Cheryl feel about what was happening between them? He wanted to ask, but maybe this wasn't the right time. "I guess we've both had a little too much excitement," he said.

She gave him a weak smile before she turned back to stare out into the night. "That's for sure. I'll be glad to get back to New York where life is safe and calm. It's been fun, cowboy, but I can't take much more of this."

There was his answer—she couldn't wait to leave. "I'm sorry you had to lie."

She spun toward him, her face pale in the starlight. "What do you mean?"

"When you told Kayla you would stay."

"Oh, that."

"What did you think I meant?"

"Nothing. It wasn't a lie. I will stay until she's better."

"What if someone else asks you to stay? Would you consider it?" His slender stalk of hope wouldn't die. He waited, afraid to breathe. He almost missed her soft whisper.

"I would have to say—no."

Disappointment burned itself deep in his heart. Turning away, Sam walked through the house and out the door.

Moments later, he found himself standing in front of Dusty's stall in the dimly lit barn. The horse stretched his neck over the stall door in greeting. Sam began to stroke the gelding's sturdy neck, drawing comfort from the sleek hide under his hand.

Cheryl had made it plain that she couldn't wait to get back to New York. She wouldn't stay. She didn't want him, just as Natalie hadn't wanted him.

Hurt and confusion churned inside him until he thought he might explode. Why did he keep falling for the same kind of woman? What was wrong with him? Why was God testing him?

"I won't play the fool again. I won't love her." Bold words, but Sam knew it was already too late for him.

Show me what to do, Lord. I don't know why You are testing me, but please help me weather this trial.

Chapter 9

Sam glanced with concern at his daughters seated beside him in the truck as he drove home from the hospital the next day. "You two sure are quiet."

Lindy looked at her sister and then back at him. "I don't think we have anything to say."

This didn't feel right. The doctor had given Kayla a clean bill of health, but Sam began to worry she'd been affected more than they realized. Only when they arrived home, and Kayla saw Cheryl did some of the animation return to her face.

Kayla climbed out of the truck and rushed to Cheryl. "You're here. When you didn't come to the hospital with Daddy, I thought you might have gone away."

"I told you I'd stay until you were better."

"I'm glad you didn't leave."

Cheryl bent down and caught the child in a hug. "I'm glad you're glad." She planted a quick kiss on Kayla's cheek.

Sam's hands clenched into fists at his side. The twins adored Cheryl already. The longer she stayed, the harder it would be for them when she left. She had no right to make them love her, then leave the way their mother had.

He felt a touch on his hand, and he glanced down at Lindy's worried face. He forced a smile to his lips.

"Aren't you glad Cheryl is going to stay, Daddy?" she asked.

He met Cheryl's gaze. "Let's not forget it's only for a few more days," he answered flatly.

For a fleeting instant, he thought he saw a look of pain in Cheryl's beautiful eyes, but the expression was gone so quickly he decided he'd imagined it.

Sam expected Kayla's bubbly personality to reassert itself once she was home, but it didn't, and he watched with growing concern as she became Cheryl's little shadow. Kayla sat quietly beside Cheryl on the sofa or out on the glider when the weather was nice, but she never moved far from her new heroine's side. Lindy hovered close by, quiet and uncertain, waiting for her sister to notice her.

Two days later, he caught Cheryl's worried glance when Kayla refused to go riding with Walter. Kayla and Lindy were both good riders, and they loved to tag along on their ponies while their great-grandpa regaled them with stories of the old days. Sam spent the day with a dejected Lindy by his side, and his concerns grew. It would break Kayla's heart when Cheryl left.

That night Kayla insisted only Cheryl could listen to her prayers and tuck her in. Sam tucked Lindy in and kissed her good-night as Cheryl did the same for Kayla. They left the children's room together and climbed the stairs.

Cheryl broke the uneasy silence first. "Sam, I'm worried about Kayla."

"She's my daughter. It's my job to worry about her, not yours."

Cheryl frowned at him. "I know whose daughter she is, but I can still see something is wrong."

"Can you? Can you see how badly Lindy feels when Kayla all but ignores her and follows you around like a puppy? Can you see how differently they act? They don't even talk the same anymore."

Cheryl laid a hand on his arm. "I see those things, but I don't see why you're angry at me."

He pulled his arm away. "Kayla turns to you now for everything, instead of her family. I think she'd get back to normal sooner if she didn't have someone interfering."

"Someone, meaning me?" Cheryl drew away from him, her voice cold and formal.

"Maybe you don't realize it, but they really care about you. Will it even matter to you that you're leaving two brokenhearted kids behind?"

"Of course I care. How can you think I don't?" When he didn't answer, she said, "I promised Kayla I would stay as long as she needed me, but if you want me to go, I will."

Sam stared at her, unable to read the expression in her eyes. He didn't want her to go. He wanted her to stay forever, but she wouldn't do that. His shoulders slumped in defeat, and he turned away feeling tired, empty and sad. "You're free to go any time."

As the adults parted, two curly heads ducked back down the stairwell. They watched their father go out the front door while Cheryl crossed to her bedroom.

"See what you did?" Lindy hissed at her sister.

"What? I didn't do nothin'."

"Cheryl's gonna leave now."

"But I don't want her to. I want her to stay and be our mommy," Kayla insisted.

Lindy propped both elbows on her knees and rested her chin on her hands as she stared at her sister. "Are you mad at me 'cause you got hurt?"

"No."

"You never want to play anymore."

Kayla sighed. "Cheryl needs me because she's so sad. We can play tomorrow."

"Okay." With that problem solved, Lindy turned to another. "Dad's mad at Cheryl because we don't talk the same anymore," she decided at last. "Cheryl won't stay and be our mommy if Daddy's mad at her."

"So?"

"So, we got to talk the same again."

"Okay," Kayla agreed with a shrug.

"And Daddy's mad cause he thinks we'll be sad if Cheryl goes away like our real mom did."

"Then we just gotta make her stay."

"I know, but how?"

"I could hide her wallet again."

Lindy shook her head. "No, Dad would know it was us."

Kayla patted her sister's shoulder. "You'll think of something."

"Maybe. But we got to pretend we don't care if Cheryl's gonna leave, then Dad won't be mad, and they won't fight. Can you do that?"

"Sure. I can pretend better than you."

"Cannot."

"Can too."

"Cannot."

"Last one to the bed is a monkey's uncle," Kayla cried and raced down the stairs with her sister in hot pursuit.

Free to go. I'm free to go. The phrase echoed over and over in Cheryl's mind as she lay in the darkness. If she was free to go, didn't that mean she was also free to stay?

Don't be stupid. It meant Sam wanted her to leave. And it was what she wanted, wasn't it? Yet, lying in bed, she found it impossible to imagine what her life was going to be like after she left here. It would never be the same again, of that much she was sure. Before, her heart had belonged only to dancing. Now, she was very much afraid it belonged to Sam and his children.

She stared at the ceiling. It wasn't possible, but even if she chose to stay with Sam, it would mean the end of her career. Half her life had been spent in the pursuit of one goal—to dance professional ballet. She couldn't picture her life without it. A life without grueling practices and constant pain? A life without reaching that special moment when the music swept her along like the current of a river and carried her twirling and spinning as effortlessly as a piece of driftwood. It was her gift. How could she give it up?

She turned over in the bed. Who was she kidding? She wasn't free to stay even if Sam asked her to. She was only here on borrowed time. It had been a mistake to stay in the first place. If Sam found out who she was now he wouldn't want her anywhere near his children. Maybe he was right. The sooner she left, the better off everyone would be.

The next morning, Sam and Walter sat drinking coffee in the kitchen when Cheryl came out of her room. She cast Sam a wary glance, but he avoided making eye contact. She filled a cup for herself and sat down at the table. Suddenly, the pounding of feet broke the uneasy quiet as the twins erupted from the stairwell and streaked into the kitchen. They skidded to a stop in front of their father.

"What's for—"

"—breakfast?"

"I'm—"

"—starved."

Mischievous eyes glanced at each other, and Cheryl was suddenly positive they could read each other's thoughts.

"I'm so hungry—"

"—I could eat—"

"—a cat!" they shouted together. With a fit of giggles, they darted out of the kitchen calling, "Here kitty, kitty," as they pounded down the stairs.

Sam raised an eyebrow at Cheryl, and she sputtered out a sip of coffee as she began to laugh.

"They're back," he said, giving her a sheepish smile.

Cheryl's heart lightened at the sight of that familiar lopsided grin. "Do you think we'll live to regret it?"

"Only if they catch the cat," Walter said dryly.

Cheryl giggled. "Yum, kitty catatori, my favorite."

It was good to see Sam smile again, Cheryl thought, as her traitorous heart soared.

Bonkers wisely remained out of sight until after

breakfast. The twins settled for pancakes. Sam and Cheryl both watched with relief as they put away enough to feed a small army.

"Can we play outside?"

"Can Cheryl come with us to see Grandma's garden?"

"Before she goes—"

"—back to New York?"

"Maybe after lunch," Sam told them. They agreed without argument, then began to gather up the dishes and load the dishwasher without being reminded.

"We're going—"

"—to clean—"

"—our room," they announced and left the kitchen.

Sam shot Cheryl a suspicious glance. "They look like—"

"—your children, and they sound like—"

"—my children, but I wonder—"

"—whose children they really are—"

"—and what have they done with mine?"

He grinned, and Cheryl burst into laugher. "That's not as hard to do as it sounds," she said between giggles.

"All you have to do is think alike," Walter said, rising and putting his plate in the sink.

Her smile faded as she and Sam stared at each other across the kitchen table. He waited until Walter had left the room.

"Cheryl, I'm sorry about last night." He hesitated a moment, then continued, "I didn't mean the things I said. I was tired and worried. I guess I've been burning my candle at both ends trying to run the ranch and trying to prove I've still got what it takes to be an architect."

"It's all right. If I thought I would hurt the girls by staying, I'd be gone in a minute."

He nodded. "I know. I overreacted," he conceded. "They seem to understand about your leaving. I just didn't want them to get hurt again."

He stared down at the cup in his hand. "They weren't even three when their mother left, but they cried for days."

He was silent for a long time as he stared into his cup, and Cheryl saw the twins hadn't been the only ones hurt by their mother's desertion. Sam had been hurt as well. He was still hurting, and Cheryl wanted nothing more than to ease his pain.

Reaching across the table, she touched his arm. "Do you want to talk about it?" she asked gently.

He gave a weary sigh. "I don't know where to start. We met in college, and it was love at first sight, or so we thought. We were married before we even knew who the other person really was. My parents had always talked about their whirlwind romance, and I thought it would be the same for me."

With a sad shake of his head, he continued. "It didn't take long for the new to wear off. We should've called it quits then, but I kept thinking we could make it work."

Gazing into Cheryl's sympathetic eyes, Sam felt a lump rise in his throat. It was hard to put into words how much his wife's desertion had cost him, but he wanted her to understand.

"She hated living on the ranch. Like a fool, I believed that if she loved me enough, she'd come to love the ranch, too. When she told me she was pregnant, I was ecstatic. My mother tried to tell me Natalie wasn't happy, but I blew her off."

He shrugged. "Anyway, the twins were born eight weeks prematurely. They were in incubators the first four weeks of their life. You'd never know to look at them now, but they were so tiny it scared me to touch them. Natalie became sick and ran a high fever after the delivery. She didn't want to see the girls. She said she was afraid she might make them sick, too. At the time, I thought she was right, so I spent every minute I could with the babies in the nursery. I knew that they needed me, needed to know that someone loved them, and I felt so bad that their mother couldn't be with them."

He moved to pour himself another cup of coffee. He hadn't been blind. For the first time, he'd admitted to himself that he'd seen all the signs of her discontent, but he had ignored them. He had been as much to blame as Natalie for the failure of their marriage.

Thank You, Lord, for helping me to see myself more clearly.

A phrase from Proverbs came to mind. *For the Lord gives wisdom, and from His mouth come knowledge and understanding.*

Cheryl said, "I've seen what a good father you are. It doesn't surprise me that you spent time with them in the hospital."

"I should have spent more of that time with my wife. Anyway, once we finally got the twins home, things were better for a while, but as the girls got older, I could see Natalie was growing more and more unhappy. She said she needed to work again, so I proposed we build our own house. The money was needed to get this ranch back on its feet, but I thought if she had a home she'd designed herself, maybe she'd be more content."

"Did it help?"

"We worked on the plans together and it was like old times for a few months. Then, after one trip she made to Kansas City, everything changed. Nothing we could get locally was good enough. She had to have special tile for the kitchen, special drapes, a dozen things that required her to travel back to KC. I never suspected she was seeing someone else.

"She filed for divorce two weeks before the girls' third birthday and gave me full custody. She said she wasn't cut out to be a mother."

"Sam, I'm so sorry."

"Now you know why I'm overprotective of them sometimes."

"I think I do."

"It took a lot of soul searching and prayer to get through that time. That's when I really turned to God. Before, I believed, but I was too busy with my life to really pay attention to what God wanted from me."

Cheryl looked down and rubbed her palms on her jeans. "I believed once myself, but after I lost my mother I didn't see how God could let such a bad thing happen. I was angry at Him. I think I thought I could punish Him by ignoring Him the way I felt He had ignored me. Silly, wasn't it?"

"No. It was human."

"I haven't prayed in years, but I prayed for Kayla when she fell."

"Did you?"

"I did. With all my heart."

Sam reached across the table. Cheryl laid her hand in his, welcoming the strength that seemed to flow from him. "And how did that make you feel?"

"I'm not sure?"

"Think about it. We all seek God in our own way. Trust Him, Cheryl. He can give you strength and hope and limitless love if only you open your heart to him."

She pulled her hand free. Sam let her go reluctantly. "I do need your help for a bit longer. I have to be in Kansas City tomorrow. If I miss another meeting, my client will start looking for a new architect," he admitted.

"I can stay a few days longer."

But not forever, Sam thought as he studied her delicate face. And that was what he really wanted. Forever.

That afternoon, Sam announced his plan to ride out and check the pastures. "I need to see if they're dry enough to start the range burning. It's got to be done soon. The grass needs at least a month of growth before the cattle are moved out onto it. That late snow has put us behind."

While he was gone, the twins insisted Cheryl spend the afternoon with them in their grandmother's garden.

"It's the prettiest place—" Kayla began.

"—in the whole world," Lindy finished.

Cheryl agreed to go with them, but she was dismayed when she saw the path they took away from the house. Narrow and steep, it curved downward around the face of the bluff, and she eyed it with unease. Getting down it on crutches might not be a problem, but getting back up could be. The girls were already skipping down ahead of her, so she gathered her nerve and followed carefully.

The path ended at a doorway in an old stone wall. It had once been a small rock house, but as Cheryl peered through the doorway, she could see the wall with the door was the only one left standing. Tall cottonwood trees shaded the ground beyond, and Cheryl followed the twins through the opening.

Twin stone benches sat on either side of a large sundial in the middle of a shady glade surrounded by masses of nodding yellow daffodils. Hyacinths in a rainbow of colors clustered close to the paving stones around the benches and added their irresistible sweet fragrance to the air. Pointed blades of iris leaves clustered along a small stone wall that ran a dozen yards out from the corner of the old house and enclosed the glade on three sides. In one corner, the long canes of a rose bush arched in budding green sprays.

Cheryl sat down on the bench and watched the girls as they gathered flowers in the dappled shade. Their arms were loaded with early-spring blooms when they came and sat down beside her at last.

"Grandma Eleanor says this is her favorite place in the whole world," Lindy told her.

"'Cause this is where she can close her eyes and hear the sounds of happiness," Kayla added.

Both girls squeezed their eyes shut tightly and listened. Cheryl watched them with amusement. They were quiet only a few moments when Lindy shook her head. "I don't hear anything. Let's go throw rocks in the water." She took off toward the creek bank. Her bouquet lay forgotten on the bench.

"Okay," Kayla jumped up, but handed Cheryl her armload of flowers. "You listen for it. Grandma says you have to have your eyes closed."

Cheryl smiled, but she closed her eyes obediently and listened.

The warm, spring wind brushed past her cheeks like the touch of soft silk and sent the cottonwood leaves rustling overhead like the petticoats of a dozen dancers crammed into one small dressing room. Birds chirped gaily, the wind sighed through the long grass on the hillside behind her, and the sound of little voices came to her.

"I see a frog."

"Where?"

"By that log."

"Oh, I see it."

"You better go kiss him."

"Yuck! Why?"

"He might be a prince."

"I don't want a prince that bad."

"Me neither."

"Hey, you should kiss Jimmy Slader."

"Double yuck! No way."

"Yeah, then maybe he'd turn into a frog." Girlish giggles filled the air.

Cheryl smiled to herself. Happiness did indeed reside in the garden. The sounds of it were everywhere.

Opening her eyes, Cheryl leaned forward to study the old copper sundial aged to a deep green. She ran her finger over the raised words that circled the rim.

A time to weep,
And a time to laugh;
A time to mourn,
And a time to dance;
Eccl. 3:4

It was if someone had written about her entire life in those four short lines.

Kayla came to sit beside Cheryl on the bench. "I like the sundial, don't you?"

"It's very pretty. Do you know what this means? 'Eccl. 3:4.'"

"It's from the Bible, silly. Grandma says it's about God's plan, how He makes a time for everything." A second later, Kayla took off in pursuit of her sister.

Cheryl's fingers lingered on the worn words that rang so true to her life. "'A time for everything,'" she whispered.

Was that true? Had God planned this time for her with Sam and the children? If Sam hadn't been on the road that night she never would have known him or the twins. If she hadn't been beside the corral that day would Kayla be alive now? The idea that she might somehow be part of a greater design gave her pause, yet a curiosity grew in her to read more of the sundial passage. Perhaps Walter would let her borrow his copy of the book.

The twins played until they grew sleepy in the afternoon heat, and Cheryl decided it was time to head up the hill. As they emerged from the stone doorway, Sam sat on his horse waiting for them on the other side. Cheryl's pulse jumped into double time at the sight of him.

"Afternoon ladies," he drawled and tipped his hat. "That's a mighty tall hill for a gal on crutches. Care for a lift?"

"Thank you, kind sir," she drawled in an imitation of him.

He swung down from the horse, took her crutches and laid them on the ground. She rested her arms on his shoulders as he grasped her waist and lifted her into the saddle.

His strong fingers gripping her waist sent a tingling straight down her spine. Cheryl glanced at his face as his hands lingered. What was it that she saw in those hazel eyes? She couldn't be sure because he released her abruptly and turned to swing the twins up, one in front of her and one behind her on the horse.

"Ready?" he asked.

"Yup!" the twins said.

"I think so," Cheryl answered dubiously as she looked up the steep, narrow path.

Sam picked up her crutches and handed them to her. "Courage is its own reward, New York."

"That's virtue, cowboy."

"What's virtue?" Kayla asked.

"You explain that one," he suggested. He turned and started up the hill leading his horse.

"Thanks, cowboy. It means being very good, Kayla."

Lindy leaned around Cheryl. "God wants us to be good, doesn't He, Daddy?"

"That's right."

"I'm good," Kayla declared.

"You are not," her sister stated. "You wanted to turn Jimmy Slader into a frog. That's not nice."

"Oh. I forgot that."

"You better tell God you're sorry."

Kayla raised her face to the heavens and called out, "I'm sorry I wanted to turn Jimmy into a frog, God." After a moment of silence, she said, "Daddy, how do I know if God forgives me?"

"God forgives everyone when they are truly sorry, Honey. We have His word on that."

Would He forgive her omissions and half-truths, Cheryl wondered. Would Sam if he ever found out?

At the front of the house, Sam stopped the horse and handed the twins down. He took the crutches from Cheryl and gave them to the girls.

Cheryl wished she could get off by herself, but before she could think of a way, his hands gripped her waist again. When her feet touched the ground, she found she couldn't move away from his touch. She avoided looking at him, afraid he would read the longing in her eyes.

He reached up to gently brush a strand of hair away from her face. "I don't know why I try to resist you," he whispered.

Her glance flew to his face. Her breath seemed to stick in her throat. He was going to kiss her. A small sound reminded her of the children staring with rapt curiosity.

"Ah, Sam," she said leaning back.

"Hmm?"

"We have an audience."

He turned his head and leveled a stern look at the twins. "Don't you two have something to do?"

Each twin held out a crutch. Cheryl reached over and took them. The girls scooted for the house.

Sam removed his hands from Cheryl's waist with reluctance. He hated to let her go. It felt so good when she was close to him. Maybe he was playing the fool, but did he care? Just to touch her made him feel alive in a way he'd never known. He shoved his hands into his pockets. He was letting his heart rule his head. That was a sure ticket to disaster.

"I need to go to Kansas City tomorrow. Will you be okay with Walter and the girls while I'm gone?"

"I can manage without you."

He sighed and led Dusty toward the barn. "That's exactly what I'm afraid of," he told the horse.

Chapter 10

"It's your move," Walter said as he sat across from Sam at the chess board several evenings later.

Sam tried to study the board and plan his next move, but his mind wasn't on the game. His gaze drifted to where Cheryl and the twins stood by the billiard table. She'd given in to their pleading and agreed to teach them some of the basic moves of ballet. They were using the side of the table like a dancer's barre.

"The barre is used to help you keep your balance while you practice, like so." She touched the pool table rail lightly. She wore a ballet slipper on one foot, and she rose lightly onto her toes as she held her injured foot extended in front of her.

"It's your move, Sam," Walter said again, louder this time.

"What? Oh, sure." Sam moved a dark pawn and returned to watching the dancers.

Walter's gaze traveled between Sam and Cheryl, then his lips tightened into a thin line. "I know you don't want an old man sticking his nose in your business, but you're riding for a fall with that one, Sammy. She's as out of place here as a hothouse flower."

"I don't know what you mean." He ignored Walter's snort and moved another pawn, then he glanced at the dancers once more.

She was a natural with children, Sam thought as he watched her showing them different positions. Each girl had her full attention as she gave them praise and gentle corrections. She seemed to know when they needed encouragement and when to step back and let them try on their own.

"Sam, since that was my pawn you moved, I'm going to put it back, and we can continue this game when your mind is less occupied."

Sam pulled his attention back to Walter. "I'm sorry. What did you say?"

"I said your mind isn't on the game." The elder Hardin leaned back in his chair. "We can start burning pasture soon. The snow put us behind, but the grass should be dry enough by the first of next week."

Cheryl crossed the room and sat down with the men as the girls continued to practice. "Don't look at your feet," she called.

Walter smiled at her. "You're in for a treat, Cheryl. You can help us with pasture-burning next week."

"Not me!" She held up one hand and shot them both a look of disgust. "You go play with fire if you want to, but I'm staying right here. I have no intention of going back to New York with all the hair singed off my head."

"You'll be perfectly safe with us. Tell her, Sam."

"She can make up her own mind. Are you going to make a move or will I have to wait another six months to finish this game?"

Walter cast a speculative look between the two, then turned his attention back to the game. Cheryl rose and went back to the twins.

Sam caught a glimpse of the hurt look in her eyes before she turned away and hated himself for causing it. He was acting churlishly, and he knew it. But every time she mentioned going back to New York, he felt as if he'd taken a blow to the midsection.

He wanted her to love the ranch, to love his kids, to love him. But she already had a life she loved. A life he couldn't be a part of. She wasn't going to stay. Why couldn't he get that through his thick head? The wooden chess piece in his hand snapped in two. Sam stared at the broken queen. He rose from the table and left the room without a word.

"Where is Daddy going?"

"Doesn't he want to watch us dance?"

Cheryl's eyes followed Sam's retreating form. "I don't know where he's going."

Walter came up beside them. "I want to see you dance."

Cheryl flashed him a grateful look, and he gave her a sympathetic smile in return.

It was Walter who told Cheryl the next morning that Sam had gone to Kansas City.

"Did he say when he'd be back?" she asked, biting her lip.

"No, but he can't be gone long because there's a lot to be done here in the next few days. If he thinks I plan to work like a dog while he's off enjoying the bright lights, he's got another think coming."

Cheryl kept herself occupied and tried not to let her

thoughts dwell on Sam as the days dragged by. The one good thing was that no more cryptic letters arrived for her.

To pass the time, she began helping her first students master the basic ballet positions and steps. The twins were a delight to teach. They were eager and gifted with a desire to learn, and she had discovered something new about herself in the process—she liked teaching.

"Plié means to bend," she demonstrated for the girls, "and demi-plié means a half bend, like this. Remember to do it slowly, Lindy. You don't want to look like a jack-in-the-box popping up."

"Why don't you just say *bend* if you mean bend?" Walter asked, as he lounged in a leather chair watching them. "Makes more sense. Shouldn't they be on their toes?"

"French has been the language of ballet for about four hundred years, and no they shouldn't be up on their toes. Toe dancing can't be done until a qualified teacher decides a pupil is ready for it. It's very hard on young bones."

"How old were you when you started?"

"I was very old, almost fourteen, but it was love at first sight. Once I'd seen a ballet, I never wanted to do anything else. It wasn't easy to start training at that age, but I was lucky. My cousin knew a wonderful dancing master who took me on as a private pupil. I had a natural flexibility and lots of determination. It's much better if a child starts learning at age six or seven."

"It won't do Lindy and Kayla any good to start this young," Walter said, standing up.

"Why do you say that?" She frowned at him.

"Who'll teach them after you're gone?"

Cheryl didn't have an answer, and some of the joy she felt went out of the day. The girls were so eager to learn. Surely they would be able to continue.

"There must be a dance school in town?"

"I don't think so," Walter scoffed.

"Maybe not in Council Grove or Strong City, but in Manhattan they must have some."

"An hour's drive from here? I doubt Sam will want to take them that far for dancing lessons."

"You think dance lessons would be a waste of time, don't you?" she asked, amazed at his attitude even though she knew she shouldn't be.

He shrugged, but didn't answer. He didn't have to. She read the answer on his face, and her temper flared. "If it doesn't teach them to cook, mend fences or haggle a better price out of some cattle buyer, it's a waste of time, right?"

She planted her hands on her hips. "You've been past the cattle crossing at Bazaar. You know the world is a lot bigger than this ranch, and these children deserve the chance to discover for themselves where their heart's desire lies."

Walter's eyes narrowed, and he watched her silently for a long moment. "There's something about you that doesn't add up."

Taken aback, she stiffened. "I don't know what you mean."

"For one thing, you know a lot more about ranching than you let on. And when you're mad, that New York accent fades faster than the flavor of penny bubble gum. Who are you?"

Cheryl stared at him, her mind racing. She'd gotten careless again. Her gaze fell before the suspicion in his eyes. "I'm nobody special. But I do care about the twins, and about Sam."

"Do you?"

Her gaze snapped back to his. "Yes," she answered firmly.

His gaze grew stern. "Then maybe you shouldn't tempt them with things they can't have."

They stared at each other silently. He wasn't talking about dance lessons, and she knew it. Jamming his hat on his head, he left the room, and she chewed her lip as she watched him walk away. Was that what she'd been doing? Tempting Sam, and herself, with something they couldn't have?

Maybe Walter was right. She didn't have a reason to stay now. She had her wallet back, and she could tag along with her company once she caught up with them. Kayla was fully recovered.

Only, she didn't want to leave. She wanted to be a part of this family. She'd never felt so torn in her entire life.

She missed Sam, Cheryl realized as she turned her attention back to the girls and corrected Kayla's foot position. She missed his boyish grin and hearty laughter. She missed the amused glances they shared when the twins provided some unintentional humor. She missed him a lot. If it was like this after he'd been gone only two days, what would it be like when she left for good?

Sam showed up in the kitchen for breakfast the next day. He wore an enormous grin on his face. The twins raced to hug him and he scooped them both up before stopping in front of Cheryl. "They bought my design."

"For the house in Kansas City?" she asked.

"Yup."

"Oh, Sam, I'm so glad."

"You and me both. We start construction in two weeks. And we're gonna burn pasture today," he announced, twirling around once with the girls in his arms.

"Cheryl, you got to—"

"—come and watch," the twins told her.

"I will be able to see it from here. That's close enough," she assured them.

"Girls, leave Cheryl alone. If she's too chicken to come and set the world on fire, then she should stay home."

"Chicken? Who are you calling a chicken, cowboy?" she demanded.

"Hey, if the feather fits…" He put the girls down, folded his arms and flapped his elbows like wings. "Chicken!"

"Chicken! Chicken!" The twins took up the chant.

"Come on, it'll be fun," Sam coaxed.

He grinned when she folded her arms across her chest, raised one eyebrow and looked at him in disbelief.

"Please come, Cheryl," the twins begged. "Please."

"All right. But only to prove to your father that I'm not a chicken."

An hour later, she sat in Sam's pickup and rested her arms on the open window as she watched the activity going on around her. She'd seen the huge fires when she was a child, but she'd never helped set them. Three trucks lined up along the fence inside an immense pasture. A plump, elderly woman wearing a pink shirt and faded jeans tucked into cowboy boots stood handing out donuts and coffee to the men as they grouped around the tailgate of one truck. Sam took her elbow and separated her from the cowhands. He led her over to the truck where Cheryl sat.

Cheryl was thankful for the wide round sunglasses that hid her eyes. Sam stopped beside her.

"Cheryl, this is Mrs. Webster. It's her pasture we're burning today."

"And I can't thank you enough for doing this, Sam." Mrs. Webster said. "With my Simon laid up after his heart surgery I never would have gotten this work done."

"It's my pleasure."

"I'd better be getting back to the house. Simon gets fit to be tied if I'm gone long. I wish I could pay you with more than coffee and donuts."

Sam slipped an arm around her ample shoulders. "Your donuts are worth their weight in gold, Mrs. Webster, and that's a fact."

"Still, it don't seem right, you and your crew doing this for nothing."

"You would do the same for us if the shoe was on the other foot. In fact, when Dad passed away, you and Simon were the first ones to come with food and offers of help."

"I'm blessed to have such good people for friends and neighbors. How is your sister doing? I heard your mother went to Denver to stay with her."

Sam winked at Cheryl. "It's hard to keep a secret in a small town, isn't it?"

Cheryl swallowed hard and hoped her guilt didn't show on her face.

Sam didn't seem to notice. "Becky has been in and out of the hospital twice with early labor. Mom is staying to help out. We miss her, but we know Becky needs her at a time like this."

"I'll remember you and all your family in my prayers, Samuel. It's the least I can do to repay all you've done for me and mine." She wiped her eye with her sleeve, then hurried away.

Cheryl studied Sam's face. "You like helping people, don't you?"

His smile lightened her heart. "Do unto others. That's the way I was taught to live."

Her father would have finished the quote with *before they do it to you.*

Sam wasn't like the ranchers her father had bad-mouthed and stolen from. Only, maybe those ranchers had been good men, too. She once told Angie that she didn't regret anything she had done in the past. It seemed that was no longer true. Not if she had hurt people like Sam or Walter or Mrs. Webster.

Shaking off her deep thoughts, she pointed to the men waiting to get started. "Tell me about this job. Why three trucks?"

He explained, "The first truck lights the grass afire from a torch pulled along behind it. The second truck is equipped with a pressurized water sprayer, and it puts out the blaze as it follows alongside the torch. The third truck follows the others putting out any little fires that are missed. This way we create a burn line that will contain the main fire."

"You backfire the whole pasture that way?"

He gave her a look of surprise. "That's right. Once we get a strip done around the entire perimeter, we'll fire the grass inside and let the wind push the blaze across the range. When the fire reaches the strip on the other side that's already burnt, it dies out from lack of fuel."

"You do this every year?"

"Some ranchers do. I prefer a three-year rotation because it gives the wildlife a break. Prairie chickens, for instance, prefer newly burned pasture for feeding and mating. They like to nest in the two-year-old grass, but they prefer to seek cover in the thicker grass that's three years old or older."

Cheryl shot him a skeptical look. "How do you know what a prairie chicken prefers?"

Sam pushed the brim of his hat up with one finger and grinned. "Well, ma'am, I asked them."

She tried, but couldn't smother a chuckle.

Walter came to stand beside Sam. "I think we're ready."

Both men moved away to talk with the rest of the crew.

Cheryl pulled her sunglasses off and looked for the twins. They were busy gathering long branches of snowy blossoms from a thicket of wild sand plums growing along the pasture fence.

After a detailed check of all his equipment, Sam ordered the burning started. He watched as the sprayer truck followed closely behind Walter, then he headed back toward his pickup and called to the twins. A small gust of wind crossed the freshly burned strip and carried a flurry of ashes toward the truck.

Cheryl pulled back from the window and gave a cry of pain as she covered one eye with her hand.

Sam was beside her in an instant. "What's the matter?"

"Something blew in my eye."

"Don't rub it. Let me see." He opened the truck door, jerked off his gloves, and bent close. With gentle fingers, he removed a cinder from the corner of her eye.

Cheryl blinked rapidly. "Thanks, cowboy."

"You're welcome, New York," he replied softly. His gaze was drawn to her tempting lips. Ever so slowly, he bent toward her.

"Cheryl, look at—"

"—all the flowers we found."

The twins squirmed in between them and held up grubby hands filled with flowers and clumps of clinging dirt. Sam drew back.

"They're beautiful, girls," Cheryl said, taking the offered bouquet. "These wild plums smell wonderful, don't they? But I'm afraid this old milkweed will make me sneeze."

Sam frowned. "I didn't think they had milkweed in New England. It's a prairie plant."

Cheryl's gaze shot to his, and her eyes widened. Suddenly, she smacked the flowers into his chest, and he jumped. "What on earth?"

"Bee! Sam, there's a bee on you. I'll get it." She hit him again, spreading dirt and petals across his shirt.

The twins watched with puzzled faces. Lindy said, "I don't see a bee."

"Me neither," Kayla added.

"It's gone now." Cheryl dropped the tattered remains of her bouquet and put her sunglasses on. "Don't you think we had better catch up with the others, Sam? Come on, girls, get in the truck."

Sam brushed the dirt from his shirt as he walked around to the driver's side. What had that been all about? He didn't have time to ponder the question. The other trucks were pulling ahead of them.

The twins climbed in with Cheryl. They both wanted to sit beside her, and she forestalled an argument by lifting Kayla over her lap and placing one child on each side. She looked at Sam as he got behind the wheel, and he gave her a rueful grin.

"Can we—" Lindy started.

"—see the fire?" Kayla asked.

"Will it make—"

"—lots of smoke?"

"What makes the smoke go up?"

"Where does it go after it goes up?"

Sam said, "Remind me to leave them at home next time."

Cheryl grinned at him. "I would have had to stay at home with them."

"You're right. Remind me to let them ride with Walter."

"Now that's a good idea, cowboy."

By late afternoon, the thrill had worn off for the twins, and Sam looked over to see both girls asleep as they leaned on Cheryl. Even Cheryl's head was nodding as he followed slowly behind the others occasionally stopping to put out a small fire the main water truck had missed. It was boring work, but the entire pasture perimeter had to be backfired carefully before the main fires could be lit.

The trucks were nearly back at the starting point when a movement off to his right caught Sam's attention. A white-tailed doe sprang out of a brushy ravine as the wind carried the smoke in her direction. Sam watched as she bounded back into cover only to reap-

pear a moment later. Nervously, she watched the trucks
and stamped her front leg in a signal of alarm. After a
moment, she bounded back down the ravine.

She's got a fawn down there, Sam thought, slowing
his truck. He glanced at Cheryl and the girls. The twins
dozed quietly, and only Cheryl's eyes opened when the
truck stopped.

"Are we done?" she asked, trying to stifle a yawn.

"We're back where we started from, but we're a long
way from done." He smiled as she gave a sleepy nod
and closed her eyes again.

"I'll be back in a minute," he said, stepping out of the
truck. He didn't want Cheryl or the girls to know about
the deer. Area wildlife would head for the creeks and
ponds when the grass started burning, but a newborn
fawn wouldn't stand much of a chance. He decided to
check the ravine and see if the doe had hidden a baby
too young to run.

Cheryl heard Sam leave the truck. She opened her
eyes long enough to see him start toward a deep gully
that cut between two loaf-shaped hills. She sat up and
rubbed her eyes. The twins slept soundly as they leaned
against her.

Several minutes had passed when the radio crackled,
and Walter's voice came over the speaker. "The wind is
gusting a bit harder now, Sam. I'm going to get started."

It was a moment before her sleepy brain processed
the fact that Walter's truck had turned and was coming
back toward them. He had set fire to the grass inside
the burnt strip, and the breeze was already pushing the
flames out across the prairie.

She grabbed the mike and fumbled with it an instant

before she was able to call out, "Walter, stop! Sam went down into that ravine."

His truck veered off the grass and stopped.

His voice barked over the radio to the other truck. "Get the sprayer going and put this out. Sam's in front of the fire!"

Cheryl saw the men on the second truck scrambling to get the water sprayer started again. The wind kicked up in a sudden brisk gust, and the fire gained momentum, crackling and snapping as the flames swept through the tall, dry grass.

Walter jumped out of his truck and began running toward the gully, yelling Sam's name. Thick gray-white smoke rose in a dense curtain from the flames and obscured everything beyond it. A swirling column of hot air sprang up in the blazing grass, and a spark-laden whirlwind danced ahead of Walter spreading the fire even faster. He threw his arms in front of his face and backed away as a wall of flames flared in front of him. He was still shouting Sam's name.

Sam walked down the ravine slowly scanning the underbrush for the white dotted pattern of a fawn's back. A rustling in the brush ahead of him and the flash of a white tail bounding away gave him a clue, but he nearly stepped on the little thing before he saw it.

"Your mama did a good job of hiding you, didn't she?" he spoke softly as he knelt down beside the huddled fawn.

He gathered the quivering infant into his arms. "You can't be more than a few hours old. It's just your bad luck to be born so early in the spring. Someone forgot to tell your mama you weren't supposed to be born for another month. Let's get you out of harm's way, shall we?"

He looked into its liquid brown eyes and sighed. "Those girls of mine will want to keep you. I can just see it. In a year's time, I'll have a six-point buck in the house with a big red bow around his neck. I hope you like cats."

Sam heard Walter calling him as he made his way back up the steep ravine. Suddenly, the crackling of fire drowned out Walter's voice. Smoke swirled down into the draw, and the fawn began to struggle in his arms.

Sam spun around and sprinted down the gully away from the fire. Of all the witless blunders he had pulled in his life, this was the stupidest. He'd walked off without telling Walter, and he'd assumed the men in the other trucks had seen him. It was a careless mistake that might cost him his life.

He knew a small creek curved across the prairie a quarter of a mile from the base of these hills. It was a slim chance but it was all he had. To make it, he'd have to run the race of his life. He wasn't going to die without a fight—his girls needed him. He glanced down at the tiny deer. If he was going to have any chance, he knew he'd have to leave the fawn behind.

Cheryl watched as Walter backed away from the blaze. She stared in stunned disbelief as the fire engulfed the ravine Sam had entered. Her mind recoiled in horror as the flames shot higher when they reached the thick brush that grew there.

A moan escaped her lips, and she swayed in the seat. The radio mike dropped from her nerveless fingers. She clapped her hands over her own mouth to keep from screaming. Tearing her gaze away from the fire, she looked down at the twins. They continued to sleep quietly on either side of her. *Dear God, please don't let them wake up and see this.*

The men on the water truck fought a losing battle as the fire spread out in front of them. One man jumped from the truck and ran to pull Walter away from the fire's edge. Walter shook him off and staggered back to his pickup. He braced both arms on the hood and bowed his head. After a long moment, he walked to the open truck door, leaned in and grabbed the radio mike. Cheryl didn't hear any sound from her set. He'd turned the radio to the emergency channel, she realized, and he was calling for help. He dropped his head onto his arms when he finished and leaned on the truck door as if it were the only thing in the world that could hold him up.

The other cowboy took the mike from him and laid a hand on his shoulder. Walter straightened and looked toward Cheryl. He began to walk slowly toward her.

At the bottom of the ravine, Sam paused and looked back. The flames were gaining on him. Upward and to his left, he saw the hill ended in a rocky outcropping. The crumbling limestone cliff was free of brush, and a shelf of stone jutted out like a small cave. It was a better gamble than the creek, and he scrambled upward with the fawn still cradled in his arms.

He stretched out under the low rock shelf and prayed he didn't find himself sharing it with a copperhead. It would be just his luck to survive the fire and die of snakebite. The fawn squirmed in his arms, but he held it tightly as the fire swept around the hill below them.

Thick smoke choked him, and he pulled his bandanna up to cover his nose and mouth.

A picture of Cheryl with her arms full of plum blossoms flashed into his mind. He regretted now he hadn't kissed her at the truck. If he were going to die, he'd much rather die with the memory of her sweet kiss still on his lips.

He huddled under the rock ledge as burning embers fell beside him from the hilltop's grassy overhang. Heavy smoke billowed around him, the heat became intense as the fire devoured the heavy brush at the foot of the cliff a few feet below him. The fawn stopped struggling, and he wondered if it had passed out from the smoke. He sheltered its small body as best he could and he prayed for deliverance.

Walter stopped at the open window beside Cheryl. She saw the agony in his ancient eyes, and her heart trembled.

"It's good that they're asleep. They shouldn't see this," he said when he saw the girls on the seat beside her.

"Sam?" she whispered.

"He's got a chance. There's a creek a little ways below these bluffs." From the look in his eyes, Cheryl knew the chance wasn't a good one.

"I want you to take the girls home and wait for us."

"No! Walter, don't make me leave. I can't."

His lips thinned in a tight grimace of pain, and she read the determination in his face. "Sam wouldn't want his children here no matter what happens, and you know it."

She glanced at the twins and nodded in resignation. "Yes, you're right."

She had to take care of Sam's children even if her soul screamed out the need to stay.

As one of the young cowboys drove them back toward the ranch, Cheryl turned in her seat and looked through the rear window. Towering columns of smoke obscured the hills as the line of orange flames raced across the prairie leaving behind only flat, black ash smoldering with a thousand tiny plumes of white smoke. The other cowboys gathered beside Walter. It was a grim-faced group of men who stood together and waited for the fire to sweep past the base of the hills before they began their grisly search.

Chapter 11

"Where's Daddy?"

Cheryl turned away from the balcony door to see Kayla and Lindy standing in the middle of the room. Sirens sounded in the distance, and she slid the door closed against the eerie wailing. "He's still out at the pasture with Grandpa Walter."

Cheryl tried to keep the twins occupied, but she couldn't keep her eyes off the clock. Sam had to be all right. He was a strong man, he could have outrun the fire and made it to safety. Any minute now, he would come through the door and tell some exciting tale about sharing the creek with catfish and rabbits. Any minute now.

Please, dear Lord, he is such a good man. Bring him home safe to his children.

The minutes became an hour, then two, and still no word. She refused to give in to the despair that threatened her. She couldn't accept that she would never see him again. Her nerves were stretched to the breaking point when she heard the sound of a car pulling into the driveway, and she hurried to the open front door.

It wasn't Sam or even Walter who got out of the car in the drive, it was Merci Slader.

She didn't try to hide her dislike of Cheryl. "I was on my way home and Sam asked me to come by and tell you and the girls that he's okay."

"He's safe?" The welcome fact penetrated Cheryl's mind, and her knees nearly buckled with relief.

"He has a few scrapes and bruises and some mild smoke inhalation, but when I left the hospital, he was getting cleaned up and ready to leave. They were able to save the fawn, but the vet wants to keep it a few more days."

Cheryl stared at her in confusion. "What fawn?"

Merci walked past Cheryl into the house. "I'll let Sam tell you that story. I still can't believe he risked his life to save a stupid deer."

The twins came racing up the stairs, then stopped short. "Hi, Mrs. Slader," Kayla said.

"Hello, girls. I have a treat for you. How would you like to come and spend the night at my house? Your dad thought it was a great idea."

"I guess." They cast each other a dubious glance.

She bent toward them. "We're going to have pizza and go to a movie. Doesn't that sound like fun?"

The girls looked at Cheryl. She smiled and nodded. "A movie sounds like lots of fun. It was very nice of Mrs. Slader to offer. Go get your pj's and toothbrushes."

The twins went back downstairs without arguing, and Merci turned to Cheryl. "I thought Sam might need some time to recover from his ordeal. Obviously, he's going to need some rest and quiet. I know he can't get that with those girls in the house. I mean, I'm sure you do your best, but they do need a firm hand."

"Are you sure Sam is all right?"

Merci studied her closely. "I'm sure."

Cheryl knew her relief must be plastered across her face. She only hoped her love for Sam wasn't plain to see, as well.

Sam saw Cheryl standing out on the balcony when he came in later that evening. He watched her for a long moment through the windows. She stood with her arms clasped tightly across her middle as she faced the night. Beyond her, the southern sky glowed with the eerie orange light of prairie fires.

A soft south wind carried the faint scent of smoke drifting to him through the open sliding glass door. The same breeze fluttered the edges of her blue skirt and toyed with her loose hair. Her pale curls seemed to reach out and beckon him.

"It does look as if the whole world is on fire." She spoke without turning.

"It's a long way off. You don't have to worry about it coming this way," he said, moving to stand behind her. Her scent filled his nostrils and stirred a fierce longing to hold her in his arms once more. He closed his eyes and bowed his head. He was tired of fighting this attraction to her.

He placed his hands gently on her shoulders and pulled her against his chest. She leaned back with a sigh as he folded his arms around her and rested his cheek against the softness of her hair. The silky strands caressed his face as the breeze stirred them. He didn't want to let her go, not tonight, not ever.

"Oh Sam, I was so frightened," her voice trembled.

"Hush, don't talk. Just let me hold you," he whispered. For a long time they stood together and watched the distant hills burning brightly in the night.

Cheryl welcomed Sam's warmth and strength. She needed to be held in his arms. She needed to feel that he was real and whole. After a time, she turned in his arms. "I prayed you would come to back to me safe and sound."

"And I prayed for a chance to do this." He lowered his head and captured her lips in a sweet and thrilling kiss that sent her heart flying with happiness.

When they drew apart at last, Cheryl looked up into his eyes. They glittered with reflected starlight. She had never felt like this about anyone before in her life. The power of the emotions he stirred scared her to death.

She drew away from him unsure of what to say. In spite of how she felt, she knew any relationship between them was doomed. She didn't want to hurt him. Not ever.

No, what she wanted was to throw herself back in his arms and hang on to the first good thing that had come into her life in a long time. But staying here would mean facing her past, her grandmother and the community that once shunned her.

"I'm sorry," Sam said, dropping his arms to his sides. "Maybe the kiss was out of line, but I don't regret it. I care for you a great deal."

It was so much more than she deserved.

He spoke again quickly. "It won't happen again. I hope this doesn't drive you away."

"No, of course not." Because she wanted to be near him for whatever time she had left. "I know you need help watching the girls. I'll stay another week, but I can't promise more. My sister will be home from her honeymoon then. After that, I'll be going to stay with her."

It was late the next morning when Sam woke. He stretched stiff, sore muscles that creaked in protest after a day of fire fighting. After dressing, he left the bedroom and saw Cheryl out on the balcony, cradling a steaming cup in her hands as she leaned a hip against the railing. She was dressed in a pair of jeans and a yellow shirt. Her hair was pulled back in a long ponytail, and her shoulders were slumped. It struck him that she looked more like a lonely kid than an elegant dancer.

She turned around at the sound of the sliding glass door opening and smiled. He smiled back, but wondered why she often seemed so sad when she thought no one was looking. "'Morning."

"'Morning? It's almost noon, lazy bones. Walter left to check the fence in the west pasture an hour ago. He told me to tell you to feed the horses."

"Okay. Come on, I could use some help."

"Doing what?"

"Someone has to explain to Dusty why his breakfast is late."

Cheryl followed Sam out to the barn, happy to be included in his day. She drank in the sight of him as he worked. He lifted the heavy bales of hay effortlessly as the muscles of his broad back and shoulders bunched and flexed beneath his faded denim shirt. She was leaning against the barn stall when she felt a nudge at her back and turned to find Dusty looking for some attention.

Sam finished his chores and came to stand beside her as she patted the horse's neck. "Want to see something cute?"

"Another new calf?"

"Think smaller, but kind of hard to get to."

"What and where?"

"I can't tell you what, but where is in the hay loft."

She pointed to her cast. "Sam, I can't climb up there."

"Sure you can. Do you trust me?"

"Maybe."

"Yes or no?"

"I think so. Why?"

"Good." He grabbed her and hefted her over his shoulder.

"What are you doing?" she shrieked. "Put me down!" She pummeled his back as he strode to the front of the barn.

"You can't climb the hayloft ladder with that cast on, New York. I'm helping you up."

"Oh, no you don't! You are *not* going to carry me up a ladder like this!"

"Relax. You don't weigh any more than a flea. I've carried sacks of grain up there that were bigger than you."

"Oh, that's great. How many of them have you dropped?"

"Not more than five or six. Hey, grab that horse blanket."

"Why should I?"

"The hay is soft, but it's prickly. Take my advice and grab the blanket."

Cheryl snatched the dark blue blanket off the stall door as he walked past. At least if he dropped her, she'd have something to break her fall.

He quickly started up the wooden ladder beside the front door. With a squeak, Cheryl squeezed her eyes shut and grabbed on to his belt as the barn floor dropped away beneath her.

"Okay, you can let go now," Sam said as he stepped onto the solid floor and set her down.

She glared at him. "That was not fun, Sam!"

He grinned. "Yes, it was."

"Look, you big, bull-headed cowboy. If you think for one minute that I enjoyed that!"

He touched his finger to his lips. "Hush."

"I will not be hushed."

"You'll wake the babies."

She scowled at him. "What babies?"

He walked to a stack of bales, dropped to his belly in the hay and motioned for her to do the same. "Come see."

Cheryl lay on the hay beside him and looked into a space between the hay bales. A small gray cat looked back at her with luminous green eyes. Beside her, four long-haired, yellow, newborn kittens slept nestled together.

Sam grinned at Cheryl. "I found them yesterday morning. I think Bonkers is a father."

Her giggle was music to his ears. A lifetime with this woman wouldn't be enough. His grin faded, and he sobered at the thought. What if she didn't stay? What if all he had wasn't enough for her? *Please, God, don't let it happen again.*

The days that followed were some of the happiest Cheryl could remember. One afternoon, Sam installed a long wooden barre and a full-length mirror on the rec-room wall. Delighted, Cheryl spent hours practicing and teaching the twins to use it properly. While Sam and Walter finished burning the range, Cheryl took care of the house and the children. She dusted off her cooking skills and beamed with pride when Sam complimented her meals.

Sitting at the table in the evenings, she listened to Sam and Walter discuss the ranch work and their breeding programs. It was strange and yet wonderful to feel so included in the lives of the people she'd grown to love. Was this what belonging to a family was supposed to feel like?

The next afternoon, the twins persuaded her to help them fly their kites, and she followed them across to the hillside opposite the house. As they passed the old oak tree, she saw that someone had nailed wooden strips to its slanted trunk, and a few planks were visible in its leafy branches.

"Is this your tree house?" Cheryl asked as she sat down in the shade. Bonkers climbed into her lap for attention.

"It was Daddy's and Aunt Becky's."

"When they were little like us."

"I see." Cheryl smiled as she imagined a young Sam the budding architect constructing it.

The twins ran to launch their kites, and the western breeze carried them quickly out over the valley below the hillside. Cheryl leaned back against the trunk of the tree and watched as the red-and-yellow kites dipped and soared in the wind silhouetted against the blue sky and the fluffy white clouds that drifted by. She closed her eyes and took a deep breath of fresh air on a glorious spring day.

A meadowlark sang somewhere in the tall grass, and the wind stirred the branches overhead and set them to whispering. The children laughed and shouted, and on her lap Bonkers purred in contentment.

"A penny for your thoughts," a voice spoke above her.

She opened one eye and squinted up at Sam as he towered over her. He tipped the brim of his hat up and leaned his broad shoulder against the tree trunk. "Or aren't they worth that much?"

"I was just thinking how brave your parents were."

His brow wrinkled. "What do you mean?"

"To spend all that money to send you to college to study architecture after they saw your early work." She pointed above them.

He glanced up at the haphazard tree house. "You might not believe it, but I had a beautiful set of blueprints to follow. That was when I discovered an architect is only as good as his builder. I also discovered I was much better with paper than with a hammer and nails." He sat down beside her. "Mind if I share your tree?"

"Not at all, just promise me you won't haul me up to see your tree house first-hand." Cheryl could have bitten her wayward tongue as a speculative gleam leapt into Sam's eyes. He studied the boards above them but slowly shook his head.

"It's an idea, but I don't think those old timbers could take the stress," he said as he grinned at her.

She shot him a look of disgust. "Don't you have some ranch work to do?"

He leaned close and whispered in her ear, "I do, but I'd rather spend the time with you. Unfortunately, I'm needed in one of the pastures. I just stopped to tell you that Gramps and I'll be in late for supper." He rose and tipped his hat in her direction, then strode away.

She sat up straight and gave her attention to the children while trying to ignore the happy hum of her pulse.

As much as Cheryl liked the girls, watching two active and imaginative kids turned out to be harder than she believed possible.

Sam came into the house the next afternoon as she was cleaning up, followed by two contrite-looking children. Cheryl stared at them in surprise. She'd thought they were downstairs watching TV. In fact, she could still hear the sounds of cartoons coming up the stairwell.

His tone was stern as he crossed his arms and said, "Show Cheryl what you did."

Lindy glanced once at his set face then held out her hands. Messy globs of vibrant pink covered her fingertips as she held out an empty bottle of nail polish. Cheryl took the vial and looked to Sam for an explanation. She'd used her favorite shade of Rose Petal Pink just that morning, and she was sure she'd left the bottle on the dresser in her room.

"Apologize for taking something that didn't belong to you," Sam said.

Kayla's face was downcast. "We're sorry."

"We just wanted to—"

"—look as pretty—"

"—as you do." They fell silent and stared at their feet.

"Tell her the rest," Sam said sternly.

"Let me guess," Cheryl said, looking at Sam. "Bonkers is now pink?"

"No, but not because they didn't try."

"He wouldn't hold still," Lindy said, looking contrite.

"Harvey held still," Sam told her. "My prize breeding bull has hot pink hooves."

While Cheryl had learned that Harvey really was a gentle giant, she blanched at the thought of these two crawling into his pen and painting his feet. He could have trampled them without even trying. "Sam, I'm so sorry. I thought they were downstairs, honest."

"They're going to be—in their room until supper time and no TV tonight. Is that understood?"

"Yes, Daddy," they agreed together, and left the room.

When they were out of earshot, Cheryl burst into laughter. "A bull with pink toenails. This I've got to go see."

Sam shook his head, but he was grinning too. "I plan on moving him into the Hazy Creek pasture with four new cows on Saturday. I just hope the heifers don't get jealous. Buying nail polish for the entire herd could bankrupt me."

"I'm out of pink, but I've got some red you can borrow if that will help keep the peace."

Sam chuckled. "No thanks. I came in to tell you that Walter's going into Council Grove tomorrow. If you want, you and the twins can ride along. Kayla says her boots are pinching her toes. Do you think you can help her find some new ones? I would take her, but I've got another meeting with my firm."

Cheryl hesitated. Each time she went to town, she was courting disaster. What if someone recognized her?

Sam noticed her hesitation. "Forget I mentioned it. I can't keep adding more and more to your duties."

How could she deny him anything? In truth, she

didn't want to. "I think a temporary ninny should be able to manage a new pair of shoes."

"Thanks. And I mean for everything you do."

Cheryl held the memory of his warm gaze close to her heart all day long.

Finding a new pair of boots in town Friday afternoon turned out to be easy enough. Cheryl and the girls finished their shopping a full half hour before the time Walter had agreed to pick them up.

"What shall we do now?" Cheryl asked.

"We could get some ice cream," Lindy suggested.

"That sounds good," Cheryl agreed.

She began walking toward the river that divided the town. The girls skipped along beside her, chattering happily. They crossed the bridge, and Cheryl saw the town had added a new statue on the east bank as she passed a larger-than-life bronze figure of a Kaw Indian warrior. Across the street stood the monument of the Madonna of the Plains, a pioneer woman looking westward with her children at her side. The small Kansas town was fiercely proud of its place in the history of the West.

The bright red ice-cream shop stood sandwiched between the street and the sloping bank of the river. Once they had their cones, the girls ran back to play around the Indian statue, and Cheryl followed along behind them. She was admiring the artist's work when the sound of squealing tires pierced the stillness. She looked up to see a battered green-and-white pickup swerving to miss a car that had stopped to turn. The pickup accelerated and sped out of town.

Cheryl watched with a sense of unease as the weaving green-and-white truck disappeared down the highway. She turned to the girls. "We told Walter we'd meet him in front of the shoe store. We'd better hurry."

The twins eagerly displayed their new boots for Walter, but Cheryl herded the girl into his truck and quickly climbed in after them, happy to be heading back to the seclusion of the ranch.

The twins came barreling into Cheryl's room early the next morning. Kayla tried to wrest the covers away from Cheryl while Lindy jumped up and down on the bed.

"Come on!"

"You've got to get dressed."

"We'll be late for church—"

"—if you don't hurry."

"Girls, please," Cheryl pleaded. "I'm not going to church."

"What?" Lindy collapsed in a heap at the foot of the bed. Kayla let go of the blanket and the sisters exchanged shocked looks.

"But it's Sunday," Kayla said.

Lindy leaned forward. "We all go to church on Sunday."

Cheryl pulled the covers up to her chin. "Sunday is a day of rest, right? Okay, I'm resting."

The twins moved to stand side by side at the foot of the bed. They exchanged puzzled glances.

Lindy said, "How will God know you're thankful for the things He's given you if you don't go to His house and tell Him?"

They waited for her to answer.

Looking at their serious faces, Cheryl couldn't find it in herself to offer another excuse or to dismiss their beliefs out of hand. Their faith was important to them. A faith as strong as the one Sam and his family shared was something that had been missing in her own life. She found it was something she wanted to learn more about. After all, she had many, many things to be thankful for.

Kayla took her hand. "Please come with us."

Perhaps now was the time to show some courage. "Okay, you've convinced me. Scoot out of here so I can get dressed."

They exchanged glowing smiles and dashed from the room. Cheryl heard them yelling the news at their father. She couldn't hear his reply, but she was certain that Sam would be every bit as pleased as the twins.

Later that morning, inside the pretty stone church on the edge of Council Grove, Cheryl found herself seated between Sam and the girls. She had worn her hair down so that it partially hid her face if she kept her head bowed. Glancing around carefully, she saw several faces in the crowded pews that looked familiar. Speculative glances were being cast in her direction but she couldn't tell if it was because she looked familiar to them or if it was because she was with Sam. Maybe this hadn't been such a good idea, after all. She took a deep breath to keep from bolting out the door.

The organist began playing and the congregation joined in the hymn. Sam held his songbook so that she could see the words. The tiny invitation lightened her heart and made her forget for a moment that she had anything to hide. She added her voice to the chorus and set her worries aside.

After the hymn, the young pastor moved to the pulpit. "Good morning, brothers and sisters. In case any of you haven't noticed, it's springtime outside."

That brought a sprinkling of laughter from the people around her, and Cheryl smiled as well.

"Springtime," he continued. "A time for new beginnings. A time for renewal, both of the land and of our hearts. And of our spirits. I'd like talk to you today about learning to accept the way God has chosen to arrange our lives. How for us, His children, He has made a time for everything. I would like to read to you now from Ecclesiastes, chapter three. There is a time for everything, and a season for every activity under heaven:

> a time to be born and a time to die,
> a time to plant and a time to uproot,
> a time to kill and a time to heal,
> a time to tear down and a time to build,
> a time to weep and a time to laugh,
> a time to mourn and a time to dance,
> a time to scatter stones and a time to gather them,
> a time to embrace and a time to refrain,
> a time to search and a time to give up,
> a time to keep and a time to throw away,
> a time to tear and a time to mend,
> a time to be silent and a time to speak,
> a time to love and a time to hate,
> a time for war and a time for peace."

Cheryl listened to his sermon with a sense of wonder. It was as if God had arranged the world so that she would be here to listen to these passages today. The words on the sundial came to life in the voice of the young pastor and Cheryl opened her heart to hear them.

A time to mend. A time to be silent and a time to speak. Was God offering her a chance to mend her life? Was the time to be silent passing and the time to speak out at hand?

She looked over at Sam and caught his eye. He smiled and she was so very glad the twins had convinced her to come. This was the life Sam wanted her to know. Was it possible? If only she dared believe that it could be.

At the end of the service, her old fears came creeping back. She made her way out of the church slowly on her crutches. Outside, she saw the congregation had broken up into smaller groups of friends and families eager to visit and exchange news. Many of the people were looking at her with frank curiosity. She kept her head down.

Sam remained at her side. "Are you okay?"

"My foot is aching terribly. Can we go home?" She used her ready excuse to avoid meeting Sam's friends and neighbors.

"Sure."

His solicitous care the rest of the day pricked her conscience, but she wasn't ready to bare her soul, to risk her happiness on the chance that she wouldn't be accepted. But that night, she asked Walter if she could borrow his Bible. She took it to her room and read until the early hours of the morning.

Monday morning Kayla came into the kitchen and laid several envelopes on the counter. "Is there anything for us? Grandma said she'd write to us."

"Let me see." Cheryl picked up the mail and sorted through it until she discovered a white envelope with her name on it. It didn't have a return address or a postmark, she noted. Someone must have left it in the mailbox.

"Nothing for you," she told the girls. When they left the room, she tore open the letter, pulled out a single sheet of paper, and stared at the message. In block letters in the middle of the page were the words,

LEAVE NOW!

Chapter 12

Who could have written the ominous note and why? Cheryl continued to puzzle over the question two days later while she waited for Dr. Carlton to finish examining her foot. Merci Slader was the obvious choice, but she didn't seem to have trouble voicing her sentiments in person, so why the cryptic nature of the note? The other possibility was that someone had recognized her. Someone who didn't want to confront her face-to-face.

"Your fractures are healing well," Dr. Carlton's voice interrupted her thoughts. "I think we can trade in this cast for a heavy splint if you promise to take it easy."

Cheryl agreed and waited impatiently as he cut through the thick plaster. The footgear he replaced it with reminded her of a cumbersome ski boot.

When he was finished, the doctor scribbled a note on her chart, then paused and peered at her over the edge of his glasses. "How's Sam feeling?" he asked.

"Fine." She couldn't help the foolish grin that spread across her face.

"That's good," Dr. Carlton muttered absently.

A light tap sounded on the door, and Merci opened it. "Doctor, you have a call holding." She ignored Cheryl completely.

Cheryl stood and tested her balance on the new splint.

"Thank you, Merci," he said. "If you'll wait a second, I'll be done with this chart. Ms. Steele, these are your instructions for care of this splint. Oh, by the way," he said, glancing at Cheryl, "I solved the mystery of why I thought I'd met you before."

"You did?" Cold prickles of fear crept down Cheryl's spine.

"Yes, you bear a striking resemblance to a patient I had—oh—it must have been about fifteen years ago." He continued writing on her chart. "Such a beautiful, sad woman. I only saw her once."

"And you remember her after all this time?" Merci asked.

"Yes. She came in with a broken wrist. From the type of fracture and other bruises, and after meeting her husband, I suspected that he might have done it. I never found out for sure. She died tragically in a car accident right after she left my office."

Cheryl felt the blood drain from her face, and she groped behind her for the exam table.

"Her name was Mira Thatcher," he added, snapping the chart shut. "I don't suppose you could be related? The resemblance is remarkable."

Cheryl gripped the edge of the table. He'd known her mother. He must have been one of the last people to see her alive. Dozens of questions poured through her mind. She wanted to ask him about everything that had happened that day. She looked up and met Merci's speculative stare across the room.

"You mean that thieving Thatcher bunch?" Merci asked with a sneer, taking the chart he handed her.

Cheryl turned and reached, with a hand that wasn't quite steady, for her purse on the chair against the wall.

Dr. Carlton said, "They're not exactly the sort of relatives one would want to claim. They're rather infamous, locally. Doris Thatcher still lives on the family ranch."

"And you know she isn't playing with a full deck," Merci said. "She's in this office every other week with some new complaint. The woman is a hypochondriac."

"Merci," the doctor chided. "We can't talk about our patients in front of others. You know that."

"Well, the whole family is a bunch of no-good thieves."

The doctor scowled at her over the rim of his glasses. "They aren't exactly the James Gang."

"Close enough. Even the kids helped the old man steal cattle. My dad's cousin was one of the deputies that arrested them. He said Hank and his son gave up easy enough, but the older girl lit out of the barn on a big, black horse before anyone could stop her. She ran down one of the deputies and nearly killed him. They chased her across country for more than five miles before her horse gave out."

"What happened to them?" Cheryl asked, desperate to know if her whereabouts was common knowledge.

Dr. Carlton stroked his chin with one hand. "The father and son went to prison. I believe Hank died there. Liver cancer, if I remember right. The son got out about a year ago."

Merci nodded. "He lives out with the old woman.

Cattle still disappear around here. We know who's responsible, but the sheriff says he can't prove it. One of these days, Thatcher will slip up and go straight back to prison where he belongs."

The doctor stuffed his pen in his pocket. "I don't know what happened to the girls. Doris never mentions them."

Merci's eyes narrowed. "Are you okay, Ms. Steele? You look a bit pale."

Cheryl forced a smile to her stiff lips. "I'm fine. At least you didn't hang them. Isn't that what they do to—what's the term?"

"Rustlers," Dr. Carlton supplied.

"Ah, yes." Cheryl nodded.

He chuckled. "We don't hang horse thieves or rustlers any more, Miss Steele. Kansas has modern law enforcement, just like they do in New York."

"Of course. I guess I've seen one too many movies." Cheryl felt tiny droplets of sweat forming on her forehead. The air seemed thick and heavy, making it hard to breathe. She fought to remain calm. No one had forgotten or forgiven her and her family. She had been so foolish to stay.

She left the doctor's office and crossed the parking lot to the pickup Sam had loaned her for the day just as Merci Slader caught up with her. "Ms. Steele, you forgot your instructions."

Cheryl took the paper Merci held out. "Thank you."

"I thought you'd be gone long before now."

"Did you?" Cheryl struggled to keep her composure as she opened the truck door.

Merci's hand shot out and grabbed the door. "I think

we both know it's time for you to move on. Sam and the girls don't need the help of an outsider."

Cheryl looked the woman in the eye. "I think that's for Sam to decide, not you. I don't like threats—of any kind. That includes the notes you've been sending me."

"I don't know what you're talking about."

"I think you do. Now, if you will excuse me, I have to get back to the ranch." She jerked the door out of Merci's hand,

"You don't belong here. I won't stand by and watch Sam be hurt again." With that, Merci spun on her heels and walked away.

Cheryl sank onto the truck seat, and her shoulders slumped in defeat. Merci was right. It was past time for her to leave. If Dr. Carlton had recognized her resemblance to her mother, then others could, too. She was risking everything she had worked for by staying.

In her head, she knew she should go, but in her heart, she longed to find a way to hold on to the first true taste of happiness she had ever known. With a weary sigh, she bowed her head and sought help. *God, if You're listening to me, please show me what to do.*

Sam and Walter stood in the barn, watching as Doc Wilson carried the tiny, spotted fawn in from his van. The vet settled the baby on a bed of thick straw and began showing the twins how to bottle-feed him. Sam and Walter stood outside the stall and watched as the girls made over their new pet.

Lindy grinned. "He's so cute."

"We'll call him Bambi," Kayla stated.

"Why does he have spots?"

"Won't Bonkers love him?"

"Can he sleep in our room?"

"Please!" they pleaded together.

Bonkers stalked up to his competition with his tail stiff in the air. He stretched out his neck and sniffed at the fawn with obvious suspicion. The deer sneezed, and Bonkers jumped in fright. Everyone burst out laughing as the cat took off.

Doc slapped Sam's shoulder. "He's your problem now, Sam. If you need me for anything else, just call."

The twins sat cross-legged in the straw and took turns holding the bottle as the fawn nursed eagerly.

"Can Bambi come in the house?" Lindy asked.

"No," Sam stressed. "You aren't to take him outside of this stall. Is that understood?"

"Yes, Daddy." Lindy's lips tightened briefly in a pout.

"What are you going to do with him when he gets too big for the stall?" Cheryl asked from behind them.

"I don't have a clue." Sam smiled at her, feeling foolishly happy. Whenever she was out of his sight, he worried that he'd seen the last of her. Whenever she was near him, he felt as happy and carefree as a kid again.

"If we bottle-raise him, he'll be too tame to turn loose," Walter said.

"Why don't you see if the zoo in Wichita or Kansas City will take him?" she suggested.

"That's a good idea," Walter admitted.

She stepped inside the stall and knelt down. "He is an adorable baby, isn't he?" she said, stroking his sleek head. "Won't he be lonesome out here in the barn?"

The men glanced at each other and rolled their eyes.

"Speaking of babies," Walter said. "What's the latest on Becky?"

"Mom called today," Sam said. "Becky is still on strict bed rest at home. Mom couldn't give me any idea when she'll be able to come home. It looks like she'll be there until the baby's born. It could be another month."

"Poor Becky," Walter said. "I'll bet she's ready to go nuts staying in bed while Eleanor runs her house."

"I'll bet she is, too," Sam agreed. "Doc, I've got a mare who's overdue. Can you take a look at her for me before you go?"

"Sure."

"It's Flying Lady's first foal, and I'm a little worried." Sam and Walter walked out of the barn with the young vet, and Cheryl stayed behind with the twins.

"What happened to Bambi's mommy?" Kayla asked.

"She ran to safety when the pasture was burned," Cheryl replied, petting the fawn's head.

"Why did she leave her baby behind?"

"I think he was too little to run away, and she knew that we would take care of him."

"Will he miss her?" Lindy asked.

Cheryl stroked his slender neck and watched him guzzle his milk as she pondered her answer. "He will, but not very much if you give him lots of love and attention."

Lindy smiled at Cheryl. "Like you give us?"

"What?" Cheryl's heart stumbled a beat as her glance flew to Lindy's face.

Kayla slipped her arms around Cheryl and laid her head against her side. "You give us lots of love—"

"—like a real mommy does," Lindy added.

Kayla sighed wistfully, "I wish you could be our mommy."

"For real," Lindy said.

A lump rose in Cheryl's throat. A longing she'd been unable to put into words swept over her. She stroked Kayla's soft curls and bent to kiss the top of her head. "Darlings, that's the sweetest thing anyone has ever said to me."

The fawn finished his bottle, and Lindy turned to Cheryl.

"So, why can't you—"

"—stay and be our mother?"

Cheryl stared at their upturned, trusting face. "It's so complicated."

"Don't you like us?"

Cheryl reached out and drew Lindy close. "Of course I do, it isn't that."

"Is it 'cause you have to be a ballerina?" Kayla asked.

"That's part of the reason."

"Don't ballerinas have kids?" Lindy looked at Cheryl with a puzzled frown.

"Some of them do," Cheryl admitted.

"Then why can't you be our mommy *and* a ballerina?" Kayla insisted. "You could go to work like Daddy does. Grandma would take care of us while you're gone."

"Honey, it isn't that easy." She gazed at their eager faces. Their world was still so simple and so innocent. They would never know a brutal and unkind father because they had Sam. She had no way to make them understand what her life had been like—the shame and humiliation she had known for simply being who she was. The same shame and humiliation that waited for her now if her identity were discovered.

She pulled the girls into a tight embrace. "I can't stay. I wish I could, but I can't. I love both of you very much. Always remember that. Promise me you'll always remember that, no matter what anyone tells you."

"We promise," Kayla said, and Lindy nodded.

Sam watched Cheryl toy with her food at the supper table while the twins talked nonstop about their new pet. They finished the meal quickly and begged to be allowed to go back to the barn. A nod from him sent them running out the door.

"You're quiet tonight, New York. Is your foot bothering you? I noticed you got rid of your cast."

She gave him a weak smile. "It aches a little. This splint is lighter, and I can walk better, but it still leaves something to be desired as far as footwear goes."

"Oh, before I forget, you got a letter today." He rose and searched through the stack of mail by the phone. "Here it is."

She stared at the long, white envelope for a moment, then took it and stuffed it in the pocket of her jeans.

"Do you think you can ride in that splint?" Sam asked.

"Ride?" She shot him a puzzled look.

"I thought we might go for a ride tonight. The moon will be full. It might be fun to try it without the snow. What do you say?"

Her eyes brightened and a smile curved her beautiful mouth. He'd never get tired of seeing her smile, he realized. The phone rang before she could answer him.

"Hold that thought," Sam said and answered the phone.

"Hi, Sam." The sound of Merci's low voice purred in his ear.

"Hi, Merci. What can I do for you?"

"I was wondering if I could catch a ride to the school board meeting with you tonight? My car's in the shop."

"Merci, I don't think I can make it tonight."

"The bond issue is being voted on, Sam. You have to come. We need your support on this."

She was right. He couldn't let his responsibility to the community slide because he wanted to go for a moonlight ride. "Okay, sure, I can give you a lift."

"If it's not too much trouble, that would be wonderful."

Sam glanced at Cheryl. He'd much rather spend the evening with her, but he said, "It's no trouble. I'll see you in thirty minutes."

He hung up the phone and turned to Cheryl. "I'm sorry. I completely forgot about the school board meeting tonight. Maybe we can work in that ride after I get home?"

"Sure."

The brightness left her eyes. She looked down and began to toy with her food again. For a minute, he was tempted to skip his meeting, but his sense of duty got the better of him. The bond issue was important to his children's future.

Cheryl watched Sam leave, then pulled her letter from her pocket and stared at it with dread. The phone rang again, but she let the machine pick up until the sound of a familiar voice made her grab the receiver.

"Angie?" she asked in delight. "Oh, Angie, it's so good to hear your voice."

"I just got your message, Cheryl. What's going on? What are you doing in Council Grove? How bad are you hurt?"

"One question at a time, sis. Where are you?"

"San Francisco. We wanted to spend a few days here before we came back. If Jeff hadn't called home to pick up his messages, I'd still be thinking you were dancing your way across the country. Why didn't you call me? I left you the number of the hotel in Hawaii."

"And ruin your honeymoon? No way."

"Well, thanks for that. But I can't believe you stayed in Council Grove all this time. The sister I know would have crawled on her bloody hands and knees all the way to New York rather than spend one night in Morris County."

"Believe me, I wanted to, but twelve inches of snow nixed that idea. It's a long story, but I ended up staying and playing nanny here on the Hardin ranch."

"Hardin? You don't mean Ol' Hard-as-Nails Hardin from school, do you?"

Cheryl smiled at the once-popular nickname for Sam's stern, no-nonsense mother. "Her son, actually."

"You've got to be kidding! And you as a nanny? I can't believe that."

Cheryl couldn't stop the wistful note in her voice. "It's been wonderful."

"Wonderful?"

"Yeah, wonderful."

"Oh, honey. You've got it bad."

Cheryl didn't pretend to misunderstand. "I've got it bad. For a cowboy with a pair of five-year-old twin girls," she admitted.

"My big sister's in love. It's about time. And what does the cowboy think about it?"

"It doesn't matter."

"Doesn't matter?" Angie exclaimed. "What do you mean, it doesn't matter? Oh, don't tell me he's married!"

"No, of course not."

"So what's the problem? There's nothing wrong with cowboys or ready-made families."

"You know I can't stay here." Cheryl's voice quivered. "I can't face it all again. And besides, I have my career to think about."

"He doesn't know who you are, does he?"

"Does he know he's been sheltering one of the 'thieving Thatchers'? That he's letting a reform-school grad babysit his kids? No, I haven't told him. I've tried, but I can't. I'm such a coward."

"No, you're not. You are the bravest and best sister in the world."

"When will you be home?" Cheryl asked, determined to change the subject.

"Early tomorrow afternoon."

Tomorrow. It would be her last day with Sam and the children. How would she bear it? Sighing, she asked, "Can you put me up for a few weeks?"

"You know I can."

"Don't you think you'd better check with Jeff?"

Angie laughed. "He's still head over heels in love with me. If I say I want you to stay, he'll pretend he's thrilled."

Cheryl had to smile at her sister's confidence. She sobered as she considered how to ask the next question on her mind. There wasn't any easy way to bring up the subject. "Angie, did you know that Jake's out of prison?"

A long silence greeted her question. Finally, Angie said, "Yes, I knew. He was at my wedding."

Cheryl almost dropped the phone. "What? Are you sure? I didn't see him. How did he know about it?"

"Yes, I'm sure," Angie answered calmly. "Jake knew

because I invited him, and you didn't see him because he's as stubborn as you are."

"I don't understand."

"Let's face it, Jake's had the same address for fourteen years. How many letters and visits did he get from you?"

"None," she whispered, ashamed to admit how totally she had cut herself off from her brother.

"He said he wouldn't impose himself on you unless you were willing to see him. He made me promise. I tried to talk to you about him—"

"And I refused to discuss anything about our family. I'm sorry we put you in the middle."

"When I didn't invite him into the dressing room, he simply stayed out of sight in the choir loft. He was the guitarist."

Cheryl sank onto a kitchen chair. Such beautiful, haunting music. "I remember he used to play. I didn't know he was so good."

"There are a lot of things you don't know. Like the fact that he pled guilty and waived his right to trial in exchange for the judge going easy on you."

"What?" Cheryl couldn't believe her ears.

"He made a deal with the district attorney and took the maximum sentence in order for you to get the minimum time."

Cheryl rubbed a hand across her stinging eyes. This was like opening a photo album and seeing the faces of strangers on all the familiar family pictures. Her half brother had sacrificed years of his life to help her. Why?

"I didn't know any of this. Why didn't you tell me?"

"To be honest, I didn't know it either until the last time I went to visit Harriet. Beside, I didn't think you would approve of my staying in contact with Jake. You wanted a clean break with the past. I tried to respect your wishes. Harriet said when you were ready, you'd ask the questions, but until then, you wouldn't be able to hear the answers."

"She was such a wise woman. She was right, I wouldn't have been able to hear anything good about Jake."

"Cheryl, if you're thinking about staying, we need to talk."

"I'm not staying!"

She'd been hiding the truth from Sam for weeks. She couldn't ask him to understand and forgive that. And even if by some chance he did forgive her, she couldn't give up her career to live out here. Sam needed someone to be mother to the twins. She loved the girls, but what kind of mother could she be if she were two thousand miles away? It was a no-win situation.

"We'll talk in person. Not over the phone. Come and get me, Angie."

When Cheryl hung up the phone, she slowly unfolded her letter. It read,

Leave or I'll Make You Sorry.

Chapter 13

Sam held the door open for Merci as they left the high-school gym after the meeting. The full moon had disappeared behind thick clouds, and raindrops dashed any hope he still harbored of a moonlit ride with Cheryl.

"How about some coffee at my place?" Merci asked.

"I don't think so. It's late, I should be getting home."

"I haven't seen much of you lately." Merci laid a hand on his arm. "I've missed you," she said quietly.

Sam found himself at a loss for words.

"Actually," she continued, "I need your professional help with something."

"Are you taking up cattle breeding, Merci?"

She gave a short laugh. "No. I'm going to remodel that dinky house of mine, and I need some advice on which walls I can knock out. I've got the original blueprints at home. Whenever you get some time, maybe you could look at them for me."

The rain began coming down in earnest as Sam gazed at Merci's hopeful face, and his conscience pricked him. Merci had been a good friend to him after his divorce. If her attentions occasionally made him uncomfortable, that was his fault, not hers. He hadn't been ready to resume a relationship with anyone and he knew he had sometimes hurt her feelings.

"Never mind, Sam. It can wait."

"No, I'd be happy to take a look at them for you."

He drove her to her home at the edge of town and followed her through the front door. A high-school-aged girl came out of the living room as they walked in.

"Thanks for babysitting tonight, Susan. How much do I owe you?" Merci asked, opening her purse.

Susan held out a lock of her waist-length blond hair with a large pink glob in it. "It's free if you know a way to get this gum out of my hair without cutting it. Your son's a brat!"

"Oh, Susan, I'm so sorry." Merci cast Sam an embarrassed look. "He's not really a brat, he's just spirited. Come in to the kitchen. Some peanut butter will take care of this."

"Peanut butter in my hair? How yuck!"

Sam hid a laugh with a cough. "I'll wait in the living room."

Sitting on the sofa, he listened to Susan list the abuses she'd endured. *Brat* sounded like a good description of Jimmy Slader, Jr. The peanut butter worked, but Sam doubted Susan would sit for Jimmy again any time soon.

He picked up the newspaper while he waited for Susan to leave. With a bark of laughter, he held it up as Merci walked into the room. "I hope you've read it," he said with a smile. It was full of holes, and he wiggled a finger through one.

Merci's eyes widened, and she snatched it away from

him. "I can't believe Susan didn't watch him any better than this. She knows not to let him play with scissors."

"I'd say she was lucky to find gum in her hair and not her hair on the floor."

Merci folded the paper into a tight square and sat down on the sofa beside him. "He does it to annoy me—to get attention. He's getting to be a handful. His father never has time for him now that he has a new wife and a baby on the way. What Jimmy needs is a full-time father. You know how it is. Your girls are getting to the age when they need a mother full time, too."

Sam shifted uncomfortably on the sofa. "Mom does a great job with them."

"Of course she does, but she's not getting any younger. At her age, she should be enjoying herself, not running after the two of them day in and day out."

"She'll let me know when it gets to be too much for her."

"I'm sure she will." Merci smoothed the creases in the paper she held. "I ran into Cheryl Steele at the hospital today. Did she tell you?"

"No, she didn't mention it."

Merci smiled, "She's ready to get out of the boonies and back to New York, isn't she?"

Sam frowned. "Did she say that?"

"You can't blame her. This is a far cry from what she's used to."

"Did she say she wanted to leave?" he insisted.

"Not in those exact words. In fact, she said she was enjoying the diversions ranch life had to offer, but she missed the excitement of the big city and her work."

"I'm sure she does." Sam stared down at his boots. A diversion, was that all he was?

"It was the strangest thing," Merci continued. "Dr. Carter mentioned the Thatcher family, and I swear, she turned as white as a ghost. Why do you suppose that was?"

"I have no idea. Where are those blueprints?" he asked abruptly. He didn't intend to discuss Cheryl with Merci.

It was late when he finally arrived home, but he found himself standing outside Cheryl's room anyway. He raised his fist to knock, but hesitated and lowered his hand.

A diversion. Was he being used to help pass the time and nothing more? He didn't believe that. Their attraction was mutual, he was sure of it. He raised his fist again, but still he hesitated.

An attraction wasn't the same as love. She'd never said anything about love. And neither had he.

Could he risk telling her that he loved her, then watch her walk away as Natalie had done? Could he face that? He stuffed his hands in his pockets.

He'd never considered himself a coward, but this scared him to death. Feeling more confused than ever, he turned away from her door and headed down the stairs.

He was surprised to see Walter lining up a shot at the billiard table when he walked down into the rec room. Sam glanced at his watch. "What are you doing home? I thought you and Fred Barns were on for a game of checkers at the café."

Walter took his shot and sent the cue ball flying down the length of the table. It bounced off the cushion, rolled back and gently kissed the eight ball into the corner pocket.

He picked up his glass of iced tea from the rail and took a drink. "Fred had to leave early. After that, the company went downhill. Jake Thatcher was there."

"That's funny. Someone else mentioned the Thatchers tonight. Was he making trouble?"

"Not by the time I left. But he rode in on a shiny, new motorcycle. Makes a man wonder where a jailbird gets that kind of money?"

"I hear he's been doing a good job on his grandmother's spread. Cattle prices are up. Maybe he sold some steers."

"Yeah. I wonder who they belonged to? Maybe I should've asked him."

"Don't go looking for trouble, Gramps. A man your age should have more sense."

"Speaking of looking for trouble, isn't that what you're doing?"

"What's that mean?"

Walter walked around the table and began pulling the balls out of the pockets and rolling them to one end. "It means, one day I see you making eyes at a certain blonde, and tonight I see your truck parked outside the house of a certain redhead."

Sam walked to the table and caught the balls Walter rolled his way and placed them in the rack. He picked up a stick. "I wasn't making eyes at anyone. Merci and I are friends. I don't need to defend myself if I want to see her."

Walter lined up the cue ball and made the break. Colored balls careened madly around the table, but none of them dropped into a pocket. "Funny choice of words, *defend.*"

Sam took his time as he searched the table for the best shot. He picked a striped ball near the side pocket and sank it with a quick stroke. "Merci wanted me to look at some house plans, that's all." The next ball he tried for stalled at the edge of the pocket. He straightened and watched his grandfather study the table.

Walter missed his next shot. "So which one are you in love with, the blonde or the redhead?"

"Who says I'm in love?"

"That dopey smile you have on your face morning, noon and night. I sure hope it's the redhead."

"Why do you say that?"

Walter straightened and gave Sam a level look. "Because Cheryl doesn't belong here, and you know it."

Sam concentrated on the table for a long moment. "She could learn to like it. She's great with the girls." He took his turn and missed.

"Sure, she's great with kids, and maybe she even likes it here, but she loves it there." Walter gestured toward the barre and mirror with his chin. "There, she lights up like a hundred-watt bulb."

"She does, doesn't she?" Sam stared at the mirror, picturing Cheryl's smile when she talked about dancing and the graceful bend and sway of her body as she practiced. If he asked her to stay, he'd be asking her to give up something as essential to her as air. How could he ask her to choose?

Walter sank the rest of the balls on the table, put his stick down, then laid a hand on Sam's shoulder. "I wish she'd leave and get it over with. The longer she hangs around, the harder it's going to be on everyone. I saw you and the kids go through that once, Sam. I'd do anything in my power to keep it from happening again."

"Thanks, Gramps, but I can take care of myself."

"I hope so."

Sam didn't answer him.

Walter turned toward the stairs, then stopped. "Oh,

by the way, I was over by the Hazy Creek pasture, and I didn't see hide nor hair of Harvey."

"He was probably hiding, ashamed to be seen with his pedicure."

Walter chuckled. "Maybe. I'll check the water gap tomorrow and make sure the fence isn't down. It wouldn't hurt to call the Double R boys and see if he's slipped over in with their bunch."

"Okay, I'll take care of it in the morning."

"I put Flying Lady in the box stall next to Bambi. I think she'll foal tonight. Want me to check on her before I turn in?"

"If you don't mind."

Walter shook his head. "No trouble."

Sam watched his grandfather disappear up the stairs, then turned his attention to the ballet barre on the wall. Walking up to it, he gripped the smooth wood in his hands and leaned his forehead against the cool mirror.

In his mind's eye he could see how Cheryl looked when she stood poised in the light. It was, he realized, the only time that she let people really see her.

The rest of the time she kept some part of herself hidden. Someone or something must have caused her great pain. He wanted to know what it was. He wanted her to share her burdens as well as her joys with him. She might love dancing, but he knew she cared about him and his girls. He would tell her how he felt—tell her that he loved her—that she made his heart whole again. God had brought her into his life for that reason. He didn't doubt it. Tomorrow. He would tell her tomorrow.

With his mind made up, he crossed to his bedroom and softly closed the door.

* * *

Sam wasn't in the house when Cheryl rose the next morning. She knocked on his door but there was no reply. The twins lay curled up in their beds still fast asleep. Cheryl closed the door without waking them. After that, she made her way down to the barn.

As she stepped through the barn door, she heard Sam speaking softly from a nearby stall. She walked toward him. He didn't hear her approach. She leaned on the stall door and watched him coax a brown, spindly-legged foal to its feet.

His hands and his voice were so gentle, so at odds with his big size and rugged appearance. He glanced up and saw her. A smile lit his face. "'Morning, New York."

"'Morning, cowboy." Her heart contracted and pushed a lump into her throat. She was in love with this man. She opened her mouth to tell him so, but the sound of Walter's voice stopped her.

"What'd she have?" Walter asked as he came to stand beside Cheryl and look over the stall door.

"A nice filly," Sam said, giving her a little help to her feet. "Did you find Harvey?"

"Harvey's missing?" Cheryl asked in surprise.

Walter nodded. "The fences are all good, and I covered that pasture from one end to the other. There's no sign of him and four of our cows are missing, too. I did meet two of the Double R cowboys checking the same fence. It seems they've lost five steers sometime in the past two days."

A deep frown creased Sam's brow. "We'd better notify the sheriff."

"You think he's been stolen?" Cheryl asked. An icy feeling crept into her veins.

Walter slapped his gloves against his thigh. "Looks like it to me. I'll call the sheriff. Then I'm going to pay that thievin' Thatcher a visit to find out what he knows about this."

Cheryl steadied herself against the stall door as the edges of her vision darkened. This couldn't be happening. Not now.

Sam grabbed Walter's elbow. "Don't do anything rash. Let the law handle it."

"It's your best bull, Sam. He's a Grand Champion three times over, and four of your best cows gone with him. Years of breeding work down the drain, not to mention that he's worth thousands of dollars."

"Don't you think I know that? By now they're probably out of the state. If you warn Thatcher that you suspect him, he'll cover his tracks or skip out before the authorities have a chance to investigate."

Walter took a deep breath. "Maybe you're right. What I'd like to know is how he knew where the bull was? Harvey was in that pasture less than twenty-four hours before he was taken."

"Whoever took him must have been watching the place. If I know Sheriff Manning he'll want to check out everyone who's done work for us in the last few months. I've got a list of employees in my office."

Cheryl listened to Sam and Walter in growing horror. Her brother was the first person they suspected. And why not? He'd gone to prison twice for the same crime. It didn't take much of a stretch to think he'd try it a third time. She could find herself tarred with the same brush. She'd be investigated. No one would believe she hadn't been involved, not after she'd kept the truth from them.

She knew how easy it was to look guilty when everyone believed you were. The memory of those long, dark days in the juvenile detention center sent a shiver of fear crawling down her spine.

As much as she loved Sam, she couldn't bear to think of the look on his face when he found out who she was—what she'd been. She couldn't bear it if he thought she was guilty. Angie would arrive this afternoon unless Cheryl left a message for her at the airport. Sam didn't know she had talked to her sister. It would come as a shock, but maybe it was better this way. Better to make a quick, clean break with no time for a lingering goodbye. No time to watch her dreams fade as she tried to hide how much her heart was breaking.

Sam ran a hand over the stubble of his chin. "Look, I'll go into town and file a report, but I've got a buyer coming in to pick up some yearlings this morning. Can you take care of that for me, Gramps?"

"Are you trying to keep me away from Thatcher?"

"Yes, but more than that, I need your help now."

Walter gave his grudging consent.

"Good." Sam clapped his grandfather on the back. "The paperwork is on my desk." With a nod, Walter left.

Cheryl turned to Sam. "I need to talk."

A smile softened his features. "Good, because there's something I want to tell you."

He reached for her. She gripped his hand for a moment, then released it and clasped her arms across her chest. "My sister called last night."

He smile faded. "Your sister is back?"

"Yes. She's coming to pick me up." She stared at the tips of her shoes. She couldn't bear to watch his face.

After a long pause, he said, "I see. When?"

She heard the bewilderment in his voice, and she knew he didn't understand. "Today. This afternoon."

He turned and took a step away, then spun around to face her. Anguish marred his face. "So, this is goodbye?"

"Yes. You knew I would leave sometime." She wanted so much to reach out and hold him.

He brushed past her and headed for the workbench at the end of the aisle. He opened a cabinet door, then banged it closed and clutched the countertop in front of him. "I thought we might be enough for you, the girls and I."

"I'm sorry, Sam. I can't stay."

He turned to her. "Even if I asked you to? Even if I said—"

"Please, stop. I have to go. We both knew that at the start. I think we just forgot it for a little while."

He turned away from her. "There isn't much demand for ballet dancers out here, is there?" Bitterness colored his voice with a coldness that chilled her.

Cheryl wished she could find a way to ease the ache in her heart—and in his. Perhaps it would be best to let him believe her career was the reason she was leaving. "I've worked for years to get where I am, Sam. I can't throw it all away."

"I don't know how I could have been so stupid."

"Don't say that. What we had was wonderful. Never doubt it, and please don't belittle it."

Sam turned and stared at her for a long moment. Her pleading was so heartfelt that he knew it wasn't a charade. There was so much pain in her eyes. Why? If her career meant more to her than his affections why would he see so much pain?

"Cheryl, I was afraid of loving someone who didn't

love me in return. I thought you were afraid of the same thing. I was wrong, wasn't I? What are you afraid of?"

She turned away, but he caught her hand, preventing her escape. "I love you. I know that you love me and you love my children. I see it in your face every time you look at us. Please, whatever it is, we can work it out. Let me help you."

"Can you change the past, Sam? Can you right the wrongs done by other people? You can't. And I won't let what has happened before touch you or the girls. Please, don't make this any harder for me."

"I wish you could find it in your heart to trust me. Because of you I've learned to love again. I love the way your hair catches the sunlight, the way your eyes sparkle with delight when the girls do something funny. I love the goodness in your soul—the kindness you shower on my family. Why would I want to make it easy for you to leave?"

"If you do love me, you won't try to stop me."

His shoulders slumped in defeat. He dropped her hand. "You win. I can't change the past and whatever happened to you, but I know with God's help you can face it. You can overcome it. Until you are ready to do that, I don't know how to help you."

Cheryl watched him until he stepped out the barn door and closed it behind him, leaving her alone with her heartache. She was a coward. She didn't deserve a man as kind and good as Sam. He and the girls were better off without her. The knowledge brought a fresh stab of grief. She sank to the floor and covered her face as hot tears poured down her cheeks.

Chapter 14

Cheryl managed to regain her composure, and she was in the kitchen when the twins came running upstairs, demanding breakfast. She thought she'd cried out all her tears, but more stung the backs of her eyelids as she watched the girls slide into their chairs at the table. They were dressed in identical blue jeans, yellow Western shirts and blue cowboy hats that hung down their back by their strings.

"What's for breakfast?" Lindy sniffed. "Pancakes?"

Kayla reached for her juice. "Where's Daddy?"

Cheryl turned the cakes on the griddle. "He had to go into town this morning. I'm making your favorite breakfast—blueberry pancakes."

"Goody."

"Yum."

She slipped the golden-brown pancakes onto plates and took a deep breath before she turned around. She placed a dish in front of each child. "There's something I have to tell you."

"What?" Lindy asked, pouring too much syrup over her stack.

"My sister called me last night. She's home now and I'm going to stay with her for a while."

Kayla stared at Cheryl. "You're going away?"

Cheryl couldn't bear to see the disappointment cloud their faces. She turned away and busied herself at the stove. "Yes, I am."

"But you can't go!" Kayla insisted.

"I have to, sweetheart. I have to get back to my work."

"You can't dance, your foot is still broke," Lindy shouted.

"You said you loved us," Kayla added quietly.

Cheryl spun around and came to kneel beside her. "I do love you."

"Then why do you want to go away?" Kayla whispered. "Did we do something bad?"

"No, of course you didn't."

"Please, don't go. We'll be good, won't we?" Kayla looked at her sister, but Lindy didn't answer.

"I can't stay," Cheryl said as her heart broke into even smaller pieces.

"Are you going back to New York?" Kayla asked quietly.

Cheryl closed her eyes and shook her head. "My sister lives in Wichita. I'll stay with her until the doctor says I can dance again, then I'll leave for New York."

Cheryl struggled to keep the quiver out of her voice. "I thought we could do something really special today, anything you girls wanted. So, what will it be?"

The twins stared silently at each other for a long moment, then Kayla looked at Cheryl and said, "Nothing."

They got up from the table and walked out of the house, the untouched pancakes still on their plates.

Cheryl watched them go. It hurt nearly as much as watching Sam walk away.

She left the kitchen and wandered to the long windows and stared out at the rolling hills. She slid open the balcony door and walked out to lean against the railing. A strong south wind greeted her. The grasses on the hillside across from her nodded and swayed as they danced in the wind.

Walking around the side of the house, she checked on the twins. They were with Walter. A cattle trailer was pulling into the yard and the three of them waited for it beside the barn. Feeling very much alone, Cheryl turned and walked down the hill to the garden.

She hesitated at the stone doorway and gently ran her hand down the moss-covered stones. She leaned her head against them and gazed at the sundial in its circle of flowers. When she left here today she might never hear the sounds of happiness again. The true garden was in her heart, she realized, not on the other side of this stone wall.

Before Sam and his children, her heart had been an empty, barren space. The joy and the pain that came with loving them were both the sunshine and the rain that had made a garden of happiness grow there. Without them, she was afraid only dust would gather in the corners of her heart again. She stepped through the doorway and sat down on the cool stone bench.

She'd wanted to protect Sam and the children, but it seemed all she'd done was hurt them. Was she willing to leave and let those two children spend their whole lives believing they hadn't been good enough to earn her love? Wasn't that the way her father had made her feel?

She loved Sam so much, yet she was willing to let him believe her career meant more to her than his love. That was a sin, bigger than any she'd committed by failing to tell him the truth about her past. Sam deserved better. She had nothing to do with the missing cattle, but it wasn't fair that all his hard work would be for nothing because of her brother.

Maybe if she went to see Jake, if she could convince him to return the cattle, or at least tell her where he'd sold them, maybe it would help.

She pressed her palms to her temples. What was she thinking? She'd have to go to the ranch. She'd have to face her brother and grandmother and her bitter memories of that place. And why would Jake help her now after she had ignored him for years? Maybe he wouldn't, but she had to try. She owed Sam that much. If only she were as brave as Angie.

Clasping her hands together, she bowed her head. *Please Lord, Sam said You will give me strength, hope and limitless love if I trust in You. Help me to do the right thing. Help me find the courage I need. And help me bear the outcome with dignity, whatever that outcome may be.*

A feeling of rightness—of deep calm came over her. Filled with a determination to do what she could to help Sam, Cheryl left the garden without a backward glance.

Walter was saddling a horse beside the barn when she came around the side of the house. There was no sign of Sam. Gathering her courage, she approached his grandfather.

"Walter, I need a favor."

He looked up from his task. "What kind of favor?"

"I need to borrow your truck, and I need you to keep an eye on the girls for me while I—run an errand."

He turned back to the horse and slipped its bridle on. "Can't it wait until Sam gets back?"

"No, it can't."

"What's your hurry?"

"I'm leaving today."

That snapped his head around. "Does Sam know?"

"Yes."

He nodded toward the twins climbing on the corral fence. "Do they?"

"Yes, I told them. My sister is coming for me this afternoon."

Walter stared at her for a long moment. "Take the truck. The keys are in it. I think I'm going to miss you."

"I might just miss you, too, Walter." She smiled at him sadly. Turning away, she crossed the yard, climbed in the truck and drove out of the yard.

Lindy, sitting on the top rail of the fence, banged boot heels against the boards in frustration. "She can't leave. I don't want her to. I thought she wanted to be our mother."

"She does."

"She does not!"

"She does, too!"

"What are you arguing about?" Walter asked as he rode up next to them.

"Nothing," they answered together.

"Well, pipe down. You'll scare the cattle," he said.

"Where's Cheryl going? I didn't say goodbye." Kayla

started to climb down from the fence as Cheryl drove past.

"She's got an errand to run. She's not leaving until her sister gets here. You'll have plenty of time to say goodbye." He entered the corral and began cutting two young bulls away from the herd and driving them toward the loading chute.

"We got to find a way to stop her," Lindy said more quietly. She pushed her hat off and let it dangle down her back by the ties.

"Daddy will stop her."

"What if she leaves before he comes home? Then what will happen?"

"I don't know," Kayla admitted.

They watched silently as Walter loaded the first two cattle into the trailer, then he rode back into the herd and began to cut two young heifers away and drive them up the chute. The truck driver lowered the gate with a loud clatter when the last calf entered the trailer. He came and stood beside the girls.

"Fer a minute there, I thought I was a seein' double," he drawled, tipping his hat back. "Don't folks have trouble tellin' you apart?"

The twins nodded. "Yup," they answered together.

"Where are you—"

"—taking Daddy's cattle?"

He spat a stream of tobacco juice on the ground. "Yer daddy sold 'em, so they ain't his cattle no more. The heifers I'm takin' to a ranch over by Abilene, and them bulls are going to a farm down by Wichita."

"Wichita?" Lindy looked at her sister and smiled. Kayla stared at her a moment, then nodded slowly.

"Yup, all the way to Wichita," the man replied.

Walter rode up, dismounted and looped his reins over the fence. "Come to the house, Mr. Reed, and we'll settle the bill."

The two men crossed the yard together. They stepped apart as Bonkers darted between them and scampered toward the twins still sitting on the fence.

Cheryl turned the pickup off the highway at the familiar corner and drove slowly down the rutted lane. Weeds sprouted in a wide path between the tire tracks. The house, when it came into view, was as neglected-looking as the lane.

The once-white building was gray with age and peeling paint. The porch railing was missing a spindle or two giving the house the appearance of an old hag with missing teeth. It seemed smaller than she remembered. The yard was overgrown and wore an air of neglect.

Only the barn and corrals showed signs of repairs. A battered green-and-white pickup held a stack of new lumber and paint cans that showed someone's intent to continue the work.

Cheryl stepped out of the truck and waited. There was no sign of life. She approached the house with trepidation and climbed the steps. The front door stood open behind the screen door. She didn't have any idea what she'd say to Doris or to Jake, but she raised her hand and knocked as loudly as her wavering courage would allow. No one came. Calling out a hello, she opened the door and stepped inside her childhood home.

Little had changed, she saw as she stood in the entryway. The wallpaper was the same pattern of yellow roses, now faded to a drab gray. A glance into the living room showed her the same brown sofa, sagging more in the middle, and an overstuffed chair. The smell was different, she thought. It smelled old and devoid of life. It all seemed so familiar, and yet so foreign.

"Hello?" she called out again. Only silence answered her. Her sense of unease grew. She turned and hurried toward the front door and the fresh air and sunshine. Her hand was on the screen door when a dark figure loomed in front of her, blocking out the light.

"What are you doing here?"

For an instant, she didn't recognize his voice. Older and deeper, it carried a hard edge that sent a chill down her spine. So this was the man her brother had become. Fear flickered in the pit of her stomach. What had made her think that she could confront him? No one knew where she'd gone.

The thought of Sam and what he stood to lose stiffened her spine. Jake wasn't going to ruin all Sam had worked to achieve. Not if she could help it.

Raising her chin, she said, "I wouldn't have come at all if you hadn't stolen Harvey. Where is he? I want him back." She shoved open the screen door.

"Who?" He stepped backward as she barged out of the house.

She held her arms outstretched as she advanced on him. "Big white bull." She wiggled her fingers over her head. "Lots of curls. Pink hooves that match these." She thrust her nails in front of his face.

"I don't know what you're talking about." He took another step back and teetered on the edge of the steps.

Shoving against his chest with both hands, she sent him sprawling in the dirt. His black hat went flying. She straddled his body before he could get up. Balling her fists, she said, "You tell me where he is or I'll—I'll…"

A slow grin spread over his face, softening his features into the charming older brother she'd once known. "Or you'll do what? Spit in my eye? If I remember right, Twiggy, that's what you used to threaten me with."

Her bravado evaporated at his use of the nickname she'd hated. She dropped her fists.

"After all this time you can't even say hello?" he asked.

Slowly, she extended one hand toward him. "Hello, Goat Breath. How have you been?"

"Not too bad." After a moment, he took her hand, and she pulled him to his feet. "Nobody's called me Goat Breath in a long, long time. Sounds kind of nice."

Cheryl sank onto the porch steps behind her, and after a brief hesitation, he picked up his hat and sat down beside her.

"You didn't take them, did you?" she said.

"Take what?"

"Sam Hardin's cattle."

"No." He dusted off his hat.

"They think you did. The sheriff will be out here soon."

He settled his hat on his head. "It won't be the first time. But there's nothing for him to find."

She stared at Jake, seeing how the years had added lines to his face. He hadn't had an easy time of it. "I'm sorry I suspected you."

He shrugged. "Can't blame you. My track record ain't exactly flawless." He returned her steady regard. "You sure look like your mother."

"So I've been told."

"She was always good to me. I loved her for that. What are you doing out here, Cheryl?"

"I had a car accident on my way to Manhattan after Angie's wedding, and I broke my foot. The rest is a long story, but I've been staying at the Hardin ranch. Angie told me you were at her wedding. Your music was beautiful."

"Yeah, well, I had plenty of time to practice."

"Angie also told me yesterday about what you did for me. If it means anything after all this time—thank you."

He scuffed the ground with the heel of his boot. "Yeah, it means something."

"I wish... I'm sorry I didn't...you know...keep in touch."

"After the mess I got you into, I didn't expect you would."

"No, it wasn't right that I cut you off. I'm glad Angie had more sense. Our little sister is a lot deeper than I thought."

He nodded. "She's a good kid. I hope she's happy with Jeff."

"I think she will be. What about you? Is there anyone?"

His bark of laughter was bitter. "In this cattle country? No rancher's daughter is going to take a chance on me. Besides, I've been too busy trying to make a go of this place."

"Looks like you're making progress."

"Like you didn't know."

She frowned. "How would I know?"

He stood and shoved his hands in his pockets. "It may take a while, but I can get this place back on its feet. You'll see."

What had she said to upset him? She stood and placed a hand on his shoulder. "I'm sure you will." She smiled and gave him a gentle shake. "Although, it's just like a cowboy to fix up the barn before he fixes up the house."

"Doris won't let me touch the place. I've got a room down in the barn. I stay there and keep an eye on her. She's gotten more peculiar in her old age. She was doing a little better until she saw you."

Astounded, Cheryl said, "She saw me? When?"

"You were in Council Grove at the doctor's office after that snowstorm. It's a small town. It didn't take her long to find out Hardin had a strange woman staying on his ranch. Doris kind of went off the deep end then."

He turned to her and gripped Cheryl's shoulders. "She doesn't have anywhere else to go. She doesn't have any money. She's an old woman. I know she treated you badly when you were a kid—"

"Badly?" Cheryl jerked out of his hold and took a step away. "I can't tell you how many times she took a belt to my back. Believe me, almost a year in the girls' correctional facility was a walk in the park compared to life here."

"She beat you?"

Of course, he hadn't known. She'd never told anyone, and it wasn't fair to blame him now. She crossed her arms and stared at the ground. "After Mom died and Doris came to live with us, you got your own place. And Dad was so drunk most of the time, he didn't care. She and I didn't get along from the get go. I was mouthy and surly and mad at the world. She couldn't stand the way I acted out."

"That didn't give her the right to hit you."

"After I came back from juvie, it got a lot worse. Doris blamed me because that stupid diary I kept was the reason Dad and you were caught and went to prison the second time."

Jake shook his head. "The crimes we committed sent us to prison, honey."

"The sheriff would never have known where we were if I hadn't written about keeping the cattle out at the old Stoker place. If I hadn't gloated about what we got away with."

"I don't blame you. I never did. I never should have let Dad drag you into the business in the first place."

"I wanted to help. I wanted him to notice me, to love me. Kids will do stupid things to get noticed, won't they? In the end maybe I was more like him than I thought."

Jake drew her into a fierce hug. "No, kid. You've got too much of your mother in you to end up like him, or like me."

Tears stung her eyes as she returned his hug. "Thanks, but I don't think you turned out so badly," she muttered against his shirt front.

He held her at arms' length. "No, but it took me a long time to decide which way I was going to go. I met a good man in prison. He was a pastor and a counselor. He told me about God and about finding forgiveness. I've been trying to live the way he taught me. It hasn't been easy. If Sam Hardin wants to find his missing cattle, tell him to look for a cowhand that was fired from the Double R about a week ago."

"How do you know this?"

He gave her a wry smile. "The sheriff isn't the only one who thinks I practice my old trade. Now and then I get offers."

She managed a smile in return. "Thank you. Where

is Doris? It's past time she and I set a few things straight."

"You just missed her. She left a little while ago with a woman named Slader. They didn't say when they'd be back."

The earth shifted beneath Cheryl as a loud buzzing filled her ears. "Do you mean Merci Slader?"

"A tall redhead, doesn't smile much. Hey, you're as pale as a sheet. What's wrong?" He steadied her with both hands.

"Oh no. I should have told him." She pulled away from Jake and hurried to her pickup.

"Cheryl, wait! What's wrong?" He followed her and laid a hand on the open window as she started the engine.

"I never told Sam who I really am. Don't you see? They've gone to tell him about me. If he gets back before I do, he'll know I kept the truth from him all this time. I'm sorry, Jake, I have to go." She put the truck in gear and sped away.

Sam turned into his lane, and the image of Cheryl as he had last seen her flashed into his mind for the hundredth time. Had he imagined the regret and longing that had filled her eyes? He knew that he loved her. He couldn't, wouldn't, believe she didn't love him in return. Had she left already? He didn't know which he dreaded more, finding her gone or watching her leave.

When he pulled up in front of the house, he saw Merci Slader's dark blue Sable parked beside it. What did she want?

Walter came out of the house as Sam stepped out of the truck. "That took you long enough. How'd it go?"

"Our report's been filed. The sheriff wants to talk to the foreman at the Double R before he questions anyone else."

"He'd better make it fast. The longer he waits, the less chance we have of getting our cattle back."

"I know." Sam stared at the front door of the house. He wanted to see Cheryl coming out to greet him, to tell him she'd made a mistake and she intended to stay. Something in his face must have given him away.

"She's not here," Walter said quietly, his eyes full of sympathy. "She borrowed my truck. Said she had an errand that couldn't wait. Her sister called and left a message to say she was on her way."

"I see. Where are the girls?" he managed to ask.

Walter looked around the yard. "I'm not sure. They were here a little while ago. I thought they had gone to the house, but they're not inside."

"Has she told them she's leaving today?"

"Yes."

"Did they seem upset?"

"Not when I saw them."

"Maybe they're down in the garden." Sam shoved his hands into the pockets of his jeans. "Well, Gramps. This is where you get to say, 'I told you so.'"

Walter laid a hand on Sam's shoulder. "I think I'd rather say I'm sorry it turned out this way."

"Thanks."

Walter nodded. "Merci Slader is waiting to talk to you."

"I saw her car. Did she say what she wanted?"

"No, she wouldn't talk to me. She has Doris Thatcher with her. Said you'd want to hear what the woman had to say."

Chapter 15

Cheryl parked the truck beside the barn. Sam stood on the front porch watching her. She crossed the distance between them with lagging steps, feeling her courage ebb away. She knew by the look on his face that she was too late. She could only pray that he would understand why she had deceived him.

She stopped at the foot of the steps. The silence stretched between them. She rubbed her palms on the side of her jeans. "Sam, I can explain."

Merci stepped out of the doorway behind Sam. "I hope you enjoyed your little joke, Ms. Steele. Or should I say, Ms. Thatcher. You really had us fooled. There's hardly a trace of the poor little country girl left." Cheryl's grandmother came out of the house and stood beside Merci.

"So it's true? You're a Thatcher?" Sam asked.

Cheryl's heart sank at the sight of his expression. The pain and disbelief in his eyes told her more than words how much her deception had hurt him. "Yes, it's true."

Merci gave her a frosty smile. "You should have told

us who you were. You're quite famous around here. It's not every day a girl of twelve steals a semitrailer-load of cattle, and then rides down the officer trying to arrest her. Walter said you've had some cattle stolen recently, Sam. Perhaps Ms. Thatcher can explain how that happened?"

"I knew she was no good. She's here to make trouble and nothing else," Doris Thatcher announced. Dressed in a faded, black, shapeless garment, her gray hair drawn back in a tight bun, she looked every one of her seventy-odd years. "The sins of the father have been visited on his children. I tried to change them from their evil ways, but my words fell on deaf ears."

Cheryl studied Sam's face. Did he truly think she had helped steal his cattle? She straightened as she faced him. She'd spent a lifetime being ashamed of who and what she was—hiding from her own past. But she was more than Hank Thatcher's daughter—a lot more. She was also Mira Thatcher's daughter. Something she would be proud of until her dying day. If Sam Hardin didn't see that after all they'd meant to each other, she wasn't going to beg him to understand. *Lord, give me strength.*

"Excuse me, I have to finish packing." She marched up the steps, and the group at the top parted as she walked between them with her head held high.

She was halfway across the living room when Sam caught her arm and turned her to face him. "Why didn't you tell me the truth?"

Pride kept her back straight when what she wanted to do was fall into his arms. "I started to a dozen times, Sam, but I knew how people would react." She gestured toward the door. "Just like that. It doesn't matter what

I've done or where I've been for the last fifteen years. All that matters is that Hank Thatcher was my father and that must make me a thief."

"Cheryl, I don't believe you had anything to do with my missing cattle."

"Thank you. But others won't be so kind. My mother was a good, decent woman who never hurt anyone. All she did was try to survive a bad marriage and shelter her children. For that, she never got anything from her so-called friends and neighbors except condemnation. I didn't expect anything different."

"I'm not condemning you, Cheryl, but I thought you trusted me."

Cheryl heard the pain in Sam's voice. "I do trust you, but try to understand. I wanted you to see *me*. I didn't want who you saw to be colored by who I was. I never meant to hurt you."

Her grandmother advanced toward them, her thin frame shaking with emotion as she yelled, "You should never have come back. I told your sister, and I'm telling you—go away. You can't steal what rightly belonged to my son. The place is mine."

Cheryl studied her grandmother's worn face. She and Angie had escaped into new lives, but Doris Thatcher had stayed and faced the whispers and the snubs of this community all these years. She'd been in a prison as surely as Jake had been, only the bars were ones you couldn't see. No wonder she seemed crazed by it all.

"I don't know what you're talking about, Grandma."

"That's a lie. You've come to drive me out of my home."

Sadly, Cheryl shook her head. "No, I haven't. I couldn't, even if I wanted to."

"Actually, you could," a crisp new voice declared.

Every head turned in surprise as Eleanor Hardin walked into the room. Setting her suitcase on the floor, she crossed the room to stand in front of Cheryl.

"So you're Sam's ballerina. Oh, you've grown to look so much like your mother. I'm very glad to see you again, my dear."

"Hello, Mrs. Hardin," Cheryl whispered.

Eleanor turned away from Cheryl and faced the others in the room. "Everyone sit down," she commanded in her usual brusque manner. "I want to hear the whole story from the start."

Eleanor crossed to Sam. "Close your mouth, Samuel. You look like an astonished fish." She reached up, pulled his head down, and gave him a quick kiss on the cheek. "Did you miss me?" she asked softly.

"I wasn't expecting you for another month."

"Becky's mother-in-law came to help out. The house wasn't big enough for the both of us."

"How is Becky?"

She flashed him a bright smile. "I think she was a little glad to see me go. Doris, don't you dare leave," Eleanor called as Cheryl's grandmother gave a huff and turned on her heels.

"She can't take my home!"

"She can if she wants it. That was the deal."

Confused, Cheryl glanced from one woman to the other. "I don't understand. What deal?"

"Tell her," Eleanor commanded.

"It was blackmail, that's what it was," the old woman spat.

"Maybe, but Harriet was smart enough to make it legal."

Cheryl stared at Sam's mother in amazement. "You knew Harriet?"

Eleanor nodded. "Your mother, Harriet and I were close friends as girls together. Harriet's parents died when she was a baby. She came to live with your mother's family on the same ranch you grew up on. Your mother's father was a wise man. He wanted to make certain that both girls were taken care of after he was gone. He had the ranch placed in a trust for them.

"Harriet strongly disapproved of your father, but Mira loved him, and she married him over everyone's objections. She and Harriet had a falling-out over it, and Harriet moved to Philadelphia. She told me later that she regretted cutting herself off from Mira."

Doris interrupted her. "The ranch should have gone to my son. He was her lawful husband. It wasn't right that they kept it from him."

"But it was smart," Eleanor shot back. "Hank would have lost the place in no time."

Cheryl struggled to understand. "You mean the ranch belonged to Harriet after my mother died?"

Eleanor nodded.

"And now?"

"It's part of a trust that Harriet set up for you and Angela. Harriet was willing to let your father live on the ranch and raise you there. It wasn't until after your father died, and I contacted Harriet with my suspicions about your grandmother's treatment of you, that Harriet and I hatched this plan."

"*You* con*tacted Harriet?*"

"Yes. Your grandmother was your legal guardian, but Harriet owned the property. In exchange for transferring legal guardianship to Harriet, Doris was allowed to remain on the ranch for the rest of her life, or until either you or Angela expressed a desire to return and live there."

"The income I get from Harriet's trust fund comes from the ranch?"

"That and other investments Harriet made. I thought you knew. Your sister knows about it."

Cheryl nodded. "She would. She and Harriet's lawyer were co-executors of Harriet's estate. I was so wrapped up in my career that I never even asked where the money came from."

No wonder her grandmother hadn't wanted her to come back. She must have been afraid of being driven out of her home.

"The place is yours if you want it," Eleanor said quietly.

"No," Doris wailed. "She can't have it. Where will I go?" She sank onto the sofa and began to rock back and forth.

Cheryl watched Sam turn his back to the room and stare out the window. She had thrown away her chance at happiness here because she'd been ashamed. She had lacked the courage to share her past with Sam. He had no reason to trust her now.

"I don't want the ranch or any part of it," she said.

Sam stared out the window feeling heartsick. When Merci had confronted him with Cheryl's deception, all he could think about was how his wife had deceived him. How he'd been played for a fool again. Had Cheryl cared for him even a little? He didn't know what to think.

"Let Doris and Jake stay," Cheryl told his mother. "I have my career, and that's more than enough."

Sam shoved his hands in his pockets and closed his eyes. He had his answer from her own lips. She didn't want any part of them. Could he blame her?

"Are you sure? It was your home," Eleanor said gently.

When Cheryl didn't answer, Sam turned and met her gaze across the room. "I'm sure," she said. "There's nothing for me here."

Walter walked into the room then, and stopped short at the sight of Eleanor. "What are you doing here?"

"I came home early."

"Are the twins with you? I can't find them anywhere."

Sam frowned in concern. "What do you mean you can't find them? When was the last time you saw them?"

"They watched me load cattle this morning," Walter answered.

"The letters," Cheryl exclaimed.

Sam turned to her. "What letters?"

Cheryl strode up to her grandmother. "You sent them, didn't you? Where are the children? If you've hurt them—"

Doris shrank before Cheryl's anger. "I don't know what you're talking about."

"What letters?" Sam demanded again.

"Someone sent me threatening notes, telling me to leave or I'd be sorry."

"Do you still have them?"

Cheryl nodded. She hurried out of the room, returned with the papers and handed them to Sam.

He glanced at each sheet, then fixed his eyes on Merci. "What do you know about these?"

"Me?" She asked in obvious surprise.

"You were adamant about getting Cheryl to leave."

Merci glared at him. "I know nothing about her notes. I came here today because I thought you should know the truth about that woman. I'd never threaten your children."

Sam turned his gaze on the elderly woman on the sofa. "That leaves you, Mrs. Thatcher."

"I don't know anything."

He advanced until he towered over her and held the letters in front of her face. "Did you send these?"

She cringed away from him. "I wanted her to leave, that's all. She can't drive me away from my home."

"Where are my children?" he bit out.

Eleanor sat down beside the trembling woman. "Sam, calm down. Doris, tell us everything."

Doris kept her eyes down. "I sent the notes, but that's all. I haven't seen your girls."

Cheryl studied her grandmother's face for a long moment, then sat down beside her. "You were very cruel to me. No child deserved to be treated the way you treated Angie and I."

Doris glanced at her, but quickly looked away. "Your dad was an only child. My husband used to say I spoiled the boy, but I didn't believe it. Then, look how he turned out. I was ashamed to call him my son, but I still loved him.

"I didn't want you to turn out like he did. I thought I could beat some sense into you, but you were so stubborn. Then that stupid diary of yours sent him to prison. He died there! My son died without me by his side. You took away my son and now you want to take away my home."

Cheryl sat back and stared at her grandmother. She thought of all the fear and shame this woman had caused and she wanted to hate her, but all she felt was pity. She took a deep breath, hoping the right words would come. "The Bible tells us to forgive our enemies. I haven't had much time to study it, but that was one message I did understand. I thought forgiving you would make me a weaker person. But it doesn't. It makes me a stronger person. Someday, I hope we can find a way to get past the anger and bitterness of those years.

"I was a lonely, scared kid with no one to confide in, so I wrote down the things I couldn't tell you or anyone. I was angry at the world and I wanted to hurt someone as much as I was hurting. I wanted my dad to pay attention to me so I did the one thing he was sure to notice. I helped him steal cattle from our neighbors.

"I don't know how Angie found my diary or why she took it to school with her. I don't even know how Mrs. Hardin wound up with it."

Eleanor gave her a sad smile. "One of the boys at school, a bully, his name doesn't matter, took her book bag and dumped it out on the playground. I saw what happened and came to help her pick up her papers. The book had fallen open to the last entry you had made. I couldn't help seeing what you wrote. I *had* to tell the sheriff."

"I know. I understand. Grandmother, you have my word that you can stay at the ranch for as long as you like, only please tell us where the twins are."

"I don't know. I don't know." She burst into tears.

Eleanor sat beside the weeping woman. "I believe you, Doris. It will be okay. Merci will take you home, now."

"I'd rather stay and help find the girls," Merci announced.

Eleanor raised one eyebrow. "You brought her here, you should take her home. I think you've helped enough for one day." There was no mistaking the order in her quiet tone.

Merci helped the still-weeping woman to her feet and they left together.

"Sam, where could the girls be?" Cheryl asked, sick with worry.

He raked a hand through his hair. "A hundred places. Let's spread out and check everywhere again. Check every cupboard and closet."

Nodding, Eleanor and Cheryl began searching the house while the men searched outside.

"Anything?" Eleanor asked when they met up with Walter and Sam by the barn door.

"Nothing," Sam said. "How could two little girls disappear without a trace? Has anyone else been here?"

"Only the cattle buyer," Walter answered.

"How well do you know him?" Cheryl asked, her voice tight.

Sam looked at her in disbelief. "What are you saying?"

"I'm asking, how well do you know the man?" she snapped.

"Elmer Reed picked up the cattle," Walter answered.

"Where was the trailer headed, and when did it leave?" Sam asked, trying to rein in his growing fear.

"He was going to drop the heifers off in Abilene and then deliver the bulls to a ranch down by Wichita. He left an hour ago."

"Wichita? Did the girls know where the trailer was going?" Cheryl demanded.

Walter nodded. "Yes, I heard Reed tell them where he was taking the cattle."

"I told the twins that I would be staying with my sister in Wichita. Could they have gotten into the trailer without the driver knowing it?"

Walter shook his head. "They wouldn't be able to get in back with the cattle. There's no way they could lift the end gate. The trailer did have a side compartment, but they're too little to reach the door handle."

Cheryl's gaze flew to the bucket sitting a few feet away, and she pointed. "What if they stood on that?"

Sam followed her across the yard. Small muddy boot prints and paw prints decorated the top of an overturned white plastic five-gallon bucket.

"This is where the trailer was parked, wasn't it?" Cheryl looked to Walter and back to Sam.

"Okay." Sam bowed his head a moment. He had to think straight, he couldn't let his fear get in the way. "Walter, get the information on where those cattle are being delivered. Call the people and let them know what's going on. The trailer should be almost to Abilene by now. Then notify the Highway Patrol and have them start looking for it. Mom, check with the neighbors to see if anyone has seen the girls. This may turn out to be a wild goose chase. If it is, we'll need to organize a search party and have them spread out from the ranch on foot." He started toward his truck.

"Where are you going, Sam?" his mother called after him.

"I think Cheryl is right. I think they hitched a ride to Wichita on that trailer. I'm going to try and catch up with them. Walter, raise me on the radio if you hear anything."

"Right."

Cheryl hurried after Sam. He had started the pickup by the time she yanked open the door. He glared at her as she climbed in. "What do you think you're doing?"

She slammed the door closed. "I'm coming with you."

"No, you're not."

"You don't have time to drag me out of here, so drive."

"Your sister will be here soon."

"She'll wait."

He hesitated an instant, then he shoved the truck into gear and tore out of the yard.

He flew down the highway well over the legal speed limit. Several times, he glanced at Cheryl. She sat silent and tight-lipped beside him, a worried frown etched on her face. Twenty minutes later, he slowed for the wide spot in the road that was the town of Delavan. Cheryl continued to stare straight ahead, but he saw her lip quiver before she bit down on it.

"Are you okay?" he asked.

"Yes."

His grip tightened on the wheel. "Why didn't you tell me the truth?"

She fixed her gaze on him. "At first, because I thought I would be gone in a day or two, and it wouldn't matter."

"And later?"

She looked away. "Later, I was afraid that it would matter."

"I wish you had trusted me."

She sighed. "What was I supposed to say? 'Oh, by the way, did I mention my family used to steal cattle, and I spent time in jail for helping'? That's a little hard to work into after-dinner conversation." She stared down at her hands. "I thought if you found out, you wouldn't want me near the girls."

"I thought we had more going for us than after-dinner conversation." He couldn't help the bitterness that crept into his voice.

"I'm sorry. You're right. The truth is—I was trying to protect myself. Running away, hiding from my past had become an ingrained habit. You can't imagine what it was like, being mocked and worse because my name was Thatcher. I wanted to bury who I was and never dig her up. You helped me see that I had to face my past. You showed me how people of faith live. I wanted to be a woman like that. That's why I went to see Jake today. I was coming back to tell you everything. I never wanted to hurt you, or the children. If you can't believe anything else, I hope you'll believe that."

"I do."

She raked a hand through her hair. "I shouldn't have let them out of my sight. I knew how upset they were."

"This isn't your fault." He shook his head. "If they hadn't hitched a ride on this trailer, they would've hatched some other harebrained plan."

A small grin lifted some of the worry from her face. "They *are* imaginative."

He tried for a lighter tone. "Do me a favor, will you? When you're back in New York, keep an eye out for them. There's no telling how soon they'll think of a way to visit you."

"Maybe their father could bring them," she suggested softly.

He glanced at her. "Yes, maybe he could."

Hope began to unfurl in Cheryl's heart. Sam had been hurt by the way she had deceived him, but perhaps he could forgive her, in time.

She stared straight ahead. The highway ran west in a long silver ribbon between vast stretches of prairie. In most places, the hills were little more than acres of charred ground where the spring fires had swept across them. Boulders and stones protruded from the burnt ashes like white bones, but here and there, new green life was beginning to show as the resilient grass sprouted again.

The bright sunlight dimmed, and she realized towering thunderheads had blocked out the afternoon sun. The radio crackled as Walter's voice came on. "Sam, do you read me? Over."

Sam picked up the mike and answered him. "Go ahead, Walter."

"The trailer arrived in Abilene twenty minutes ago. The twins had been in it, but they must have gotten out somewhere along the route. All they found was one of their hats in the feed compartment."

"Did the driver say where he stopped?"

"We figure he made about eight stops, mostly at intersections. Three of those would be in towns along the route, three would be rural intersections. He says he stopped once for a train on Highway Fifteen and once at a narrow bridge to let a combine go through. He thinks that was on this side of Herington, but he can't be sure."

"Eight stops in sixty miles. That doesn't narrow the search much."

"The Highway Patrol and the county sheriff are questioning him now. They'll start working their way back from Abilene to here."

"Okay. We're just west of Delavan, Walter. Keep us posted." Sam turned on the wipers as big drops splattered the windshield.

"We'll find them, Sam. I know we will. I have faith." Cheryl didn't know if she was trying to reassure Sam or herself.

Like a hamster on an exercise wheel, her mind ran over and over all the dire possibilities. They could have been picked up by anyone—a kindly farmer or a dangerous stranger. They could be scared and hiding so that even the right people couldn't find them. She tried to ignore the possibility that they might have tried to jump out of the moving trailer and be lying injured in a ditch somewhere along this road. Her eyes searched through the rain-streaked glass for any sign of them as Sam drove westward.

The storm brought an early gloom to the late afternoon. Sam turned on the headlights. The road curved then dipped down to cross a narrow creek. Their headlights swung past an old abandoned church falling into ruins in a grove of trees at the road's edge. A yellow cat sat licking its paw on the sagging railing of a little portico. The passing headlights reflected briefly in its eyes.

Cheryl twisted around in her seat. "Sam, did you see that?"

Chapter 16

Sam braked the truck sharply. "What did you see?"

"Bonkers is back there on the church steps."

"Are you sure?"

"Yes—no! I don't know. It was a big, yellow cat. Please, we have to go check."

He turned the truck on the narrow highway and drove back, but the headlights revealed only an empty porch.

"I know it was Bonkers." Cheryl opened the door, and shouted for the twins.

"Cheryl, get in. You're getting soaked. We aren't near any of the places the driver said he stopped. There must be a hundred yellow cats between here and Abilene."

"I tell you, Sam, it was Bonkers." Determined to prove she wasn't mistaken, Cheryl crossed the overgrown churchyard and started up the dilapidated steps.

She tried the front door. It opened a few inches, but stuck fast on the warped wooden floor. From inside, she heard a faint meow. "Lindy? Kayla? Are you in there?"

"Cheryl, is—"

"—that you?"

Relief poured through her at the sound of their voices. *Thank You, dear Lord.* "Sam, they're in here."

He was beside her in an instant. "Are you girls all right?" he called.

"Yes, Daddy."

"Can you come and get us?"

"They're all right." Relief made Cheryl lightheaded.

Sam grabbed the wedged door and pulled, but stopped when a loud groaning sound issued from the building overhead. "I can't get in, girls. Can you get out?"

"No, the floor fell down."

"All by itself."

"We didn't do it."

Sam stepped back and began to look for another way in. Moving around to the side of the building, he saw that the center section of the roof had fallen in and bare rafters jutted out like broken ribs. The steeple and the ends of the building leaned precariously inward. He listened to the old boards creaking and groaning in the rising wind.

A streak of lightning flashed and thunder rolled in an ominous cadence across the prairie as the grove of trees around them bent low in a gust of wind. He glanced in fear at the slanting steeple of the old church. He had to get the girls out.

On the north side of the building, he found a large section of the wall had fallen in, and he made his way toward the gaping hole. The ground around the church lay littered with piles of old junk.

He stopped at the hole and peered in through the fallen wall. It took a moment for his eyes to adjust to the gloom. Years ago, someone had pulled up the floorboards and left only the floor joists in place. They stretched like an empty tic-tac-toe game above a deep cellar. A small section of the roof had caved in and caught on them. The twins sat huddled on a few fallen boards almost directly across the building from him.

Between him and the girls stood thirty feet of empty space. Below them lay a hazard filled pit.

People had been using the cellar of the abandoned church as a junk heap for decades. Scrap lumber, hundreds of broken bottles, rusted tin cans, rolls of barbed wire, broken bits of farm machinery and assorted debris covered the deep cellar floor.

"Daddy, come get us," Lindy called as she sat with her arms around Kayla. Bonkers lay beside them.

"Okay, honey, I will. Just stay still." Sam searched for a way to reach them. "How did you get out there?"

"We followed Bonkers in, but the floor fell down, and we couldn't get back. I told Kayla we could walk out like Bonkers did on those boards, but she's scared. She thinks she'll fall."

He blanched at the thought of the girls trying to walk across the old beams above the wreckage-filled pit. The gusty wind would make the trip dangerous even for the cat. There had to be a better way.

"Stay there, girls, don't move," he called. "I'll come and get you."

But how? Desperately, he studied the wreck of a building looking for a way to reach his children. The rain fell in earnest now. Dropping to one knee beside him, Cheryl began to undo the splint on her ankle.

"What are you doing?" he asked.

"I'm going to walk over there and carry them out, but

I can't do it with this splint on," she answered, working the straps loose.

Sam dropped beside her and grasped her wrist, stopping her. "Are you crazy? Did you look down there? Even if that old wood is strong enough to hold you, you can't do it on a broken foot. If you fall into that junk heap, you'd be lucky to walk again, let alone dance." The driving rain soaked both of them as they stared at each other.

"Have you got a better idea?" she asked. "You're the architect. Will that roof hold if the wind gets worse?"

He looked at the old bell tower leaning inward over the sagging roof and shook his head. "I can't see what's keeping it up now. It looks like it would come down if a pigeon landed on it."

"I can do this, Sam."

He studied her face for a long moment. He didn't see fear or hesitation, only determination in the bright blue eyes that stared back at him. She was willing to do this for his children. She was willing to risk her career, maybe even her life. Another strong gust of wind drove the rain into his face, and he wiped it away with his hand. Lightning flashed close by, followed by the sharp crack of thunder. The old building gave a creaking moan as it shifted.

"How can I let you do this?" he muttered.

"Hey, cowboy, the question is, how are you going to stop me?"

He gazed at her and knew she was telling the truth. She loved his daughters enough to risk everything for them.

Thunder rumbled again in the leaden sky, and Sam

rose to his feet. "I've got a rope. Maybe I can rig a safety line for you." He turned and ran for the truck.

"Hurry, Sam," Cheryl called after him. She unbuckled the last strap and pulled her foot out. Sharp needles of pain stabbed through her instep as she stood. Gritting her teeth, she began to walk back and forth testing her strength and balance. Another groan from the old timbers of the building caused her to look up in fear. She heard the twins calling, and she stepped up to the gaping hole in the wall.

"Are you coming, Cheryl?" Kayla called.

"You bet I am, sweetheart. I'll come right over."

"Hurry, please. I'm cold," Lindy called.

"It won't be long now," Cheryl promised.

Sam returned with a coiled rope. "If I can get this over one of those rafters, I'll be able to hold you up if you fall." He gave a pointed look at her bare feet. "How's the foot?"

"Okay."

"Are you sure?" He made a toss with the rope and missed.

"I'm sure."

The next toss of the rope went over the exposed rafter. He caught the dangling end and jerked on it. The beam held.

He turned to her and held out a loop. "Put this around your waist." She did, and he tightened it, then gathered up the slack. "Ready?"

She nodded and carefully tested the beam in front of her. "I think it will hold, but I'm going to need some way to secure them to me so I can have my hands free for balance."

Sam pulled a small pocketknife from his jeans, cut

a length of rope from his end, and handed it to her. She knotted it and slipped it over her head and one shoulder, then she stepped out onto the beam with her arms raised from her sides and concentrated on finding her center of balance.

The beam under her bare feet was only about three inches wide. "Now I remember why I didn't become a gymnast," she muttered under her breath as she took several steps. Her ankle felt weak and wobbly, but it would hold. It had to. *Lord, please help me do this.*

She looked at the small faces huddled together across the church, and she began to walk toward them with a smile set firmly on her face.

Gusts of wind pushed at her back like a giant hand and whipped her hair across her eyes to blind her. The old beam beneath her bare feet was rough with splinters. In places, it was wet and slippery from the rain that poured in through the hole in the roof. Each flash of lightning illuminated the danger that lay below her.

The sharp tines of a rusting, rain-slicked harrow gleamed dully in one flash, the grimy panes of a shattered window reflected her above it in the next one. She took each step with careful determination until she reached the jumble of boards where the twins sat.

"Stay still until I tell you to move. I can only take one of you at a time, so who wants to go first?" She turned around and lowered herself to straddle the beam at the edge of the fallen piece of roof.

"Lindy can go," Kayla offered. She scooted back and made more room for her sister. Bonkers climbed into Kayla's lap, and she clutched him tightly.

"Okay, good. Lindy, I want you to put your arms and

legs around me and hold on tight. I'm going to tie this rope around us to help hold you on."

"I can't. I'm scared."

"I know you are, but I won't let anything bad happen to you. Your daddy can hold us up if we fall."

Lindy shook her head and whispered, "I can't."

"Okay, this is what I want you to do. I want you to close your eyes and start saying your prayers. Can you do that?"

"Like at nighttime?"

"That's right. Just like at nighttime. But first, put your arms around my neck."

"Okay. Now I lay me down to sleep...but Cheryl, I'm not sleeping."

Cheryl tied the rope around them both. "Don't those words make you feel safe? They sure make me feel safe."

"They do?"

"Yes, they do. Now, I've got a job for you. I want you to keep your eyes closed tight and keep saying your prayers. Can you do that?"

"Yes."

Lindy did as she was told, and Cheryl stood carefully. She looked back at Kayla's pale face. "I'll be right back for you."

"Promise you won't leave me?"

Cheryl felt a lump rise in her throat. "I'm not going to leave you, baby. I'll be right back. I promise."

It was difficult to keep her balance with Lindy's added weight, and Cheryl's foot hurt with every step. She glanced once at Sam's worried face.

"You're doing fine," he coaxed. "Only few more steps."

Kayla's steady litany of people and animals she wanted God to bless droned in Cheryl's ear. It took three more steps before Cheryl grasped Sam's strong hand, and he pulled her to solid ground. Quickly, he untied the small rope and shifted Lindy to his arms. The rain poured down in torrents, and the old building shuddered in the fierce wind.

"Hurry," he said as he set Lindy on the ground and pulled the slack out of the rope.

Cheryl stepped back onto the beam and tried to do just that. She lost her balance and wobbled wildly for an instant before she steadied herself.

Behind her, she heard Sam's reassuring voice. "Easy, girl, easy. Are you okay?"

"Just peachy," she said through clenched teeth as she waited for her bounding pulse to settle.

"You can do it, I know you can."

"I'm fine." She took a deep breath and began to walk toward Kayla and Bonkers. When she reached the edge of the boards again, she smiled at Kayla. "I told you I'd be back. You and I are going to do the same thing, okay?" She sat down. "Climb on."

A sharp report sounded above their heads, followed by a grating groan that shook the boards they sat on. Cheryl glanced up, then quickly twisted around to cover Kayla's small body with her own as a shower of wooden shingles rained down from a new hole in the roof. A long piece of a splintered rafter fell, stabbing through the flimsy wood inches away from her head.

"Are you okay?" Sam's frantic voice filled the sudden silence.

"We're okay." Cheryl sat up with Kayla clutched tightly in her arms.

"Well, get out of there! This whole place is about to come down," he yelled.

"I'm not dawdling in here because I want to!" she shouted back. Another loud crack rent the air. The rafter holding her safety rope snapped in two and fell into the cellar.

Cheryl stared at the useless rope. Kayla tugged at her arms. "I'm cold. Can we go now?"

Cheryl looked down at the face of the child she loved with all her heart. "Yes, honey. Let's go home, shall we?" She threw off the useless safety line and stood.

"Come on, girls. I know you can do it."

Cheryl heard the controlled fear in Sam's voice. She shifted Kayla to her back and tightened the small rope around them. Bonkers dashed out onto the beam in front of them. He trotted a little way out, then turned around to see if they were following. He ran the rest of the way, jumped out, and stood with flattened ears in the rain.

"Show off," Cheryl muttered as she started walking.

Another sharp crack split the air. The beam under Cheryl's feet quivered wildly and shifted, and she gave a cry of alarm. A piece of falling shingle hit her head, and she struggled to maintain her balance as the beam under her dropped several inches.

Righting herself, Cheryl looked at Sam, and her heart skipped a beat before it began to thud in fear. He lay face down, holding on to the splintered end of beam she stood on. The veins in his neck stood out as he held their combined weight and the heavy beam. She began to walk quickly, praying he could hold them up. *Lord, lend him Your strength.*

Suddenly, a series of powerful reports rent the air.

An ominous moaning started low, then grew louder and louder.

"Jump!" Sam yelled.

Cheryl leaped toward the opening as the beam gave way behind her. She knew she wasn't going to make it. She landed half in and half out of the opening. She felt Kayla's weight pulling her backward as she clawed for a handhold in the wet grass.

In an instant, Sam's strong hands clamped on to her arms, and he pulled her up beside him. They scrambled to their feet and ran as the roof caved in and the ends of church toppled inward with a deafening crash.

As suddenly as it started, the sounds died away. Cheryl clung to Sam as they stood looking at a pile of wreckage where the old church had stood. With trembling hands, she began to untie the rope at her waist. Sam lifted Kayla from her back and gave the child a quick hug. "Are you okay?" he asked.

"Yes, Daddy."

He kissed her cheek, then set her on the ground.

"I want to go home," Lindy said.

"That's a very good idea," Cheryl agreed.

Sam grasped her arm. "Thank you. I don't know what I would have done without you."

"I'm cold," Kayla said with a shiver.

"Can we go?" Lindy asked.

"Bonkers doesn't—"

"—like the rain."

"He wants—"

"—to go home, too."

"Of course." Cheryl turned away and herded the girls toward the truck.

The twins told them what had happened as they drove back to the ranch.

"The man said he was going to Wichita," Kayla began after she exchanged looks with her sister.

"We decided to go and wait there for you," Lindy admitted.

"Then you'd have to bring us home, and you could stay some more."

"We were in the dark a long time." Lindy's voice grew dramatic.

"And we didn't like it," Kayla added.

"The truck stopped, and we thought maybe it was Wichita, so I opened the door to see and—"

"—Bonkers jumped out."

"We got out to catch him but—"

"—the truck drove away and left us."

"It started to rain, and Bonkers ran into the church. The door wouldn't open very far, but we got in."

"Bonkers ran over some boards to a dry place, and we followed him. Then the boards fell down, and we couldn't get out," Kayla finished in a rush.

Sam shook his head. "This was the most harebrained idea you've ever cooked up. You're grounded till you're twenty-one."

"But, Dad!"

"Two weeks, and I don't want to hear another word."

Sam radioed the ranch to let his mother and grandfather know that the twins were safe. Eleanor and Walter were waiting when he drove into the ranch yard. Cheryl recognized her sister's green Mazda parked in front of the house. Eleanor knelt down, and the girls ran to throw their arms around her in a big hug.

"Hi—"

"—Grandma."

"You girls scared me to death," she scolded.

"We're—"

"—sorry."

Walter watched them with an indulgent smile. He looked at Cheryl and said, "Your brother told the sheriff about the Double R cowboy who was looking for help to heist some cattle. His tip paid off."

"You found Harvey?" Cheryl's sadness lifted a little as he nodded. At least Sam had a chance now to get the ranch back on its feet.

"Apparently, he tried to sell them in his hometown just outside of Emporia. He had a forged bill of sale, but it seems he didn't have an explanation for why his bull had rose-pink toenails. The sale barn operator got suspicious and notified the law."

Eleanor gave the twins a small push in Walter's direction. "Take them in the house and get them cleaned up, will you?"

He nodded and took each girl by the hand. "Come and tell Grandpa all about it. How long are you grounded for?"

"Two whole weeks," Lindy admitted with a long face.

"That's not bad. Did I ever tell you about the time I got grounded for a whole year?" his voice trailed off as he led the girls into the house.

Eleanor faced Cheryl. "Your sister is here," she said just as Angie stepped out onto the porch.

Sam came up beside Cheryl. "You're leaving now?"

"Yes."

She waited for him to speak, to ask her to stay, but he didn't. She forced a smile to her face. "I'm glad you'll get your cattle back, and I'm glad the girls are safe and I'm sorry—about everything." She turned and hurried to her sister's car, determined that no one would see how much her heart was breaking.

Sam watched her go. He'd been so wrong about her. He'd let his festering pain and anguish over his wife's deceptions keep him from seeing the truth about her. He loved Cheryl, but at the first test of that love, he'd failed her miserably.

Her sister stopped in front of Sam and held out her hand. "Thanks for taking care of Cheryl."

Sam took her hand and nodded mutely.

Angie glanced toward the car where Cheryl sat with her head bowed, then back at him. "Oh, come on. You're not really going to let her go, are you?"

"She doesn't want to stay."

"You can't be that stupid." She eyed him for a long moment, then shook her head. "I guess you can." She started to walk away, but stopped and turned back to him. "She loves you, you know."

Sam's gaze moved to where Cheryl sat quietly in the car with her head up staring straight ahead. "She never told me that."

"Men. Do women have to tell you everything? Cheryl is the bravest and most loyal person I know, and you're a fool if you let her go."

She walked down the steps and joined her sister.

His mother laid a hand on his arm. "Are you okay, son?"

"You heard her. I'm a fool." Sam watched them drive away and swallowed the lump in his throat. "She's the wrong kind of woman for me. Her career will take her all over the world. She said herself that she doesn't have time for a family, or children. Yet, today, she risked everything for Lindy and Kayla. She's the wrong kind of woman in every way, except she's the only woman who can fill my heart and my life. And I just let her go."

"What are you going to do?"

"I don't know, Mom. I just don't know."

She reached up and cupped his face between her hands. "You'll figure it out, Sam. I know you will."

"I don't see how you can be so sure."

"I have faith. Besides, your mother didn't raise no fool."

Chapter 17

Cheryl completed a single pirouette on her left foot and frowned. Dressed in a leotard and toe shoes, she worked out in her sister's spare bedroom.

"Does it hurt?"

Cheryl looked up and smiled at Angie in the doorway. "Not much, but it's weak."

"You should give it a rest."

"I can't." She rose on her toes again. "I have an audition in two weeks, and I need to be ready."

"Jeff and I are going out to dinner tonight. Why don't you join us?"

"No thanks." Cheryl began another spin.

Angie walked up and stopped her by putting both hands on her shoulders. "If he hasn't called by now, he isn't going to."

Cheryl bowed her head. "I know," she admitted.

"You can call him. The phone works in both directions."

The doorbell rang, and Angie frowned at the interruption. She gave her sister a firm shake. "Go back to him or go on with your life, but don't stay in limbo."

Cheryl stared at the phone on the bedside table. It had been two weeks, and every day she had hoped and prayed for some word from Sam, but she'd heard nothing. Did she dare call him? Her sister was right—she had to go back to him and try again, or get on with her life.

She sought strength in her new faith and found it. She could not see God's plan for her, but she couldn't imagine her life without Sam and the girls in it. She had to give it one more chance. She took a deep breath and reached for the phone, but stopped at the sound of her sister's laughter.

"Well it's about time," Angie said. "What took you so long?"

"We've been grounded."

"For two whole weeks."

"It was really bad!"

"No TV—"

"—or nothin'"

Cheryl dashed into the room and froze as a wave of happiness spread over her. Sam stood in her sister's living room, looking nervous and uncertain. When he saw her, that endearing, crooked grin appeared on his handsome face.

The twins stood on either side of him. Kayla held a bouquet of roses she could barely see over, and Lindy held a giant, red, heart-shaped box of chocolates. Bonkers sat in front of them. He wore a bright-red ribbon tied around his neck with the other end firmly knotted to Sam's wrist.

Sam smiled at her. "You said the next time I wanted

to get you to come home with me, I would have to promise you chocolate and roses."

Tears of happiness stung her eyes as she walked up to him and laid her hands on his chest. "My price has gone up since then, cowboy."

"Oh? What'll it take now?"

"I won't settle for anything less than a cowboy, two kids and a cat."

"That can be arranged." He gathered her into his arms and kissed her with such fierce longing, it stole her breath away.

He drew back and studied her face. "When Natalie left me, she left a hole big enough for Harvey to walk though. I didn't know if I could ever trust my heart to another woman again. Then God brought you into my life, and before I knew it, you had mended my heart.

"I've prayed and done a lot of soul searching in the past two weeks. It wasn't that I couldn't trust anyone else, it was that I didn't trust myself. If I had been more open, less worried about getting hurt, you might have been able to confide in me."

"I'm so sorry, Sam. It was a mistake I'll never make again. I don't deserve your love, but I love you with all my heart."

"You deserve a better man than me. God willing, I'm going to spend a lifetime trying to become that man. And I don't want you to give up ballet," he said sternly. "You can go anywhere in the world to work as long as you come home to us."

"Ask her, Daddy," Lindy urged.

"Yeah, ask her," Kayla added.

Motioning to them with one hand, he said, "Just wait a minute."

He looked back at Cheryl. "The girls and I understand we're going to have to share you. We're prepared for that. I only hope ballerinas make good money because the airfare back and forth to New York is going to cost us a bundle."

"Do you think I'm worth it?" she asked with a shy grin.

He pulled her close. "Oh, yes."

"Ask her, Daddy," Kayla insisted.

Cheryl forced her face into a serious pose. "Ballerinas don't make that much money. I think all I'll be able to afford is the gas to Kansas City and back."

"What do you mean?"

She smiled broadly. "I have an audition with a ballet company in Kansas City next month."

She grew serious as she studied his face. "It will mean I'll be away working—sometimes for weeks at time. It won't be easy, Sam."

"I know." He smoothed her hair with his fingertips. "But it can't be as hard as life without you. I tried that for the past two weeks. It didn't work. I'll support you in anything you want to do."

"I want to perform for at least another two years, then I want to do something else."

"Anything. I'll never stand in your way."

"I want to teach. I want to start a dance school in Council Grove."

"I like the sound of that."

"Ask her, Dad."

"Yeah, ask her."

Cheryl grinned down at the girls. "Okay, ask me what?"

"To marry him," Lindy blurted out.

"And be our mother," Kayla added.

Sam rolled his eyes and shook his head. "Like they said—will you marry me?"

"In a New York minute. I love you, Sam." She cupped his face and kissed him with all the love she held in her heart.

The twins grinned at each other and winked.

Bonkers began to purr, but no one noticed as he wound the red ribbon around and around their boots and ballet shoes.

In the little dressing room at the back of the stone church on the outskirts of Council Grove, Cheryl Steele planted her hands on her hips. "This veil is crooked. I can't possibly wear it."

"Hush," Angie said. "Come here and let me fix it. There."

Cheryl turned around. "Well? How do I look?"

"You look…radiant…beautiful.… I don't think I can find the right words. Sam is a very lucky man. I hope he knows it."

A mischievous grin curved Cheryl's lips. "He does. I tell him every chance I get."

Angie chuckled. "I'll bet you do."

Cheryl reached out and grasped her sister's hands. "Have I ever thanked you?"

"For what?"

"For pushing me into going back to the ranch that night?"

Angie leaned close. "I might have made the suggestion, but I think the plan came from much higher up."

"I think so, too."

"I've never asked, but was it hard for you?"

"You mean facing the community and telling people who I am? Yes, and no. The day Sam and I first came to church here I was scared witless. But with his family around me, and God's grace filling my heart, it turned into a healing time. Becoming a Christian, accepting Christ as my Savior, has changed me more than I can say.

Over the past few months so many people have come up to me after church and talked about Mom. A lot of people felt they let her down. Spousal abuse wasn't talked about back then. Things have changed. For the better."

"Do you think they'll accept Jake?"

"Yes, in time. The sheriff made it known that Jake was the one who solved the theft of Sam's cattle. There will always be people with prejudices against an ex-con, but there are enough people here who believe he deserves another chance. With Walter Hardin as his outspoken supporter, Jake has a good shot at it."

"And Doris? I noticed she wasn't here?"

"Doris and I are trying to mend fences. That may take a while. She wants to shut herself away from the world. I know how that feels, but I haven't given up on her. Listen to me, I sound like a rancher's wife already. Mending fences."

"I knew those New York roots weren't as deep as you pretended."

"I guess they weren't."

A knock sounded at the door and Angie went to open it. Jake stood on the other side. Cheryl had chosen him to walk her down the aisle. His guitar rested in the front pew. She wasn't about to get married without his beautiful music as part of the ceremony. He looked at once handsome and uncomfortable in his rented tux.

He cleared his throat and pulled at the collar of his outfit with one finger. "Are you ready?"

Two little girls in matching floor-length lavender dresses pushed in past his legs. "Come on, Cheryl. We're ready," they said together. Each one grabbed her hand and tugged.

"Daddy is so nervous."

"I wish Bonkers could be here."

"Don't we look nice?"

"Did you see Aunt Becky's baby?"

"He's so cute. Grandma says—"

"—we might get a baby brother, too."

"Maybe even twins, like us!"

Cheryl let herself be led from the room by the excited pair. At the doorway, she cast a wide-eyed look back at her sister. "What have I gotten myself into?"

Angie laughed softly. "Only God knows, honey. God only knows."

* * * * *

We hope you enjoyed reading
SPRINGTIME IN SALT RIVER
by *New York Times* bestselling author
RAEANNE THAYNE
and
LOVE THINE ENEMY
by *USA TODAY* bestselling author
PATRICIA DAVIDS

Both were originally Harlequin® series stories!

From passionate, suspenseful and dramatic
love stories to inspirational or historical,
Harlequin offers different lines to
satisfy every romance reader.
Up to eight new books in each line
are available every month.

Harlequin.com

SPECIAL EXCERPT FROM

Love Inspired®

*With her family in danger of being separated,
could marriage to a newcomer in town
keep them together for the holidays?*

Read on for a sneak preview of
An Amish Wife for Christmas *by Patricia Davids,
available in November 2018 from Love Inspired!*

"I've got trouble, Clarabelle."

The cow didn't answer her. Bethany pitched a forkful of hay to the family's placid brown-and-white Guernsey. "The bishop has decided to send Ivan to Bird-in-Hand to live with Onkel Harvey. It's not right. It's not fair. I can't bear the idea of sending my little brother away. We belong together."

Clarabelle munched a mouthful of hay as she regarded Bethany with soulful deep brown eyes.

"Advice is what I need, Clarabelle. The bishop said Ivan could stay if I had a husband. Someone to discipline and guide the boy. Any idea where I can get a husband before Christmas?"

"I doubt your cow has the answers you seek, but if she does I have a few questions for her about my own problems," a man said.

Bethany spun around. A stranger stood in the open barn door. He wore a black Amish hat pulled low on his forehead and a dark blue woolen coat with the collar turned up against the cold.

The mirth sparkling in his eyes sent a flush of heat to her cheeks. How humiliating. To be caught talking to a cow about matrimonial prospects made her look ridiculous.

She struggled to hide her embarrassment. "It's rude to eavesdrop on a private conversation."

"I'm not sure talking to a cow qualifies as a private conversation, but I am sorry to intrude."

He didn't look sorry. He looked like he was struggling not to laugh at her.

"I'm Michael Shetler."

She considered not giving him her name. The less he knew to repeat the better.

"I am Bethany Martin," she admitted, hoping she wasn't making a mistake.

"Nice to meet you, Bethany. Once I've had a rest I'll step outside if you want to finish your private conversation." He winked. One corner of his mouth twitched, revealing a dimple in his cheek.

"I'm glad I could supply you with some amusement today."

"It's been a long time since I've had something to smile about."

Don't miss
An Amish Wife for Christmas *by Patricia Davids,*
available November 2018 wherever
Love Inspired® books and ebooks are sold.

www.LoveInspired.com

Uplifting romances of faith, forgiveness and hope.

His New Amish Family
Patricia Davids

Save $1.00

on the purchase of ANY
Love Inspired® book.

Available wherever books are sold,
including most bookstores, supermarkets,
drugstores and discount stores.

Save $1.00

on the purchase of any Love Inspired® book.

Coupon valid until November 30, 2018.
Redeemable at participating outlets in the U.S. and Canada only.
Not redeemable at Barnes & Noble stores. Limit one coupon per customer.

52615968

5 65373 00076 2   (8100)0 12389

® and ™ are trademarks owned and used by the trademark owner and/or its licensee.

© 2018 Harlequin Enterprises Limited

BACCOUP0918